PRAISE FO

The Yellow Eyes of Crocodiles

"Bonjour, book lovers. Get ready for best-selling French author Katherine Pancol's American debut. It's a charmer about forty-something sisters Iris and Joséphine, who have taken very different paths in life but come together when each finds herself in need of a little reinvention. Read it and ouip."

—DailyCandy

"A satisfying read." —*The Washington Post*

"Lucky you! You're about to succumb to France's most irresistible writer! At the end of this delicious, tender, funny, heartwarming novel, you'll feel as if Iris and Joséphine are part of your family."

—Tatiana de Rosnay,
New York Times bestselling author of *Sarah's Key*

"Thought Parisian women are perfect? Think again. A delicious treat about separation, sisterhood, and turning tables."

—Inès de la Fressange,
New York Times bestselling author of *Parisian Chic*

"There is a gorgeous and invigorating zip and sparkle to the writing. You read it with a big smile."

—Elizabeth Buchan, *New York Times*
bestselling author of *Revenge of the Middle-Aged Woman*

"No wonder Katherine Pancol's books are all bestsellers, reading her feels like coming home. Her characters become like friends and family members, and you long to know how they get on. *The Yellow Eyes of Crocodiles* has all the quirks, tensions, and belly laughs that family, friendship, and sisterhood can entail. It is touching, entertaining, and vibrant."

—Cécile David-Weill, author of *The Suitors*

PENGUIN BOOKS

The Slow Waltz of Turtles

KATHERINE PANCOL is one of France's best known contemporary authors. *The Slow Waltz of Turtles* was a number one bestseller in France, and to date it has sold more than 1.5 million copies in twenty-six languages. Her previous novel *The Yellow Eyes of Crocodiles* was also a number one bestseller in France. Katherine was born in Morocco, grew up in France, taught school in Switzerland, and worked as a journalist at *Paris Match*. She lived in New York City from 1980 to 1990.

The Slow Waltz of Turtles

KATHERINE PANCOL

Translated by
WILLIAM RODARMOR

PENGUIN BOOKS

PENGUIN BOOKS
An imprint of Penguin Random House LLC
375 Hudson Street
New York, New York 10014
penguin.com

Originally published in France by Éditions Albin Michel–Paris, 2008,
as *La Valse Lente Des Tortues.*

LIBRARY OF CONGRESS CATALOGING-IN-PUBLICATION DATA

Names: Pancol, Katherine, 1954- author. | Rodarmor, William, translator.
Title: The slow waltz of turtles : a novel / Katherine Pancol ;
translated by William Rodarmor.
Other titles: Valse lente des tortues. English
Description: First edition. | New York, New York : Penguin Books, 2016. |
First published in French as La valse lente des tortues
(Paris : Albin Michel, c2008).
Identifiers: LCCN 2016007385 | ISBN 9780143128175 (paperback)
Subjects: LCSH: Divorced women—Fiction. | Sisters—Fiction. |
Murder—Fiction. | Self-actualization (Psychology) in women—Fiction. |
Psychological fiction. | BISAC: FICTION / Literary. | FICTION /
Contemporary Women. | FICTION / Humorous. | GSAFD:
Mystery fiction. | Humorous fiction.
Classification: LCC PQ2676.A4684 V3513 2016 | DDC 843/.914—dc23

Printed in the United States of America

1 3 5 7 9 10 8 6 4 2

Set in ITC Galliard Std

The Slow Waltz of Turtles

♦ ♦ ♦

PART I

♦ ♦ ♦

$\mathcal{I}$'m here to pick up a package," said Joséphine, stepping to the counter at the post office on rue de Longchamp in Paris's sixteenth arrondissement.

"Foreign or domestic?" asked the postal clerk, a bottle blonde with bad skin and an empty stare.

"I don't know."

"What's the name?"

"*Joséphine Cortès. C-O-R-T-È-S.*"

"You have the delivery notice?"

Joséphine held out the yellow form.

"Can I see some identification?" asked the clerk wearily.

Joséphine handed over her ID. The clerk grabbed it from her hand and climbed down from her stool, raising first one buttock, then the other. She waddled off down a hallway and disappeared, rubbing her back. On the wall, the black minute hand of the clock crept across the white face. Joséphine gave an embarrassed smile at the line lengthening behind her.

It's not my fault the package was put in a place where it can't be found, thought Joséphine in a silent apology. *It's not my fault that it went to Courbevoie before being forwarded here. Anyway, where could it be coming from? Maybe from Shirley in England. Except that she knows my new address. It would be just like her to send some of that special tea she buys at Fortnum & Mason, a pudding, and some wool socks so I can work without my feet getting cold. Shirley always says that love exists only in the details.* Jo missed Shirley, who had moved to live in London with her son, Gary.

The postal clerk came back with a parcel the size of a shoe box.

"Do you collect stamps?" she asked, hoisting herself back onto her stool, which groaned under her weight.

The clerk blinked vacantly at the stamps, then slid the package across to Jo, who saw her name and old Courbevoie address on the coarse wrapping paper. The package's long stay on the post office shelf had frayed the equally coarse string into garlands of dirty pom-poms.

"I couldn't find it because you moved," said the clerk. "Comes from a long way off. Kenya. It's been around the block, all right! Looks like you have too."

She'd said this sarcastically, and Joséphine blushed and muttered some sort of excuse. It was true that she'd moved, but not because she didn't like her suburb, not at all. She loved Courbevoie, her old neighborhood, her apartment, the balcony with the rusted railing. To be honest, she didn't like her new place; she felt like a stranger there, a refugee. She'd moved because her older daughter, Hortense, couldn't stand living in the suburbs anymore, and when Hortense got an idea in her head, you'd better follow through or she blasted you with her contempt. Thanks to the royalties Joséphine was earning from her novel, *A Most Humble*

Queen—and a big bank loan—she'd been able to buy a handsome apartment in a nice neighborhood. It was on avenue Raphaël, near the La Muette Metro station and beyond rue de Passy with its luxury boutiques, on the edge of the Bois de Boulogne. Half town, half country, the real estate agent kept stressing. Hortense had thrown her arms around Joséphine's neck. "Thanks so much, Mom! Thanks to you, I'll finally have a life, become a real Parisienne."

"If it were up to just me, I would've stayed in Courbevoie," Joséphine murmured to the clerk, embarrassed, feeling the tips of her ears get warm.

That's new, she thought. *I didn't used to blush at the drop of a hat. Before, I knew my place—even if I wasn't always comfortable there, it was my place.*

Unlike her mother or her sister, who could make people obey or love them with a glance or a smile, Joséphine was shy. She had a self-effacing way, apologizing for being present to the point of stuttering or blushing. For a while, she thought that success would boost her self-esteem. *A Most Humble Queen* was still on the bestseller lists a year after coming out. But money hadn't brought her confidence. She'd even wound up hating it. It had changed her life and her relationships with other people. *The only thing it didn't change is how I feel about myself,* she thought with a sigh. She looked around for a café where she could sit and open the mysterious package.

It was late November, and night was falling on the city. A stiff wind was blowing, stripping the trees of their remaining leaves, which spiraled to the ground in a russet waltz. Pedestrians walked along looking at their feet for fear of a gust slapping them in the face. Joséphine pulled up her coat collar and checked her watch. She was meeting Luca at seven at the brasserie Le Coq on the place du Trocadéro.

She looked at the package. There was no sender's name.

She walked up avenue Poincaré to the place du Trocadéro and entered the restaurant. She had a full hour before Luca would join her. Since her move, they always met in this brasserie, at her request. It was a way of getting acquainted with her new neighborhood. She enjoyed creating habits. "I think this place is too bourgeois and touristy, it has no soul," said Luca dully, "but if you insist . . ." You can always tell if people are sad or happy by their eyes. They can't hide the way they look. Luca always had sad eyes. Even when he smiled.

She pushed the glass door open, spotted a free table, and went to sit down. To her relief, nobody paid her any attention. Perhaps she was starting to look like a Parisienne? She fingered the unusual almond-green hat she'd bought the week before, considered removing it, decided not to. It had three fat woolen bellows topped by a disk of ribbed velvet with a little wool stem, like a beret. With that hat, she was creating a personality for herself. Just before going to the post office she'd stopped at the lycée to see her younger daughter's main teacher, Madame Berthier. She wanted to see how Zoé was doing, what with the move and getting used to a new school. At the end of their talk, Berthier had put on her coat and the same almond-green hat with three puffy bellows.

"I've got exactly the same hat," said Joséphine, holding hers out. "Look!"

The coincidence of wearing identical hats brought the two women closer than their long conversation about Zoé had. They left the school together and headed in the same direction, still talking.

"You come from Courbevoie, Zoé tells me."

"I lived there for almost fifteen years. I liked it, even though there were problems."

"Here, the problems aren't the children, but their parents!"

Joséphine looked at her in surprise.

"They all think they've given birth to a genius, and they criticize us for not recognizing their inner Pythagoras or Chateaubriand. They bombard their children with tutoring, piano lessons, tennis clinics, sessions in fancy schools abroad. The kids are exhausted, and they either fall asleep in class or talk to you as if you were their flunkey. In fact, I just had a run-in with one of the fathers, a banker with all sorts of degrees and diplomas. He was complaining that his son had only a B average. I pointed out that a B was pretty good, and he looked at me as if I'd insulted him. His son! Flesh of his flesh! Getting a B average! I could practically smell napalm on his breath. It's dangerous being a teacher these days. I'm not afraid of the kids as much as of their parents!"

Madame Berthier clapped her hand on her hat to keep it from blowing off and laughed.

They had to part when they reached Joséphine's building.

"I live a little farther on," she said, pointing to a street on the left. "Enjoy your hat. Be sure to wear it. That way we'll recognize each other, even from a distance."

That's for sure, thought Joséphine. It stood up like a cobra rising from its basket. She almost expected to hear flute music and see the hat start swaying back and forth. She wasn't sure Luca would like it.

They had been seeing each other regularly for a year. Luca was writing a scholarly work for an academic press: a history of tears from the Middle Ages to the present. He spent most of his time in the library. At thirty-nine, he lived like a student. He had a studio apartment in Asnières, its refrigerator empty except for a bottle of Coke and a lonely chunk of pâté. He didn't own a car or a television, and in all weather, he wore a navy-blue duffel coat that served as his home away from home. Its roomy pockets held everything he needed during the day. He had a twin brother named Vittorio, who caused him endless worry. Just by looking at the furrow between Luca's eyes, Joséphine could tell if the news about his brother was good or bad. A deep furrow was a storm warning. On those days, Luca would be silent and somber. He would take Joséphine's hand and slip it into his coat pocket along with the keys, pens, notebooks, cough drops, Metro tickets, cell phone, tissue pack, and his old red leather wallet. She had learned to recognize each object with her fingertips, even the brand of the cough drops. The two of them would get together on nights when Zoé slept over at a friend's house or on the weekends when Zoé went to London to see her cousin, Alexandre.

Every other Friday, Joséphine drove her to the Gare du Nord, and Philippe and his son, Alexandre, met her at St. Pancras. Philippe had given Zoé a Eurostar pass, and she would hop on the train, eager to be in her room in her uncle's Notting Hill apartment.

"So you have your own room there?" Joséphine had exclaimed.

"Yup, even a hanging closet with lots of clothes, so I don't have to carry a suitcase. Uncle Philippe thinks of everything. He's really the best!"

In that, Joséphine recognized her brother-in-law's tact and

generosity. Whenever she had a problem, or hesitated over a decision to make, she called Philippe.

"I'm always here for you Jo," he would answer. "You know you can ask me anything." When she heard his kind voice, she immediately felt reassured. At the same time, a red flag went up: *Careful, danger! He's your sister's husband! Keep your distance, Jo.*

Joséphine's own husband, Antoine, the father of her two daughters, had died six months earlier. He'd been managing a crocodile farm in Kenya for his partner, a Chinese businessman named Wei. The business collapsed, and Antoine started drinking, getting into a strange dialogue with the crocodiles. They taunted him, refusing to reproduce, ripping down the fences, and eating the workers. Antoine spent his nights staring into the yellow eyes of crocodiles floating in the swamp, until one night he walked into the water and a croc grabbed him.

In a tearful scene, Joséphine found the courage to tell Zoé that her father was dead. Zoé had said, "Now I've got only you left, Mommy. Nothing better happen to you!" She knocked on wood to keep the danger at bay. Hortense had cried too, but then declared that it was for the best, that being a failure had pained her father too much. Hortense didn't like feelings, thought them a waste of time and energy, a suspicious self-indulgence that led only to self-pity. She had just one goal in life: to be a success, and nobody and nothing would stand in her way. She loved her father, of course, but there was nothing she could do for him, she said. Everyone was responsible for his own fate. He'd been dealt a losing hand and had paid the price.

That was last June. Hortense had passed her *baccalauréat*

exam with honors and left to study in England. She sometimes joined Zoé at Philippe's and spent Saturdays with them, but most of the time she breezed in, gave her little sister a kiss, and immediately left. She was enrolled at Saint Martins and was working like a fiend. "It's the best fashion school in the world," she assured her mother. "I know it's expensive, but we can afford it now, can't we? You'll see, you won't regret your investment. I'm gonna become a world-famous designer." Hortense had no doubt about it. Neither did Joséphine. She had complete faith in her older daughter.

How much had happened in just a year!

Within a few months, my life was turned upside down, Jo reflected. *I was alone, abandoned by my husband, rejected by my mother, harassed by my banker. I owed everyone money. I had just finished writing a novel so my dear sister, Iris, could put her name to it and bask in the limelight.*

And now, I've started a new life. I'm waiting for Luca. He'll have bought a copy of Pariscope, *and together we'll pick a movie to go see.* Luca always made the choice, but he pretended to leave it up to her. She would rest her head on his shoulder, slip her hand in his coat pocket, and say, "Go ahead, you decide." He would say, "All right, I'll pick the movie but don't complain afterward."

She never complained. She was still amazed that he enjoyed being with her. When she slept at his place, with him lying next to her, she would study the sparse decor of his studio apartment, the white light slanting through the venetian blinds, the books piled on the floor. A bachelor apartment. She snuggled closer. *I, Joséphine Plissonnier, widow of Antoine Cortès, have a lover.*

She glanced around the café to make sure no one was watching her. *I hope Luca likes my hat! If he turns up his nose, I'll squash it into a beret.*

Jo's gaze returned to the package. She untied the coarse twine and reread the address: Madame Joséphine Cortès. She carefully unwrapped the paper, glanced into the box. A letter lay on top.

Madam,

These are all the remains we found of your husband, Antoine Cortès, after the unfortunate accident that cost him his life. We want to say how sorry we all are, and remember Tonio with great affection. He was a good friend and colleague, always ready to do a favor or buy a round of drinks. Life won't be the same without him, and his seat at the bar will remain empty, in his memory.

His friends and colleagues
at the Crocodile Café in Mombasa

This was followed by a series of signatures of the people Antoine had known in Kenya. They were illegible, but even if Jo had been able to make them out, it wouldn't have done her much good: She hadn't met any of them.

She folded the letter and unwrapped the newspaper from Antoine's effects. She took out a handsome scuba diving watch with a large black dial whose bezel bore Roman and Arabic numerals, an orange running shoe size six—he hated having such small feet—and a baptism medal. One side showed a cherub in profile, its head resting on its hand. The other was engraved with Antoine's first name and birth date, May 26, 1963. The last item was a long strand of chestnut hair taped to a piece of yellow cardboard, with a scribbled note: *Hair of Antoine Cortès, French businessman.* For Joséphine, the sight of the hair was overwhelming.

This was all that was left of Antoine: a cardboard box sitting on her knees. But Jo's husband had always felt like a child she had to hold in her lap. She had let him think he was in charge, but she was always the responsible one.

"And what can I get for the little lady?"

A waiter was standing in front of her, waiting.

"A Diet Coke, please."

He walked away, a spring in his step. *I have to start exercising,* Jo thought. *I'm putting on weight.* She'd chosen the apartment so she could run in the Bois de Boulogne. She straightened up and sucked in her stomach, promising to sit up tall for several long minutes, to strengthen her abs.

She started to think about the plan for her next novel. *What would it be about? Should I set it today or in my beloved twelfth century? At least that's a period I know about. I know the era's sensibility, its romantic codes, its rules of social life. What do I know about life today? Not much. But now, I'm learning. I'm learning about relationships with other people, relationships with money, I'm learning everything. Hortense knows more than I do. Zoé is still a child, though she's changing before my eyes. She dreams of being like her sister. When I was a kid, my sister was my model too.*

I used to idolize Iris. She was my role model. Today, she's adrift in the half-light of a psychiatric clinic. The light has gone out of those big blue eyes. Her gaze wanders over me and then escapes into vague boredom. She barely listens to me. Once, when I urged her to

be nicer to the clinic nurses, who were so considerate, she asked,
"How do you expect me to live with other people when I can't live
with myself?" And her hand fell back onto the blanket, inert.

The last time Joséphine visited, Iris's tone very quickly rose
from blandly neutral to sharp.

"I've only ever had one talent," she declared, looking at her
reflection in a hand mirror that always lay on her night table. "I
was pretty. Very pretty. And I'm starting to lose even that. You
see this wrinkle? It wasn't there last night. And tomorrow there'll
be another one, and another, and another."

She banged the mirror down on the Formica table and
smoothed her black hair. It was cut short and square, and made
her look ten years younger.

"I'm forty-seven, and I've screwed everything up, my life as
a wife, my life as a mother. My life, period."

"But what about Alexandre?" asked Joséphine unconvincingly.

"Don't pretend to be stupider than you are, Jo. You know I've
never been a mother to him. I was an apparition, someone he
knew, I wouldn't even say a friend. I was bored in his company,
and I suspect he was bored in mine. He's closer to you, his aunt,
than to me, his mother, so . . ."

The questions that were on the tip of Joséphine's tongue, the
ones she couldn't ask, were about Philippe. *Aren't you afraid*
that he's going to make a new life with someone else? Aren't you
afraid of winding up alone? Asking would have been too cruel.

"Then try to become a good person," Joséphine finally said.
"It's never too late to become someone worthwhile."

"What a pain in the ass you can be, Jo. You're like a nun who's wandered into a whorehouse trying to save lost souls! You came all the way here just to lecture me. Next time, save yourself the trip and stay home. I hear you've moved, is that right? To a nice apartment in a nice neighborhood. Our dear mother told me. She's dying to visit you, by the way, but refuses to be the first to call."

Iris smiled slightly then, a scornful smile. Her big blue eyes, which had looked even bigger since she'd become sick, darkened with jealous, nasty humor.

"You have money now. Lots of money. Thanks to me. I'm the one who made your book successful, don't ever forget that. Without me, you could never have done what I did: find a publisher, handle interviews, go on stage, have my hair chopped off on TV to get attention!"

"You're being unfair!"

Iris raised herself in her bed. A strand of black hair that had escaped from her perfect square hairdo hung in front of her eyes. She jabbed a finger at Joséphine.

"We had a deal!" she shouted. "I'd give you all the money, and I'd get all the fame! I held up my end of the bargain, but you didn't! You wanted both, the money and the fame!"

"Iris, you know perfectly well that's not true. I didn't want anything. I didn't want to write the book, and I didn't want the money from the book. I just wanted to be able to raise Hortense and Zoé decently."

"Do you dare tell me that you didn't send that little bitch to rat me out on live television? 'My aunt didn't write the book,' Hortense told everyone, 'it was my mother.' Do you dare deny that? You disgust me, Jo. I was your most faithful ally. I was always there for you. I always paid for you, always watched out for you. And the one time I ask you to do something for me, you betray me. You really got your revenge too. You dishonored me! Why do you think I stay locked up in this clinic, half-asleep and numbed with sedatives? Because I don't have any choice! If I go out, everyone will point a finger at me. I'd rather die here. And when that day comes, you'll have my death on your conscience, and we'll see how you live with it."

Iris's bony arms stuck out of her the sleeves of her bathrobe, her clenched jaws raising two little hard bumps under her skin, her eyes burning with the most ferocious hatred any jealous woman ever directed at a rival.

"My God, Iris, you hate me!"

"Well, well, you finally figured it out! Now we won't have to play at being loving sisters anymore! I never want to see you again. Don't bother coming back!"

That had been three weeks earlier.

Iris resents me, thought Jo. *She resents my moving to the head of the line, to the place that was hers by right. But I wasn't the one who pushed Hortense to tell the world about our deal. I wasn't the one who broke our agreement. But how can I get Iris to accept the truth? She's too wounded to hear it.* Iris was accusing Joséphine of ruining her life. But it's easier to accuse other people than to confront yourself.

Just then, Joséphine caught a glimpse of her reflection in the café mirror.

At first, she didn't recognize herself.

Was that woman really Joséphine Cortès?

That elegant woman in the handsome tan coat with the wide

velvet lapels? That beauty with the shiny brown hair, shapely lips, her eyes full of startled light? Was that actually her? The hat with the fat bellows proudly announced the new Joséphine. She gazed at the perfect stranger in the mirror. *Pleased to meet you. How pretty you look! You seem beautiful and free. I would so love to be like you.*

Joséphine glanced at the brasserie's clock: It was seven thirty. Luca hadn't come. She took out her cell, dialed his number, got his outgoing message—"Giambelli," spoken syllable by syllable—and left a message. They wouldn't be seeing each other tonight.

She decided not to wait anymore. She would go home to Zoé and the two of them would eat dinner together. When Jo went out, she left her daughter a cold meal on the kitchen table: breast of chicken with a green bean salad, a cup of Petit Suisse with fruit, and a note: *I'm going to the movies with Luca and should be back around ten. I'll come kiss you good night. I love you my beautiful daughter, my beloved. Mom.* She didn't like leaving Zoé alone in the evening, but Luca had insisted on seeing her. "I have to talk to you, Joséphine, it's important."

She took the box with Antoine's possessions and slipped it under her coat, hugging it to her heart. As she was leaving, the waiter stopped her to say, "Madame, I have to tell you I really like your hat!"

The night was pitch black. Avenue Paul-Doumer was deserted. Joséphine walked quickly along the cemetery wall, past the gas station. Only the store windows were lit up. She tried to read the names of the avenue's cross streets and to memorize them: rue Schloesing, rue Pétrarque, rue Scheffer, rue de la Tour . . .

Boulevard Émile-Augier started at the end of avenue Paul-Doumer. She lived a little beyond it, past the Jardins du Ranelagh park. Just then, she spotted an elegant man doing chin-ups from a tree branch. It was an amusing sight, his raising and lowering himself by his arms. She couldn't see his face; he had his back to her.

That could be the start of a novel, she thought. *A man is hanging from a branch. It's completely dark, like tonight. He's wearing a raincoat and counting the chin-ups. Women turn around to look at him, then hurry home. Is he planning to hang himself or attack a passerby? What is he thinking, suicide or murder? That's how the story would begin.*

Jo was walking across the park now. It was a moonless night, and completely dark. She felt lost in a hostile forest. Rain blurred the passing cars' taillights, whose glow cast a wavering light on the park. A wind-whipped branch brushed her hand, startling her. Her heart sped up, began to pound. She shrugged and started walking faster. *Nothing bad happens in a neighborhood like this,* she thought. *Everyone's at home eating a nice dinner or watching television together. The children have taken baths and put on their pajamas and are finishing their meals while the parents discuss their day. There's no knife-wielding madman prowling around, looking for a victim.* Joséphine forced herself to think of something else.

It wasn't like Luca not to have warned her that he wasn't coming. Something must have happened to his brother—something serious, for him to forget their date. "I have to talk to you, Joséphine, it's important." He was probably at a police station somewhere, bailing Vittorio out. He always dropped everything to go get him. Vittorio refused to meet Joséphine. "I don't like that woman, she takes up all your time, and besides, she's a dimwit." "He's just jealous," said Luca, amused. Asked Jo: "Did you stand up for me when he called me a dimwit?" He smiled and said, "I'm used to it; he doesn't want me to take care of anybody but him."

The tree branches were swaying in a threatening choreography. It was like a dance of death, with the long black branches as witches' rags. Jo shivered. A splash of icy rain stung her eyes, like tiny needles prickling her face. She couldn't make out anything anymore. Of the three streetlights along the path through the park, only one was lit.

She didn't see the man sneaking up behind her.

She didn't hear his quick footsteps getting closer.

She felt herself being yanked backward, pinioned by a powerful arm. The man clamped one hand over her mouth and stabbed her repeatedly in the chest with the other. Jo's first thought was that he wanted to steal her parcel. With her left arm, she managed to hold onto Antoine's package. She struggled with all her might, but soon got winded. She fell to the ground gagging and choking. He started kicking her. As he did, she got a glimpse of his feet. She noticed that his shoes had clean, smooth soles.

She cowered, arms over her head, rolled in a ball. The package began to slip from her grasp. The man was swearing at her: "You bitch! You goddamn bitch! You fucking cunt! This'll teach you to get up on your high horse! Now you'll keep your fucking mouth shut!" The barrage of kicks increased along with the curses. Joséphine lay motionless on the ground, eyes closed, blood trickling from her mouth, as the man with the smooth soles walked away.

After waiting a long time, Joséphine stood up, leaning her

hands on her knees. She was panting, gasping for air. She tripped on the parcel and picked it up. The top of the package was slashed to ribbons. *Antoine saved my life,* she immediately thought. *If I hadn't been clutching the parcel to my chest—my husband's things, his running shoe with the thick sole—I'd be dead.*

She ran her hands over her belly, her chest, her neck. She wasn't hurt, but she suddenly became aware of a sharp pain in her left hand: It was cut and bleeding profusely.

Joséphine was so shaken, she didn't trust her legs to support her. She took shelter behind a large tree and tried to catch her breath. Her first thought was for Zoé. *I can't tell her about this, I can't tell her any of this. She couldn't handle knowing her mother was in danger. This was an accident, the man wasn't after me, he's a lunatic, he didn't mean to kill me, he's a lunatic, it wasn't me he wanted to kill.* The words were bouncing around inside her head. She leaned on her knees, making sure she could remain upright. Then she started walking to the big polished wooden door to her building.

Zoé had left her a note in the apartment entryway: *Mommy: I'm down in the basement with Paul, a neighbor. I think I've made a new friend.*

Still out of breath, Joséphine went into her bedroom and closed the door. She took off her coat and threw it on the bed, took off her sweater and skirt. Examining the coat, she found a streak of blood on a sleeve and two long rips in front, on the left. She wadded it up and stuffed it and the rest of her clothes in a big garbage bag, which she shoved to the back of her closet. She would get rid of it later. She checked her arms, legs, and thighs: no signs of injury. As she walked by the big mirror in the bathroom, she put her hand to her forehead and caught sight of her reflection. She was pale and sweaty, her eyes haggard.

He had stabbed her with a thin blade. She could have died. Joséphine had read in the newspaper that there were some forty serial killers on the loose in Europe and wondered how many there were in France. But the disgusting things he shouted suggested that he was settling a score with someone. "You fucking cunt! This'll teach you to get up on your high horse!" The curses flew through the air like daggers. *He must have mistaken me for someone else. I paid the price for some other woman.* Jo had to convince herself of that. If she didn't, life would become impossible. She would distrust everybody, she would be frightened all the time.

She took a shower, washed and dried her hair, and put on a T-shirt and jeans. She brushed on some makeup to hide any eventual bruises and added a touch of lipstick. Looked in the mirror, forced herself to smile. *Nothing happened, Zoé can't know about this, I'll act as if nothing happened.* She would have to live with the secret, unable to tell anybody. Or she would tell Shirley. She could tell Shirley anything. The thought reassured her. She opened the bathtub clean-out trap and hid Antoine's parcel inside. No one would go poking around in there.

Back in the living room, she poured herself a big glass of whiskey, then went looking for Zoé in the basement.

"Mommy, this is Paul."

A boy about Zoé's age in a black T-shirt bowed to her politely. He was skinny as a rail, with a quiff of curly blond hair. Zoé watched anxiously for her mother's look of approval.

"Good evening, Paul," Jo said wearily. "Do you live in the building?"

"On the third floor. My name's Merson, Paul Merson. I'm a year older than Zoé."

It seemed important for him to point out that he was older than the girl looking up at him adoringly.

"I heard some noise coming from the basement," said Zoé. "Boom, boom, boom! So I went down and I found Paul playing the drums. Look, Mommy, he turned his storage space into a music studio."

"And you soundproofed it?" asked Joséphine.

She was speaking with an effort, trying to ignore the staccato hammering of her heart.

"Well, yeah. Have to, 'cause I make a lot of noise when I play. People complain. Especially the guy in the next space over. He's a professional complainer, never happy. At the co-op meetings, he gets into fights with everyone."

"Maybe he has good reason."

"Dad says he's a pain in the butt. We know him well. We've been living here for ten years, so . . ."

Paul shook his head like an adult who was too smart to be taken in by appearances. He was taller than Zoé, but his face still bore signs of childhood, and his narrow shoulders hadn't widened into those of a man.

"Oh shit, here he is!" he muttered. "Run for your life!"

Paul closed the storage space door on Zoé and himself, leaving Joséphine out in hallway. A very tall, well-dressed man approached, striding along as if the basement belonged to him.

"Good evening," she managed to say, flattening herself against the wall.

"Good evening," said the man, walking by without looking at her.

He was wearing a dark gray business suit and a white shirt. The suit accentuated a powerful, muscular chest, the thick necktie gleamed, the French cuffs on his immaculate shirt sported two gray pearls. The man took some keys from his pocket, opened the door to his storage space, and closed it behind him.

Paul came back out when he was sure the man had gone.

"Did he say anything?"

"No."

"Mom says his cellar space is really well set up, with a workbench and all sorts of tools. And he has an aquarium in his apartment. It's very big with caves, plants, colored little buildings, and artificial islands. But no fishes!"

"Your mother seems to know a lot!" declared Joséphine, who realized she could learn a great deal about the building's tenants by talking with Paul.

"She's never even been invited into their apartment! Nobody visits them. I'm friends with the kids and you know what? They never have me over. Their parents won't let them. Whereas with the Van den Brocks on the second floor, they have us over all the time. They've got a TV as big as the living room wall with two speakers and Dolby surround sound. When someone has a birthday, Madame Van den Brock bakes a cake and invites everybody. I'm pals with Fleur and Sébastien. I can introduce Zoé to them, if she likes."

"Are their parents nice?"

"Yeah, super nice. He's a doctor, and she sings in the chorus for operas. She's got a terrific voice. She rehearses a lot, and you can hear her vocalizing in the stairwell. Fleur plays the violin, and Sébastien, the sax."

"I'd like to learn how to play something too," said Zoé, who must have felt left out.

"You've never played an instrument?" asked Paul in surprise.

"Er, no," she said, embarrassed.

As Joséphine observed the exchange between the two kids, she could feel herself calming down.

"It's time for dinner," she said. "And I'm sure Paul will have to go upstairs soon."

"I already ate," he said, rolling rolled up his sleeves and taking his drumsticks. "Would you mind closing the door when you go out, please?"

"Bye, Paul!" cried Zoé. "Catch you later!"

She gave him a little wave that was both bold and shy. It meant *I'd really like us to get together again sometime. . . . If you feel like it, of course.*

Paul didn't bother responding. He was fifteen years old and wasn't about to be impressed by a girl of uncertain charm. He was at that delicate age when you inhabit a body you don't know very well, and sometimes behave in ways that are unintentionally cruel. The casual way he treated Zoé showed that he expected to be the stronger of the two, and if one of them had to suffer, it would be her.

The elegant man in the gray suit was waiting in front of the elevator. He stepped aside to let Joséphine and Zoé enter first.

He asked them what floor they were going to and pressed the button for number five. Then he pressed number four.

"So you're the new tenants," he said.

Joséphine nodded.

"Welcome to the building. Allow me to introduce myself. I'm Hervé Lefloc-Pignel. I live on the fourth floor."

"I'm Joséphine Cortès, and this is my daughter Zoé. I have another daughter, Hortense, who lives in London."

Monsieur Lefloc-Pignel was very tall and serious looking. He had strong features in a rugged, angular face. A hank of neatly combed, straight black hair fell across his brow. He had very widely spaced brown eyes, heavy black eyebrows, and a somewhat broad, bumpy nose. His white teeth were immaculate.

He really is tall, thought Joséphine to herself, discreetly sizing him up. He must be over six feet two. Broad shoulders, good posture, flat stomach. She imagined him receiving a tennis trophy. A very handsome man.

Lefloc-Pignel was holding a white canvas bag flat on his open palms.

"You'll see, the building is very pleasant, most people are friendly, and the neighborhood is safe."

Joséphine frowned slightly.

"Don't you think so?" he asked.

"Yes, yes of course," she quickly answered. "But the paths aren't very well lit at night."

Jo suddenly felt her temples getting sweaty and her knees weak.

"That's a minor detail. The neighborhood is beautiful and

calm, and we're not invaded by gangs of youths or have graffiti on the buildings. And we have trees, flowers, and grass. You can hear birds singing from early in the morning, and sometimes see a squirrel running around. It's important for children to be in contact with nature."

He turned to Zoé and asked, "Do you like animals?"

Zoé kept her eyes downcast, looking at the floor. She was probably remembering what Paul said about his basement neighbor, and was keeping her distance, in solidarity with her new pal.

"Cat got your tongue?" asked Lefloc-Pignel, leaning down. She shook her head.

"She's shy," said Joséphine, apologizing.

"I'm not shy," she protested. "I'm reserved."

"I see your daughter has a good vocabulary and a sense of nuance."

"That's not surprising, I'm in ninth grade."

"Same as my son Gaétan. What school do you go to?"

"Rue de la Pompe."

"So do my children."

"Do you like it?" asked Joséphine, afraid that Zoé's polite silence was becoming embarrassing.

"Some of the teachers are excellent, others are useless. The parents have to make up for the teachers' shortcomings. I go to all the parent–teacher conferences. I'm sure I'll see you there."

The elevator had reached the fourth floor and Hervé Lefloc-Pignel stepped out, carefully carrying the white bag on his outstretched hands. He turned around, bowed, and gave them a big smile before walking away.

"Did you see that, Mommy?" asked Zoé. "Something in his bag was moving!"

"Don't be silly! He's probably just bringing up some preserves or venison. Probably has a freezer in the basement. I'm sure he's a hunter. Did you hear the way he talked about nature?"

Zoé didn't look convinced.

"It was moving, I tell you!"

"Zoé, stop making up stories!"

"I like telling myself stories. It makes my life less sad. When I'm grown up, I'm gonna be a writer. I'll write *Les Misérables*."

They ate a quick dinner, during which Joséphine was able to hide the cut on her left hand. Zoé yawned several times while finishing her Petit Suisse.

"You're sleepy, baby. Go on to bed."

Zoé trudged off to her bedroom. When Joséphine came to kiss her good night, she was already half asleep, with her doll, Nestor, next to her on the pillow. Zoé still slept with him even though he was worn out by many washes. She loved him so much that she would sometimes ask her mother, "Isn't Nestor handsome, Mommy? Even though Hortense says he's as ugly as a flea on crutches."

Joséphine found it hard not to agree with Hortense, but she lied heroically, searching for some hint of beauty in the shapeless, faded, one-eyed rag.

"Are you comfortable in your new room, my love?"

"I like the apartment a lot, but I don't like the people here. They're weird."

"They aren't weird, darling, they're different."

"Why are they different? That man we met in the elevator, he feels cold inside. It's like he's got scales all over his body so you can't get close to him, and he just lives in his head."

"What about Paul? You think he's all cold too?"

"Oh, no! Paul . . ."

Zoé stopped, then went on.

"Paul's got *zsa zsa zsu*, Mommy" she breathed. "I'd really like to be his friend."

"I'm sure you'll be his friend, sweetie."

"Do you think he feels I have zsa zsa zsu?"

"Well, he talked to you, and he offered to introduce you to the Van den Brocks. That means he wants to see you again, and he thinks you're cute."

"Are you sure? I didn't think he seemed all that interested. Boys aren't interested in me. Now, Hortense, she's got zsa zsa zsu."

"Hortense is four years older than you. Wait until you're her age, and you'll see!"

Zoé studied her mother thoughtfully, as if she wanted to believe her but found it too hard to imagine that she could someday be as beautiful and alluring as Hortense.

"Mommy, I don't want to grow up. Sometimes I'm so scared, you have no idea."

"Afraid of what?"

"I don't know. And that makes me even more scared."

The thought was so apt that Joséphine herself found it frightening.

"When do you know when you're grown up, Mommy?"

"When you make a very important decision all by yourself without asking anybody."

"You're grown up. In fact, you're very, very grown up!"

Jo would have liked to tell her that she often had doubts, often left things up to luck or to fate or put them off until tomorrow. *Suppose we never really completely grow up?* she asked herself, as she stroked Zoé's nose, cheeks, forehead, and hair, while listening as her breathing peacefully slowed. She sat at the foot of the bed until Zoé fell asleep, drawing from her daughter's reassuring presence the strength to stop thinking of what had happened to her. Then she went to her own bedroom.

Jo closed her eyes and tried to sleep. But each time she was about to drift off, she could hear man's curses and feel his kicks battering her body.

Tomorrow is Saturday. I'll call Shirley.

Talking to Shirley would calm her. Shirley put everything right.

At the age of sixty-seven, Marcel Grobz was a happy man at last, and he reveled in it. He reminded himself when he got out of bed in the morning, repeated it to the mirror while he shaved, chanted it as he pulled on his pants. He thanked God and all the saints while tying his tie. As he splashed Guerlain eau de cologne Impériale on his face, he vowed to give 10 euros to the first beggar he met in the street.

When he was showered, shaved, and dressed, Marcel went into the kitchen to pay homage to the source of all that joy: the crème de la crème of femininity, the Everest of sensuality: his companion Josiane Lambert, who was known as honeybunch.

At that moment, she was busy at her AGA range, the model with the triple layer of vitreous enamel. She was frying eggs for her man. Swathed in the vaporous nimbus of a pink negligee, she watched her every move with furrowed brow and grave concentration.

"How you spoil me!" exclaimed Marcel. "Such care, such refinement! And the best of all is the love you give me. You're my happiness, honeybunch. You make me lyrical, happy, even handsome. I've become good looking, don't you think? Women turn around in the street to look me over. I stroll along without saying anything, but I love it."

"They're checking you out because you're talking to yourself!"

"No, honeybunch, no! It's all the loving that makes me shine like a star. Look at me: Since we've started living together I've gotten handsomer. I'm younger, I glow. I'm even putting on muscles."

Marcel slapped his stomach, after sucking it in.

"How's the son and heir?" he asked. "Did he sleep well?"

"He woke around eight, I changed and fed him, and he dozed off again. He's still sleeping so don't go and wake him up!"

"Come on! Just one little kiss on the tip of his right foot!" Marcel pleaded.

"No. Babies need to sleep. Especially at seven months."

"But he looks twelve months older than that! You saw he already has four teeth. And when I talk to him, he understands everything. Just the other day I was wondering if I should open a new factory in China. I was talking to myself, thinking he was busy playing with his toes. Well, he lifted that adorable face to me and he said yes. Twice! I swear!"

"You're hearing things, Marcel Grobz. You're completely off your rocker."

"I even think he said, 'Go, Daddy, go!' He speaks English, too. Did you know that?"

"At seven months!"

"That's right!"

"Just because you put him to sleep with that Assimil language program? You don't really believe that stuff works, do you? I worry about you, Marcel, I really do."

Every evening when he put his son to bed, Marcel turned on a CD designed to teach English. He'd bought it in the children's section at WH Smith on rue de Rivoli. Marcel took off his shoes, stretched out near the crib on the carpet with a pillow under his head, and repeated the sentences of lesson number one in the darkness. "My name is Marcel, what is your name? I live in Paris, where do you live? I have a wife. . . . Well, sort of a wife," he corrected in the dark. The soft female voice on the disc lulled him to sleep. He had never gotten past the first lesson.

"Okay, he doesn't talk it fluently, I'll grant you that. But he does babble a few words. Anyway, I distinctly heard him say, 'Go, Daddy, go.' I'd bet my life on it!"

"Then you better go buy some life insurance!" said Josiane. "Get a grip, Marcel. Your son is perfectly normal. That doesn't mean he's not a very beautiful baby, very alert and lively."

"I'm just telling you what I see and hear. I'm not making anything up."

Marcel jabbed a chunk of buttered toast into his fried eggs and sloppily mopped the plate with it.

Josiane couldn't help but smile. Marcel senior and Marcel junior were going to make a hell of a pair of rascals. It was true that Junior was smart and grasped things very fast. At seven months he sat bolt upright in his high chair and pointed an imperious finger at the object of his desire. If she didn't do as he wanted, he would frown and glare at her. She didn't know a lot about babies' usual behavior, but she had to admit that Junior seemed very advanced for his age.

Life had given Josiane two men, a big one and a little one, and they were sewing her a mantle of joy stitch by tiny stitch. She wasn't about to let life take them away from her. Marcel had made her the woman who shared his life and repudiated Henriette, the long-nosed, shrewish wife they called the Toothpick. End of story, thought Josiane, and the start of my happiness.

She had spotted Henriette prowling around their building, ducking behind street corners so as not to be noticed. But she was wearing her usual hat—the one that looked like a big pancake—and it was a dead giveaway. If you want to play undercover detective, you have to change your headgear, or you'll soon be discovered.

It worried Josiane to have her happiness spied on by a bony woman with knobby knees. It gave her the shivers. *She's on the hunt, looking for something. Looking for an opportunity. She's stalled the divorce proceedings dead in the water with her demands. Won't give an inch.*

Marcel pushed his plate back and looked up at her.

"Something the matter, honeybunch?"

"I'm a bundle of nerves today, I don't know why . . . Everything's going too well for us, Marcel. Some old raven is going to come perch on us—some stinking, croaking black thing, full of misery."

"No, it won't! We've earned our happiness. It's our turn to set off the fireworks."

"Yeah, but when has life ever been fair, huh? When has it been just? Ever seen that, you?"

Iris reached for her mirror, feeling around on the night table without finding it. They'd taken it away! Probably afraid she would break it and use the glass to slit her wrists.

Who do they think I am? And why shouldn't I have the right to end my life? Why would they deny me that ultimate freedom, considering what life has in store for me? At forty-seven and a half, it's over. The wrinkles are getting deeper, the collagen is gone, little pads of fat are gathering in the corners. I can see it happening every day. I use my compact mirror to inspect the skin behind my knee, spying the buildup of fat. And I won't lose it by lying around all day long. I'm wasting away in this bed. My color's as waxy as a church candle. I can see it in the doctors' eyes. They don't look at me. They talk to me like a graduated glass they pour full of drugs. I'm not a woman anymore, I'm a laboratory beaker.

She grabbed a glass and hurled it against the wall.

"I want to see myself!" she screamed. "I want to see myself! Give me back my mirror!"

She picked up a spoon she took her medicine with, rubbed it on the sheet, and turned it around to see her reflection. All she saw was a face deformed as if it had been stung by a swarm of bees. She threw the spoon against the wall as well.

Before, I existed because others looked at me, lent me thoughts, talent, style, elegance. Before, I existed because I was Philippe Dupin's wife, I had Philippe Dupin's credit card, I had Philippe Dupin's address book. People feared and respected me, flattered me with their lies.

She tipped her head back and gave a bark of angry laughter.

It's a poor success if it doesn't belong to you, if you haven't made it, if you haven't built it brick by brick. When you lose that, you may as well go crouch in the street with your hand out.

Iris was lucid, which magnified her unhappiness. She could be unfair when she got angry, but she quickly became reasonable again, and cursed herself. She cursed her cowardice, her frivolousness. *Life gave me everything when I was born, and I didn't do a thing with it. I let myself float along on a bubble of ease. I have to find myself another husband, and quickly. Richer, stronger, more important than Philippe. A huge husband. Someone to dazzle and subjugate me, someone I'll kneel before like a little girl. Someone who will take me in hand, get me into the social whirl again. With money, connections, dinners out on the town. I'm still pretty. As soon as I get out of here, I'll become the beautiful and magnificent Iris I was before.*

Joséphine and Zoé were eating breakfast when the telephone rang.

"Joséphine. It's Luca."

"Luca? Where in the world were you? I tried calling you all day yesterday."

"I couldn't talk. Are you free this afternoon? We could go for a walk around the lake."

Joséphine's thoughts were racing. Zoé was going to the movies with a classmate. She would be available for three hours.

"How about three o'clock, near the boathouse?"

"I'll be there."

He hung up without a word. Joséphine held the telephone in the air, surprised at how sad she felt. Luca had been curt, without an ounce of tenderness in his voice. Her tears rose, but she blinked them away.

"Is something the matter, Mommy?"

Zoé was looking at her with concern.

"That was Luca," she said. "I'm afraid something must have happened to his brother. You know, Vittorio."

"Ah," murmured Zoé, relieved that her mother was just worried about some stranger.

"Do want some more toast?" asked Joséphine.

"Yes, please!"

Jo stood up, sliced the bread and toasted it.

"With honey on it?" she asked.

She was careful to sound enthusiastic so Zoé wouldn't notice the sadness in her voice. She felt her heart had been emptied. *With Luca, I'm happy intermittently. I steal my happiness from him, wrestling it away. I break into him like a burglar into a house. He closes his eyes, pretends not to see me, lets me rob him. I love him in spite of himself.*

"Hortense's special honey?" asked Zoé.

Joséphine nodded.

"She wouldn't be happy if she found out we ate it when she's not here."

"But you're not going to finish the whole jar, are you?"

"One never knows," said Zoé with a greedy smile. "When's Hortense coming back, Mommy?"

"I don't know."

"What about Gary?"

"I have no idea, darling."

"How about Shirley? Do you have any news?"

"I tried to phone her, but she didn't answer. She must've left for the weekend."

"I miss them," said Zoé. "We don't have much family, do we, Mommy?"

"That's true. We were shortchanged in the family department," said Joséphine playfully.

"What about Henriette? Couldn't you make up with her? That would make at least one grandmother, even if she doesn't like us calling her that."

Everybody used Henriette's first name, and she refused to be called "Grandma" or "Granny."

"At least you have *one* uncle and *one* cousin, Philippe and Alexandre. That's a start."

"It's not much. The girls in my class have real families."

Zoé's expression turned serious. *What is she thinking about?* Jo wondered, gazing at her daughter. *Something's on her mind.* Zoé squinted and widened her eyes, they changed color, and her eyebrows knitted and relaxed. After a while she looked her mother in the eye and anxiously asked, "Do you think I look like a man, Mommy?"

"Of course not! Whatever makes you say that?"

"You don't think my shoulders are too square?"

"Not at all! What a strange idea!"

"Because I bought a copy of *Elle*. All the girls in my class read it."

"So?"

"Nobody should read *Elle*. The girls in the magazine are too beautiful. I'll never be like them."

Her mouth full, Zoé was eating her fourth slice of toast.

"Well, I think you're very pretty and I don't think your shoulders are too square."

"Yeah, but you're my mother, so of course you don't."

"Do you have any homework to do for Monday?"

Luca was waiting near the boathouse. He was sitting on a bench, hands in his pockets, legs outstretched, his long nose aimed at the ground, a hank of brown hair across his face. Joséphine stopped and looked at him before approaching.

The problem is, I don't know how to love lightly. I want to throw my arms around the neck of the one I love, but I'm so afraid of scaring him that I extend a humble cheek for his kiss. Luca, you and I have been seeing each other for a year, and I don't know any more about you than what you revealed on our first date. In love, you're like a man who has no appetite.

Luca had seen her. He stood up and gave her a light, almost brotherly peck on the cheek. Joséphine pulled away, already feeling the dull pain caused by the kiss. *I'm going to talk to him today,* she decided with the boldness of the very shy. *I'm going to tell him my misfortunes. Why have a lover if you have to hide your pains and fears from him?*

"How are you, Joséphine?"

"Things could be better."

Come on, hang in there, just be yourself. Talk to him. Tell him you were attacked.

"I've just spent two awful days," he immediately said. "Vittorio disappeared Friday afternoon, the day I was supposed to meet you."

He gave her a pained smile.

"He had an appointment with the therapist who is treating him for his outbursts, but he didn't keep it. We looked for him everywhere. He only returned this morning and was in terrible shape. I feared the worst."

He took Joséphine's hand. "I'm very sorry I stood you up."

Feeling Luca's long, dry fingers moved her. She pressed her cheek against the sleeve of his duffel coat, as if to say that it didn't matter, that she forgave him.

"Yesterday I spent the whole day and night on his sofa, waiting for him," Luca continued. "When he came back this morning I was there. He was haggard and looked at me as if he didn't know me. He ran to the shower without a word. I persuaded him to take a sleeping pill and to get some rest. He was exhausted."

Luca was clutching Joséphine's hand as if to convey the anguish of his two days of waiting and dread.

"I'm really worried about Vittorio," he said. "I don't know what to do anymore."

"I have problems too," said Joséphine.

Luca raised an eyebrow in surprise.

"Something very violent happened to me," she said, trying to make light of it.

Just then, a black Labrador sprinted past them and dove into the lake. Distracted, Luca watched as it swam in the oily, greenish water, which made rainbow-sheen ripples. The dog's jaws were open, and he was panting as he swam. His owner threw him a ball, and he paddled out to fetch it, his glossy black coat catching liquid pearls and water splashing in his wake. Some nervous ducks took to the air, cautiously settling a little farther away.

"Those dogs are unbelievable!" exclaimed Luca. "Look!"

Then, turning back to her:

"You were saying, Jo?"

"I was saying that . . . that someone almost killed me."

"Almost killed? You? That's unbelievable!"

"Friday night on my way back from our failed meeting, a man stabbed me in the chest. Right here!"

She patted her heart to underscore the drama of what she was saying. As she did, she felt ridiculous. She just wasn't credible as a victim in some news story. *Luca must think I'm being dramatic to compete with his brother.*

"Your story doesn't make any sense!" he said. "If you were stabbed, you'd be dead!"

"I was saved by a shoe. Antoine's shoe."

She calmly explained what happened. He listened while watching a flight of pigeons.

"Have you told the police?"

"No. I didn't want Zoé to find out."

Luca looked at her dubiously.

"For heaven's sake, Jo! If you were attacked, you have to go to the police!"

"What you mean, *if* I was attacked!"

"But suppose this man attacks someone else! You'd be responsible! You'd have a death on your conscience."

Not only was Luca not taking her in his arms to reassure her, not only was he not saying, "I'm here, I'll protect you," he was guilt-tripping her and thinking of the next victim instead! Joséphine looked at him helplessly. *What do I have to do to get this man to show some feelings?*

"Don't you believe me?"

"Of course I believe you. I'm just suggesting you should go to the police and file a complaint against persons unknown."

"You seem very well informed!"

"With my brother, I'm used to police stations. I know practically every one in Paris."

Joséphine now stared at him in astonishment. Luca had brought everything back to his own story! He'd taken a little detour to listen to her, then closed the circle around his own unhappiness. He put his arm on her shoulder and pulled her close. In a low, weary voice, he murmured, "Joséphine, I can't handle everyone's problems. Let's keep things light, all right? I feel good when I'm with you. You're the only part of my life with any cheer, laughter, or tenderness. Let's not spoil that. Please."

Jo nodded, feeling resigned.

She thought to ask what he had wanted to tell her the other evening at the brasserie, but decided against it. Luca's hand was stroking her shoulder, but it seemed to want to escape.

That day, a little piece of her heart broke away from him.

At nightfall, Joséphine sought refuge on her balcony.

When she was looking for a new apartment, the first question she put to the real estate agent—before knowing the price, how much sunlight it got, what floor it was on, the neighborhood, the Metro station, the state of the roof and gutters—was always, "Does it have a balcony? A real balcony where I can stretch out and look at the sky?"

Joséphine wanted a balcony so she could talk to the stars. She wanted to talk to her father.

Lucien Plissonnier had died on July 13 when Jo was ten years old. Firecrackers were going off, people were twirling on dance floors, and the fireworks lighting up the sky were making dogs howl.

Since then, Jo had developed a habit. Whenever she felt sad, she would wait until dark, wrap a quilt around her, go out on the balcony, and talk to the stars.

All the things that father and daughter hadn't said to each other while he was alive, they now shared via the Milky Way. She always followed the same ritual. She sat down in the corner of the balcony, propped her elbows on her bent knees, and looked up at the sky. She found the Big Dipper and the little star at the end of the handle, and started talking. It seemed to twinkle on and off as if to say, "Go ahead, darling, I'm listening, tell me."

"Daddy, my life has become a whirlpool, and I'm being sucked under.

"Do you remember when I was a little girl and almost drowned? You watched from the beach and couldn't do anything because the sea was rough and you didn't know how to swim? Do you remember?

"It was calm when Mom, Iris, and I started out. Mom was ahead of us, swimming strongly as usual. Iris was next, and I was a little way back, trying not to be left behind. I must've been seven. All of a sudden the wind came up, the waves got bigger and bigger, and the current caught us. We were being swept away, and you were just a tiny figure on the beach waving your arms in alarm. We were going to die. That's when Mommy decided to save Iris. She might not have been able to save both of us, but she chose Iris. She wedged Iris under her arm and towed her to the beach. She left me all alone, gulping salt water, thrown around by the waves, tumbling like a rock. When I realized she'd abandoned me, I tried to swim toward her and hang on, but she turned and yelled, 'Let go of me!' and shoved me away with her shoulder. I don't remember how I managed to get to shore. It was as if a hand took me by the hair and pulled me to the beach.

"I know I almost drowned.

"Today it's the same thing. The currents are too strong, they're carrying me away too far. Too far, and too fast. Too alone. I'm sad, Daddy. Sad from having to deal with Iris's anger, the stranger's violence, Luca's indifference. It's too much. I'm not strong enough."

Her head between her knees, Joséphine listened to the wind, listened to the night. A thought occurred to her: *Luca didn't take the attack seriously because I don't take it seriously, either.*

Luca doesn't pay more attention to me because I don't pay attention to myself.

Luca treats me the way I treat myself.

He didn't hear the danger in my words or the fear in my voice. He didn't feel the stabbing of the knife because I didn't feel it.

I know it happened to me, but I feel nothing. Someone stabs me, but I don't go to the police and ask for protection or revenge or help. Someone stabs me and I don't do anything.

It slides off me.

I present a fact, the words are there, I speak them aloud, but there isn't any feeling to give them color. My words are mute.

Luca doesn't hear them, he can't. They're the words of a dead woman, someone who died a long time ago.

I'm that dead woman, draining the color from her words, draining the color from her life. Ever since the day Mother decided to save Iris instead.

That day, she erased me from her life. In fact, she erased me from life itself. It was as if she said, "You aren't worth existing, so you no longer exist."

And I, a little girl of seven, shivering in the icy water, looked at her, baffled at her gesture, the shoulder that shoved me aside into the waves.

I died that day. I became a dead woman behind the mask of a living one. I act without ever connecting what I do with myself. I'm not real anymore. I've become virtual.

Everything slides off me.

When I managed to crawl out of the water, when Daddy carried me off, yelling at Mother, saying she was a criminal, I told myself that she didn't have any choice. She couldn't save both of us, and she chose Iris. I don't complain, I think it's normal.

Everything slides off me. I don't demand anything, I take nothing for myself.

I pass the agrégation *exam in classics. Fine.*

I'm recruited by the Centre National de la Recherche Scientifique. I'm one of three people hired out of a hundred and twenty-three applicants. Fine.

I get married, I become a gentle, supportive wife. My husband's absent-minded love evaporates.

He cheats on me. That's no surprise, he's unhappy.

I don't have any rights; nothing belongs to me because I don't exist.

But I continue to act as if I did. One-two, one-two. I write articles, give talks, publish, write a habilitation *thesis. I'll end up being a research director, and my career will have reached its peak. Fine. . . .*

It doesn't resonate in me; it brings me no joy.

I become a mother. I give birth to a baby girl, then a second one.

That's when I come alive. I rediscover the child in myself, the little girl shivering on the beach. I take her in my arms, I rock her, I kiss her fingertips, I tell her stories to help her sleep, I warm her honey. I love her. Nothing is too beautiful for the little girl who died at seven whom I bring back to life with hot compresses, kisses, and care.

My sister asks me to write a book that she'll put her name to. I agree. The book becomes a huge success. Fine.

It pains me that I don't get credit for the book, but I don't protest.

When my daughter Hortense goes on television to tell the truth and thrusts me into the spotlight, I disappear. I don't want people to see me, I don't want them to know me. There's nothing to see, nothing to know. I'm dead. Nothing can touch me because I stopped existing that day in the raging sea in the Landes.

Since then, things happen to me but make no impression.

I'm dead. I have a bit part in my own life.

Joséphine looked up at the stars. The Milky Way seemed illuminated, twinkling with a thousand pearly lights.

I should buy some white camellias.

Joséphine loved white camellias.

"Shirley?"

"Joséphine!"

The way Shirley said it, Jo's name sounded like a trumpet call. Launched from the first syllable, it rose into the air, weaving arabesques of sound: *Joooséphiiine!*

"Shiiirley!" said Jo, echoing her. "I miss you! Please move back to Paris, I'm begging you. I've got a big apartment now and I can house you and your entourage."

"Actually, there's a chance that I might show up one of these days, pay a little visit to the arrogant frogs."

"Not a visit, an invasion! A good old-fashioned Hundred Years' War."

Shirley burst out laughing.

Ah, Shirley's laughter! It papered the walls, hung up curtains and paintings, filled the whole room.

"When are you coming?" asked Joséphine.

"At Christmas, with Hortense and Gary."

"But you'll stay for a while, won't you? Life isn't the same without you."

"That sounds like a declaration of love."

"Declarations of love and friendship are very similar."

"So . . . how are you doing in your new apartment?"

"I feel like a guest in my own house. I perch on the edge of the sofa, I knock before entering the living room, and I spend all my time in the kitchen. It's the one place I feel most comfortable."

"Knowing you, I'm not surprised!"

"To think I bought this apartment to make Hortense happy, and she goes off to live in London."

Joséphine heaved a sigh. *It's always that way with Hortense. You're always setting your offerings before a closed door.*

"Zoé's like me," she said. "We feel like outsiders here. The only person who seems alive is the concierge. Her name's Iphigénie, and she dyes her hair a different color every month. She goes from Iroquois red to glacier blue, and I never recognize her, but she gives me a real smile when she brings the mail up."

"Iphigénie, eh? She'll come to a bad end, that one. Sacrificed by her father . . . or was it her husband?"

"She lives in the concierge apartment with her two children, a boy of five and a girl of seven. She takes out the garbage cans every morning at six thirty."

"Let me guess: you two are going to be friends. I know you. How's life otherwise?"

Joséphine murmured that things could be better, then told the whole story. Shirley interrupted a few times to register her astonishment and anxiety with, "Oh, shit! Joooséphiiine!" She asked for specifics, thought for a moment, then decided to tackle the problems one at a of the time.

"Let's start with the mysterious killer," she said. "Luca's right, you should go talk to the cops. Because it's true, he might do it again! Just imagine if he killed a woman beneath your window."

Joséphine nodded.

"Try to remember everything when you give your statement. Sometimes a detail will put them on the right track."

"He had smooth soles."

"You mean the soles of his shoes? You saw them?"

"Yeah. They were smooth and clean, as if the shoes had just come out of the box. Nice ones, like from J.M. Weston or Church's."

"I see," said Shirley. "If he's wearing Church's, he's not some pikey punk from a council estate. But it doesn't help the investigation."

"Why not?"

"Because smooth soles don't tell you anything about the person's weight or size, or where he's been walking. A good worn sole can reveal valuable information. Any idea how old he was?"

"No, but he sure was strong. Oh yes! When he was cursing,

he had a nasal voice. That I remember very well. He sounded like this . . ."

Talking through her nose, Joséphine repeated the attacker's curses.

"And he smelled good. I mean he didn't stink or smell sweaty."

"Which suggests he acted in cold blood, not in a fit of rage. He prepared his action, thought it over, set the stage. He probably wanted revenge. He was righting a wrong that was done to him. I learned that when I was working in intelligence. And you say there was no aqueous discharge?"

The phrase was unexpected, but it didn't surprise Joséphine. Those two words—aqueous discharge—said a great deal about Shirley's past and her knowledge of the world of violence. To hide the secret of her royal birth, she had worked for a time in Queen Elizabeth's secret service. She'd been trained as a bodyguard, and learned to fight and defend herself, to read faces for people's intentions and impulses. She had spent time around ruthless men, uncovered plots, learned to penetrate the criminal mind. Joséphine admired her nerve. "Any one of us could stoop to crime," Shirley liked to say (when Joséphine asked her about her past). "What's surprising isn't that it happens, but that it doesn't happen more often."

On the phone, Joséphine heard a whistling in the background that died away with a sigh. Shirley must have turned off the gas. It was teatime. She imagined Shirley in her kitchen, phone propped on her shoulder, pouring nearly boiling water over the fragrant leaves. She owned an assortment of teas in colored metal boxes, and when you open their lids, they released intoxicating smells. Green tea, red tea, black tea, white tea, Prince Igor, Czar

Alexander, Marco Polo. Shirley took the leaves from the teapot after exactly three and a half minutes of steeping, timed to the second.

"As far as Luca's indifference, what can I tell you?" she continued, moving from one topic to the next without being distracted. "He's been that way since the beginning, and you let him keep his emotional distance. You've always done that with men. You apologize for breathing, you thank them for deigning to look at you."

Joséphine told her what she had just realized while looking at the stars and talking to the Big Dipper.

"You mean you're still talking to the stars?"

"Yeah."

"Well, I suppose it's as good as therapy, and it's free."

"I'm sure he hears me and answers me from up there."

"If that's what you believe . . . I don't need to climb to the stars to tell you that your mother is a criminal and that you're a ninny who has let people walk all over you since the day you were born."

"I know, I finally understood that—at forty-three. You're right. I'll go see the police. It's so good to talk to you, Shirley. Everything becomes clear when we talk."

"It's always easier to see things from the outside, when you're not involved. Is the writing coming along?"

"Not really. I'm going around in circles. I need a subject for a novel, and I can't think of one. I come up with a thousand stories during the day, but they disappear at night."

"Go to the movies, take a walk, look at people in cafés. Let your imagination wander, and one day an idea for a story will just pop into your head."

"How about the story of a man who stabs lonely women in parks at night!"

"Why not?"

"No! I want to forget all that. I'm going to start working on my *habilitation* thesis again."

"What's a *habilitation* thesis?"

"It's a body of publications that includes a major thesis and all the work you've produced in articles and conferences. You present it to a jury. It's a big chunk of work. I already have about forty pounds of stuff!"

"What's it good for?"

"You can lead a research group and supervise doctoral students."

"And earn tons of dosh!"

"No. Academics aren't drawn to money. It's more the crowning of a career. You become somebody, you're spoken to with respect. People come from all over the world to consult you. Everything I need to make my mark."

"Joséphine, you're wonderful!

"Hold on, I'm not there yet! I still have a two or three years of hard work to do before I can defend my thesis. What about you, what are you up to?"

"I've created a nonprofit to fight obesity. I go into schools and teach the kids how to eat properly. We're creating a society of fatties."

"That's something neither of my daughters has to worry about."

"Of course not. You've been fixing them nice balanced meals since they were babies. By the way, your daughter and my son are spending all their time together."

"Hortense and Gary? You mean they're lovers?"

"I don't know, but they're seeing a lot of each other."

"We'll quiz them when they come to Paris."

"I ran into Philippe too, the other day at the Tate. He was standing in front of a red and black Rothko."

"Was he alone?" asked Joséphine, surprised to feel her heart speed up.

"Er, no. He was with a young blonde. He introduced her as a painting consultant who was helping him acquire artworks. He's building a collection. Since stepping away from the business world, he has a lot of free time."

"What was the consultant like?"

"Not bad."

"If you weren't my friend you'd go so far as to say she was . . ."

"Not bad at all. You should come to London, Jo. Philippe is attractive, rich, handsome, and at leisure. For the moment he's living alone with his son. That makes him a perfect prey for hungry she-wolves."

"I can't, and you know it."

"Iris?"

Joséphine bit her lip without answering.

The next morning she went to the local police station. After a long wait in a hallway that smelled of cherry-scented floor polish, she was ushered into a narrow, windowless office. It was lit by a yellowish ceiling light that made the room look like an aquarium.

She explained the facts of the attack to a police captain, a young woman with thin lips and an aquiline nose, her brown hair in a bun. She was wearing a light blue blouse and navy cargo pants, and had a small gold earring in her left ear. The plaque on her desk read CAPITAINE GALLOIS.

She had Joséphine give her name, first name, and address, and reason for being at the police station. She listened to Joséphine's story in silence, her face impassive. She was surprised that Joséphine had waited so long to report the attack and offered to have her see a doctor. Jo declined. She asked her to describe the man and if she had noticed any detail that might help the investigation. Joséphine mentioned the smooth, clean soles, the nasal voice, the absence of perspiration. Capitaine Gallois raised an eyebrow, surprised by the detail, then went on typing the statement. She asked if there was a reason anyone would want to hurt her, and whether robbery or rape had occurred, and then summarized the facts in a mechanical, emotionless voice.

Joséphine felt like weeping.

Hortense stepped over the clothes tossed helter-skelter on the living room floor. Her flatmate was a pale, anemic French girl who stubbed out her cigarettes everywhere, heedlessly burning holes at random. Agathe must have gotten undressed where she stood, because the rug was strewn with her jeans, thong, tights, T-shirt, turtleneck, and jacket.

Agathe was enrolled at the same school as Hortense, but didn't show nearly the same commitment to studying or keeping the apartment clean. She got up if she heard the alarm clock. Otherwise, she stayed in bed and caught the following class. Dirty dishes piled up in the kitchen sink, dirty clothes covered what were once sofas, the television was always on, and empty bottles littered the glass coffee table amid cut-up magazines, dry pizza crusts, and ashtrays overflowing with the butts of old joints.

"Agathe!" screamed Hortense. When no sound came from the room where she was most likely buried under her covers, Hortense started listing all of her roommate's shortcomings punctuating the violence of her tone with kicks on her door. "This can't go on! You're disgusting! You can make a mess in your room, but not in our shared space! I just spent an hour cleaning the bathroom. There's hair everywhere, everything's clogged up, the toothpaste is leaking, there's a used Tampax in the toilet. Were you raised in a barn? You're not living alone here, you know! I'm warning you, I'm gonna get another apartment. I can't stand this anymore!"

The problem is, I can't really move, thought Hortense. *The lease has both our names on it and I've already paid a two-month deposit. . . . I wouldn't even know where to go.*

She looked at the coffee table with a grimace of disgust, fetched a big garbage bag, and stuffed everything on and under the table into it. Holding her nose, she tied the bag shut and tossed it out on the landing, to be taken downstairs later. *If Agathe had to fish her jeans out of the garbage, it might get her attention. But maybe not even that would do it,* Hortense grumbled. *She would just buy herself another pair with the money she gets from one of her old and disgusting gangster boyfriends, guys who smoked cigars in the living room while Agathe the anorexic was pasting her false eyelashes on. Where does she even find them? One glance at their camel hair coats and raised collars makes you want to run and hide. They give me the creeps, coming and going every night.*

"Do you hear me, you lazy slut?"

She listened at the door. Agathe didn't stir.

Hortense put on some rubber gloves, took a sponge, and started mopping up. Gary was coming to get her in an hour, and there was no way he was going to set foot in a pigsty.

When I have money, I'll have a cleaning woman. When I have money . . .

"But you don't have any money, so shut up and clean," she muttered under her breath.

Her mother was the one who paid for her rent, school, gas, electricity, council tax, clothes, telephone, even a sandwich in the park at lunchtime. Joséphine paid for everything, in fact. And in London, nothing was free: 2 pounds for a Tropicana in the morning, 10 pounds for a sandwich at lunch, 1,200 pounds for her share of a two-bedroom apartment with a living room, though admittedly in a nice neighborhood: Notting Hill, Royal Borough of Kensington and Chelsea. Agathe's parents must have money, or maybe the mafiosi in camel hair coats supported her. Hortense couldn't figure out which. She sniffed the cleanser on her hands and wrinkled her nose. *I'm gonna stink of Domestos. The odor seeps right through the gloves.*

She stepped over to Agathe's bedroom and kicked the door again.

"I'm not your goddamn maid! Get that through your thick skull!"

"Too bad," came the answer. "And too late. I was raised with a couple of maids. That should shut you up since your family was probably on welfare."

Hortense stared at the door in astonishment. Welfare? She'd dared call her poor?

What was I thinking when I chose her out of everyone to be my roommate? I must've had fog in my eyes that day.

Gary lived in a big flat on Green Park just behind Buckingham Palace, but he'd made it very clear that he wasn't going to share it.

"Sixteen hundred square feet just for you, it's not fair!" groused Hortense.

"Maybe, but that's the way it is. I need silence and space. I need to be able to read, listen to music, think, walk back and forth in peace. I don't want you bugging me, Hortense. And whether you mean to or not, you take up a lot of space."

"I would stay in my room and be quiet as a mouse!"

"No dice," said Gary. "And don't insist or you'll be like those girls I hate, always whining and complaining."

That brought Hortense up short. There was no question of her being like anybody else. She was unique, and she worked hard to remain so. There was also no question of her losing Gary's friendship. He was probably the most desirable young bachelor in London. Royal blood flowed in his veins. Nobody was supposed to know, but she did. She had heard her mother talking with Shirley, et cetera, et cetera. Long story short, Gary was the queen's grandson. His granny lived in Buckingham Palace. He occasionally wandered over there, and he knew his way around.

He got invitations to soirées, club openings, shows, brunches, lunches, and dinners, and absentmindedly flipped through the cards that piled up on his entryway table. He always wore the same black turtleneck, the same shapeless jacket, the same pants, and the same reprehensible shoes. Gary simply didn't care how he looked. He didn't care about his black hair, his big green eyes, or any of the other details that Hortense felt made him so handsome.

Gary wanted to be a musician, a poet, or a philosopher. He studied piano and took philosophy, theater, and literature classes. He watched old movies while eating organic chips, wrote down his thoughts in ruled notebooks, and recited lines from Oscar Wilde, *Scarface*, and this one from *Children of Paradise*: "If the rich all wanted to be loved, what would be left for the poor?" He dropped into an arm chair that once belonged to George V and contemplated the beauty of the line, chin in hand. Hortense had to admit that Gary was charming, brilliant, and original. He was pitted against the consumer society and barely tolerated having a mobile phone. He was completely indifferent to modern technologies and gadgets.

When he shopped for clothes, he bought items one at a time, even if shirts, for example, were on sale at two for the price of one.

"Take the second shirt!" urged Hortense. "It's free."

"I've only got one chest!" he answered.

To top it all, he's handsome, she continued musing while sniffing her gloves. *Tall, handsome, rich, the whole package in sixteen hundred square feet with a view of Green Park. And he didn't have to lift a finger for any of it. How unfair!*

She was vacuuming when she spotted cockroaches in the living room rug: a whole swarm that made her gasp. She put the hose over them, imagining their painful death. She thought, *I'll set fire to the bag to make sure they're good and dead.*

She looked around the living room. It was now in perfect order, and smelled nice and clean. Gary could come in without slipping on a thong or a dollop of guacamole.

She looked at herself in the mirror: She was perfect too.

She stretched her long legs, studied them with satisfaction, and picked up the latest *Harper's Bazaar*. "100 Beauty Tricks to Steal from Stars, Pros, Pals." She read the article, decided it had nothing to teach her, and went to the next: "Jeans, but Which Ones?" She yawned. It was the three hundredth article she'd read on the same topic. The fashion editors needed to have their heads reamed out. *Someday, when I've created my brand, I'll be the person they come to interview.*

Just then Agathe came out of her room, drinking from a bottle of Marie Brizard. She stumbled in like a sleepwalker, belched, plopped onto the sofa, and peered blearily around for her clothes. She took another swig of liquor to wake herself up and rubbed her eyes.

"Wow, it's clean! Did you use a fire hose on the place?"

"That's a topic I don't want to talk about. Otherwise I'd want to beat you to a pulp."

"Care to tell me where my things are?"

"You mean the rags you scattered on the floor?"

The skinny blonde nodded.

"They're in a garbage bag out on the landing."

"Those are my favorite jeans! Designer jeans, two hundred thirty-five pounds! You're gonna pay for them. I'm gonna send Carlos to kick your ass!"

"That sun-tanned runt of yours? He has to stand on a chair just to reach my chin."

"You won't be laughing when he tears your tits off with a pair of pliers."

"Ooooh, God, I'm so scared! I'm quaking in my boots."

Bottle in hand, Agathe trudged to the door to retrieve her possessions, and bumped into Gary, who was about to ring the bell. He stepped into the living room, picked up *Harper's Bazaar*, and slipped it in his pocket.

"Are you reading chick magazines now?" cried Hortense.

"I'm cultivating my feminine side."

Hortense picked up her purse and shot a last look at her roommate, who was on all fours pulling her jeans from the garbage bag while shrieking like a frightened piglet.

"Come on, Gary, let's get out of here."

In the stairwell they ran into the notorious Carlos: five feet tall, a hundred and fifty pounds, hair dyed coal black, face pitted with old acne scars. He slowly looked them up and down.

"What's with him?" asked Gary. "Does he want my picture?"

The two men's eyes met.

Hortense grabbed Gary by the arm and pulled him along.

"Never mind. He's one of the knuckle-draggers who's always sniffing around Agathe."

"You two have another fight?"

Hortense stopped and turned to him. Putting on her most appealing and moving expression, she said pleadingly, "Hey, Gary, won't you let me live—"

"No, Hortense! It's out of the question. You work things out with your roomie. I'm staying at my place, in peace and alone!"

The king-size bed filled half the room and was surrounded by the clothes they had stripped off before jumping under the covers.

Where am I? wondered Philippe, gazing around the bedroom. *And how old is she?* In the pub the night before, he would have said twenty-eight or thirty. Looking at the walls of her flat this morning, he wasn't so sure. He couldn't quite remember how he had approached her. Snatches of dialogue came back to him. They were always the same; only the pub and the woman changed.

"Can I buy you a beer?"

"Sure."

They'd drunk one, two, three beers standing at the bar, bending elbows while half watching a Manchester–Liverpool match on TV. Soccer fans were shouting and slamming their glasses on the bar. They wore team jerseys and jabbed each other in the ribs at each notable play. Behind the bar, a waiter in a white shirt frantically yelled orders to a second one, whose arms seemed welded to the taps.

After a while, Philippe had whispered, "Fancy a quickie?"

"All right. My place or yours?"

He preferred going to her apartment. Alexandre and the nanny lived at his.

These days I spend my time waking up in rooms I don't know with bodies I don't recognize. I feel like an airline pilot, changing hotels and partners every night. More critical people would say I'm going through puberty again. Pretty soon I'll be watching Sponge-Bob SquarePants *with Alexandre, and we'll recite Squidward Tentacles's lines together.*

He felt like going home to watch his sleeping son. Alexandre was changing, coming into his own. He had taken to English ways very quickly. He drank milk, ate muffins, learned how to cross the street without getting run over, took the Tube and the bus by himself. He went to the Lycée Français but in a few months had become a proper little Brit.

To make sure he didn't forget his native language, Philippe decreed that only French could be spoken at home. He also hired a French nanny, a stocky, fiftyish Breton from Brest. Her name was Annie, and she and Alexandre seemed to get along well.

The boy went on trips to the museum with his father and asked questions when he didn't understand something. "How do you know something's going to be beautiful or ugly before anyone else?" he once asked. "When Picasso started painting everything sideways, a lot of people thought it was ugly. Now they think it's beautiful. Why?" At times his questions were more philosophical ("Should you love to live or live to love?") or ornithological ("Daddy, do penguins get AIDS?").

The only subject Alexandre never raised was his mother. When they went to visit Iris in her room at the clinic, he sat in a chair, hands on his knees, staring into space. One time, Philippe had left the two of them alone, imagining that his presence kept them from talking to each other.

Afterward, getting into the car, Alexandre said, "Daddy, don't ever, ever leave me alone with Mommy again. She scares me. Really scares me. She's there but she isn't there. Her eyes are empty." As he fastened his seat belt, he spoke again, sounding like a doctor. "She's lost a lot of weight, don't you think?"

Philippe had all the time in the world to spend with his son, and he did. He was still the head of the Paris law firm, but his role was purely supervisory. He continued to pocket fees, which were sizable, but the work no longer required his engaged and exhausting daily presence, as it had a year earlier.

For the time being, there was nothing particular he felt like doing. It was like having a hangover that went on and on. The break with Iris had been both abrupt and progressive. He had gradually grown detached from her. He was at loose ends, getting used to the idea of not living with her anymore. Another feeling, a mix of contempt and pity, had replaced the love he'd felt for her for so many years. *I loved an image, a very beautiful image. But I was a picture too: the picture of success.*

A new man had been born, stripped of appearances, pretense, and social airs. A man he was getting to know, who sometimes disconcerted him. *What role had Joséphine played in that man's emergence?* he wondered. She had played some role, he was sure, in her own discreet, low-key way. *Joséphine is like a healthful vapor that envelops you and helps you breathe freely.* Philippe remembered their first, stolen kiss in his Paris office. He had seized her wrist, pulled her close and . . .

He had chosen to settle in London, abandoning his Parisian life to take stock of himself in a foreign city. He had friends here, or rather acquaintances, and he belonged to a club. His parents lived nearby. Paris was only three hours away, and he went there often, taking Alexandre to see Iris. He never called Joséphine. It wasn't time yet. *I'm going through a strange period. I'm waiting. In neutral. I don't know anything anymore, I have to learn everything anew.*

He freed his arm, sat up in bed, fumbled for the watch he had dropped on the carpet. Seven thirty. Time to go home.

What was her name again? Debbie, Dottie, Dolly, Daisy?

He put on his underpants and shirt, and was about to pull on his trousers when she turned around and blinked, shading her eyes against the light with her arm.

"What time is it?"

"Six o'clock."

"It's the middle of the night!"

He could smell stale beer on her breath, and pulled away.

"I have to go home. I . . . I have a child waiting for me and . . ."

"And a wife?"

"Er, yes."

She abruptly turned away from him, hugging her pillow.

"Debbie . . ."

"Dottie."

"Don't be sad, Dottie."

"I'm not sad."

"Yes, you are. Your back tells me you're sad."

"As if."

"I really do have to go home."

"You treat all women the same way, Eddy?"

"Philippe."

"Do you buy them with five beers and shag them, and then it's good-bye without even a thank you?"

"What I'm doing right now isn't very classy, you're right. But I don't want to hurt your feelings."

"Too late."

She still had her back turned, and was clutching her pillow.

"Is there something I can do for you? Do you need money, advice, someone to talk to?"

"Go fuck yourself, you wanker! I'm not a slut, and I'm not a loser. I'm an accountant at Harvey and Fridley."

"Okay. At least I tried."

"Tried what?" screamed the woman, whose name he was struggling to remember.

"Listen, er . . ."

"Dottie."

"Look, Dottie, we shared a cab and a bed for a night, let's not turn this into a drama. This isn't the first time you've picked up a man in a pub."

Don't ask for her number. Don't say, "I'll call you, we'll get together." It would be cowardly. He wasn't ever going to see her again.

He picked up his jacket and scarf. Without a word, she watched him go.

Closing the door, Philippe found himself out on the street, blinking at the sky. *Did the same gray sky stretch all the way to Paris? She must be asleep at this hour. Did she get my white camellia? Did she put it out on her balcony?*

"Some passions grip the soul and stifle it," Blaise Pascal wrote, "while others expand it and cause it to break its bounds." Since Marcel Grobz left her to set up house with his secretary, Josiane Lambert, Henriette Grobz was experiencing a passion that gripped her soul: the thirst for revenge. All she could think of was repaying Marcel a hundred times over for the humiliation he had inflicted on her. Someday, she wanted to be able to tell him: "You robbed me of my place in society and my comfort. Now I'm punishing you, Marcel. I'm dragging you through the mud, along with your cheap slut and your beloved son."

Revenge, revenge! cried her whole being, from the moment she awoke. She wandered through her bare apartment, which lacked the huge bouquets that the florist Veyrat used to deliver. There was no butler to draw up the menus, no ladies' maid to care for her clothes, no servant to bring her breakfast in bed, no chauffeur to drive her around Paris, no daily sessions with her dressmaker, hairdresser, or masseuse, no visits to the salon for a pedicure and manicure. She was ruined. At the jeweler's on Place Vendôme the day before, she'd collapsed into a chair when she saw the bill for replacing her Cartier watchband. She no longer bought her beauty products in a salon, but at the drugstore. She shopped at Zara and had given up Hermès date books and Ruinart blanc de blancs champagne. Each day brought a new sacrifice.

Marcel paid the rent on her apartment and gave her an allowance, but it wasn't enough to satisfy Henriette's voracity. Without enough money, she was nothing. That other woman had it all!

That other woman. It gave Henriette nightmares. She would wake up choking with rage, her nightgown soaked through, and would have to drink a big glass of water to cool the fury that filled her chest. The nights ended by the wavering light of dawn with her mulling a revenge that she continually refined. Sunk in her soft pillows, she hissed, "I'll have your hide, Josiane Lambert, and your son's hide, too."

To settle her nerves, she hung around her rival's house, following Josiane as she walked the son and heir in an English pram full of lace and combed wool blankets.

Henriette considered acid. Throw acid at mother and child, disfiguring and blinding them, scarring them forever.

But her revenge had to be secret, anonymous, and silent.

So she decided to study her enemy's terrain. She started by trying to bribe the little maid who worked at Marcel's, to get her to talk about her mistress's friends, relations, and family. Henriette knew how to talk to servants, to put herself at their level, adopt their points of view, reinforce their imagined fears. She poured it on, flattering them, encouraging their dreams, showing herself to be a friend, to extract the piece of information she needed: Did Josiane have a lover?

"Oh no, madame would never do that!" said the maid, blushing. "She's too good a person. And too honest, too. When something's bothering her, she comes right out and says it. She's not the kind of person to hide things. Madame Josiane is very much in love, and so is monsieur. They're always kissing each other, and if Junior wasn't there to keep an eye on them, they would be doing it in the kitchen, the entry, and the living room. When it comes to loving, they really love each other. They're like two candies in a box, stuck together."

Henriette tapped her feet angrily.

"You mean to say they're still fooling around with each other? That's disgusting!"

"Oh no, madame, it's charming! If you could only see them. It gives you hope. Working for them, it makes you really believe in love."

Henriette stalked off, holding her nose.

Joséphine's plan was to work at the library, then go to Zoé's school at six thirty for the regular quarterly parent–teacher meeting. "You won't forget, will you, Mommy?" Jo had smiled and promised to be on time.

So Joséphine was sitting in the Metro facing forward, her nose against the window. She was thinking about the organization of her work, the books she had to reserve, the forms to fill out, the sandwich and coffee she'd eat at some café. She was writing a paper on medieval girls' costumes. Clothing varied by region, and you could tell where a woman came from by her clothes. A peasant girl would wear a dress and a hood, with small purses hanging from her belt; people didn't have pockets in the Middle Ages. Over the dress she would wear a surcoat, which was a kind of coat often lined with vair, the white fur from a squirrel's belly. Today, of course, you could have your eyes put out if you were caught wearing squirrel fur!

Joséphine turned and glanced at her neighbor in the Metro. He was studying a chapter on three-phase current for a lesson about electricity. She tried to read his notes, a tangle of red arrows and blue circles with square roots and divisions. A title underlined in red ink read, *What is a perfect transformer?* Joséphine smiled. She had read it as, "What is a perfect man?" Her relationship with Luca was on hold. She was no longer sleeping at his place. He had taken Vittorio in, who was becoming more and more agitated. Luca was worried about his brother's mental state. "I'm reluctant to leave him alone, but I don't want to have him committed," he said. "He's really fixated on you. I have to prove that he can rely entirely on me." Luca's publisher had moved up the deadline of his book on tears, and he had to correct the galleys. He occasionally called Jo to talk about movies or shows they could see together but didn't make a date. *He's avoiding me*, she thought. One question nagged at her: What had Luca wanted to tell her, that night when he didn't meet up with her? "I have to talk to you, Joséphine," he'd said. "It's important." Was he referring to his brother's violence? Had Vittorio threatened to harm her? Or had he turned on Luca?

An awkwardness had grown between them since she told

him about the attack. She wound up feeling she should have kept it to herself. Not bothered him with her problems. Then she caught herself. *Hold on a minute!* she snapped. *Stop treating yourself like you're nothing, Joséphine. You're a terrific person. I have to train myself to think that way. I'm a terrific person. I'm worthwhile. I'm not just a bump on a log.*

Luca was as much of a mystery as her Metro neighbor's chapter on three-phase current. *I would need a diagram with little arrows for me to understand him and touch his heart.*

A train coming in the opposite direction stopped alongside hers, and she studied the people sitting in the car. She observed them, imagining their lives, loves, and regrets. Tried to guess which ones weren't single, tried to grasp snatches of dialogue on their lips.

Her eye fell on a fat, scowling woman who was wearing a coat with a pattern of big squares. *Squares aren't a smart choice when you're fat. And that frown! I bet she's a peevish spinster.* Next to the woman sat a man with slumping shoulders wearing a red turtleneck and a worn gray jacket that was a little loose on him. He had his back turned to her. When another woman went to sit down, he moved to let her by. Joséphine saw his face and was rooted to the spot. It was Antoine! He wasn't looking at her and his eyes were vacant, but it was him.

She knocked on the window, yelling, "Antoine! Antoine!" She stood up, pounding on the glass. The man turned and looked at her in surprise. He gave a little wave, as if he was embarrassed and wanted her to calm down.

Antoine!

He had a long scar on his right cheek and his eye was shut.

Antoine?

Now she wasn't so sure.

Antoine?

He didn't seem to recognize her.

The doors closed and her train started to move. Joséphine sat and craned her neck around, desperate for another glimpse of the man who looked like Antoine.

It couldn't be him. If he were alive, he would have come to see her.

Joséphine spent the afternoon at the library, but had a hard time working. She couldn't concentrate. She kept seeing the Metro car and its occupants, the fat woman in the squares, the petite woman with the green eyeliner, and Antoine in the red turtleneck. She shook her head to clear it and went back to studying her notes.

At quarter to six she put her files and books away, and took the Metro in the other direction. At the Passy station, she looked around for a man in a red turtleneck. *Maybe he's homeless and living in a subway car. He chose the number six line because it runs above ground, you can see Paris looking like a postcard and admire the glittering Eiffel Tower. At night he sleeps bundled in an old coat under an elevated train buttress. A lot of people find refuge in the subway. He doesn't know where I'm living now. He's wandering like a hermit. He's lost his memory.*

At six thirty, she entered Zoé's school, where the teachers were holding their meetings in individual classrooms. The parents lined up in the hall, waiting for their turn to discuss their child's problems or accomplishments.

Joséphine noted Zoé's teachers' names and room numbers, and her appointment times. She went to stand in line for her first meeting, with the English teacher, Mademoiselle Pentell.

Joséphine glimpsed her neighbor, Hervé Lefloc-Pignel, coming out of a classroom. He gave her a little wave, and she smiled back. He was alone, without his wife. Then it was her turn to meet with the English teacher. Mademoiselle Pentell assured her that everything was fine. Zoé was doing very well, was comfortable in English, and had a very good accent. She had nothing special to point out. Joséphine blushed at so many compliments and knocked her chair over as she got up to leave.

It was the same thing with the math, Spanish, Earth sciences, history, and geography teachers. Jo went from classroom to classroom gathering laurels and praise. All the teachers congratulated her for having such a smart, funny, conscientious daughter. She was a good classmate too: Zoé had been asked to tutor a student who was having trouble. Joséphine took these compliments as plaudits that she awarded herself. She too admired effort, perfection, and accuracy. Aglow, she cheerfully headed to her last meeting, with Madame Berthier.

Lefloc-Pignel was waiting at the classroom door. This time, his greeting wasn't as warm as before. He was leaning against the open jamb, steadily tapping on the door with his index finger. The regular, repeated sound must have bothered Berthier because she looked up and wearily asked, "Would you mind stopping that noise, please?"

Her green bellows hat lay on a chair next to her, its fat rings at rest.

"It won't gain you any time, and you're keeping me from concentrating," she said.

Lefloc-Pignel contained himself for a moment, then started tapping again, this time with his finger bent, as if he were knocking on the door.

"Monsieur Lefloc-Pignel," said Berthier, "I would appreciate it if you waited your turn patiently."

"You're already thirty-five minutes late! That's unacceptable."

"I'll take as much time as necessary."

"What kind of the teacher are you if you don't know that punctuality is a politeness that students must be taught?"

"What kind of a parent are you if you can't listen to other people and adapt to them? This isn't a bank. We look after children here."

"You're in no position to be teaching me lessons!"

"That's too bad," Berthier said with a smile. "I would have been happy to have you as a student. You would've had to mind your *p*'s and *q*'s."

Stung, Lefloc-Pignel drew himself up to his full height.

"It's always like this!" he snapped, trying to enlist Joséphine in his cause. "The first meetings are fine, but after that they run later and later. There's no discipline! And this one deliberately makes me wait, every time. She thinks I don't notice, but I'm not fooled!"

He had raised his voice enough so Berthier could hear. She got up and briskly closed the door. The other parents stood in abashed silence.

"Did you see that? She slammed the door in my face!"

He stared at it, livid.

Jo would have given anything to be elsewhere and decided to make her escape.

Later, she told Zoé about the visit. She stressed the good opinion her teachers had of her and described the scenes of near riot she'd witnessed.

"You kept your cool because you were happy," said Zoé. "Maybe other parents are having lots of problems with their kids, so they got angry."

"Then they're mixing everything up. It isn't the teachers' fault."

As she started to clear the table, Zoé came over and wrapped her arms around her mother's waist.

"I'm very proud of you, my love," murmured Joséphine.

Zoé hugged her tighter. She sighed and asked, "Do you think Daddy would have been proud of me too?"

Joséphine started. She had forgotten about the man in the Metro. Again she saw the red turtleneck, the scarred cheek, the blind eye. She tightened her grip on Zoé, and murmured, "Of course he would. Of course."

When Iphigénie brought Joséphine the mail the next day, she told her that a woman had been stabbed the night before in the bushes near Passy.

"They found a hat next to the body," she said. "A funny almond-green hat with bellows. Exactly like yours, Madame Cortès."

PART II

♦ ♦ ♦

◆　◆　◆

*T*he recipe said, "Easy, straightforward; prep and cook time 3 hours." It was Christmas Eve, and Joséphine was cooking a turkey. A turkey stuffed with real chestnuts, not the insipid frozen chestnut purée that sticks to the roof of your mouth. Chestnuts are smooth and savory when fresh, dull and pasty when frozen. To go with the turkey she was also puréeing celeriac, carrots, and turnips. The rest of the meal would consist of appetizers, a salad, a plate of cheeses she'd bought at Barthélémy in rue de Grenelle, and a *bûche de Noël* with meringue dwarves and mushrooms.

What's the matter with me? she wondered. *Everything feels oppressive and boring. I usually enjoy cooking our Christmas turkey. Each ingredient is full of memories and takes me back to my childhood: I'm perched on a stool watching my father bustle about in his big white apron with the embroidered blue letters that say,* I'M THE CHEF, AND I GIVE THE ORDERS. *I'm wearing that apron now, running my fingers over the raised letters, reading my past in Braille.*

Jo's eye fell on the turkey lying pale and limp on the butcher paper. Plucked, wings folded, belly swollen, reddened skin dotted with black, the picture of an unhappy turkey ready for the sacrifice. Next to it lay a long knife with a gleaming blade.

Madame Berthier had been stabbed to death. She was found lying on her back, legs apart. Joséphine was summoned to the police station, where Capitaine Gallois noted the similarity between the two attacks: same circumstances, same modus operandi. Lips pursed, she heard Joséphine out. Jo could tell she was thinking, *She was saved by a shoe.*

"You're lucky to be alive," said Capitaine Gallois, shaking her head as if she couldn't believe it. "Madame Berthier was stabbed extremely violently. We estimate the cuts to be four to five inches deep. The killer is a powerful man and knows how to use a knife. He's not an amateur."

She had asked Jo to bring Antoine's parcel, so the police lab could examine it.

"Did you know Madame Berthier?"

"She was my daughter's main teacher. We walked home from school together one evening."

"Do you remember anything in particular that you talked about?"

Joséphine smiled, about to mention an odd detail. The captain would think she wasn't taking her seriously.

"Yes, I do. We had the same hat. A funny wool hat with three layers. It was a bit extravagant and I was afraid it would attract attention. She encouraged me to wear it."

The captain took out a photo.

"Is this the one?"

"Yes. I was wearing it the night I was attacked," Jo murmured.

"Very well," said Capitaine Gallois. "Please remain available. We'll be in touch if we need you."

Joséphine told herself to stop thinking about Madame Berthier and the killer, but she couldn't help it. She wondered whether he lived in the neighborhood and if he meant to stab her when he attacked Madame Berthier. *After failing the first time, he tried again, but picked the wrong victim. He spotted the hat and thought it was me: same size, same gait. . . .* "Stop it!" cried Joséphine. "Stop! You're going to spoil the evening!" Shirley, Gary, and Hortense had arrived from London the day before, and Philippe and Alexandre were joining them for dinner.

I need to create a quiet space for myself, the way I do when I prepare my talks, she decided. *Work calms me. It focuses my mind, keeps it from wandering off into gloomy thoughts.* Cooking also brought Jo back to her beloved medieval studies. *There's nothing new under the sun,* she reflected, working her fingers raw peeling chestnuts. The Middle Ages had fast food, too. Not everybody had a kitchen of her own. Lodgings in town were too small. Bachelors and widowers ate out. There were caterers, cooks, and *chaircutiers* who set up tables outdoors and sold sausages, little pâtés, and tarts to go: the ancestors of the hot dog and Big Mac. Cooking was a major part of daily life, and the markets were well stocked. Olive oil from Majorca, crayfish and carp from the Marne, bread from Corbeil, butter from Normandy, and lard from Ventoux all made their way to the Paris Halles.

Jo's worries lifted when she returned to the twelfth century, the time of Hildegard of Bingen. It was hard to ignore Hildegard, because she took an interest in everything: plants, food, music, medicine, and the humors of the soul that act on the body, making it strong or weak depending on whether you laughed or brooded. She wrote: "If a man acts in accordance with the soul's desire, his works will be good. If he follows that of the flesh, they will be bad."

"Sausage. Mix the chestnuts with sausage meat, minced liver and heart, chopped thyme, salt and pepper."

I need to get back to my habilitation thesis. I don't have any ideas for another novel. No ideas and no desire. I should trust myself. One of these days, the beginning of a story will come to me, take my hand, and make me write. I have plenty of time. She peeled the chestnuts' hard husks, taking care not to cut her fingers.

Monsieur and Madame Van den Brock paid Joséphine a visit after learning of Madame Berthier's death. They rang her doorbell, looking as solemn as pallbearers. The woman's eyes kept wandering this way and that, and she struggled to keep them focused on one point. The man frowned, waving long skinny fingers about like gigantic blades. As a couple, they looked like Snow White and Edward Scissorhands. *How in the world did they manage to make babies?* Joséphine wondered. *Maybe he landed on top of her in a moment of distraction, folding his long, sharp fingers so as not to scratch her. Two clumsy dragonflies mating in midair.*

"We have to protect our children," Madame Van den Brock was saying. "If he's attacking women, he might attack the little ones too."

They suggested starting a nightly neighborhood patrol by the fathers, the heads of households. Joséphine smiled and said she didn't happen to have that item on hand. They didn't seem to understand, so she added, "I mean a father who is the head of the household. I don't have a husband." It took them a moment to realize that she was not joking.

"I'll tell Hervé Lefloc-Pignel to come up see you," said Van den Brock firmly. "He's very concerned. His wife is afraid to go out anymore. She won't even open the door to the concierge."

"By the way, don't you think that concierge of ours is a little strange, changing her hair color every three weeks?" asked Madame Van den Brock anxiously. "Maybe she has a boyfriend who—"

"Who just got out of prison and is holding a big knife behind his back?" asked Jo. "No, I don't think Iphigénie is mixed up in this."

"I heard that her boyfriend was in trouble with the police."

The couple left, promising to send Lefloc-Pignel over as soon as they saw him.

The Pinarelli family, a son and his mother, lived on the ground floor of Joséphine's building. He was around fifty; she was in her eighties. He was tall and thin with dyed black hair, and looked like an older version of Anthony Perkins in *Psycho*. He had an odd smile. When he ran into you, a corner of his mouth shot up, as if he distrusted you and wanted you to get out of his way. He didn't work for a living, and probably served as his mother's companion. They went shopping every morning, walking slowly hand in hand, he pulling their cart like a greyhound on a leash, she clutching their shopping list.

Joséphine lived in Building A and didn't know the tenants in Building B, on the other side of the courtyard. There were more of them because A had just one apartment on each floor, whereas B had three. Iphigénie told her that the tenants in A were richer, that the ones in B hated them, and that the co-op meetings often disintegrated into furious arguments, with the tenants quarreling and insulting each other. The A's always won, to the dismay of the B's, who were saddled with fresh services and construction and resented paying for them.

Joséphine looked up at the big IKEA clock: it was six thirty already! Hortense, Gary, and Shirley had gone out to do last-minute shopping and would be back at any minute. Zoé was locked in her room, making her presents.

Since the London contingent arrived, the house had been full of noise and laughter, and the phone rang nonstop. Joséphine showed off the apartment when they arrived, proud of the space she was putting at their disposal.

Hortense had opened the door to her room and flopped on her bed, arms outstretched, crying, "Home sweet home!" Joséphine couldn't help but be touched by her exclamation. Shirley requested a whiskey. "What are we eating tonight, Joséphine?" asked Gary, who was sitting on the sofa wearing headphones. "I'm sure you've fixed us something delicious." Doors opened and closed, snatches of conversation flew, different music poured from every room. Joséphine realized what she didn't like about the apartment: It was too big for just Zoé and her. When it was full of laughter, shouts, and open suitcases, it warmed up.

Every morning, Joséphine put on her sweats and running shoes and went for a run around the lake in the Bois de Boulogne. On her way to the lake she jogged along, observing the lawn bowlers, bike riders, and other runners while dodging dog turds and jumping into puddles. There was nothing she liked more than stomping in a pool of rainwater. She did it when she was alone, so no one would think she was crazy. She liked the sound her shoes made as they hit the water and the splash that shot up around her. When Jo reached what she pompously called "My circuit," she picked up the pace, circling the lake in twenty-five minutes. Out of breath, she stopped to stretch, so she wouldn't be sore the next day.

Every morning she encountered a man who also circled the lake, but walking. He kept his hands in his pockets and wore a navy pea coat buttoned up to his mouth, a watch cap pulled down to his eyebrows, dark glasses, and a scarf. He was wrapped up like a mummy, and Joséphine had dubbed him "the Invisible Man." He strode along at a dogged, mechanical pace, as if following a doctor's prescription: "Once or twice around the lake every day, preferably in the morning, back straight, breathing deeply." They occasionally passed each other, but the man always ignored her, without even a nod to acknowledge her presence. *Why would a lonely and stubborn man walk around a lake every day between ten and eleven in the morning?* Joséphine wondered.

A drop of boiling water shot from the saucepan and scalded her. Jo yelped and turned the flame down. Then she poured in the first batch of chestnuts and continued peeling the rest.

Boil the chestnuts for 30 minutes. Remove the second skin as you take them from the water.

Does Philippe know how to cook? She looked around for a tissue while scratching her nose with the tip of the vegetable peeler. *Philippe.* Her heart began to pound whenever she thought of him. "Forget me not." Those were his last words to her on a train platform back in June. They hadn't seen each other since then.

When she learned that he and Alexandre would be alone on Christmas Eve, she invited them over.

The carrots, turnips, and celeriac that Joséphine planned to purée were simmering in their copper pans. The chestnuts would soon be cooked and peeled. She had decided on foie gras as an appetizer, along with slices of wild salmon. Zoé loved wild salmon.

She was in her room, probably still making her presents. Using cardboard, lengths of wool, fabric, staples, glue, paper clips, and glitter, she made beautiful dolls, pictures, and mobiles. Unlike Hortense, Zoé didn't like buying things. *My daughter's an old-fashioned girl,* thought Jo. *She doesn't like change. She likes to do the same thing every year, eat the same special meal, hang the same Christmas balls and decorations on the tree, listen to the same Christmas carols. I preserve the ritual for her. When Zoé tastes her slice of* bûche de Noël *before digging in, she's expecting it to taste like all the other* bûches *she's had before, maybe including those she ate with her father. Where is the man I glimpsed in the Metro spending Christmas Eve? Could it possibly have been Antoine? He had a scar and a half-closed eye. If he's alive and looking for us, he must be hanging around the Courbevoie building. There's a new concierge there, who doesn't know us. My name isn't listed.*

Zoé had asked Joséphine to leave an empty seat at the table on Christmas Eve.

"You'll see, Mommy, it'll be a surprise. A Christmas surprise."

"She's bringing in some homeless person," predicted Hortense. "If she does, I'm out of here."

Add cheese and prunes to the stuffing. Mix well. Stuff the turkey.

That's what Jo liked best when she was little, filling the turkey with thick, fragrant stuffing.

Sew the cavity shut with string. Dot the bird with butter or margarine. Salt and pepper. Put the bird in a hot oven. After about 45 minutes, lower heat to medium. Cook for 1 hour, basting frequently.

The doorbell rang, once, and briefly. Joséphine looked at her watch: It was seven o'clock. They must have forgotten their keys.

It turned out to be Hervé Lefloc-Pignel. He came up to apologize for the noise he was likely to make that evening; he and his wife had family visiting. He was wearing a tuxedo with a bow tie, a pleated white shirt, and a black satin cummerbund. His hair was slicked down and parted as straight as a French garden hedge.

"No need to apologize," said Jo with a smile. "We're likely to be noisy too."

It occurred to her that she should offer him a glass of champagne. She hesitated, and then, as he didn't seem to be leaving, invited him in.

"I don't want to take up your time," he said apologetically, striding into the entry.

After wiping it on her dishcloth, Jo extended a slightly greasy hand to shake.

"Would you mind coming with me to the kitchen? I need to keep an eye on the turkey as it's roasting."

As he followed her, he said, "I wanted to ask you. How did, er . . . how did your daughter react to what happened to Madame Berthier?"

"It was a shock. We talked about it a lot."

"I ask, because Gaétan isn't talking about it."

He looked concerned.

"What about your other children?" asked Joséphine.

"Charles-Henri, the oldest, didn't know her; he's in high school. And Domitille didn't have her as a teacher. Gaétan is the one I'm worried about. And because he's in the same classes as your daughter, I thought they might've talked."

"She hasn't said anything about it."

"I heard you were called in by the police."

"Yes. I was attacked not long ago."

"In the same way?

"Oh, no! It was nothing compared to what happened to poor Madame Berthier."

"That's not what the chief told me. He agreed to a meeting at my request."

"You know people tend to exaggerate in police stations."

"I don't think so."

Lefloc-Pignel said it severely, as if he meant, *I think you're lying.*

"Anyway, it doesn't matter, since I'm not dead! I'm here, drinking champagne with you!"

"I don't want the man going after our children," continued Lefloc-Pignel. "We should request a police presence in front of the building."

"Around the clock?"

"I don't know. That's why I came to talk to you."

"Why would the police do that just for our building?"

"Because you were attacked. Isn't that reason enough?"

They were interrupted by the arrival of Shirley, followed by Gary and Hortense. Arms loaded with presents, noses and cheeks ruddy from the cold, they clapped their gloved hands together, blew on their fingers, and noisily demanded champagne. Joséphine made the introductions. Lefloc-Pignel bowed to the women.

"Delighted to make your acquaintance," he said to Hortense. "Your mother has often spoken of you." *Really?* thought Jo. *We've never talked about Hortense.* Hortense gave him her most charming smile, and Joséphine realized he had grasped her daughter's true nature. Flattered, Hortense would think the world of him.

"I hear you're studying fashion," he said.

How does he know that? Jo wondered.

"Yes, in London."

"If I can ever help you, just ask. I know a lot of people in the world of fashion, in Paris, London, and New York."

"Thanks very much. Trust me, I won't forget! As it happens, I need to find an internship soon. Do you have a number where I can reach you?"

Joséphine watched in fascination as Hortense danced around Lefloc-Pignel, spinning her web. She was chatting, nodding, recording his cell number, thanking him in advance for the help he would give her.

The moment he left, Hortense cried, "Now there's a man for you, Mom!"

"He's married and the father of three!"

"So what? You can get it on with him without his wife knowing, can't you? No need to mention it to your father confessor."

"Hortense!" Jo cried scoldingly.

"This champagne is wonderful," said Shirley, trying to change the subject. "What year is it?"

"I don't know. It's probably on the label."

Joséphine had answered distractedly. She didn't like Hortense's comments about her neighbor. *I mustn't let this pass. Hortense has to understand that love is a serious commitment, that you shouldn't just hook up with the first handsome man who comes along.*

Turning to her daughter she asked, "What about you darling? Are you . . . involved with anyone these days?"

Hortense sipped her champagne.

"So here we go! Back home, and I'm already on the hot seat. You want to know if I've met a handsome, rich, intelligent man and fallen madly in love with him, right?"

Joséphine nodded, full of hope.

"Well, no." Then she paused, leaving Jo in suspense. "On the other hand . . ."

She held out her glass for her mother to refill it, then continued. "On the other hand, I did meet a guy. Drop-dead gorgeous!"

"Ah," said Joséphine softly.

Shirley was following the exchange between mother and daughter. *Don't fool yourself Jo,* she thought in a silent prayer. *Your daughter is too much for you to handle.* Gary was smiling, expecting the end of the conversation to be painful for a soft-hearted mother like Joséphine.

"For two weeks, we were swept up in an all-consuming passion."

"And then?" asked Joséphine hopefully.

"After that, no more zsa zsa zsu. Nothing! Total flameout. Men in love are so boring!"

The doorbell rang again, interrupting their exchange. Philippe came in carrying a case of champagne, accompanied by a silent, somber Alexandre, who looked upset.

"Champagne for everyone!" cried Philippe.

Hortense jumped for joy. "Roederer rosé! I love that champagne!"

Philippe signaled to Joséphine to follow him into the entry hall, using the excuse of hanging up his and Alexandre's coats.

"Let's get to the presents quickly," he whispered. "We just left the clinic, and it was pretty grim."

"All right," she said, surprised by his forceful tone.

"Isn't Zoé here?"

"She's in her room, I'll go get her."

"Are you okay?"

He had caught her arm, and pulled her close. She could feel the warmth of his body under the damp wool of his jacket, and knew her ears were turning red.

"Yes, yes, I'm fine, would you mind looking after the fire while I get dressed and brush my hair?" She was talking fast, trying to ignore how unnerved she felt. He put a finger on her lips, gazed at Jo for what felt like a long time, then regretfully released her.

A fire was crackling in the fireplace. The pile of Christmas presents gleamed on the chevron-pattern parquet floor. Two clans had formed: the elders, awaiting only the joy of giving, secretly hoping they had guessed right, and the younger generation, secretly longing for the fulfillment of dreams built around nighttime wishes. The slight anxiety of the first group was matched by the tense expectancy of the second, unsure if they would have to hide their disappointment or be able to show their joy freely.

Joséphine didn't like the ritual of presents. Each time, she felt an inexplicable sense of despair. As if it was a proof of the inability to love properly and well and a guarantee that she would never be satisfied with the expression of her love.

She turned to listen to Shirley, who was telling Philippe about her work to fight obesity in English schools.

"Worldwide, there are eight thousand seven hundred deaths a day because of those sugar sellers! And four hundred thousand more overweight children each year in Europe alone! After working slaves to death growing sugarcane, now they're going after our children, sprinkling them with poison!"

Philippe raised a hand in protest.

"Aren't you exaggerating a little?"

"They're sticking it everywhere," said Shirley. "They put vending machines with soda and candy bars in the schools, rotting our kids' teeth and making them fat. And it's all about money, of course. Don't you think that's outrageous?"

Philippe wasn't really listening. He and Alexandre had gone to see Iris. They had left the clinic in silence and walked along the little gravel path, hands in their pockets, each staring at his footprints in the white frost. They were like two orphans at a boarding school, left behind at the holidays. It wouldn't have taken much for their hands to join, but they resisted, walking tall and dignified under their mantle of pain.

Alexandre seemed to ignore the pile of shiny presents at his feet. He was staring into space, seeing a gloomy room that held his silent, emaciated mother, arms crossed on her chest, arms that hadn't opened to him when she said good-bye. "Have fun," she hissed between pinched lips. "You might think of me if you have time and get a chance." Alexandre left, keeping the kiss she hadn't asked for. He watched the dancing firelight, struggling to understand why his mother was so cold. *Maybe she never loved me. Maybe you don't have to love your child.* The thought opened a dizzying void in him.

"What are we waiting for, Joséphine?" cried Shirley. "Let's open the presents!"

Jo clapped her hands and announced that for this once, they would open the presents before midnight. Zoé and Alexandre would play Santa Claus, taking turns sticking an innocent hand into the big, beribboned pile. A Christmas carol arose, draping a sacred veil over the evening's undercurrent of sadness. "Silent night, holy night / All is calm, all is bright . . ."

Zoé closed her eyes and reached into the pile.

"For Hortense, from Mom," she announced, pulling out a long envelope. She read from the little note: "Merry Christmas to my darling beloved daughter."

Hortense seized the envelope and opened it apprehensively. Was it a Christmas card? Or a stern letter pointing out that life and study in London was expensive and paying for it was a major effort, so any Christmas present would be purely symbolic? Hortense's tense face relaxed, reinflated by a gust of pleasure when she read: "For my darling love, this coupon is good for one day of shopping together."

Hortense ran to hug her mother.

"Thanks, Mom! How did you know?"

I know you so well, Joséphine wanted to say. *I know that the one thing that can bring us together without blows or ill feeling is a mad rush through the stores in a spending spree.* But she said nothing, and was moved when her daughter kissed her.

"So we can go wherever I like?" asked Hortense, still surprised. "For a whole day?"

Jo nodded. She had guessed right, even if her prescience made her a little sad.

She held Hortense in her arms for a moment, murmuring in her ear, "You're my darling, beautiful daughter, and I love you madly."

"I love you too, Mom," Hortense said in a breath.

Joséphine sensed she was telling the truth, and felt a surge of joy that cheered her up, reawakening desire and appetite. Life would be beautiful if Hortense loved her, and Jo was prepared to write twenty thousand more checks to gain her daughter's whispered declaration of love.

The rounds of gift giving continued, punctuated by Zoé and Alexandre's announcements. Shirley got a handsome pair of boots and the works of Oscar Wilde. Philippe received a long sky-blue cashmere scarf and a box of cigars. Joséphine got the complete set of Glenn Gould CDs and an iPod. "But I don't know how to make those things work," she said. "I'll show you," promised Philippe, putting his arm around her shoulders. Zoé's arms were so full of gifts, she wasn't able to carry them all to her bedroom. Alexandre grinned with delight at his presents.

The melancholy of the afternoon had evaporated. Philippe opened a bottle of champagne and asked how the turkey was doing.

"Oh, my God! The turkey!" cried Joséphine, leaping up.

She ran to the kitchen and opened the oven to see how far cooked the bird was. Still very pink, was her diagnosis. She decided to turn up the heat.

She was standing in front of the oven, wearing the big white apron and squinting as she tried to baste the turkey without spilling the juices, when she sensed a presence behind her. She

closed the oven, turned around, spoon in hand, and found herself in Philippe's arms.

"It's good to see you again, Jo. It's been a long time"

She looked up at him and blushed. He hugged her close.

"The last time," he remembered, "you were dropping off Zoé
so I could take her and Alexandre to Évian."

"You had signed them up for riding lessons."

"You and I wound up alone on the platform."

"The kids had gone to buy drinks."

"You were wearing a suede jacket, a white T-shirt, a check-
ered scarf, and earrings that brought out your hazel eyes."

"You asked, 'Are you okay?' and I said yes."

"I really wanted to kiss you."

Joséphine looked him in the eyes.

"But we didn't," he said.

"No."

"We figured we couldn't. . . . That it was forbidden."

She nodded.

"And we were right."

"Yes," she whispered, trying to pull away.

"Forbidden."

"Completely forbidden."

He pulled her close again and stroked her hair, murmuring,
"Thank you for this family party, Jo."

His lips brushed hers. She shuddered, turned her head away.

"Philippe, you know . . . I think that . . . We don't want . . ."

He straightened, looked at her as if he didn't understand
what she was saying. Then he wrinkled his nose and exclaimed,
"Do you smell that, Joséphine? Do you think the stuffing may be

leaking into the roasting pan? It would be terrible if the turkey dried out."

Joséphine turned around and opened the oven. He was right: The turkey was slowly leaking, creating a brown avalanche with caramelized edges. She was wondering how to stop the hemorrhage when Philippe's hand came to rest on hers. Carefully handling the spoon, the two of them pushed the overflowing stuffing back into the turkey's cavity.

"Is it good?" asked Philippe, speaking into Joséphine's neck. "Did you taste it?"

She shook her head in reply.

"And did you marinate the prunes?"

"Yes."

"In water with some Armagnac?

"Yes."

"Good."

He was murmuring into her neck and she could feel his words being imprinted on her skin. With his hand still on hers, he guided it toward the fragrant stuffing, took some of the chestnut, prune, and cheese mixture, and very slowly brought the steaming spoon to both their lips. Eyes closed, they sampled the delicate, mouthwatering stuffing. They heaved a sigh and their mouths joined in a long, tender, delicious kiss.

"Could use a touch more salt," he said.

"Philippe," she pleaded, pushing him away. "We shouldn't."

Smiling, he pulled her closer. Noticing a fleck of gravy at the corner of his mouth, she felt an urge to lick it off.

"You make me laugh," he said.

"Why?"

"You're the funniest woman I've ever known!"

"Me?"

"Yes, you're so incredibly serious, it makes me want to laugh, and to make you laugh."

His words continued to fall on her lips like a gentle mist.

"Philippe!"

"That stuffing really is delicious, Joséphine."

He took another sample before closing the oven, raised the spoon to her lips, and bent toward her as if to say, "Can I have a taste?" Their lips intertwined, his lips brushing hers. Soft, full lips flavored with roasted prunes and a hint of Armagnac. In a flash of anticipatory happiness, Jo realized that she had stopped making decisions, that she had gone beyond the very limits she had promised never to pass. *At some point, we have to understand that the limits we set don't keep other people at a distance or protect us from problems or temptations,* she said to herself. *They just lock us in, cut us off from life.*

"I can hear you thinking, Jo. Stop examining your conscience!"

"But—"

"Stop it, or you'll make me feel as if I were kissing a nun!"

But there are some limits too dangerous to pass, limits I absolutely shouldn't cross. But that's exactly what I'm doing, and my God, how good it feels to have this man's arms around me!

"It's just that I feel—"

"Joséphine! Kiss me!"

He pulled her tight, shutting her mouth with his as if he wanted to bite her. His kiss became brutal and imperious as he pushed her against the warm oven door. She tried to pull away but he pressed her, forced his way into her mouth, searching it as if he were after some more stuffing, the stuffing she had mixed. It was as if he were licking her fingers mixing the stuffing, the taste of prunes filling his mouth.

"Philippe," she moaned. "Oh, Philippe!" She clung to him, opening her mouth to his.

"I've wanted this for so long," he said. He attacked her white apron, rumpled it, pulled it off, pushed her against the oven's glass window, entered her mouth, kissed her neck, parted her white blouse, caressed her warm skin, ran his fingers down to her breasts, put his mouth on every inch of bare skin freed from the blouse and the apron, ending days of tortured waiting.

A burst of laughter from the living room startled them.

"Wait!" whispered Joséphine, freeing herself. "Philippe, they mustn't—"

"I don't care! You have no idea how much I don't care!"

"We can't do this again."

"Can't do what again?"

"I mean—"

"Joséphine! Put your arms around me again. I didn't say we were finished."

This was a new voice, another man, one she didn't know. Philippe was right. She didn't care either. She just wanted to do it again. Was that what a kiss was? Like in books, when the earth splits open, mountains crumble, and you're ready to die with a flower on your lips? A new strength lifted her up, made her forget her sister, her two daughters in the living room, the scarred bum in the Metro, and Luca's sad eyes, and propelled her into this man's arms. And not just any man! Her sister's husband! She pulled back, but Philippe grabbed her and pulled her close again, pressing against her from her toes to the curve of her neck, as if he were taking a stand, forever. He whispered, "And now we stop talking, or do it silently!"

Zoé watched them from the kitchen door. She stood there, looking at her mother in her uncle's arms, then bowed her head and slipped off to her room.

"Who are we missing this time?" asked Shirley. "It's an evening of magicians, you keep disappearing one after another."

Philippe and Joséphine had come from the kitchen with a story about saving the turkey from drying out. Their obvious excitement stood in such contrast to the evening's earlier reserve that Shirley gave them an intrigued look.

"We're waiting for Zoé and her mysterious visitor," said Hortense, sighing. "We still don't know who it is."

"Could it be someone from the building?" asked Shirley. "Maybe she ran into a lonely man or woman and invited them."

"I don't see who it could be," said Joséphine thoughtfully. "The Van den Brocks are having family over, and so are the Lefloc-Pignels. The Mersons—"

"Did you say Lefloc-Pignel?" asked Philippe. "I know someone by that name, a banker. His first name's Hervé, I think. A handsome man, quite serious, married to a young woman from a very good family. Her father owns a private bank, and put his son-in-law in charge."

"That must be the same man," said Joséphine, "but I've never seen her."

"She's blonde, unassuming, very low key. She hardly speaks,

lets her husband take up all the room. They have three children, I think. If I remember correctly, they lost their first one, run over in a parking lot when he was nine months old. His mother set him down in his child seat and was looking for her keys when another car hit him."

"My God!" cried Joséphine.

"It was awful. None of Lefloc-Pignel's co-workers dared even mention it. The moment they tried to mumble their condolences, he glared at them! I used to do business with him. He's a touchy man, not easy to get along with. Yet he's also cultured and charming, and a natural leader. We called him Janus behind his back."

"Because he had two faces, I suppose," said Jo, amused.

"He's smart, too. Has degrees from all of the big schools: National School of Administration, Polytechnique, Mines. Taught at Harvard for four years, and MIT tried to recruit him. When he talked, people listened."

"I'll plate the salmon and the foie gras," said Joséphine. "You all go and sit down. I wrote everyone's name on place cards."

"I'm coming with you," said Shirley.

Once they were in the kitchen, Shirley closed the door behind her and pointed a finger at Joséphine

"All right, tell me everything!"

Jo blushed, took out a plate for the foie gras, and said, "He kissed me!"

"Well, none too soon! I was starting to wonder what he was waiting for."

"It felt so good, Shirley, I can't tell you. Better than I could've imagined. I trembled from head to foot, even with the hot oven handle poking me in the back."

"It was about time, don't you think?"

"Go on, make fun of me."

"Not a bit of it. Full marks for the hot, torrid kiss."

"I loved it when he kissed me. I want him to do it again. Oh, Shirley, it's so good! I don't want to stop. Do you think I'm going to suffer?"

"Great suffering often goes with great passion."

"That's an area where you're a specialist, aren't you?

"I am indeed."

Joséphine thought for a long moment, looked lovingly at the oven door handle.

"I'm so happy, Shirley," she said, sighing, "even if this great happiness only lasts ten and a half minutes. I'm sure some people don't have ten and a half minutes of great happiness in their whole lives."

Joséphine was leaning against the oven, eyes half closed, her arms around her chest as if she were cradling a dream.

Shirley shook her arm.

"Let's bring in the foie gras. People are going to wonder what we're up to."

In the living room, everyone was now waiting for Zoé.

Hortense was leafing through the Oscar Wilde tome and reading passages aloud. Gary was fanning the fire with the bellows. Alexandre was sniffing his father's cigars, a disapproving look on his face.

Joséphine and Philippe were on the sofa near the fire. He reached behind her and seized her hand. She turned crimson and looked at him, silently begging him to release it. He did nothing of the sort. Instead he gently stroked her open palm, turned her hand over, and stroked between each finger. Joséphine couldn't free herself without jerking her hand away, which might attract attention. So she just sat there, her hot hand in his, absentmindedly listening to the Oscar Wilde quotations. She tried to laugh when the others did, but was always half a beat late, and they noticed.

"What's up, Mom?" exclaimed Hortense. "Are you drunk or something?"

That was the moment Zoé chose to enter the living room and solemnly declare: "Everyone to your places and then I'm turning out the lights."

They headed for the table, sought their place cards, sat down, and unfolded their napkins. Then they turned to Zoé, who was holding something behind her back.

"Now everybody close your eyes, and no cheating!"

They did so. Hortense tried to glimpse what was going on, but Zoé had turned off the lights and she could only make out a stiff, square shape sliding over to the table, supported by Zoé. *What the hell is that?* Hortense wondered. *Must be some old guy who can hardly stand. She's bringing us some broken-down bum as her mystery guest. Talk about a surprise! He's gonna puke on us or blow a blood vessel the first time he belches. We'll be calling for an ambulance or the fire department, and Merry Christmas to all!*

"I'm turning on the lights and you can open your eyes," announced Zoé.

They shouted with surprise. At the empty place stood . . . Antoine. A life-size photograph of Antoine in his safari clothes, glued to a foam panel.

"Ladies and gentlemen," said Zoé, her eyes shining, "here's Daddy!"

They gaped first at the Antoine figure, then at Zoé, then back at Antoine, as if he might come to life at any moment.

"I thought it would be nice if Daddy was with us this evening because Christmas without Daddy isn't Christmas. Nobody can take a daddy's place, nobody. So I'd like us to raise a glass in his memory and toast to his return that we are awaiting anxiously."

Zoé must have memorized her little speech, because she gave it all at once while gazing at the picture of her father.

Joséphine recognized the photo. It had been taken just before Antoine was let go from the Gunman company, when the future still looked bright, before talk of mergers or layoffs. The effect was striking. They all felt as if Antoine were at the table with them.

Recoiling in shock, Alexandre knocked over his chair, making the picture totter and fall.

"Don't you want to give him a kiss, Mommy?" asked Zoé, as she propped her father's effigy back in front of his plate.

Joséphine shook her head, petrified. She just sat there, facing this cardboard Antoine, trying to understand.

"Zoé, please . . ." she stammered.

With a strand of hair wrapped around her finger, Hortense looked at the picture of her father.

"What the hell are you up to, Zoé? You doing a remake of *The Invaders*?"

Zoé didn't answer, and Hortense went on. "She didn't think

this up all by herself, you know. This is a 'Flat Daddy.' It's an American idea. It started with the wife of a soldier stationed in Iraq when she realized their four-year-old daughter didn't recognize her father when he came home on leave. US National Guard families started doing the same thing, and it spread. Now the families of every American soldier stationed abroad can request a Flat Daddy, and it'll be mailed to them. Zoé didn't invent anything. She only wanted to screw up our evening!"

"No I didn't!" cried Zoe. "I just wanted to have Daddy here with us."

Hortense leaped to her feet.

"So what do you want? To make us feel guilty? Prove that you're the only one who hasn't forgotten him? The only one who really loves him?"

Joséphine burst into tears, threw down her napkin, and left the table.

"Great job, Zoé!" yelled Hortense. "You have any more surprises up your sleeve, to give us a chuckle? Cause we're dying of laughter here."

Gary, Shirley, Alexandre, and Philippe all waited, embarrassed. The foie gras blushed on its plate, the toast points shriveled, and the salmon began to sweat. A smell of something burning came from the kitchen.

"The turkey!" shouted Philippe. "We forgot to turn off the oven!"

Just then, Joséphine reappeared, wearing the big white apron.

"The turkey burned," she announced with a grimace.

Gary heaved a sigh of disappointment.

"It's eleven o'clock and we still haven't eaten! You Cortèses and your psychodramas are a pain in the ass. I'm never spending Christmas with you again!"

"What's going on?" cried Shirley. "Is this war?"

"That's right!" cried Zoé, grabbing the Flat Daddy and marching off to her room.

Slumped in her chair, Joséphine looked gloomily at the table, while stroking the embroidered words on the apron: I'M THE CHEF, AND I GIVE THE ORDERS.

"What time are they coming?" asked Josiane, emerging from the bathroom rubbing her back.

She'd been sleeping badly for the past two weeks. Her neck was stiff, and her back as if it had been used for target practice by a circus knife thrower.

"Twelve thirty," said Marcel. "Philippe will be here too, with Alexandre. Plus someone called Shirley and her son, Gary. They're all coming! I'm so happy, I'm purring. You're my little sweetie-pie, and I get to introduce you to them. This is a big day, and not just because it's January first."

"You sure it's a good idea?"

"Joséphine was the one who thought of having a lunch. She invited us to her place, but I thought you'd be more comfortable if we had them over here. Think of Junior. He needs a family."

"They aren't his family."

"No, but since we don't have any, we'll just borrow someone else's."

Marcel fell back on the bed with his arms spread wide and his giant thighs barely covered by his white shirttails. This was Marcel Grobz, a bundle of reddish hair and rolls of fat, his freckled flesh illuminated by eyes as blue as forget-me-nots and sharp as sword points.

He was freshly shaved and perfumed. On a nearby chair lay a gray alpaca suit, blue necktie, and matching cuff links.

"You're making yourself handsome," said Josiane, plopping down on the bed next to him.

"I *feel* handsome, honeybunch, that's different. Today I'm the Great Mamamouchi."

"But a lot sexier than a mamamouchi."

"Stop it, you're turning me on. Scope out my shorts: stiff as a ship's mast in a storm! If we climb under the covers now, it'll be a while before we get up again."

In bed, Marcel was still insatiable. The man was made to eat, drink, laugh, and come. To climb mountains, plant baobabs, pocket thunder, and snuff lightning. *And to think that viper Henriette wanted to turn him into a powdered lapdog!* thought Josiane, who had been dreaming of her again. *What the hell is that woman doing, prowling through my nights?*

"You have any news about Henriette?" she asked cautiously.

"Still won't grant me a divorce. Her demands are outrageous, and I'm not giving in. Why do you ask? Do you want to make me lose my hard-on?"

"She's been showing up in my dreams."

"Ah, so that's why you haven't had much zip recently."

"I feel as sad as a lone sock on a clothesline. Nothing interests me."

"Not even me?"

"Not even you, my big honey bear."

The ship abruptly lost its mast.

"Are you serious? What about Madame Suzanne, have you been seeing her?"

"No."

Marcel sat up, now gravely concerned. If Madame Suzanne wasn't being called in, the situation was serious. The fortune-teller had predicted their move into the big apartment, Junior's birth, Henriette's fall, even the death of a person close to them in the jaws of an animal. Madame Suzanne closed her eyes and saw things. "The eye is a liar," she claimed. "You see better with your eyes closed. True sight is interior." She was never wrong, and when she didn't see anything, she said so. To keep her gift intact, she never asked for money, instead earning her living as a pedicurist. Madame Suzanne trimmed toenails, sounded souls, and divined destiny.

She came to the Grobz apartment once a month, wearing the serious expression of a spirit dowser. Whenever Marcel engaged in sharp trading or pulled off some dirty trick, he would entrust his plantar arches to her, because he was determined to keep her good opinion of him. She would explain that in the merciless business world in which he moved, cheating and using the same weapons as his rivals could be forgiven, provided he didn't harm someone weaker than himself.

"I feel as if I've been drained dry," continued Josiane. "I'm not myself. It's like I've been split in two. You see me, but I'm not here."

Marcel listened, incredulous. Josiane had never said anything like that before.

"Could you be having a nervous depression?"

"I might, though I've never heard of it. We didn't have that, growing up."

Marcel was perplexed. He felt Josiane's forehead. She didn't have a fever.

"Maybe you have a touch of anemia. Have you had any tests done?"

She shook her head, frowning.

"Well, we ought to start with that."

They were seated side by side on the bed, leaning against each other, pondering this strange illness. Josiane felt enveloped by a languor that dulled her zest for life—her appetite, her sexual desire, all the things that had sustained her since she was a child.

The lunch was a success. Sitting at the head of the table in his high chair, Junior reigned like the lord of the manor. He would bang his baby bottle against his chair to indicate his desires. He liked to see the table properly set, with glasses, knives, and forks all in their proper places. If by chance a guest upset the alignment, he banged his bottle until the culprit had rectified the error. Junior frowned hard, seeming to follow the conversation. He was so concentrated, he looked fit to burst.

"I think he's taking a dump," Zoé whispered to Hortense.

Marcel had placed presents on everyone's plate. Each of the children got a 200-euro bill. Hortense, Gary, and Zoé gasped when they found the big yellow bill folded in an envelope. Zoé almost asked, "Is it real?" Hortense gulped and got up to kiss Marcel and Josiane. Gary looked at his mother in embarrassment, silently asking if he should object. Shirley shook her head, signaling him to say nothing, otherwise he would make Marcel angry.

Philippe received a bottle of 1947 Château Cheval Blanc, Saint-Émilion Premier Grand Cru Classé (A).

On Joséphine and Shirley's plates, Marcel had placed a white gold bracelet set with thirty diamonds, on Josiane's, a pair of earrings, each with a huge Tahitian cultured pearl studded with diamonds. Shirley protested that she absolutely couldn't accept the bracelet. Marcel warned her that if she refused his gift, he would be offended and leave the table.

"I love playing Santa Claus," he said. "My bag of presents is overflowing, so I have to empty it from time to time."

"This is really too much, snuggle bunny," said Josiane, thoughtfully stroking her earrings. "I'm going to look like a big rock."

Joséphine murmured, "Marcel, you're crazy."

"Crazy with happiness, little Jo. Just having you here for lunch is such a gift, you can't imagine. I'd have never thought that . . . Ah, I almost feel like crying."

Junior chose this moment to lighten the mood by banging his bottle on the arms of his chair. This meant, *Enough of this playacting! I'm bored, I want action!*

They turned to him in surprise. He gave them a big smile, leaning his head forward as if to encourage them to make conversation.

"You'd almost think he wants to talk," said Gary in surprise.

"See how he stretches his neck?" remarked Hortense. Privately, she thought Junior was looking especially ugly, his head on a long, flexible neck, mouth agape, eyes bulging.

"You have to talk to him all the time or he gets bored," said Josiane with a sigh. "And you can't say just anything, otherwise he gets angry! You have to make him laugh, surprise him, or teach him something."

"Go ahead and test him," said Marcel. "You'll see, he's a genius."

Hearing the word *genius*, Junior gurgled happily. To prove his father right, he pointed his bottle at a ceiling spotlight and very distinctly said, "Lamp."

Seeing their astonished faces, he gave a throaty laugh. Then, with an amused glint in his eye, he said it in English: "Light."

"That's—"

"Incredible!" said Marcel. "See? Nobody believed me."

"*Luz*," continued Junior, still pointing at the spotlight.

"Spanish, too! This child makes me—"

"*Deng.*"

"Ah, now that one's nonsense," said Shirley, feeling reassured. Marcel corrected her.

"No, it means 'sun' in Chinese."

"Help!" cried Hortense. "The dwarf is a polyglot!"

Junior gave Hortense an affectionate look, thanking her for recognizing his talents.

"He's not a dwarf, he's a giant!" said Gary with a whistle of admiration. "Do you see the size of his hands and feet?"

"*Shushu!*" cried Junior, spitting water from his bottle at Gary.

"What does that mean?"

"'Uncle,' in Chinese," said Marcel. "He's chosen you as his uncle."

"Now I understand why you might be feeling tired, Josiane," said Joséphine. "Can I hold him? It's been a long time since I've had a baby in my arms, and I want to take a good look at a baby like this one."

"As long as it doesn't give you any ideas," muttered Zoé under her breath.

"Wouldn't you like to have a little brother?" asked Marcel teasingly.

"And who would be his father, if you don't mind my asking?" she answered, glaring at Joséphine.

"Zoé!" she stammered, taken aback by her daughter's vehemence. She was standing next to Josiane, who had picked Junior up and was bending over to kiss his red curls. Junior looked at her, scrunched up his face, and vomited a stream of carrot purée that spattered Joséphine's shirt and Josiane's silk blouse.

"Junior!" scolded Josiane, patting him on the back. "I'm terribly sorry, Joséphine!"

"It's not a big deal," said Jo, wiping her blouse. "It just means that he's eaten well."

"It's gotten all over you too, honeybunch," said Marcel, relieving her of the baby.

"Joséphine, why don't you come with me, and we'll get cleaned up?"

In her bedroom, she offered to lend Joséphine a clean blouse. Jo accepted and took hers off.

"Your son is really surprising!"

"I sometimes wonder if he's normal."

"He reminds me of a story about a baby who defended his mother at a trial in the Middle Ages. The mother was accused of having sinned in conceiving him, giving herself to a man who wasn't her husband. She was sentenced to be burned alive and appeared before the judge holding her baby in her arms."

"How old was he?"

"The same age as Junior. The mother held the child up and said, 'My beautiful son, I'm going to be put to death because of you. I don't deserve it, but who would believe the truth?'"

"What happened then?"

"The child spoke, and said, 'You will not die because of me. I know who my father is and I know you did not sin.'"

"He could talk that well?"

"That's what the book says. He finished by telling the judge, 'And I know better who my father is than you do yours!' That put the judge in his place, and he acquitted the mother."

"You didn't make that story up to make me feel better, did you?"

"Not at all. It's one of the tales from the Knights of the Round Table."

"It sure is nice to be educated. I didn't get much schooling."

"But you've learned about life, and that's more useful than any diploma."

"That's sweet of you to say. I sometimes miss not having any culture. And you can't catch up, with stuff like that."

"Of course you can, sure as two plus two makes four."

"That much, I know."

Relieved, Josiane gave Joséphine a friendly poke in the ribs. Caught by surprise, Jo paused, then poked her back.

And that's how they became friends.

As Philippe drove them home, Joséphine was thinking how much she liked Josiane. On the few times she'd gone to Marcel's warehouse on avenue Niel, she'd only gotten a partial picture of her: a gum-chewing secretary behind a desk. What her mother said did the rest. Henriette called Josiane, "that slut of a secretary," spitting out each syllable. So the half-image of the secretary gave way to that of a common floozy, easy and venal, made up like a carnival mask. *She turns out to be completely the opposite,* thought Jo with a sigh. *She's kind and gentle. Attentive. A softie.*

Shirley and Gary had gone for a walk in the Marais, and Joséphine was heading back to the apartment with Philippe, Alexandre, and the girls. Philippe drove the big sedan in silence, a Bach concerto playing on the radio. Alexandre and Zoé were chatting in the back. Hortense was caressing the envelope with her 200 euros. The rain mixed with snow made hesitant circles on the windshield that the wipers erased in a steady ballet.

Joséphine looked out at the bright Christmas decorations hung on the shivering trees along the Champs-Élysées and avenue Montaigne. Christmas! New Year's! January first! So many rituals to give the trembling trees a reason to be garlanded with lights.

Philippe's warm hand closed around hers, gently stroking it. She squeezed his back, but freed herself, afraid the children would catch them.

In the building lobby they ran into Hervé Lefloc-Pignel, who was hustling his son Gaétan along by his jacket collar. Stopping in front of the big mirror, Hervé yelled, "Take a look at yourself, you little shit! I forbade you to touch her."

"But I just wanted to give her some air! She's bored too, you know. We're all bored at home. We can't do anything! And I'm tired of always wearing prescribed colors. I want to wear plaid! Scotch plaid!"

Gaétan had yelled those last words. His father shook him violently to make him be quiet. When the frightened boy raised his arms to protect himself, he dropped something round and brown that fell to the floor and bounced.

"Look what you've done!" yelled Hervé. "Pick her up!"

Gaétan bent down and cautiously held it out to his father. He took it and set it gently on his palm, stroking it.

"She's not moving!" Hervé shouted. "You killed her!"

Leaning close, he spoke to the thing softly.

Because of the way the lobby mirrors were arranged, Philippe and his group were able to observe the whole episode without being seen. He gestured to them to not make any noise, and they stepped into the elevator.

"Well, that's certainly the Lefloc-Pignel I knew," he said. "He hasn't changed. Amazing, how worked up people can get sometimes."

Joséphine and Philippe were in the kitchen. Alexandre and the girls were in the living room, watching television.

"There was so much hate in his voice," said Jo. "I thought he was going to kill him."

"Oh, please! Don't exaggerate!"

"No, I mean it. I could feel the hatred and the resentment. It creeps into everything."

Philippe hugged her and said, "Come on! We'll open a good bottle of wine and forget all about it."

Joséphine smiled absently. Her mind was elsewhere. There was something familiar in the scene she'd just witnessed: violence, a shout, a gesture that trailed like a long scarf. She searched her memory, trying to remember. She didn't succeed, but for some reason felt threatened. *How can I explain this nameless, ghostly fear that steals in and envelops me? I'm alone. No one can help me. No one can understand. We're always alone. I have to stop fooling myself in order to feel better, stop running to take refuge in charming men's arms. That's not an answer.*

"What's going on, Joséphine?" he asked, a worried look in his eye.

"I don't know."

"You can tell me anything, you know."

She shook her head. She'd been struck, as if with a knife, by the twin certainties that she was alone and that she was in danger. But she didn't know why she was so positive. She looked at Philippe resentfully. *How can he be so sure of himself? Sure of me? Sure of being able to make me happy? As if life were that simple!* She felt his need to protect her as intrusive, his protective declaration as arrogant. It was intolerable.

"You're wrong, Philippe. You're not a solution for me. You're a problem."

He gaped at her, shocked.

"What makes you say that?"

Jo gazed off into space, if she were reading in a big book, a book of truths.

"You're married," she said. "To my sister. You'll be going back to London soon. Before you do, you'll go see Iris. She's your wife, so that's normal. But she's also my sister, and that's not normal."

"Joséphine! Stop it!"

She gestured for him to be quiet, and continued. "Nothing will ever be possible between us. We've been telling ourselves stories. We've been living a fairy tale, a Christmas story. But I've come back down to Earth. Don't ask me how, because I don't know."

"But these last days, you seemed to—"

"These last days, I've been dreaming. But I've started to understand, now."

He stared at her as if he didn't recognize her. He'd never seen this tough, determined Joséphine before.

"I don't know what to say," he said. "You may be right or you may be wrong."

"I'm very much afraid I'm right."

She had pulled away and stood looking at him, her arms crossed on her chest.

"I'd rather suffer right now, all at once. I don't want to pine away."

"If that's really what you want."

She nodded, backing away and hugging her chest tighter to keep him from approaching. At the same time, an inner voice was crying, *He'll protest, he'll shut me up, gag me, call me crazy, my crazy darling, the crazy woman I love, my crazy-daisy, why are you talking crazy? Remember us!*

He stood motionless, looking at her somberly. His look held their last days together, fingers touching under a table, hands clasped in the darkness of the foyer, caresses stolen while hanging up a coat, holding a door, picking up keys, stolen kisses and the long, long kiss against the oven handle, the taste of black prunes and stuffing and Armagnac. The images reeled by like a silent black-and-white film, and she could read their story in Philippe's eyes. Then he blinked, and the film stopped. He ran his hands through his hair, as if to keep from touching her. Without a word, he went to leave the kitchen. He stopped on the threshold for a moment, about to say something more, but changed his mind and closed the door behind him.

Jo could hear him calling to his son: "Alex, change of plans: We're going home."

"But we haven't finished watching *The Simpsons*. There's just ten more minutes."

"No, right away! Get your coat."

"Ten minutes, Daddy!"

"Alexandre."

"You're a drag!"

"Alexandre!"

Philippe's voice had climbed a notch; it was harsh and imperious. Joséphine shivered. It was a voice she didn't recognize. She didn't recognize this man who gave orders and expected to be obeyed. She listened to the silence that followed, hoping the door would open, that he would come back and say, "Joséphine . . ."

Instead, she heard the front door slam and Zoé shout, "Why are they leaving? We aren't done watching *The Simpsons*."

Joséphine bit her fist so as not to cry out in sorrow.

Next day, the telephone in the kitchen rang.

"Do you still remember me, Joséphine? Or have you forgotten?"

It was Luca!

"Hello, Luca," Jo answered in a casual tone. "How are you doing?"

"How polite you are!"

"Did you enjoy the holidays?"

"I hate this time of year, when people feel they have to be nice to each other and cook those awful turkeys."

Jo could feel the taste of the turkey in her mouth, and closed her eyes. Ten and a half minutes of fleeting happiness.

"I spent Christmas with a tangerine and a can of sardines," he said.

"All alone?"

"Yes. It's a habit of mine. I hate Christmas."

"Habits change, sometimes. When we're happy."

"What a vulgar word!"

"If you say so."

"What about you, Joséphine? Your Christmas was merry, apparently."

She could hear the condescension in his statement, but ignored it. She didn't want to get into a fight, just wanted to understand what was happening inside her. Without her being aware of it, a sort of knot was loosening and falling away. An old, shriveled piece of her heart. She didn't feel anything for Luca anymore, she realized. The longer she spoke, the more he faded. The handsome Luca who once made her tremble when he took her hand and slipped it into his duffel coat pocket was fading like a figure in the fog. *You fall in love, and then one day you wake up and you're not in love anymore. When had this end of loving begun?* Jo remembered very clearly: walking around the lake, the splashing black Lab, Luca not listening to her. Their love had eroded that day. Philippe's kiss against the oven handle had done the rest. Without noticing it, Jo had slipped from one man to another. She had stripped Luca of his finery and dressed Philippe in it. The love had evaporated.

"Would you like to go to the movies?" Luca was asking. "Are you free this evening?"

"Not really. Hortense is here and I want to take advantage of that."

Silence fell. She had offended him.

"I get it. A mother's tender heart."

Luca's mocking tone irritated her.

"Is your brother better?"

"His condition is stable."

"Ah."

"Don't feel that you have to ask about him, Joséphine. You're being too polite. Too polite to be sincere."

Jo felt her anger rising. Luca was becoming a pest, someone she didn't feel like talking to. She paused, observing this new feeling with surprise and a certain confidence.

"Are you still there, Joséphine?"

His tone was light, teasing. Taking her courage in both hands, she said, "You're right, Luca, I don't give a damn about your brother. He's always calling me a dimwit, and you never saw anything wrong with that."

The words came tumbling out as if she'd held them back for too long. She could feel her heart pounding and her ears getting hot.

"Oh, ho! It's the fighting nun!"

Luca was starting to talk like his brother!

"Good-bye, Luca."

"Did I hurt your feelings?"

"I don't think there's any point in our calling each other anymore."

She could feel herself taking the high ground. Then she repeated it, with a kind of studied indifference, an intoxicating, calculated slowness: "Good. Bye."

Jo hung up, then stared at the telephone as if it were a weapon. She was amazed at her boldness, full of respect for this new Joséphine who had just hung up on a man. *Is this really me? Did I do this?* She burst out laughing. *For the first time in my life I've dared to break up with a man, I've dared! Me, the clumsy, ordinary one, the one left to drown, ditched for a girl in a hail salon, riddled with debt, oppressed and manipulated. I did it!*

She ran to wake Shirley and tell her the good news.

Henriette Grobz got out of the taxi and smoothed her raw silk dress. At the driver's window, she asked him to wait for her. When the man muttered that he had other things to do, Henriette sharply promised him a good tip. He nodded reluctantly and turned his radio on.

Henriette had come to retrieve her daughter.

"This has gone on long enough," she had warned Iris on the phone. "You've had a nice, long rest. You're not going to rot in a room in some clinic. You're just giving in, that's all. Pack your bags and get ready to leave."

The doctors had agreed, and Philippe paid the bill.

"What am I going to do now?" asked Iris, when she was seated in the taxi with her hands on her knees. "Besides getting a good manicure, that is."

"You're going to fight. Get your husband and your position back. Also, get your looks back, which you've tended to neglect."

"I'm washed up," said Iris calmly, as if stating a fact.

"Nonsense! You start working out, get in shape, fix yourself up, and you'll get your husband back. You can snag any man with a good belly dance."

"Philippe comes to see me out of charity," she said, sighing.

"Just try!"

"I don't feel like it anymore."

"You'll feel like it again, otherwise you'll wind up like me: wearing scratchy sweaters and eating canned peas and grocery-store tuna in crankcase oil."

At that, Iris straightened, a hint of amusement in her eyes.

"Is that why you got me out of there? Because you don't have any more money and you're counting on Philippe to bail you out?"

"Ah, I see you're doing better already. You're showing some spirit!"

"You didn't visit very often during my months in the clinic. Your absence was noticed."

"It depressed me."

"And now all of a sudden you come because you need me— or rather you need Philippe's money. Now that's depressing!"

"What's depressing is that you're giving up, whereas Joséphine is on parade. She went to have lunch at that pig Marcel's place. On your husband's arm!"

"I know, he told me."

"And you let him get away with it?"

"What can I do? Burst into tears? Cling weeping to his legs? That might've worked back in your day, but pity doesn't cut it anymore. Besides, I'm not even sure I love him. I don't love anyone. I'm such a monster, I don't even care for my son. So my husband . . ."

"I'm not going to let you give in to despair, Iris. That's too easy! I'm taking you in hand, my girl. Trust me!"

Iris smiled with a kind of calm disenchantment, and turned her lovely, sad face to the window. Fumbling in her purse for her compact, she opened it and looked at herself in the mirror. Reflected back at her were two wide expanses of blue. *My eyes! I still have my eyes. As long as I have them, I'm saved*, she thought. *Eyes don't grow old*. Feeling reassured, she said, "It's nice to be outside."

Then, peering at the apartment blocks lining the rain-swept street, she exclaimed, "How ugly it is! How do people manage to live in those cages?"

"Think long and hard," said Henriette. "If you don't want to wind up in one of those ugly buildings, you better get your husband back. Otherwise you'll discover the charms of poverty."

She didn't much like my remark, thought Henriette, secretly observing her elder daughter's stubborn profile. *Whenever Iris is confronted with an unpleasant reality, she tries to get around it. She never faces it. She's always dreaming of being off in some fairy-tale world where the wave of a magic wand makes all problems vanish, solves all difficulties. She'll listen to any charlatan pitching her any kind of happiness that doesn't require the slightest effort. She'll yield to any master who fulfills her, be it Botox or God. She would become a nun and lock herself away in a convent just so as not to have to fight. Everybody thinks she's so strong, when she's actually a facade of cheap glitter. She'll do anything rather than get her hands dirty, grubbing in the muck of reality.*

Iris was wiping the condensation off the car window with the tip of her finger and asking herself what her life was going to be like. *I'm going to have to go out, face people,* she thought, sighing. *I need to find a Trojan horse, a trick to play to get back in the game of this cruel and foul high society. Could the answer be a man? A rich and powerful man, a fashionable man who would notice me?* A nervous laugh escaped her lips. *I'll just have to seduce my husband.*

Standing in the bathroom in her long nightgown back home, Henriette gazed with affection at the scar on her thigh. It was an old burn, a pale rectangle of pink flesh now smooth and soft.

To think that's how it all began! she thought. *A little household accident and I'm back in the saddle again. What a good idea it was to curl my hair myself that day.*

She remembered the moment very well. It was early December, and she'd gone to get her curling iron in the bathroom closet—it had been ages since she'd last used it—and plugged it in. She had combed her lank hair, which snagged on the comb like dry hay, separated it into two hanks, then waited patiently for the iron to heat up. Once it was hot, she would smooth each of the hanks, then braid them into in a bun on top of her head.

A clumsy gesture knocked the white-hot iron against her thigh, burning her terribly. Whole strips of flesh came away when she pulled off the iron, and the scorched skin bled. She ran screaming downstairs to the concierge, displayed her wound, and begged the woman for some ointment or to ask the pharmacist at the corner for help. Instead, the woman led her into her apartment and picked up the telephone. With a mysterious look, she dialed a number.

"In a few minutes it won't burn anymore," she assured Henriette, tapping on the dial with a conspiratorial glance. "And in a week your skin will be nice and pink again." When the other party—a woman called Chérubine—answered, the concierge handed Henriette the phone.

And that's exactly what happened. The burning disappeared and the swollen flesh became smooth, as if by magic. Every morning, Henriette studied the instantaneous cure in amazement.

Still, it cost her 50 euros. She tried to object, but Chérubine stood firm. That was her price, she said. Otherwise she would blow into the phone and the pain would return. Henriette agreed to pay. Later, when she had the precious phone number, she called the woman she had already dubbed "the Witch." She thanked her and asked for the address to send the check. As she was about to hang up, she heard Chérubine say, "If you need any other services . . ."

"What do you do besides healing burns?"

"Sprains, insect bites, snakebites, shingles . . ." Mechanically, she listed the services on offer. "Inflammations of various kinds, vaginal discharge, eczema, asthma—"

Seized by a sudden idea, Henriette interrupted her.

"What about souls? Do you work on souls?"

"Yes, but that's more expensive. Attracting love, lifting depression, repelling spirits, countering spells—"

"Do you cast spells, too?"

"Yes, but that's even more expensive, because I must protect myself from the energy rebound."

Henriette thought it over, and made an appointment to meet her.

So one fine day just before the Christmas holidays, which would underscore her loneliness and poverty, Henriette went to a rundown building on rue des Vignoles in the twentieth arrondissement.

Chérubine opened the door, and Henriette squeezed into an apartment barely big enough to contain its fat owner's girth.

Everything in the place was pink, pink and heart-shaped: pillows, chairs, picture frames on the wall, plates, mirrors, and crêpe paper flowers. Even Chérubine's shiny, bulging forehead was decorated with pomaded spit curls.

"Did she bring me a photograph?" asked the Witch, lighting pink candles on a card table covered with a pink tablecloth.

From her purse, Henriette took a full-length photo of Josiane and set it in front of her. The fat woman's chest wheezed as it rose and fell. Her color was pale, her hair thin. *She must be anemic*, thought Henriette, wondering if she ever went outside. *She's so fat and the apartment is so small, maybe she came in one day and wasn't able to get out.*

As Chérubine fetched a work box from under the table, Henriette glanced up to see a large statue of the Virgin Mary with a golden crown on her white veil on the corner of a dresser. The sight of Mary bending toward her, palms joined, made Henriette feel better.

"What exactly does she want?" asked Chérubine with the same devout air and posture as the statue.

"I don't especially want my husband's love," she explained. "I want my rival, the woman in the picture, to become deeply depressed. I want everything she touches to turn to ashes, and make my husband come back to me."

"I see, I see," said Chérubine, closing her eyes and folding her hands over her ample bosom. "That is a very Christian request. The husband should remain with the woman he has chosen as his companion for life. These are the sacred bonds of marriage. The person who undoes them risks divine fury. So we will ask for a first-degree spell. She does not wish the woman dead?"

"Er, what exactly is a first-degree spell?"

"This woman will feel very tired, will have no appetite for anything, no taste for the sexual act, strawberry tarts, gossip, or playing with her children. She will begin to fade like a cut flower. She will lose her beauty, her laughter, her enthusiasm. In a word, slowly wither away, have dark and even suicidal thoughts. Like a cut flower, that's the best way I can put it."

"And will my husband come back?"

"Boredom and disgust will spread to everything around this woman. Unless he is driven by an extraordinary love, one stronger than the spell, he will turn away from her."

"That's perfect," said Henriette, straightening up. "I want him to be in good shape to run his business and earn money."

"Then he will be protected. She will have to bring me a photograph of him."

Oh God, that means I'll have to come back here! Henriette's mouth twisted in a grimace of distaste.

"Does he have children with this woman?"

"Yes, a son."

"Does she wish him to be affected as well?"

Henriette hesitated. After all, he was just a baby.

"No. I want to get rid of her first."

"Very well. She may leave now, and I will concentrate on the photo. The effects will be immediate. That will be six hundred euros, cash. Does she understand?"

Henriette practically choked.

"I've only got three hundred euros on me."

"That is no problem. She can give them to me and come back with the rest when she brings the husband's photo. But she has to return quickly," Chérubine added with a hint of menace, "because if I start working . . ."

Three weeks later, Henriette went to Parc Monceau, looking for the little maid who took Junior out for walks. She found her on a bench reading a magazine. In his pram, the baby was deep in the contemplation of a sticky candy wrapper.

"Good morning," said Henriette, sitting down.

"Morning," said the girl, looking up from her magazine.

"Did you have a nice holiday?"

"So-so."

"You have all my best wishes for the new year," said Henriette, who thought the maid wasn't making much of an effort to keep the conversation going.

"Thanks. You, too."

"What is he doing, there?" she asked, pointing at the boy with the tip of her shoe.

"That's the wrapper from his Carambar," said the maid, leaning over to wipe caramel smears from the baby's cheeks. "He loves Carambars. He's working his teeth on them."

Henriette let the maid rattle on about Junior, the amazing progress he made every day, his playful or angry moods, the state of his teeth, his feet, his well-shaped stools. She concluded by saying, "The only thing he can't do is talk, and that'll be coming soon, if you ask me."

Henriette tried to look interested, endured a few more surprising anecdotes about the child and his age, then cut the girl off. She wasn't about to get gaga over a rug rat drooling on a Carambar wrapper.

"What about his mother? Is she well? I haven't seen her in the park lately."

"Oh, don't mention it. She's so unhappy."

"How can you tell?"

"She has no energy at all."

"But she has so many wonderful things in her life!"

"I don't get it," said the maid, shaking her head. "She spends whole days in bed, cries all the time. It just hit her one morning. She woke up, sat up in bed, put one foot on the floor and said to me, 'I think I'm coming down with the flu. I feel weak and everything's spinning.' So she went back to bed. And she's just been dragging herself around ever since. Poor Monsieur Marcel is at his wits' end. He's got scabs on his scalp from scratching his head so much. Even little Junior has stopped gurgling."

Henriette listened in delight. She could've kissed the air around her. So it was working! It was just like the burn. Josiane was going to disappear by magic.

"Monsieur just paces back and forth," the maid added. "She stays in bed all day long, doesn't want to see anyone. Won't even let me open the curtains; the light hurts her eyes. Things were okay until Christmastime. At Christmas she got up, even had company over. But since then, it's been awful!"

The girl was giving Henriette an account of her triumph.

"I have to do everything. Cleaning, cooking, and laundry, plus taking care of the kid! I don't have a minute to myself, except when I take him out for a walk. Then I have a chance to catch my breath, maybe read a book."

"These depressions do happen, you know," said Henriette. "In my day we called them 'the baby blues.'"

"Madame won't go to the doctor. She won't do anything! Says she has black butterflies flying inside her head. I swear, that's what she said: black butterflies!"

"My God!" said Henriette with a sigh. "It's as bad as that!"

Her gaze fell on the baby, who was looking at them intently, as if trying to understand what was being said above his head.

"Poor little sweetheart," Henriette murmured. "He's so cute, with his red curls and his gummy smile."

She leaned down, intending to pat Junior's head, but he stiffened and shrank back in the pram to avoid her caress. He screamed and put raised thumbs and index fingers together in a kind of threatening gesture.

"Well, will you look at that!" cried the maid. "It's like you were the devil. In *The Exorcist*, that's what you do to ward off the devil."

"Don't be silly, it's my hat! It scares him. Children often find it frightening."

"It's a strange one, for sure, like a flying saucer. Must be a nuisance in the Metro."

Henriette had to hold her tongue not to tell the woman off. *Do I look like someone who takes the Metro?* She pursed her lips, stifling a retort. She needed this girl.

"Well, I'll leave you to your reading," said Henriette, standing up. She had slipped a bill in the girl's half-open purse.

"Oh, you mustn't! I know I've been complaining, but they're very good to me."

Henriette walked away, a smile on her lips. Chérubine's work was first class.

Gary and Hortense were enjoying a cappuccino in a Starbucks. He had come to pick her up during her lunch break, and they watched the passersby while dipping their lips in the thick white foam. It was one of those winter days that the English call "glorious." Blue sky, sharp cold, dazzling light. In the morning, they would cry "What a glorious day!" to each other with big, satisfied smiles, as if they were personally responsible for it.

"My grandmother called me in last night," he said.

"To the palace?"

He nodded. The cappuccino had left a thin white mustache above his lip. Hortense rubbed it off with her finger.

"Any particular reason?"

"Yeah. She said I've wasted enough time lying around, that I have to decide what I'm going to do next year. This is January, when you have to apply to universities. She gave me the choice between a military academy and law school, something like that. She pointed out that all the men in the family spent time in the military, even that old pacifist Charles."

"They'll shave your head and stick you in a uniform!"

"I'm not attending any military academy, I'm not going into the army, and I won't study law, business, or anything else."

"Well, that's clear at least. So what's the problem?"

"The problem is the pressure she's going to put on me. She doesn't give up easily, you know."

"It's your life. You have to make up your mind, and tell her what you want to do."

"I want to do music, but I don't know how, exactly. Maybe I'll be a pianist. Is that a career?"

"It is if you're talented and you work like crazy."

"My teacher says I have perfect pitch and I should continue. But it's tough at my age to decide what I'm going to do for the rest of my life. I want to make music. That's the only thing I'm sure of. I don't smoke, I don't drink, I don't do drugs, I don't shop for clothes to give myself a look, I don't zone out seeking God, and I don't have expensive tastes. But I do want to do music."

"Well, just tell her that."

"As if it were that easy!" he said, rolling his eyes.

Gary paid the bill, and they went outside to sit on a little wall. He pulled his pea coat collar up.

"Listen, Gary, you have the luxury of being able to do whatever you like. You don't have money problems. If you don't try to do the one thing in life you're passionate about, who can?"

"She won't understand."

"Since when do you let someone else decide your life?"

"You don't know my grandmother! She's gonna pressure my mom, who will feel guilty for not looking after me 'seriously.'" Gary made air quotes around the word. "And she'll get involved."

"What if you ask her to trust you for a year?"

"A year wouldn't be enough! You need more time than that, if you're serious about music. It's not like I'm taking cooking classes!"

"Enroll in a music school, then, a good one. One with a name."

"She won't hear of it."

"You can do it anyway."

"Easier said than done!"

"You know, it's strange. Until today I never thought of you as a loser."

"Ha-ha, very funny."

"Gary! You're giving up before you've even tried. Prove to her that it's serious, and she'll trust you."

"Is that how you manage to do it?" he asked, looking at Hortense as if her answer could change his life.

"Yes."

"And that's working for you?"

Gary was watching her so seriously, it gave her goose bumps.

"Yes, up and down the line. But you have to work hard. I wanted my *baccalauréat* with honors, and I got it. I wanted to come to London; I came here. I wanted to go to this school; I was accepted. And I'm going to be a great designer, maybe even a great couturier. Nobody has moved me off my path because I made up my mind that nobody would. It's pretty simple, really."

"Is there anything else that you've sworn you would get?" he asked, aware of the importance of this moment, when Hortense's guard was down.

"Yes."

She said it without trembling, knowing exactly what he was asking about but refusing to answer. They stayed that way for a moment, looking into each other's eyes.

"Like what?"

"None of your business!"

"Yes, it is. Tell me."

Hortense shook her head.

"I'll tell you when I get it!"

"Because you'll get it, right?"

"Of course."

He gave her an enigmatic little smile, as if conceding that she might be right, but that the matter was far from settled. A few formalities still had to be dealt with.

This was followed by a moment of great solemnity that led the two of them into an area they had never entered before: that of surrender. They were tasting their inner souls, their hearts' tenderness, and could reveal exactly what they thought, except that they didn't say it in words but with their eyes. As if it didn't exist, or wasn't supposed to exist yet. They did a few brief tango steps with this heartfelt gentleness, and their souls kissed. Then they floated back down to the honking street.

A brisk breeze had come up and Gary's nose was reddening. He shoved his hands into his pockets as if he wanted to burst them, and scraped the ground with his shoe tip. He seemed to be focused on an inner monologue. Hortense observed him, amused. They had known each other for so long. She was closer to Gary than anyone else in the world. She stepped close, slipped her hand under his arm, and rested her head on his shoulder.

"You never give up, do you?" he complained.

She looked up at him and smiled.

"Never. And you know why?"

"Why?"

"Because I'm not afraid." Then she glanced at her watch and cried, "Rats! I'm going to be late!"

"You're just like your mother. You never say 'shit.'"

"Thanks for the compliment."

"It's a nice compliment. I'm very fond of her."

Hortense didn't reply. Whenever her mother was mentioned, she closed down.

He walked her to her school near Piccadilly Circus.

"You know what else my grandmother said? She talked about my 'romantic conquests,' with that look of royal delicacy of hers. That's what she calls those sluts I've been going out with. 'Gary dear, when you give away your body, you also give away your soul.' Hearing stuff like that, you never want to fuck again."

"Stop complaining! You're privileged—never forget it. There aren't a lot of guys whose grandmother is the queen of England. Besides, you have the best of both worlds: You're in the royal family but nobody knows it. So shut up!"

In front of Hortense's school, she gave him a quick peck on the cheek and went in.

Gary watched as Hortense disappeared into the flood of students pouring into the building. That girl was a master in the art of solving problems. She didn't waste time with useless worries. She focused on facts and facts only, and she was right. He was going to look for a music school. He would learn solfège and practice scales. Hortense had given him a kick in the butt, and a kick in the butt moves you forward and drives away gloom.

"What a glorious day!" Gary cried, admiring the sight of a double-decker bus bright red against the blue sky. The bus would soon be replaced by an ordinary single-decker, but that didn't matter. Life would go on, because life was beautiful. He was going to take it in hand and ditch all the dark baggage he was lugging around.

Hortense's first class of the day was art history.

The professor was a slow-talking little gray man with ivory skin and a burgundy vest over a potbelly. *His collar makes him look like a cheapskate,* thought Hortense, sketching on her blank page. *It needs more fullness. The sleeves and shirttails too. Get some sea breeze blowing on him.* The teacher was explaining how art and politics sometimes walked hand in hand and sometimes pulled in opposite directions.

"When did the first political parties appear?" he asked the sleepy classroom.

"You mean in the world?" asked Hortense, looking up from her notebook.

"Yes, Miss Cortès. But in particular in England, because the first parties were born in England. Despite your revolution, France isn't the flower of democracy. So?"

Hortense had no idea.

Glancing to her left, she spotted her roommate. Agathe had her head on her arm as if she were taking notes, but she was dozing. From the front, you would think her absorbed in the professor's talk, but from the side it was obvious she was asleep. She had come in at four in the morning, and Hortense heard her vomiting in the bathroom. *That one'll never be a fighter,* thought Hortense. *She crawls and lets stocky dwarves walk all over her.*

They came to fetch Agathe almost every evening. They didn't even call to warn her, just showed up, shouted, "Get dressed. We're going out!" and she followed. Hortense couldn't believe Agathe fancied any of them. They were vulgar, condescending, brutal gnomes. Their odd voices were like hot coals blowing in your face, burning you and sending shivers up and down your spine.

Hortense avoided the men, but also trained herself not to be overwhelmed with fear when she encountered them. She kept them at a distance, putting a mental mile between her and them. It was a difficult exercise because in spite of their forced smiles, they were terrifying.

Still, Agathe had talent as a designer. She was inspired, understood patterns, didn't bother making sketches, and would instinctively grasp an item's correct drape or cut. Then she would add the little detail that narrowed the waist or lengthened the figure. She knew how to handle fabric, but she had no interest in effort and hard work.

Out of a hundred and fifty students, Agathe and Hortense had been chosen as candidates for an internship with Vivienne Westwood. Only one of them would be taken, and Hortense was determined to be the one. She read up on the history of the brand so that she could make informed comments during her interview and have the advantage. That was something Agathe almost certainly hadn't thought of. She was too busy going out, dancing, drinking, smoking, and swinging her hips. And vomiting.

"Don't you want to go to London?"

Her eyes downcast, Zoé shook her head.

"Don't you ever want to go to London again?"

Zoé heaved a sigh that meant no.

"Did you have a fight with Alexandre?"

Zoé looked away. Nothing on her face revealed whether she was feeling angry, unhappy, or intimidated.

"Talk to me, Zoé!" cried Joséphine in irritation. "How can I guess what's happening? In the old days you used to turn cart-wheels at the idea of going to London, and now you don't want to go anymore! What happened?"

Zoé glowered at her mother and said, "It's five to eight. I'm going to be late for school."

She swung her backpack onto her shoulders, tightened the straps, and made for the front door. Before going out, she turned around and said, "And don't go into my room. It's forbidden!"

"Zoé! You didn't even give me a kiss!" shouted Jo, seeing her daughter's back disappearing.

She rushed to the stairwell and ran down the stairs. In the lobby, she caught a glance of herself in the mirror: she was in pajamas, wearing a sweatshirt that said DEATH TO CARBS!, a gift from Shirley. Gaétan Lefloc-Pignel was standing next to Zoé. Joséphine felt embarrassed to have the boy see her this way and turned tail. Retreating to the elevator, she bumped into a young blonde woman who looked as disheveled as she did.

"Are you Gaétan's mother?" she asked, happy to finally meet Madame Lefloc-Pignel.

"He forgot to take his banana for recess," she said. "His blood sugar drops sometimes, and he needs a snack. I was running to catch up with him. I didn't have time to get dressed so I went out just as I was."

She'd slipped a raincoat over her nightgown and was bare-foot. She kept rubbing her arms, avoiding Joséphine's eye.

"I'm happy to meet you," said Jo. "I never see you around."

"Oh, that's because of my husband. He doesn't like me to . . ."

She stopped, as if someone was listening in to her.

"He would be furious to see me in the elevator, not properly dressed."

"I'm just as bad as you!" exclaimed Jo. "I was running after Zoé. She left without kissing me. I don't like starting my day without a kiss from my daughter."

"Neither do I! Those children's kisses are so sweet."

Madame Lefloc-Pignel looked like a child herself. She was delicate and pale, with big, frightened brown eyes. She looked down, hugging the raincoat around her. The elevator stopped at her floor and she stepped out. She said good-bye several times, but kept holding the door open with her thin arm. Jo wondered if she wanted to tell her something. Strands of blond hair had escaped her two thin braids. She was glancing nervously right and left.

"Would you like to come up for a cup of coffee?" asked Joséphine.

"Oh no! That wouldn't be . . ."

She was rubbing her arms again.

"I have my list of things to do. I can't be late."

She spoke as if she were terrified at the idea of forgetting something.

"It's very nice of you to offer. Some other time, maybe."

She continued to hold the elevator door open.

"If you see my husband, please don't tell him that you saw me this way, not dressed. He's very . . . he's very strict about manners."

Finally, as if regretfully, she let the door close. Joséphine gave her a friendly little wave. *She must take tranquilizers. She's shaking like a leaf, jumps at the slightest sound. She must not be much fun as a mate, or a very present mother.* Joséphine never saw her at the school or at the neighborhood grocers. *Where does she do her shopping? Maybe she's like me, who still goes back to the Intermarché in Courbevoie. A habit I've kept from my old life.* She still had her Intermarché rewards card. Antoine had one too. Two cards on the same account. She never canceled his; it was a connection with him she still maintained.

She went home and decided to go running.

Joséphine had completed one lap around the lake and was considering a second when she encountered the unknown man coming in the other direction. He had his hands in his pockets and his cap pulled down his forehead. He walked by without looking at her.

Joséphine stretched, lifted her arms, bent her head, shook her arms and legs. She missed Philippe. He came to mind all the time. He stole into her head, filling it up. *Come back,* she whispered. *Come back, and we'll lead a secret life, we'll hide, steal moments of happiness while waiting for time to pass, for Iris to get well, for the girls to grow up.* She stopped at the thought. *The girls! Maybe Zoé knows. Children know things that we don't know ourselves. You can't hide anything from them. Does Zoé know Philippe and I kissed? When she comes close to me, is it possible that she can sense his kisses?*

Joséphine massaged her legs, did one final stretch. *I really have to talk to her. Get her to talk to me.*

She took a few steps and started jogging. She was running, her mind elsewhere, when she heard someone call her name: "Joséphine!"

She turned around to see Luca coming toward her, his arms wide, a big smile on his face.

"Luca!" she cried.

"I knew I would find you here. I know your habits."

Joséphine could hardly believe it: Luca, the coldest man in the world, was pursuing her. She felt her knees shaking. She wasn't used to sparking passion and still didn't know how to behave. On the one hand, she was grateful to him; his attention made her feel important and attractive. On the other hand, she thought he looked about as attractive as a stick.

They walked to the lakeside café. Luca got two cups of coffee and set them down. She crossed her legs, tucked her feet under her chair, and prepared herself.

"How are you doing, Joséphine?"

"I'm all right."

Jo wasn't very good at keeping men at a distance. Wasn't used to it. She preferred to let them talk.

"Joséphine, I've been unfair to you."

She excused this with a wave.

"I behaved badly," Luca continued. "I miss you, Joséphine. I'd gotten used to your presence, your thoughtful attention, and your generosity."

"Oh!" she exclaimed in surprise.

Why hadn't he said these words before, when there was still time? When she was so eager to hear them? At a loss, she studied him. He saw the sorrow in her eyes.

"You don't feel anything for me anymore, do you?"

"It's just that I waited for a sign from you for so long that I think I—"

"Got tired of waiting?"

"Yes, in a way."

"Please don't tell me it's too late!" he said playfully. "I'll do anything to get you to forgive me."

Joséphine felt tormented. She tried to retrieve some scrap of love, some thread that she could draw out, pinch, ravel, and curl so she could fashion it into a big bow. She looked into Luca's eyes, searching for the beginning of such a thread, something she could hold on to, but didn't find anything. Her probing was unsuccessful.

"You're right, Joséphine. It's no accident that I'm alone at my age. I've never been able to hold onto someone. You at least have your daughters."

"But you have your brother. He needs you."

Frowning, Luca looked at her as if he didn't understand. He seemed to try to get what she was referring to, then caught himself and laughed sarcastically.

"Vittorio!"

"That's right, Vittorio. You're his brother and the only person he's able to turn to."

"Forget about Vittorio!"

"I can't forget about him, Luca. He always stood between us."

"Forget him, I tell you!" he commanded angrily.

She pulled back, startled by his change of tone. They remained silent for a long moment. He played with a sugar packet, crushing it with his long fingers, pressing it, rolling it, flattening it.

"You're right, Joséphine, I'm a dead weight. I drag everybody down."

Their coffees had gotten cold. Jo grimaced when she tasted hers.

"Do you know what we're going to do, Joséphine?"

He raised his head, a determined look on his face.

"I'm going to give you a key to my place, and—"

"No!" she protested, frightened by the responsibility he was putting on her.

"I'm going to give you a key to my place, and when you've forgiven me for my indifference and my clumsiness, you'll come. I'll be waiting."

"Luca, you shouldn't."

"It's something I've never done before. It's a proof of . . ."

She waited for the word he was about to say, but he didn't. Instead, he said, "A proof of our connection."

He stood up and took a key from his pocket and set on the table next to the cold coffee. He kissed her on the head.

"Good-bye, Joséphine."

As she watched him leave, she picked up the key. It was still warm. She closed her hand around it, the useless proof of a dead love.

Zoé didn't want to talk.

Joséphine was waiting for her when she got back from school.

"We have to talk, darling," said Joséphine. "I'm open to anything you want to tell me. If you've done something that you're sorry for or you're ashamed of, tell me. We'll talk about it, and I won't get angry because I love you more than anything."

Zoé set her backpack down in the foyer. Took off her coat. Went to the kitchen. Washed her hands. Picked up a towel. Wiped her hands. Cut three slices of bread, and buttered them. Put the butter back in the refrigerator, the knife in the dishwasher. Took two bars of dark chocolate with almonds. Put everything on a plate. Went to get her backpack and, without listening to Joséphine—who repeated, "We have to talk, Zoé, we can't go on like this"—closed her bedroom door and stayed in there until dinnertime.

Joséphine reheated the braised chicken she had cooked. Zoé liked braised chicken.

They ate dinner together, but separately. As Jo choked back her tears, Zoé spooned up the chicken sauce without once looking at her mother. Rain was beating against the kitchen window, running down in fat, soft drops. *When the drops are thick and heavy, they stick to the glass and you can count them.*

"What in the world have I done?" Joséphine finally yelled, out of words, out of patience, out of arguments.

"You know perfectly well," said Zoé imperturbably.

She picked up her plate, glass, and silverware and put them in the dishwasher. She carefully wiped off her section of the table, taking care not to touch the crumbs on her mother's side. Then she folded her napkin, washed her hands, and left.

Joséphine jumped up from her chair and followed her. Zoé closed the door to her bedroom. Joséphine heard the lock turn twice.

"I'm not your maid!" she cried. "Thank me for dinner, at least."

Zoé opened the door and said, "Thank you. The chicken was delicious."

Then she closed it again, leaving Joséphine speechless.

She returned to the kitchen and sat down at her plate, which she hadn't touched. Gazed at the chicken in its gelid sauce, the weary tomatoes, the shriveled peppers.

Jo put her head on her arms on the table and sat there for a long time. A Beatles song could be heard from Zoé's room: "Don't pass me by, don't make me cry, don't make me blue, 'cause you know darling, I love only you." *It's useless,* Joséphine thought. *There's no point in forcing someone to confide in you. You can't fight the dead, let alone the living dead.* She laughed bitterly. She had never laughed that way and didn't like it. *I have to get to work. I have to find a research supervisor and plan my* habilitation *thesis defense. Studying has always saved me from bad situations. Whenever life throws me for a loop, the Middle Ages come to my rescue. I used to describe the symbolism of colors to the girls to hide my anxiety about tomorrow or my sorrow from yesterday. Blue, the color of mourning. Purple, connected to death. Green, hope and rising sap. Yellow, sickness. Red, in both fire and blood, like the cross on a Crusader's chest or an executioner's hood. Black, the color of hell and darkness. The girls listened, open mouthed, and I forgot about my problems.*

The telephone interrupted her thoughts. She let it ring for a while and then got up and answered.

"Joséphine?"

It was Iris.

Her voice was playful, her tone carefree and gay.

"Yes," Jo said. She swallowed hard, clutching the phone.

"Have you lost your voice?"

Joséphine laughed in embarrassment.

"It's just that I really didn't expect—"

"Well it's me, all right! Back in the land of the living. And with no ill feelings, I should say. It's been a long time hasn't it?"

Joséphine was silent.

"Are you okay, Jo? Because you don't seem to be."

"Oh sure. I'm fine. What about you?"

"I'm in great shape."

"Where are you?" asked Joséphine, trying to make a connection.

"Why do you ask?"

"No reason."

"Yes, Jo. I know you. You have something in mind."

"No, really. It's just that—"

"The last time, I was a little harsh with you, that's true. I apologize. I'm really sorry. And to prove it, I want to invite you to lunch."

"I would so like it if we would stop fighting."

"Take a pencil and write down the address of the restaurant."

She did: Hôtel Costes, 239 rue Saint-Honoré.

"Are you free day after tomorrow?" asked Iris.

"Yes."

"All right, then, Thursday at one. I'm counting on you, Joséphine. It's very important to me that we get together."

"It is to me too, you know," she said, and added quietly, "I missed you."

"What did you say?" asked Iris.

"Nothing. See you Thursday."

Joséphine grabbed her quilt and went to sit on the balcony. She raised her head and looked up at the stars. It was a beautiful starry sky, lit by a moon as full and brilliant as a cold sun. She found her little star at the very end of the Big Dipper's handle. Clasping her hands, she said, "Thank you for bringing Iris back to me. Thank you. It feels like coming home. And make Zoé come back too. I don't want us to be fighting. As you know, I'm not much of a fighter. Help us start talking to each other again. Tonight, I promise you that if you give me my daughter's love back—I'm promising, you hear?—I promise to give up Philippe."

Philippe had become a man of leisure, a man who hung out in hotel bars reading books and art catalogs. He liked the bars in big hotels, enjoyed the lighting, the hushed atmosphere, the background jazz, the foreign languages people spoke, the graceful way the waiters moved with their trays. He could imagine himself in Paris, New York, Tokyo, Singapore, or Shanghai. He was nowhere, he was everywhere. It suited him very well. He was on the rebound from love. *Not a very virile state of mind*, he told himself.

He put on a severe look, the look of a businessman busy studying serious matters. In fact he was reading Auden, Shakespeare, Pushkin, Sacha Guitry, all the authors he'd never read in his previous life. He wanted to understand emotion, feelings. He would leave the great affairs of the world to others. To others who were like he used to be. When he was serious, in a hurry, his hair neatly combed, his shirt well buttoned, his tie well striped, two cell phones in his pockets. A man full of figures and certainties.

In the morning he stopped by his Regent Street office and checked on a few cases in progress. He phoned Paris, talked to Raoul Frileux, who was running the firm in his name. In the beginning, everything had gone well, but Philippe could now feel the man's barely veiled irritation. *Raoul can't stand my idleness. He can't stand the fact that I'm collecting fees without breaking a sweat.* Then he would phone Magda, his former secretary, who had given Raoul the code name they used: "the Toad." Magda, who now worked for Raoul, would talk quietly so the Toad couldn't hear, and tell Philippe the latest office gossip.

The Toad was a sexual obsessive, she said.

"The other day I almost threw him out the window," she said with a chuckle, "because of his roaming hands."

The Toad stayed at the office until eleven o'clock at night. He was ugly, sneaky, hateful, and vain.

"But he's a terrific businessman!" said Philippe. "He's doubled our revenue since taking over."

"Yes, but he's liable to explode at any moment! Be careful, because he hates you. His vest buttons practically pop off after he talks with you."

Philippe raised the salaries of the firm's two lawyers, to be sure to be protected. You had to watch out in this world of hammerhead sharks. The Toad was a shark, and a brilliant one.

Philippe was the firm's rainmaker, lunching with prospective clients. So as not to waste time, he focused on the ones who were rich, pleasant, and cultured. He would start the initial discussions, then turn them over to the Toad in Paris. In the afternoon he would choose a hotel bar and a good book, and read. Around five thirty he would pick up Alexandre at school and they would walk home together, talking. They would often stop at a museum or an art gallery or go to the movies, if Alexandre didn't have too much homework.

Philippe no longer wanted to waste time, and so had decided to work less. He had dropped his art consultant. He was clearing his personal space, unburdening himself. *Maybe that's why Joséphine slipped away. She thought I came with too much baggage, was too encumbered. She's ahead of me. She's learned to make do with less. I'll learn. I have all the time in the world.*

He missed Zoé's weekend visits and the long conversations between Zoé and Alexandre, on which he would subtly eavesdrop.

Alexandre didn't ask after his cousin, but Philippe could tell he missed her from the way he looked sad on Friday evenings. She would come back, he was sure. He and Jo had moved too quickly by kissing on Christmas Eve. There were too many unresolved things between them. And there was Iris . . . He thought about their last evening in Paris. Iris had been discharged from the clinic, and they'd eaten at home. "We'll have a bite together, just the three of us," she said. "It would be lame to go to a restaurant." Iris cooked. It wasn't exactly a success, but at least she had tried.

Philippe put his book down, and picked up another: Sacha Guitry's plays. He closed his eyes and thought, I'll open it at random, and meditate on whatever line I happen on. He concentrated, opened the book, and read the following:

"You can make people who love you look away, but not people who desire you."

I won't look away, he resolved. I'll wait, and I won't give up.

The only woman whose presence he could stand was Dottie. They had run into each other by accident at a party at the Tate Modern.

Seeing her, Philippe asked, "What are you doing here, er . . . ?"

He couldn't remember her name.

"Dottie. Now do you remember?"

She burst out laughing. Her open mouth revealed three fillings in need of work.

"What are you doing here, Dottie?" he repeated, with a slightly superior air, as if she didn't belong there.

He immediately regretted his arrogant tone, and bit his tongue.

Stung, she snapped at him.

"Why? Don't I have the right to be interested in art? Maybe I'm not smart enough, or chic enough, or—"

"Touché!" Philippe admitted. "I'm a pretentious moron."

He took her to dinner at a little restaurant.

"Oh-ho! I'm rising in the ranks," she smirked. "Now I get treated to a restaurant with white tablecloths."

"It's just for tonight. And because I'm hungry."

"I forgot that monsieur was married and didn't want to get involved."

"That's still true."

Dottie looked down, busying herself with reading the menu.

He wound up at her place, without knowing quite how it happened, and they spent the night together. His performance wasn't brilliant, but she made no comment.

Next morning, he got up early. He didn't want to wake Dottie, but she opened her eyes and put her hand on his back.

"Are you running off or do you have time for coffee?"

"I think I'm going to run off."

She leaned up on her elbow and studied him as if he were an oil-soaked seagull.

"You're in love, aren't you? I can tell. You really weren't with me last night."

"I'm very sorry."

"No, I'm sorry for you."

She hugged a pillow against her breasts and asked, "What's she like?"

"Are you determined to make me talk?"

"You don't have to, but it might be better. We're not destined for a grand passionate love affair, so we may as well be friends. So, what's she like?"

"Prettier and prettier."

"Does that matter?"

"No. When I'm with her I see life differently, and it makes me happy. She lives surrounded by books and jumps into puddles with both feet."

"How old is she? Twelve and a half?"

"She acts twelve and a half, and everybody takes advantage of her: her sister, her daughters. Nobody treats her the way she deserves, and I'd like to protect her, make her laugh, make her head spin."

"Sounds like you're hooked!"

"And no further along than when I started. Will you make me some coffee?"

Dottie got up and put the water on.

"Does she live in London?"

"No, Paris."

"So what's keeping you from living out your great love story?"

Philippe stood and picked up his shirt.

"That's all I'm telling for now. And thank you for last night, even though I was particularly pathetic."

"Want to get together again, even if you're not Tarzan of the Sheets?"

"That's up to you."

Dottie appeared to think it over.

"All right, but on one condition," she said. "I want you to tell me about modern art and take me to the theater and the movies. In a word, teach me. Since she's in Paris, it shouldn't be a problem."

"I have a son named Alexandre, and he always comes first."

"Do you go out with him in the evening?"

"No."

"So is it a deal?"

"It's a deal."

They shook hands on it, as pals.

He started calling her. Took her to the opera, explained modern art to her. She listened, a model student, writing down names and dates with genuine interest. He took her home. Sometimes he came upstairs and fell asleep in her arms. Sometimes, moved by her yielding, her innocence, and her simplicity, he started kissing her and they fell onto the king-size bed together.

Eventually he asked her how old she was. Twenty-nine.

"See? I'm not a baby anymore."

As if she was hinting: I can take care of myself, and I'm getting what I want out of this strange relationship too.

He felt deeply grateful to her.

While they awaited word from Vivienne Westwood as to which of them would be selected for the internship, the atmosphere between Agathe and Hortense crackled with tension. They hardly spoke, just ran into each other at the flat. They hid their notes and their sketchbooks. Agathe began to get up early, go to class, stay in at night. She had started working, and an unusual calm reigned in the apartment. Hortense was pleased. Now she could work without wearing earplugs. That was progress.

One evening Agathe brought home some Chinese food and offered to share it. Hortense was dubious.

"All right, but you taste the dishes first," she said.

Agathe burst out laughing like a little kid, rolling on the sofa and holding her stomach.

"You really think I'd try to poison you?"

"Nothing would surprise me, coming from you," grumbled Hortense, who realized she was being silly, but felt cautious just the same.

"Listen, if it makes you feel better I'll eat some first, and then pass you the container," said Agathe. "I'm just as nervous as you are, you know."

"I'm not nervous, I'm serene. I'm going to win the internship, and I hope you'll be a good loser."

"There's going to be a party at Cuckoo's tomorrow evening. The whole French school is going to be there. You know, the ESMOD gang."

Besides Saint Martins and Parsons in New York, there was also ESMOD in Paris. Hortense hadn't wanted to go there, because she wanted to get away from Paris and her mother, but it was a first-class fashion school, with alumni like Vannina Vesperini, Fifi Chachnil, Franck Sorbier, and Catherine Malandrino. London had been all the rage five years ago, but Paris had returned to the center of the fashion world, with a French specialty: *modélisme*. At ESMOD, you learn to master the techniques of making a model, molding and cutting fabric, and patternmaking—valuable skills that Hortense very much wanted to learn.

She hesitated.

"Are your mafia buddies gonna be there?"

Agathe pouted in a way that meant, "Can't be helped."

"Those guys are really no bargain," said Hortense. "They're fat pigs."

"But they can be nice too, you know."

Hortense snorted. "Nice, really?"

"Sometimes they help me," said Agathe. "They encourage me, give me wings."

"If pigs could fly, we'd have heard about it."

Hortense wound up agreeing to go to the party with her. But when they took the taxi, Agathe gave the driver an address that wasn't the club's.

"Do you mind if we stop at their flat to see them first?"

"Their place?" screamed Hortense. "I'm not going anywhere near those guys."

"Please! If you're with me, I won't be so afraid. They scare me when I'm alone."

Agathe was begging her. She really looked frightened.

Hortense eventually went up to the flat with her, ranting every step of the way.

The men were waiting in the living room, which was glittering with bad taste. It was all marble, gold, chandeliers, curtains with golden cords, showy Bergère chairs, and overstuffed arm chairs.

Five men in black, sitting on their fat pig asses. Hortense didn't like it when they all got up and walked over to her. And she liked it even less when Agathe disappeared, claiming she had to go to the bathroom.

"So, we're not talking so big anymore, are we?" asked a stocky man. "Hey Carlos, is it just me, or do you think the kid's wetting her pants?"

Hortense said nothing, watching for Agathe to come out of the bathroom.

"So tell me, chickie, you know why we had you brought here?"

Hortense realized she'd fallen into a trap, like a ninny. There was no more a party at Cuckoo's than there was good taste in this living room.

"No idea, but I'm sure you're going to tell me."

"We wanted to talk to you about something. After that, we'll leave you alone."

They're going to ask me to turn tricks, she thought.

A lot of the women students did that, to pay for their studies or to go skiing at Val-d'Isère. Special agencies hired them by the weekend. They would fly to some country in the East, spend the night with a fat slob, and come back with full pockets.

"We're gonna ask you a kind of special favor, and you better say yes. 'Cause otherwise, we're gonna get mad. Very mad."

"Oh really?" asked Hortense. She drew herself upright, but could feel fear filling her with a cottony whiteness that made her knees knock.

"Here's what you're gonna do. You're gonna be a sweetheart and drop out of the competition with Agathe. Let her have the internship with Vivienne Westwood."

"Never!" said Hortense who suddenly understood the Chinese food, her roommate's sudden cleanliness, the studious atmosphere in the flat.

"You got five minutes to think it over. Be a pity to get yourself messed up."

Hortense's mind was racing. *Of course, it would also be a pity to miss the opportunity to get in the fashion world so easily. They're using Agathe to gain entrance unnoticed. There is no way I'll help them do that. Not a chance!*

As the five minutes ticked by, Hortense inspected the place

as carefully as a tourist in Versailles: the gilt dressers with their curved drawers and display of silverware—*To make it look like they were taking tea, maybe?*—the clock pendulum silently swinging in the air, the beveled mirrors, the polished parquet floor.

Then she looked at her watch, and announced, "Time's up. I'm leaving now. Delighted to meet you, and I certainly hope I never see you again."

She turned on her heel and headed for the door.

One of the wannabe mafiosi got up and blocked Hortense's way, then hauled her back into the room. Another put on a CD—the overture to Rossini's *The Thieving Magpie*—and turned the volume up full blast. They were clearly planning to beat her up.

"You take over, Carlos," said the tallest of the goons, who seemed to be in charge.

"Okay, boss."

He shoved Hortense into the bathroom, threw her to the floor, and left. She got to her feet and stood there for a moment, her arms crossed. *He's leaving me here to give me time to think. I could see that one coming a mile away. I'm not going to waste my time waiting in here.*

She stepped out of the bathroom, joined them in the living room, and asked, "So what's going on? You chickening out?"

The tall, bossy one angrily rushed over, dragged Hortense back to the bathroom, and threw her to the tiled floor. He yelled, "You cunt!" Then he went out, slamming the door.

I got him angry, Hortense told herself. *That's a point for me. It won't make the punches any gentler, but at least they know I won't roll over for them.*

She straightened her jacket, dusted off her shoulders. She

stood erect and dignified, which was all she had going for herself. The air was still white and cottony, and she felt like throwing up.

She could hear the one they called Carlos coming. He always had to make noise, yelling so people would know he was on his way. And suddenly there he was, in the bathroom. There was white everywhere. Not a speck of color to hang onto or to base a shred of resistance on. Carlos was five feet high and five feet wide, a cube. A bald, fat cube. A real gnome.

Carlos's chunky shape blocked the frosted glass ceiling light, casting shadows everywhere. Seeing the violence in him, Hortense forgot everything. His eyes gleamed with so much rage, she couldn't even look at them. If she wanted to maintain some self-possession, she'd do better to stare at the shower curtain. It was completely white, like the cottony white rising within her and choking her. The walls were white, too. So was the mirror, the little window, the medicine cabinet above the sink, the sink itself, the bathtub. Even the bathmat was white.

Carlos reached down and pulled out his belt, and told her to drop her jeans.

"In your dreams!" she said, gritting her teeth to push the suffocating white away.

"Drop 'em, or I'm getting the razor."

Hortense thought fast. If she dropped her pants, he would take out the razor afterward. She'd be erased pretty quickly.

"In your dreams," she repeated, searching for some sort of color in the bathroom.

He laid the belt on the bathtub rim, opened the medicine cabinet, and took out a long, black folding razor.

"I'm not afraid," she said spotting a rolled-up yellow towel in the tub.

"From red to green all the yellow dies away," wrote Apollinaire. Her mother had taught them that line when they were small. Her mother had told her the story of colors, too. Blue, green, yellow, red, black, purple. Hortense had recently drawn on this when writing a paper on the theme of harmony and colors, earning the best grade in the class. "You got a good education," said the teacher.

Her fear retreated by a good ten inches. If she could find another color detail, she'd be saved.

"Agathe, get your scrawny butt in here!" yelled the cube.

Agathe slouched in, shoulders hunched, eyes to the ground. She was sticky with fear. Hortense tried to catch her eye, but Agathe's gaze slithered away like an eel.

"Show her your toe!" ordered the cube.

Agathe leaned on the white bathroom wall, unbuckled her shoe, and displayed the stump of her little toe. It was a tiny, shriveled thing, lopped off at the root. It was disgusting to see: a chunk of flesh, all purple with some red. There was a little toenail left. But it was red. Vinegary red, twisted red—but red!

"Okay, wrap it up and get out of here."

Agathe left the way she'd come, hugging the wall. Hortense could hear her moaning on the other side of the door.

"You see how we keep girls in line?"

"I'm not a girl. I'm Hortense, Hortense Cortès. And you can eat shit!"

"Are you getting the picture, or do I have to spell it out for you?"

"Go ahead. I'll turn you in. I'll go to the cops. You have no idea what kind of trouble you're going to be in."

"I know big shots, too, chickie. Maybe not the nicest kind, but they travel in the best circles."

He had put down the razor and picked up the belt.

The first blow hit her full in the face. She hadn't seen it coming. She didn't move. She couldn't let them see that she was hurt or frightened. When the second blow came, she let it. She didn't duck, and gritted her teeth so as not to cry out. It felt like being shot, with the bullets starting high and going down to her belly.

"Go ahead, I don't care," she said. "I won't change my mind. You're wasting your time."

Another blow, on her breasts. Then another one, in the face. Carlos was hitting her with all his might. She could see him draw back before swinging. He looked serious, concentrating on the task at hand.

"I warned my boyfriend," said Hortense, panting, her mouth full of saliva. "If I'm not back by midnight, he's calling the cops. I gave him your name, and Agathe's, and the club's. They'll find you."

She couldn't feel the blows anymore. She was only thinking of the next word she would add after each of the words she'd just said. She was using the excuse to talk to turn herself a little sideways so as to not take everything head on.

"You know him," she spat between two blows. "The tall guy with dark hair who comes to my flat all the time. His mother works in the royal secret service. You can check. She's part of the queen's protection detail. Those people aren't sissies. You'll be sorry when they get their hands on you."

Carlos must have been listening because he wasn't hitting

her as hard. His arm seemed to hesitate slightly. Hortense tried not to scream, because if she started screaming, he would figure he'd almost beaten her down and would go crazy. She had the feeling that her skin was flayed and bloody, her teeth loosened. She could hear the blows echoing in her jaw, on her cheeks, on her neck. Her tears were flowing, but Carlos probably couldn't see them. It was too dark, and besides he blocked all the light with his bully's chest, his bully's arms, his bully's panting.

At a certain point, Hortense felt nothing except a great swirling where only the words she was trying to say, trying to stay as close as possible to her thinking, making her thoughts as precise and determined as she could, were all that kept her from giving in and falling to the floor. As long as she was on her feet, she could talk. Among equals. Actually, she was a good head taller than Carlos. *It must annoy him to have to stand on tiptoe to hit me.*

"You don't believe me, maybe? If I weren't so sure of myself I would've already collapsed at your feet."

She spat in his face.

The next blow split her upper lip. She gasped in shock, and the tears spurted without her being able to hold them back. The leather strap hit her again. He was starting to go berserk.

"His name's Weston, Paul Weston," she said, quickly inventing a name. "You can check. His mother's Harriet Weston, one of the queen's bodyguards. Her last lover was shipped off to Australia because otherwise they were going to fit him with cement boots and drown him."

Hortense's voice was full of blood and tears, but she wasn't giving up.

"And her boss . . . Her boss is Zachary Gorjiak. He's got a

daughter named Nicole, who's a cripple, and that makes him very angry at guys like you. Nicole's in a wheelchair because of some gangster. So Zachary doesn't like guys like you."

That last part was all true. Shirley had told Hortense and Gary that Zachary was a born killer. He was deadly with a knife, slashing anybody who tried to intimidate him or rip him off. He stabbed them calmly, dropping them where they stood.

Shirley told them how one of the gangsters took revenge by running over Zachary's daughter, crippling her for life. He became even crazier, even more violent, even more determined to track people down and cut them up.

The cube was starting to waver. His blows were less accurate. Hortense could stand them now. The good thing about pain is that after a while you don't feel it anymore. It becomes just one more echo, a little echo, and then it vanishes into the mass.

She laughed then, and spat in his face again.

He put his belt down and left the bathroom.

She looked around. One of her eyes was so swollen she couldn't see out of it, or even blink without wincing, but the other was working. She had the feeling she was locked in a box, a damp white box. She stayed on her feet, in case he came back. Touching her face, she found it sticky with blood, tears, and sweat, her tongue thick and viscous. She swallowed the salty saliva in her mouth.

They must be talking things over in the next room, thought Hortense. The cube's telling them everything I said about Her Majesty's Secret Service. They probably know the name Zachary Gorjiak.

Hortense stepped over to the sink, turned on the faucets, then changed her mind. *If they came in, it might give them ideas, like shoving my head in the water and drowning me. I'm not sure I could resist that.* She looked around, saw a lock on the door, and turned it.

Back at the sink, she rinsed her face. The cold water hurt so much she nearly screamed.

That's when she noticed the frosted window over the bathtub. A little dormer. She quietly opened it. It gave onto a terrace. *These pigs live in a nice neighborhood. The place has flowered terraces.*

She climbed up to the window, raising first one leg, then the other, and slipped through. She landed gently, tiptoed through the dark to the next terrace, and then to another and another, until she made her way to the street.

She turned around and noted the address.

She hailed a taxi, covering her face so the driver wouldn't be frightened when he saw her.

The taxi stopped for her. Grimacing in pain, she gave Gary's address. Her upper lip must really be split. She could almost fit a finger between the edges of the cut.

"Jesus!" she moaned. "What if I wind up with a hare lip?"

Collapsing on the seat, she burst into tears.

PART III

♦ ♦ ♦

◆ ◆ ◆

One evening when Joséphine wasn't due home until late, Paul Merson knocked on Zoé's apartment door.

"Want to come down to the basement?" he asked. "Domitille and Gaétan will be there. Their parents are out, gone to the opera. You know, tuxedo, ball gown, all that crap. They'll be back pretty late."

"I've got homework to do."

"Stop being such a teacher's pet! It's gonna give you problems at school."

He was right. Kids were already starting to give Zoé funny looks. Her pen case had been stolen twice, she was jostled in the stairs, and nobody wanted to walk home with her after school.

"All right," she said. "Sure."

Paul turned on his heel and stalked away, carefully executing a walk he had practiced in front of the mirror. Then he stopped and came back, with his thumbs in his pockets and arms akimbo.

"Is there any beer in your fridge?"

"No, why?"

"Never mind. Bring some ice cubes."

Zoé didn't feel good about this. She liked Gaétan Lefloc-Pignel, but his sister, Domitille, made her uncomfortable, and Paul Merson intimidated her.

She went down to the basement around nine thirty. A few candles gleamed in the darkness.

"I can't stay long," she said.

"Do you have the ice?" asked Paul.

"This is all I found," she said, opening a plastic container. "I have to remember to bring the box back."

"A perfect little housekeeper!" snickered Domitille, who was sucking her finger.

Paul pulled out a bottle of whiskey and four jelly glasses, and filled them halfway.

"Sorry I don't have any Perrier," he said, capping the bottle and hiding it behind a big pipe covered with heavy black tape.

Zoé took her glass and nervously studied the amber-colored liquid. To celebrate the success of *A Most Humble Queen*, her mother had opened a bottle of champagne and offered some to Zoé. She tasted it, then ran to the bathroom to spit it out.

"Don't tell me you've never had a drink before!" said Paul, snickering.

"Leave her alone," said Gaétan. "It's no crime not to drink."

"But it tastes so good!" said Domitille, stretching her legs out on the concrete floor. "I couldn't live without booze."

What a show-off! thought Zoé. *She's pretending to be all cool and sexy, and she's a year younger than I am.*

Zoé felt on the spot. If she didn't drink, they would think she was a loser. She decided to discreetly dump the whiskey behind her back. In the darkness, nobody would see. She went to lean against the pipe. Then she moved her arm, slid the glass along the ground, and slowly emptied it.

Paul took the whiskey bottle out again.

"Anybody want another little hit?" he asked.

Domitille stretched out her glass. Gaétan said no thanks, not for now, as did Zoé.

"Is there any Coke?" she asked cautiously.

"No."

"Too bad."

"Bring some next time! All of you, bring something next time, and we'll have a real party. We can even plug into the basement outlet and set up a sound system. I'll handle the music, Zoé can do the food, and Gaétan and Domitille the liquor."

"We can't do that!" exclaimed Gaétan. "We don't get any pocket money."

"Okay. In that case, Zoé will take care of the food and drinks, and I'll chip in for the booze."

"But I don't—"

"C'mon, your family's loaded! Your mother's book is a best-seller. My mom told me so."

"That's not fair!"

"You gotta make up your mind. Do want to be in the gang or not?"

Zoé wasn't sure she wanted to be in the gang. The basement smelled moldy, and it was cold. Bits of gravel were digging into her butt. She kept hearing weird noises, imagining rats, bats, and abandoned pythons. She felt sleepy and she didn't know what to say. She had never kissed a boy.

Finally, she smiled agreement.

"Good for you," said Paul. "Gimme five."

He stuck out his palm and Zoé half-heartedly slapped it. *Where in the world am I going to find the money to go shopping?* she wondered.

"What about them, what are they going to do?" she asked, pointing to Gaétan and Domitille.

"We can't do shit, we don't have anything," grumbled Gaétan. "With our dad, it's like being in jail. If he knew we were down here, he'd kill us."

"They do go out some evenings, though," said Domitille, sucking the rim of her glass. "We can find out ahead of time."

"What about your brother, won't he snitch on us?"

"Charles-Henri? No, he's cool."

"So why didn't he come down?"

"He's got homework. Besides, he's covering for us in case they come home early. He'll say we went down to the courtyard because we heard a noise, and he'll come get us. It's best for him to be on the lookout because if we get nailed, we're screwed. I mean really screwed."

"My mom is cooler than cool," said Paul, who couldn't stand not being the center of attention. "She tells me everything. I'm her confidant."

"Your mom's really built," said Gaétan. "How is it that some chicks have great bodies and others look like dump trucks?"

"It's 'cause when you have sex the right way, lying down all comfy and focused, you make nice, smooth lines and that creates great-looking women," said Paul. "When you're just fucking head over heels, twisting this way and that, you create big, lumpy fatsos."

They burst out laughing. All except Zoé, who thought her mother and father must've made love nice and straight to create Hortense, and all twisted to make her.

"If you fuck on a bag of nuts, for example, you're sure to make a little sausage full of cellulite," Paul continued, proud of his thesis and determined to milk its comic potential.

"I can't even imagine my parents making love," muttered Gaétan. "Or maybe under threat. My dad must point a gun at her head. I can't stand him. He terrifies us."

"Then stop pissing him off," said Domitille. "He's easy to fool. If you keep your eyes down and walk straight, he doesn't see shit. You can do whatever you like behind his back. Your problem is, you always confront him."

What in the world are they talking about? wondered Zoé. They all seemed to know something she didn't. *It's as if I were out sick that day and missed a class. I'm never coming back to this basement. I'd rather stay home alone.* She decided to go back upstairs. She felt around for the ice-cube box in the darkness, and started rehearsing an excuse to leave. She didn't want to look stupid, or chicken.

That was the moment Gaétan chose to put his arm around Zoé's shoulders and pull her close. He kissed her hair and rubbed his nose against her forehead.

Zoé suddenly felt all soft and weak. She could feel her breasts swelling. She stretched out her legs, gave a happy little laugh, and laid her head on Gaétan's shoulder.

Hortense rang Gary's doorbell at two o'clock in the morning, covered with blood.

"Oh, my God!" he muttered.

He quickly let her in, and was soon swabbing the cuts on her face with hydrogen peroxide and a scrap of cloth. "I'm sorry I don't have any tissues or cotton balls, dear," he said. "I'm a bachelor."

Hortense described the trap she'd fallen into.

"And don't say, 'I told you so' because it's too late now and it would just make me scream and that hurts too much."

Gary treated her injuries inch by inch, with precise, gentle gestures. She looked at him, feeling reassured and moved.

"You're getting more and more handsome, Gary."

"Stop moving!"

She heaved a long sigh, then stifled a cry of pain when he touched her upper lip.

"Do you think I'll have a scar?"

"No, it's superficial. It'll be visible for a few days and then it'll shrink and scab over. The cuts aren't very deep."

"Since when did you become a doctor?"

"I took a first aid course in France, remember?"

"I skipped those classes."

"Oh yeah, I forgot. Taking care of other people isn't your thing."

"That's right. I concentrate on myself. And I've got work to do: Check it out."

She pointed at her face and frowned. Smiling hurt too much.

Gary had sat her on a chair in the living room. Glancing around, Hortense noticed his piano, scores, metronome, pencil, and solfège notebook. There were open books everywhere: on a table, a window ledge, a sofa.

"I have to talk to your mother and get her to help me," she

said. "If there are no reprisals, those guys'll try again. In any case, I'm never going back to my flat!"

She gave him a pleading look, silently begging for shelter.

"You can stay here," he said, unable to refuse. "We'll talk to my mother tomorrow."

"Can I sleep in your bed with you tonight?"

"Hortense!"

"Otherwise I'll have nightmares."

"All right, but just for tonight. And you stay on your side."

"I promise! And I won't jump you."

"That's not it, as you know very well."

"All right, all right!"

Gary straightened up and studied her face, going over a few places here and there. She grimaced.

"I'm not touching your breasts," he said, handing her the bottle and the cloth. "You can do that yourself."

Hortense went to stand in front of the mirror over the fireplace and cleaned her cuts one by one.

"I'm going to be wearing sunglasses and a turtleneck tomorrow."

"You can tell people you were mugged in the Tube."

"And I'm gonna track down that bitch Agathe and tell her a thing or two."

"She won't be coming back to school, if you ask me."

"You think?"

When they went to bed, Hortense curled up on one side of the bed, with Gary on the other. She kept her eyes open and waited for sleep to find her. *If I close my eyes, I know I'll see the whole scene again, and I don't want that.* She listened to Gary's irregular breathing. They spent a long time spying on each other, until Hortense felt his arm reach across to her.

"Don't worry," he said. "I'm here."

She closed her eyes and promptly fell asleep.

The next day, Shirley came over. She gave a cry when she saw Hortense's swollen face.

"Wow! They did a real number on you!" she said. "You should file a complaint."

"That won't do any good. We have to scare them."

"Tell me the whole story," Shirley said, taking Hortense's hand. *This is the first time I've been affectionate with her,* she realized.

"I didn't give the guy your name. I made up names for you and Gary, but I did tell him your boss's name, Zachary Gorjiak. That calmed him down. At least enough for him to leave the bathroom and go talk to the other dwarves."

"All right, I'll tell Zachary," said Shirley thoughtfully. "I don't think they'll dare make a move after this. But in the meantime, be careful. Do you plan to go back to your school?"

"I'm not about to leave the field free to that bitch! I'm going back this afternoon, and we're gonna have it out."

"Where do you plan to live in the meantime?"

Hortense looked at Gary.

"With me," he said. "But she'll have to find another flat."

"Why can't she stay here? It's big enough."

"I need to be alone, Mom."

"This is no time to be selfish, Gary!"

"That's not it. It's just that there are a lot of things I have to figure out, and I need to be by myself to do that."

Hortense said nothing.

She seems to be agreeing with him, thought Shirley. *What a surprising connection those two have!*

"Oh, and Shirley, one more thing," said Hortense. "There's no way you can tell my mother about any of this. No way, understand? If she knows, she won't be able to stand it. She'll worry herself to pieces, lose sleep over it, and be a major pain in the butt."

Gary had guessed right: Agathe didn't show up at school. Hortense's arrival, on the other hand, drew a crowd with a volley of questions and horrified exclamations. She had to speak to each student looking at her with disgust or compassion. Someone asked her to take off her sunglasses to show the extent of her injuries. She refused.

"I'm not a sideshow freak," she said. "Anyway, we're done here."

Then she went to pin a note on the school bulletin board. It said she was looking for a female roommate who didn't smoke or drink, and if possible, was a virgin.

A week later, she got a call from a girl looking for a roommate. Her name was Li May, she hailed from Hong Kong, and seemed very strict; she had kicked her last roommate out for smoking a cigarette on the balcony of her bedroom. The flat was well located, just beyond Piccadilly Circus on a high floor, and the rent was reasonable. Hortense took it.

She invited Gary out to dinner. Peering through his hank of black hair, he examined the menu with the gravity of a CPA reviewing a year-end balance sheet. He considered both sea scallops

Melba and spiced partridge with fresh vegetables, opted for the partridge, then waited for his entrée in silence. He ate each mouthful as if he were nibbling on a communion wafer.

Over dessert, Hortense said, "I enjoyed our living together." She sighed. "I'm going to miss you."

Gary didn't answer.

"You could be polite and say, 'I'll miss you too.'"

"I need to be alone."

"I know, I know."

"You can't focus on yourself and someone else at the same time. It's already so much work to know what you yourself want."

"Oh, Gary!" Hortense sighed again, and rolled her eyes. Then she abruptly changed the subject.

"Did you notice that I've stopped wearing sunglasses? I slathered my makeup on with a trowel to hide the bruises."

"I notice everything about you," he said evenly. "Everything."

Under his steady gaze, Hortense faltered and looked down, playing with her fork, drawing parallel lines on the tablecloth.

"What about Agathe? Any news?" he asked.

"Didn't I tell you? She quit school, right in the middle of the year. One of the teachers announced it at the start of a class: 'Agathe Nathier has left us, for health reasons. She has returned to Paris.'"

Gary closed his eyes to savor the last bite of his honey-baked apple with Calvados sorbet.

A waiter brought the check, and Hortense laid some bills on it with a triumphant, "Ta-dah!"

"This is the first time I've bought a man dinner!" she said. "Oh God, I'm on a slippery slope."

They walked across the park arm in arm, discussing the Glenn Gould biography Gary had just bought. He looked around for squirrels, but didn't see any. They must be asleep. It was a beautiful night, the sky sprinkled with stars.

If he asks if I know the names of the stars, he's not a man for me, thought Hortense. *I hate people who want to teach you the names of stars, capital cities, foreign currencies, highest mountains—all the trivia you read on the back of cornflakes boxes.*

"Some people can't stand Glenn Gould," Gary was explaining, "and others are so crazy about him, they even revere his old broken-down chair."

"It isn't good to worship someone. Every person has faults."

"His father built the chair for him in 1953, and he always kept it with him, even when it was falling apart. It was like a talisman."

Gary's voice quavered that he said these last words.

"Why are you looking at me that way?" he asked abruptly, catching Hortense's eye.

"I don't know. You looked flustered all of a sudden."

"Me? Why?"

Hortense couldn't have said. They walked on in silence. *How long have I known him?* she wondered. *Eight years? Nine years? We've grown up together, but I don't think of him as a brother. It would be more practical if I did. Then I wouldn't worry about him falling in love with someone else, like really in love. It's just that I have so much to do before I can let that happen to me.*

"Do you know the names of the stars?" Gary asked, looking heavenward.

Hortense stopped and jammed her fingers in her ears.

"What are you doing?" he asked worriedly.

"Nothing," she said. "It's all right. Not a big deal."

There was so much concern in his eyes and so much tenderness in his voice, it unnerved her. *Time for me to move out,* she thought. *I'm starting to get terribly sentimental.*

Joséphine paused at the entrance to the Hôtel Costes restaurant, as snatches of conversation and bursts of excited voices rang from adjacent dining rooms. The place looked like something out of *The Arabian Nights*: deep sofas, puffy cushions, statues of bare-breasted women, hanging plants, snow-white wild orchids, glittering carpets, low couches, a jumble of mismatched furniture. The waitresses looked as if they had stepped out of a modeling catalog and were hired by the hour as walk-ons.

Joséphine felt nervous. Iris had postponed their lunch date several times, claiming first an appointment for a wax job, then a date at her hair salon, and finally to have her teeth whitened. Each time, Joséphine had felt diminished. Whatever pleasure she'd felt the first time Iris called had vanished. All she felt now was a dull anxiety at the idea of seeing her sister again.

"I'm meeting Madame Dupin," she told the miniskirted beauty at the front desk.

"Follow me, please," said the dreamlike creature, striding on her dreamlike legs. "You're the first of your party to arrive."

Joséphine followed the miniskirt as it threaded its way among the tables, taking care not to bump into anything. She felt heavy and clumsy. She'd spent two hours searching through her clothes closet, trapped in a tangle of hostile hangers. She had finally selected her most beautiful outfit, but now felt she should have worn a pair of old jeans.

She was seated in an overstuffed red arm chair that was so low, she almost fell over. She grabbed the round table, yanked the tablecloth, and nearly brought the plates, glasses, and cutlery crashing to the floor.

She folded her feet under the table—*I shouldn't have worn these shoes*—hid her hands in the white napkin—*My nails are crying for a manicure*—and waited for her sister. There was no way she could miss her. Their table was the focal point of the whole restaurant.

So I'm going to see Iris again, she thought.

Joséphine had been buffeted by a storm of contradictory thoughts lately. *Iris, Philippe. Iris, Philippe. Philippe . . . Forget him! It's an impossible situation,* hissed the storm raging in her head. *Of course I have to forget him, and I will. It shouldn't be too hard. You don't make a love story out of ten and a half minutes leaning against an oven handle. It's ridiculous.*

Then Iris made her entrance.

Joséphine watched her sister's arrival, and marveled. The storm in her head subsided, replaced by a little voice that said, "How beautiful she is! God, she's so beautiful!"

Iris confidently sauntered in, parting the air as if entering conquered territory. She was wearing a beige cashmere coat, high deerskin boots, and a long aubergine jacket with a wide belt. Necklaces, bracelets, long dark hair, blue eyes that scissored space with their icy edges. She handed her coat to a worshipful cloak-room attendant and bestowed an absent smile on the tables nearby. Then, having gathered every glance in the place into a bouquet of offerings, she made her way to the table where Joséphine slumped, feeling crushed.

Confident and amused to see her sister sitting so low to the ground, Iris turned a radiant gaze to her.

"Have I kept you waiting?" she asked, pretending to just now realize that she was twenty minutes late.

"Oh no! I was early."

"I'm so happy to see you," said Iris, gracefully sitting on an identical low chair without knocking her purse over. "You simply have no idea."

She had taken Joséphine's hand and was squeezing it. Then she leaned over and kissed her on the cheek.

"Me too," murmured Jo in a voice thick with emotion.

The last time I saw her, three months ago, her hair was very short. And her face was as sharp as a knife blade.

"I hope you weren't angry at me for putting our lunch date off. I had so much to do! I have long hair now, did you notice? Hair extensions. Beautiful, isn't it?" She enveloped Joséphine in her deep blue gaze, and continued. "I'm so terribly sorry, Jo. I behaved unforgivably at the clinic. It was all those drugs they gave me. They made me miserable."

She sighed, lifting her mass of thick black hair.

"Please, let's not even mention it," murmured Joséphine in embarrassment.

"But I absolutely must apologize," insisted Iris, leaning back in her chair. She was looking at Joséphine with grave candor, as if her fate depended on her sister's generosity, as if hoping for a gesture that would say she had forgiven her.

Joséphine half stood, reached out, and hugged her.

"So we'll forget all about it?" asked Iris. "Put it behind us?" Joséphine nodded.

"Then tell me what you've been up to," ordered Iris, picking up the menu.

"No, you first!" insisted Joséphine. "I don't have much to tell. I've gone back to work on my postdoc thesis. Hortense is in London. Zoé—"

"Philippe has told me all that," said Iris, interrupting her. She turned to the waitress and said, "I'll have my usual."

"I'll have the same as my sister," Jo hurriedly added, panicky at the idea of having to read the menu and choose a dish. "So how are you doing?"

"I'm okay. I'm slowly getting my taste for life back. I came to understand a lot of things while I was in the clinic, and I'm going to try to put them into practice. I've been stupid, frivolous, incredibly superficial. And selfish. I've only thought about myself. I was swept up in a whirlwind of vanity. I wrecked everything. I'm not very proud of myself, you know. I'm even ashamed. I've been a terrible wife, a terrible mother, and a terrible sister."

Iris continued in this vein, beating her breast, listing her shortcomings, her betrayals, her dreams of false glory. The waitress brought a green bean salad, followed by a chicken breast. Iris nibbled a few beans and tore off a piece of chicken. Joséphine didn't dare eat for fear of seeming crude, insensitive to the flood of confidences coming from her sister's mouth. Whenever she was in Iris's company, Jo became her servant. She picked up the napkin Iris dropped, poured her a glass of red wine and followed it with some Badoit water, tore off a tiny piece of bread, but especially, and forever, listened.

The two women talked of their mother, how Marcel's leaving had made life difficult for Henriette, and of her financial straits.

"I almost lost my husband too, so I know what she's going through," said Iris.

Joséphine jerked upright with a gasp. She waited for the rest of the story, but Iris paused and asked, "You don't mind if we talk about Philippe, do you?"

"Oh no!" Jo stammered. "Why not?"

"You're never going to believe this, but I was jealous of you! Yes, I was. For a moment I thought he was in love with you."

Joséphine felt the blood rising to her ears where it started to clang like a hammer on an anvil. The sound was deafening, all enveloping. She could catch only one word out of every two. She was forced to crane her neck, bringing her ear almost to Iris's mouth to catch what she was saying.

"I was crazy! Going out of my mind! But the last time he came through Paris . . ."

She paused suspensefully, as if about to deliver a great piece of news. Her greedy, rounded lips promised the item would be succulent. But before speaking, Iris held it in her mouth, savoring it.

"Philippe was in Paris?" asked Jo in a dull voice.

"Yes, and we got together. It was just like old times. I'm so happy, Jo! So happy!"

She clapped her hands as if to applaud the immensity of her joy, then caught herself, not wanting to tempt fate.

"I'm moving very slowly. I don't want to rush him. I have a lot to apologize for, but I think we're on the right path. That's the advantage of being an old couple. We understand each other at a word, forgive each other with a glance, and then we hug, and it's all said and done."

Joséphine had stopped hearing her. She was struggling to

remain upright and silent while what she wanted was to twist and scream.

"Is something wrong, Jo?"

"No. It's just that you talk so . . ."

Whatever happens, she mustn't start crying, thought Iris irritably. *That would ruin everything I'm trying to accomplish. I set up this lunch to show everyone who matters in Paris that we've reconciled.*

Iris shifted her chair aside, took her sister in her arms, and rocked her.

"There, there," she whispered. "Take it easy, Jo."

So I was right, there is something between them. A stirring of feelings, an attraction. I'm sure she's in love with him. I have the proof right here. But what about him? Jo has charm, no question about it. She's even become pretty. She's learned to dress, fix her hair, use makeup. She's lost weight, too, and she even has a slightly shopworn appeal. I'll have to tread carefully.

Jo calmed down, freed herself from Iris's embrace, and apologized.

"I'm terribly sorry. Excuse me."

She didn't know what to say. *Sorry for falling in love with your husband. Sorry for kissing him. Sorry for still having childish dreams. This naive part of me is rooted like a weed.*

"Excuse you? Whatever for, darling?"

"Oh, Iris," Joséphine began, wringing her hands.

She was about to tell her everything.

Iris caught the hesitation in Jo's eyes. *If she reveals her secret I'll have to appear offended, consider her an enemy, push her away. It'll be our final break. We'll separate, and I'll be leaving the field to her. She'll be free to see him again. I absolutely have to keep her from saying anything now.*

"I'm going to tell you a secret, Jo," she said, abruptly breaking the silence. "I'm so happy to have come back to life that nothing, and I mean nothing, can spoil my pleasure."

Joséphine wasn't listening anymore. She smiled, defeated. She wasn't going to say anything. She would never see Philippe again.

And would never again taste that Armagnac kiss.

Anyway, isn't that what she'd promised the stars?

Joséphine decided to walk home. After admiring Place Vendôme's perfect beauty, she took rue de Rivoli and its arcades, and walked along the quais on the Seine. Leaving behind the winged chariots of the Alexandre III bridge, she headed for the Trocadéro.

She had to pull herself together. Iris's presence had suffocated her, as if her sister had sucked all the air out of the restaurant. When she was with Iris, she felt asphyxiated.

She crossed the park, instinctively hunching her shoulders. She couldn't help it. Madame Berthier's body had been found nearby.

Pushing open the door to her building, she heard shouts coming from the concierge's apartment.

"It's outrageous, and you're responsible!" a man was yelling. "The place is disgusting! You have to clean the garbage-bin room every day. There are beer cans, empty bottles, and wads of tissues all over the ground. We're constantly tripping over trash!"

Jo recognized Pinarelli *fils* as he stormed out of Iphigénie's apartment, still yelling. Pale as death, Iphigénie was standing behind the curtained glass door, the card stating her work hours dangling on a chain. When Monsieur Pinarelli turned back and raised his arm as if to hit her, she locked the door. Joséphine rushed over and grabbed his arm, but he freed himself and knocked her down. Jo's head slammed against the wall.

"You're crazy!" she cried, overwhelmed.

"Don't you dare defend her! This is what she's paid for. She has to keep the place clean! Bitch!"

A thread of saliva hung from his trembling chin, red blotches dotted his skin, and his Adam's apple jerkily bobbed up and down.

He spun on his heel and stormed off to his apartment.

"Are you okay, Madame Cortès?" asked Iphigénie.

Trembling, Joséphine rubbed her painful forehead. Iphigénie gestured her to come her into the apartment.

"Do you want something to drink? You look all shaken."

She made her sit down and handed her a glass of Coke.

"What did you do to put him in such a state?" Jo asked, gathering her wits.

"I clean the garbage room, I swear. I do my best. But people are constantly throwing things in there, stuff too nasty to talk about. So if I forget to go in there for a day or two, it gets dirty pretty quick. But this is a big building and I can't be everywhere."

"Do you know who's doing it?"

"No. At night, I'm asleep, if I'm lucky. This place is a lot of work, and when the day's over, I have to take care of my kids."

Joséphine looked around the apartment. A table, four chairs, a faded sofa, an old sideboard, a TV, a galley kitchen with chipped Formica counters, yellowing linoleum on the floor. Beyond was a shadowy space behind a dark red curtain.

"Is that the children's room?"

"Yeah. I sleep on the sofa, but it's as if I were sleeping in the hallway. I can hear the front door slam all night long when people come in late. I just toss and turn."

"Your apartment could use some fresh paint and some new furniture. It's a little gloomy."

"That's why I dye my hair all those colors," said Iphigénie with a grin. "It brightens up the place."

"You know what we're going to do? On your break tomorrow, we'll go buy everything you need: beds for the children, a table, chairs, curtains, dressers, a sofa, a sideboard, carpets, a stove, and pillows. Then we'll go to Bricorama, pick out some nice colors, and paint the place. You won't need to dye your hair anymore."

"But what are we gonna use for money, Madame Cortès? If I showed you my pay stubs, you'd weep."

"I'll pay for it."

"I'm telling you right now, the answer's no!"

"I don't care," said Joséphine. "I'll go by myself and have everything delivered to your apartment. You don't know me; I'm stubborn."

The two women faced each other in silence.

After a moment, Jo continued. "The thing is, if you come with me, you'll be able to choose. We might not have the same tastes. And it really would be better if you put the colors on the walls instead of on your head."

Iphigénie ran her hand through her hair.

"Yeah, I know, I screwed up the dye job this time. But it's not easy. The shower's out in the courtyard, there's no light, and I can't always finish during my break. In winter I have to be fast, or I'll catch cold."

"What? Is your shower really in the courtyard?"

"Well, yeah. Next to the garbage room."

"I can't believe it!"

"Sad but true, Madame Cortès."

Joséphine noticed Iphigénie's daughter, Clara, standing at the children's room threshold. A startlingly serious little girl, her drooping eyes looked sad and resigned. Her brother, Léo, joined her. Whenever Joséphine smiled at him, he hid behind his sister.

"I think you're being a bit selfish, Iphigénie. I bet your kids would love living with lots of colors around them."

Iphigénie looked at her children and shrugged.

"Me, I'd like to have the room painted pink," said Clara, chewing on a strand of hair. "And I'd like a quilt that's green like an apple."

"Nah, pink is for girls!" cried Léo. "I want yellow all over, and a red quilt with vampires."

The two children danced around their mother, crying, "Say yes, Mommy! Please!"

Iphigénie rapped on the table for silence. To Jo she said, "All right, but in exchange I'm gonna clean your apartment till it shines. Take it or leave it."

The next day, Joséphine drove Iphigénie to IKEA.

They went through the Bois de Boulogne, headed for La Défense, and parked in front of IKEA. Armed with a tape measure, notebook, and pencil, they plunged into the store's labyrinth. Joséphine wrote items down, filling the notebook with orders.

Iphigénie protested.

"It's too much, Madame Cortès! Much too much!"

"Can't you call me Joséphine? After all, I call you Iphigénie."

"Oh no! To me, you're Madame Cortès. Mustn't mix the rags and the towels."

At Bricorama, they chose a canary yellow for the kids' area, raspberry red for the main room, and bright blue for the kitchen. Joséphine caught Iphigénie gazing hungrily at parquet floor samples, and ordered a new floor, then added a shower and tiles.

"Who's gonna put all this stuff in?" asked Iphigénie.

"We'll find a plumber and somebody who knows how to do tile work."

At the checkout counter, Jo gave the concierge apartment's address, and asked that everything be delivered.

The two women walked back to the car and sank into their seats, exhausted.

"You're completely off your rocker, Madame Cortès! I'm gonna polish your apartment till it shines. You'll be able to eat off the floor."

Then she added, happily, "This is the first time anybody's ever been nice to me. I mean nice without expecting something in return. Because I've run into supposedly nice people, but they always wanted to rip me off, somehow. But you . . ."

Iphigénie puckered up and blew a loud raspberry, trumpeting her surprise.

"The worst of them was my husband. I say 'husband,' but we never made it official. He beat up anything that stood in his way, starting with me. It cost me two teeth, and I had to work hard to replace them. He just blew up all the time. One day he punched out a cop who asked for his I.D., and he got six years in jail. I was pregnant with Léo and was happy to see him locked up. He's getting out soon, but he'll never think to look for me here. Nice neighborhoods scare him. They're full of cops, he used to say."

"Don't the children ask after him?"

Iphigénie repeated her trumpeted raspberry, this time as a sign of contempt.

"They never knew him, and it's just as well. When they ask me where he is and what he does, I tell them he's an explorer in the South Pole, the North Pole, the Andes. I make up voyages with eagles, bears, and penguins. The day the kids meet him, if that lousy day ever comes, he better be wearing a beard and a pith helmet!"

It had started to rain. Joséphine wiped the fog from the windshield with the back of her hand and turned on the windshield wipers.

"Hey, Madame Cortès, I wanna thank you, but please don't tell the people in the building that you paid for all this, okay?"

"I won't, but you don't have to justify yourself."

"At the next co-op meeting, you can spread the word that I won the lottery. Only poor people win the lottery. The rich aren't allowed to."

As they passed the Intermarché where Joséphine used to shop when she lived in Courbevoie, Iphigénie asked if they could stop in; she needed some Duck toilet cleanser and a whisk broom.

They wound up at the register with two full carts. When the checker asked if they had an Intermarché card, Joséphine took hers out and used it to pay for Iphigénie's purchases. This made her angry.

"Hey, no dice!" she snapped. "That's enough, Madame Cortès! You keep this up, and we won't be pals anymore!"

"But this way I'll earn even more points."

"I bet you never use your points!"

"I don't, actually," Joséphine admitted.

"Next time I'll come along and you can use them. It'll save you money."

The two women ran to the car though the pelting rain, taking care not to drop anything.

Marcel drove to Casamia, his business, where his longtime friends and employees René and Ginette also lived. Ginette was brewing the morning coffee when she heard the knock on her door.

"Just a sec!" she cried, as she watched the boiling water soak into the grounds.

"Take your time," came Marcel's voice. "It's just me."

Marcel? What's he doing here so early?

"Is something wrong?" she called. "Did you forget the keys to the office?"

"I have to talk to you."

"I'll be right there. I just need a minute."

She poured in the rest of the water, put down the kettle, and wiped her hands on a dishtowel.

Through the door she said, "I better warn you, I'm in my nightgown."

"I don't care! You could be wearing a thong and I wouldn't even notice."

Ginette opened the door and Marcel came in with Junior in a baby carrier on his belly.

"Well, this is a doubleheader!" she exclaimed. "Two Grobzes on the same welcome mat!"

"Something terrible's happened to us, Ginette," he moaned. "We're up shit creek, and we never saw it coming!"

"Why don't you start at the beginning? Otherwise I won't understand anything."

Marcel sat down and took Junior out of the carrier. He propped the baby on his knees and gave him a piece of bread to chew on.

"Here you go, kid. Grow yourself some teeth while I have a chat with Ginette."

"What a sweetheart he is! How old is he?"

"He's about to have his first birthday."

"You know, he seems a lot older. And so strong! But why are you bringing him to work with you?"

"God, I don't know if I can even tell you!"

Marcel looked stricken. His head was slumped on his chest, he hadn't shaved, and a grease spot glistened on his jacket lapel.

"Come on, out with it!" she urged.

Gloomily, Marcel began his tale of woe.

"Do you remember how happy we were, the last time Josie and I had dinner with you?"

"I sure do! You guys got us so drunk, we almost passed out."

Marcel spread his arms helplessly, closed his eyes, and sighed. The baby tottered but Marcel's big hands caught him and began to stroke him.

"Is it Josiane? Is she sick?"

"She's worse than sick, Ginette: She has the blackwater blues. And that can't be cured."

"Oh, come on! It's just postpartum depression. All women have it. They get over it."

"No, this is worse. A lot worse."

Marcel leaned close and asked in a whisper:

"Is René around?"

"Yeah, he's inside getting dressed. Why?"

"Because . . . Because what I'm gonna tell you is completely secret. You absolutely can't tell him."

Ginette looked scandalized.

"Keep a secret from René? Not on your life! You keep your secret, I'm keeping my husband."

Marcel ran his hand over his skull and bit his fist. He was flushed and agitated. The chair groaned under his weight.

"My God, you're really in a bad way!" said Ginette.

"With me it's just anxiety, but Josiane . . . If you could see her! White as a sheet! Looks like a ghost! She's gonna float away to heaven."

Marcel hunched over and began to sob.

"I can't take it anymore," he said. "My brain's on the fritz. I wander around the apartment like an old buck who's lost his antlers. I've cried myself out, my pillow's wet. I'm a soggy mess. I don't know what I'm signing, I don't know my name, I'm not sleeping, I'm not eating, my guts are in an uproar. I stink of evil."

Propped on his elbows, Marcel was bellowing now. *"Evil has come into my home!"*

René burst into the kitchen.

"Damn, what's happening to the poor guy? He's gonna rouse the dead."

Ginette realized she had to take the situation in hand. She settled Junior on the sofa and wedged him upright with pillows. Then she set the fragrant coffee pot in front of Marcel and René, cut and buttered some bread, and passed them the sugar.

"First, the two of you are going to eat some breakfast. Then I'm staying behind while Marcel spills the beans."

"You don't want to talk it over with me?" asked René suspiciously.

"It's kind of special," said an embarrassed Marcel. "I can only talk to your wife about it."

The three of them ate together in silence, then René snatched his cap and stalked out.

"Is he pissed off?" asked Marcel.

"I'm sure his feeling are hurt."

Ginette glanced over at Junior who was sitting among the pillows and listening.

"Maybe we should get Junior something to occupy him."

"Give him something to read," said Marcel. "He loves that."

"I don't have any baby books!"

"Doesn't matter. He reads everything. Even the phone book."

Ginette went to fetch the telephone directory.

"I only have the Yellow Pages," she said.

Marcel dismissed the objection with a wave. Junior took the book and opened it, put a finger on a page, and started to drool on it.

"You know, your kid is kind of strange!" she said. "Has he been seen by a doctor?"

"If that were the only strange thing in my life, I'd be the happiest man alive."

He sniffed, and blew his nose in the paper napkin Ginette handed him. Then with a fearful look at her, he said, "It's Josie. She's bewitched."

"Bewitched! Oh, come on! That stuff isn't real!"

"Yes, it is, I'm telling you. It's like someone's sticking pins into her."

"Poor Marcel!"

"In the beginning, I was like you, I didn't want to believe it. But I had to admit that . . ."

"What happened? Did she grow horns?"

"She doesn't enjoy anything. Feels as drained as an old bathtub, lies in bed all day long, doesn't even snuggle with the baby. That's why he's growing up so fast. Wants to get out of diapers so he can help her."

"You guys have gone 'round the bend!"

"If only Josiane hadn't stopped seeing Madame Suzanne"

"You're just worn out, that's all."

Ginette came over and gently rubbed Marcel's bull neck. He laid his head on his folded arms moaned:

"Help us, Ginette. Please!"

"Who else have you told about this?"

He gave her a distracted look.

"Who could I possibly tell? They'll think I'm crazy. These things exist, Ginette. We don't talk about them because we all have science bouncing around our brains, but they're real."

"Well maybe, but only in voodoo countries like Haiti or Burkina Faso!"

"No! Everywhere! Someone casts an evil spell, and awful things happens to the victim. It's like Josie's trapped in a spiderweb. She can't move, can't do anything without triggering bad stuff. She wanted to take the kid to the park the other day, and you know what? She sprained her ankle and somebody stole her purse. She tried to iron one of my shirts, and the ironing board caught fire."

"But who would hate Josiane so much to want her dead? Or both of you."

"No idea. I didn't even know that sort of thing existed, so . . ."

Ginette sat down next to him. She was thoughtful.

"So that's why she doesn't come to see us anymore."

"How could she explain it to you? Besides, she's ashamed. We've gone to all the specialists, had tons of scans, X-rays, tests. They didn't find anything. Nothing!"

On the sofa, Junior was staring at the phone book, trying to decipher it. Ginette spent a long moment observing him. *He really is a strange kid,* she thought. *At his age, babies play with their hands or toes, or a stuffed toy. They don't read phone books.*

Junior glanced up then and looked her full in the face. He had the same blue eyes as his father, she realized.

"Witch-doc-tor," he babbled wetly. "Witch-doc-tor."

"What's that he said?" she asked.

Marcel jerked his head up, stunned. Junior repeated the phrase, straining so hard to speak that the cords stood out on his neck and a tangle of purple veins appeared between his eyes. He was putting all of his baby energy into making himself understood.

"Witch doctor," Marcel translated.

"That's what I thought!" said Ginette. "But how—"

"He must've spotted a display ad for one of those cheesy fortune-tellers."

My God, thought Ginette. *Now I'm the one going crazy.*

Henriette was exultant. She had just seen Josiane and the little maid in Parc Monceau. What a state she was in! A specter, lacking only cobwebs dangling from her wrists. Josiane shuffled along on thick crepe-soled shoes. She was hunched over, swaying from side to side, lost in her navy blue gabardine coat, her hair lank and stringy. The little maid guided her, watching her like a hawk. They rested at every bench they came to. Chérubine's sorcery was doing wonders.

It's working! And to think I went so long without knowing about these magic powers. How many clever plots I could've laid! How many enemies I could've dispatched! And what a fortune I could have amassed! If I had only known!

It was enough to make her head spin.

Back home, Henriette took off her big hat, and patted her hair to get rid of the indentation from the weight of the huge pancake. She smiled radiantly at herself in the mirror. She had discovered a new dimension: that of total power. The laws that controlled the rabble would no longer apply to her. From now on, she would go straight to her goal, with Chérubine on hand for the dirty work, and regain her former luster. Hermès day timers, Guerlain soaps, twelve-ply cashmere, lavender linen essence, Cassegrain business cards, Royal Hotel spa treatments, and a fat bank account were all within reach.

She was dying to call Chérubine. Not to congratulate or thank her—the wretch might feel flattered and get conceited—but to ensure her loyalty. The woman could prove a valuable ally. Henriette dialed her number and heard Chérubine's familiar slow drawl.

"Chérubine, this is Madame Grobz, Henriette Grobz. How are you, my dear?"

She didn't expect Chérubine to respond, and promptly went on. "You can't imagine how satisfied I feel. I just saw my rival in the street. You know, that revolting woman who stole my husband and—"

"Madame Grobz?"

Surprised at not being immediately recognized, Henriette introduced herself a second time, then continued. "She is in pathetic shape! Pathetic! I practically didn't recognize her! What do you expect the next stage of her decrepitude will be? Will she decide to end—"

"I believe she owes me money . . ."

"But Chérubine, I paid you what I owed," Henriette protested.

She had personally delivered the amount demanded, in small bills. She'd been forced to take the Metro, and martyred herself by being pressed against sweaty, shapeless bodies, clutching her hat and purse under her arm.

"She owes me money," said Chérubine. "If she wants me to pursue this, she will have to pay. . . . She seems to be pleased with my services . . ."

"But I thought we were . . . that we had . . . that I—"

"Six hundred euros. Before Saturday."

A dry click echoed in Henriette's ear.

Chérubine had hung up on her.

Next morning, after Zoé went to school, Joséphine entered her daughter's lair. She sat down on the edge of the bed so as not to leave a mark. She didn't feel comfortable sneaking in like this, and would never consider opening a letter or reading something Zoé had written in a diary. She would have felt like a burglar. She just wanted to share a bit of Zoe's intimacy.

Jo glanced over the messy room, noticed a wrinkled T-shirt,

a dirty skirt, and mismatched socks, but didn't touch anything. She wasn't allowed to straighten up.

She breathed in the scent of the Nivea cream Zoé used, the woodsy flavor of the scent she wore, the warm sweat of her sheets. She perused the clippings Zoé had cut out and tacked on the wall. Flat Daddy Antoine grinned at Jo from the corner of the room, standing tall and proud in his tan shorts, his foot propped on a big cat. She itched to knock it over. She shouted at him mentally: *Come on, be brave! Get out of the shadows and face me instead of making me miserable from afar. It's too easy to stir a teenager's imagination with your mysterious messages.* After a few seconds of mental berating, she was ashamed when she imagined his shredded corpse. She remained sitting on the bed, thinking.

She was feeling sad and empty, the way she did whenever she felt helpless. She couldn't see any way to break through the seamless barrier Zoé had erected. Her daughter came home from school and locked herself in her room. After eating dinner, she ran downstairs to listen to Paul Merson drumming. Then she came up, said, "Good night, Mommy," and went to her room.

Zoé had grown up all at once, Jo realized. Small breasts were beginning to show under her sweaters, and her hips were rounding. She was putting gloss on her lips, mascara on her eyelashes. She would be fourteen soon, and as pretty as Hortense.

When Joséphine felt truly hopeless, when she'd been working so long she couldn't read another word, she switched off her computer and took refuge in Iphigénie's apartment, which was being painted by a Monsieur Sandoz. The IKEA furniture would soon be delivered, and the place first had to be painted and the floor laid. The National Employment Agency social services office had sent Sandoz to them. When Joséphine explained the work to be done, he said, "No problem. I know how to do painting, electrical, plumbing, carpentry—all that stuff."

Jo lent him a hand from time to time, as did Clara and Léo when they came home from school. Sandoz gave them brushes and watched them paint, smiling sadly. He came to Iphigénie's apartment every morning wearing a suit and tie, and changed into painter's overalls. At noon, he put his suit and tie back on, washed his hands, and went to eat lunch in a bistro. Sandoz prized his self-respect. He'd almost lost it a few years earlier, snatched it back at the last moment, and made sure he didn't lose it again. Joséphine asked him no questions. She could sense pain and unhappiness just below the surface. She didn't want to stir things up just to satisfy her curiosity.

Sandoz had very nice eyes. They were deep blue, but melancholy. He looked like Buster Keaton being chased by the brides. He and Joséphine occasionally had long talks, often sparked by some detail.

"How old are you, Monsieur Sandoz?"

"Old enough not to be wanted anymore."

"Can you be specific?"

"Fifty-nine and a half. Ready for the trash heap."

"And you feel like an old man?"

"I feel like a lost soul. Today, being young isn't just a period in your life, it's a condition for survival. It wasn't like this in the old days."

"That's where you're wrong!" said Joséphine. "In the twelfth century, they used to toss old people out into the street."

"How do know that?"

"I study the Middle Ages, and I enjoy finding the similarities between then and now. There are a lot more of them than you might think! Young people's violence, their hopelessness at not feeling they have a future, nights of drinking, gang rapes, piercings, tattoos—you can find all that in the fabliaux."

"So people were just as unhappy then."

"And just as frightened. They were afraid of a changing world that they didn't recognize anymore. The world never changed as much as it did during the Middle Ages. Chaos and renewal. That's always the way."

The two of them then got back to work, sanding, painting, smoothing, and mixing plaster and stucco. They were sometimes interrupted by Iphigénie.

"You know what we could do when this is all finished, Madame Cortès?" she asked one day. "Invite the building tenants in for a party. Wouldn't that be *simpatico?*"

"It would, Iphigénie. *Muy simpatico.*"

Iphigénie rang Joséphine's doorbell with the mail one morning, bringing letters, magazines, and a small parcel.

"Hey, Madame Cortès, the co-op meeting is next week. You haven't forgotten, have you?"

Joséphine shook her head.

"You'll tell me what they say, won't you? I mean about the party. It would do the whole complex good. There are people who have lived here for ten years without ever talking to each other. You could invite your relatives, if you like."

"I'll ask my sister to come. That way, she'll be able to see my apartment at the same time."

"And we'll go shopping for the party at Intermarché, all right?"

"Sure."

"Enjoy your reading, Madame Cortès," she said, pointing at the parcel. "I think that's a book."

It came from London. Jo didn't recognize the writing. She opened it carefully. Was it a fashion sketch by Hortense? A little book on the ravages of sugar in English schools, with a preface by Shirley? Photos of leaping squirrels by Gary?

It was indeed a book, *Les Neufs Célibataires* by Sacha Guitry, a rare edition bound in cherry calfskin. A line of tall writing in black ink on the frontispiece leaped out at her: *You can make the people who love you look away, but not the people who desire you. I love and desire you, Philippe.*

Joséphine clutched the book to her chest, aglow with happiness. He loved her! He loved her!

Closing her eyes, she kissed the cover of the book. But she had promised the stars . . . She would become a Carmelite nun and disappear behind the convent bars in eternal silence.

"So what happened?" asked Dottie. "Did she answer you?"

They were going to the opera that evening.

Before heading over to Dottie's, Philippe had eaten dinner with Alexandre, who said, "Mom phoned. She wants to come on Friday and wants you to call her back."

Alexandre reported this while studying his steak (well done) and putting his fries to one side, saving them for later. He ate steak out of duty, saving his appetite for the fries.

"Oh?" said Philippe, caught unprepared. "Do you and I have any plans this weekend?"

"Not that I know of," said Alexandre, chewing his steak.

"Because if you want to see Mom, she can come. We're not angry at each other, you know."

"You just don't agree on how you view life."

"That's right. You got it."

"Can she bring Zoé? I'd really like to see *her*. I miss her."

He had stressed the word *her* as if his mother's plan didn't involve him.

"I'll give it some thought," said Philippe, reflecting on how complicated life was getting.

"Are you going out tonight?"

"I'm going to the opera with a friend, Dottie Doolittle."

"Will you take me, when I'm older?"

"It's a promise."

Philippe kissed his son and walked to Dottie's apartment, hoping a solution would come to him on the way. He didn't want to see Iris, but he also didn't want to keep her from seeing her son or rush the question of separation or divorce. *I'll raise the subject when she's better,* he said to himself, before ringing Dottie's doorbell. He was always postponing.

He was now perched on the edge of the bathtub, a glass of whiskey in his hand, watching Dottie put on her makeup. When he raised his glass, his elbow brushed a plastic shower curtain from which a radiant Marilyn Monroe blew kisses to the world.

In front of him, wearing black tights and bra, Dottie busied herself amid a colorful jumble of jars, brushes, and powder puffs.

"So, did she answer you, or not?"

"No."

"Nothing at all? Not even an eyelash in an envelope?"

"Not a thing."

"If I ever really fall in love with a man, I'll mail him one of my eyelashes. It's a true sign of love, you know, because lashes don't grow back. You're born with a certain supply, and you mustn't waste it."

Dottie had pulled her hair back, holding it with a pair of over-size clips. She looked like a teenager experimenting with makeup in secret.

"Saying things like that is what's going to make some man fall in love with you," said Philippe, thereby pointing out that he wasn't that man.

"Handsome men who love language don't exist anymore. They grow up talking to their Game Boys."

"She didn't succumb to Sacha Guitry's wit," he said thoughtfully. "It was a beautiful line, though."

"You'll think of something else. I'll help you. There's no one better than a woman to seduce another woman! You've just lost your touch."

He watched her, fascinated as her hands danced from the orange stick to the kohl bottle she handled without spilling a speck of it.

"You can be Christian and I'll be Cyrano," she said. "In those times, a man could enlist another to speak on his behalf."

"Did you finish the book?" he asked, wiping his hands on a towel. He had bought her a copy of *Cyrano de Bergerac* in English.

"I loved it. It's so French!"

She waved her mascara brush as she recited: "Philosopher and scientist, / Poet, musician, duelist— / He flew high, and fell back again! / A pretty wit—who's like we lack— / A lover . . . Not like other men."

She paused. "It's so beautiful, I thought I'd die! You know, my values have completely changed, thanks to you. I go to bed listening to a Scarlatti sonata, I read plays. Before, I used to dream of fur coats, cars, jewels. Now I hope for a book or an opera. As mistresses go, I'm a bargain."

"You're not my mistress, Dottie, you're my friend."

"A friend you sleep with is a mistress," she assured him, recalling his passion the night before.

In bed, he had shouted her name as if he was discovering a new world: "Dottie!" It wasn't the cry of a friend, it was the cry of a lover bending to the yoke of pleasure. She knew that cry. She could draw conclusions from it. He surrendered last night.

"Dottie!"

"Yeah?" she murmured, fixing a lash that was curling the wrong way.

"Dottie, are you listening to me?"

"Um, sure," she said with a sigh, unwilling to hear. "Where are you taking me tonight?"

"To see *La Gioconda*."

"Who's it by?"

"Ponchielli."

"Brilliant! I'll be ready for Wagner soon. A few more

evenings and I'll be able to handle the Ring Cycle without batting an eye."

"Dottie!"

She dropped her hands, and her reflection in the mirror showed the pained face of defeat. She didn't look so cheerful anymore, and a black line of mascara ran down her cheek.

He took her hand and pulled her close.

"Do you want us to stop seeing each other?" he asked. "I'd understand perfectly, you know."

She stiffened and looked away. *Would he even care if we stopped seeing each other? He doesn't need me. Go on mate, hurt me! Put salt on the wound, I'm not dead yet. I hate men, I hate needing them, I hate feelings, I'd like to be a bionic woman who kicks anybody who tries to kiss her and doesn't let anyone come close.*

Her gaze was elsewhere, her body an unstrung puppet's. She sniffled.

"Blow your nose," he said, handing her a tissue.

"Sure, why not? And spoil Yves Saint Laurent foundation that costs like a million pounds!"

He crumpled the tissue and tossed it aside.

The storm that had been gathering finally broke. Mascara was now running down Dottie's blotchy cheeks. "You're all alike!" she screamed. "You're all cowards! Bloody cowards, that's what you are! There isn't a real man among you!"

Philippe glanced at his watch. They were going to be late.

Dottie was raging now, as if challenging all the men who had taken advantage of her, all the men who used her for a night and dumped her by text message. Finally the two of them fell silent, stubbornly entrenched in their doubts, their loneliness, and their anger. Dottie was on pins and needles. *I want to feel a man's skin against mine, the skin of a man who talks to me and loves me,* she thought. Philippe was miles away thinking: *I wish Joséphine hopped on a train to see me and gave herself to me for one night.*

"Philippe, love me! Please!" implored Dottie.

"Damn it Joséphine! I'm asking for only one night!" cried Philippe.

No answer came from the ghosts their silent pleas went to. They were facing each other, embarrassed by a love they couldn't trade.

"Life is beautiful!" Zoé sang to herself, coming out of a bakery. "Life is sooooo beautiful!" She felt like dancing in the street, grabbing passersby and saying: *Hey, you know what? I'm in love! For real! How do I know? Because I keep laughing to myself all the time, and when we kiss I think my heart's gonna burst.*

When do we kiss, you ask?

Right after school we go to a café and sit way in the back where we're sure no one'll see us, and we kiss. In the beginning I didn't know how to do it, 'cause it was the first time, but he didn't either. So the first time I opened my mouth wide, and he said, "You're not at the dentist's!" After that, we did it the way they do in the movies.

Hey, you know what? His name's Gaétan. It's the most beautiful name in the world. First, because it has two A's, and I like A's. And then there's a G. I like G's. And when you put it all together, it makes, "Ga-é-tan."

What's he like?

Taller than me, blond hair, with small, serious-looking eyes. He likes sunshine and cats. Hates turtles. He's not really built, but when he hugs me, it's as if he had three million muscles. He doesn't wear cologne but he smells good, I love the way he smells. He likes walking better than taking the Metro, and his girlfriend is Zoé Cortès!

I didn't know it would feel like this. I want to shout it in the street. Well, actually no, I want to whisper it to everyone, like a secret that you can't help telling. I'm getting mixed up. Okay, it's like a secret, a super-important secret that I can't tell anyone but I want to shout from the rooftops.

This afternoon, we decided to go to the movies after school. He made up an excuse for his parents. I didn't need one, 'cause my mom and I aren't speaking anymore. She disappointed me too much. When I'm with her, all I can see is her kissing Philippe on the mouth, and I don't like it. Not at all.

But what the heck, it doesn't really matter 'cause I'm happy. So happy!

I'm not the same person anymore. And yet I am. It feels as if I had a big balloon in my throat, as if I were full of air. And when I know I'm going to see Gaétan, my heart jumps up and makes a clatter like pots and pans, and I get scared that I'm not pretty enough, that he's stopped loving me or something. I'm afraid all the time. I go to meet him on tiptoe, I'm so scared he'll change his mind.

When we kiss, it makes me want to laugh, and I can feel his lips smiling. I don't close my eyes. I like seeing his closed eyelids.

When we walk in the street, he holds me by the shoulder so tight, our friends complain that we aren't walking fast enough.

That's right! Because of Gaétan, I have lots of friends now.

Yesterday, he said, "Zoé Cortès is my girlfriend," and he looked real serious and hugged me tight, and I was so happy I thought I was gonna die.

Yesterday I felt like kissing him, just like that, out of the blue, right in the middle of a sentence. He laughed when I kissed him and then when I got mad, he apologized and said, "It's just because I'm happy." And that made me want to kiss him more.

I want him to hold me all the time. I don't want to make love with him, just be with him. We haven't made love, in fact. We don't talk about it. He hugs me real tight, we're happy and it's like we're flying.

I haven't told my mom anything. It kills me when I think about that. I wonder if her stomach gets all fluttery when she thinks about Philippe. I wonder if love is the same at every age.

Joséphine opened the door to the co-op owners' meeting just as they were choosing a person to chair the session.

It looked like a high school examination room. Some forty people were sitting at desks with papers in front of them. She went to sit in the back next to a man with a round face and unkempt hair. He was sprawled so casually in his chair that if you added an umbrella and some sun block, you'd think he was at the beach.

"Hello," said Joséphine, taking the chair to his. "I'm Madame Cortès, fifth floor."

"I'm Monsieur Merson, Paul's father," he replied with a cheerful grin that smoothed his wrinkles. "And Madame Merson's husband."

"Nice to meet you," she said, blushing.

Merson shot her a look that seemed to go right through her clothes, as if he were trying to read the tag on her bra.

"Is there a Monsieur Cortès?" he asked, leaning close.

Feeling rattled, Joséphine pretended not to have heard.

Pinarelli *fils* raised his hand, volunteering to chair the meeting.

"Hey, he came without his mommy!" said Merson. "How daring!"

In front of Merson, a stern-looking woman of about fifty wheeled around, glaring at him. She was thin, almost emaciated. With her helmet of jet-black hair and bushy eyebrows, she looked like a scarecrow set out in a field to frighten birds away.

"A little decency, please!" she croaked.

"I was joking, Mademoiselle de Bassonnière," Merson said with a big smile. "Just joking."

Joséphine looked around the room. She recognized Hervé Lefloc-Pignel, sitting in the front row next to Monsieur Van den Brock. The two men were exchanging papers. Pinarelli was a little farther down the same row, having carefully left three empty chairs between them.

The building manager was wearing a gray suit and a gentle, conciliatory smile. Looking around vaguely, he decreed that Monsieur Pinarelli would chair the session. Next up was the selection of a secretary and two note takers. Hands shot up, eager to be recognized.

"This is their moment of glory!" whispered Merson. "You'll see what it's like to be drunk with power."

The agenda listed twenty-six items to be covered and voted on, and Joséphine wondered how long the meeting would last. The first topic of debate was the Christmas tree that Iphigénie had set up in the lobby during the holidays.

"Eighty-five euros for a pine tree!" yelped Pinarelli. "The concierge should pay for that herself. She obviously put it there to pressure us for her New Year's bonus. As co-op owners, I don't think we get a penny's worth of value from the money collected. I therefore propose that she pay for the tree and the Christmas decorations and reimburse us for any other expenses this year."

"I agree with Monsieur Pinarelli," said de Bassonnière, drawing herself up. "And I would like to express my reservations about this concierge, whom we were forced to hire, as usual."

"For heaven's sake, what's eighty-five euros divided forty ways?" asked Lefloc-Pignel, exasperated.

"It's easy to be generous with other people's money!" she screeched.

"Aha, the first skirmish!" said Merson aside to Joséphine. "They're in good form this evening. Usually it takes them longer to get worked up."

"Just what are you insinuating?" asked Lefloc-Pignel, standing to face his adversary.

"I'm saying that it's easy to spend money when you haven't earned it by the sweat of your brow."

Lefloc-Pignel's head jerked up, his face livid. Joséphine thought he was going to pass out.

She leaned closer to Merson and asked, "What are they talking about?"

"She's down on him for being the head of his father-in-law's bank. It's a private business bank. But this is the first time she's ever been so specific. It must be in your honor; a kind of initiation rite. Also a warning not to cross her, otherwise she'll start rummaging through your past. She has an uncle who works in domestic intelligence and has files on all the tenants."

"I won't participate in this meeting if Mademoiselle de Bassonnière doesn't apologize!" roared Lefloc-Pignel to the embarrassed building manager, who was gazing out over the audience.

"Absolutely not!" riposted his enemy, eagerly saddling her high horse.

"Same old, same old," said Merson. "They're sparring, sizing each other up. You have nice legs, do you know that?"

Joséphine blushed and spread her raincoat over her knees.

"Mademoiselle, I won't leave because of item eighteen, which requires my presence," said Lefloc-Pignel. "But know this: If you weren't a woman, I'd ask you to step outside."

"Oh, I'm not afraid of you. Considering where the gentleman comes from! A country bumpkin."

Lefloc-Pignel took a step toward the older woman, and for a moment Joséphine thought he was going to slap her, but Van den Brock intervened. He stood up and whispered something into Lefloc-Pignel's ear. He eventually sat down, though not without glaring angrily at the viper. The whole scene had an odd whiff of violence. It was like the rehearsal of a play in which the actors all know how it ends but are determined to play their parts to the hilt.

"My God, they're so nasty!" exclaimed Joséphine. "I would never believe that—"

"It's like this all the time," said Merson with a sigh. "Monsieur Lefloc-Pignel makes the co-op spend money and this drives Mademoiselle de Bassonnière crazy, 'cause she's a skinflint. He wants the building to shine because it makes him look good." Merson looked Joséphine over with a big smile. "You really do have fine wrists and ankles. Very fine, very attractive. They cry out to be caressed."

"Monsieur Merson!"

"What can I say? I like pretty women. In fact, I like all women.

I worship them. Especially when they surrender. That's when female beauty reaches almost mystical perfection. In my eyes, it's proof that God exists."

Having provoked Lefloc-Pignel, Mademoiselle de Bassonnière then turned her guns on Merson about a carelessly parked scooter. She made a reference to his uncontrolled sexuality, but that merely made him smile complacently. Seeing that her jab tickled instead of wounded, she wheeled on Van den Brock and his wife's piano playing.

"I want that racket that comes from your floor every hour of the night and day stopped."

"It isn't a racket, madame, it's Mozart."

"The way your wife plays, I can't tell the difference," she hissed.

"Adjust your hearing aid, then. Its circuits are overloaded!"

"Go back where you came from! Here in France, we're the ones who are overloaded."

"I'm French, madame, and proud of it."

"Van den Brock? That's French?"

"Yes, madame."

"A jumped-up blond half-breed who sexually assaults his patients and plants little bastards in them."

"Madame!" screamed Van den Brock, stunned by the enormity of the accusation.

The exhausted building manager had long since thrown in the towel. His pen was drawing circles and squares on the first page of the agenda and his elbow no longer seemed able hold up the weight of his head. There were still thirteen items to discuss and it was already seven o'clock. He witnessed the same scenes at every meeting and wondered how these people managed to co-exist during the rest of the year.

"That woman is dangerous," said Joséphine. "She radiates hatred."

"She's actually been roughed up twice," said Merson. "Once at the post office by an Arab she called a social parasite, and another time by a Pole she mistook for a German and accused of being a Nazi. We change concierges every two years because of her. She harasses and torments them, and the building manager eventually caves in. But Pinarelli is no slouch either. He can't stand Iphigénie, calls her an unwed mother. 'Unwed mother!' Talk about a phrase from another century!"

"But she has a husband! Problem is, he's in jail." Joséphine giggled.

"How do you know?"

"She told me."

"Are you two friendly?"

"Yes, I like her a lot. And I know she wants to throw a little party in her apartment when the remodeling is done. That's going to be a challenge!"

Joséphine sighed as she contemplated the group.

Merson burst out laughing, which echoed through the room like a thunderclap. Everybody turned to look at him.

"It's nerves," he said apologetically, smiling broadly. "But at least it'll calm things down! Mademoiselle de Bassonnière, you're not worthy of belonging to our community."

The older woman nearly choked at the word *community*, then slumped in her chair, muttering that it was too late anyway, that

France was going down the drain, the damage was done, vice and foreigners ruled the country.

A murmur of disapproval arose, and the building manager took advantage of the relative calm to return to the agenda.

Joséphine decided to drift off toward a blue ocean with palm trees and a white sand beach. She imagined little waves licking her ankles, the sun on her back, sheets of sand on her belly, and relaxed. From time to time she would hear snatches of speech— jarring terms like *constitution of special provisions, consultation modalities,* and *roofing and infrastructure*—that intruded on her paradise, but she continued to daydream.

An hour earlier, she had told Shirley what Philippe had written on the book's flyleaf.

"So when do you do the deed, Jo?"

"Don't be stupid!"

"Hop on the Eurostar and go see him. No one will know. I'll lend you my flat, if you like. You won't even need to go out."

"I told you, Shirley, it's impossible. I can't."

"Because of your sister?"

"Because of a thing called conscience. Ever hear of it?"

"Is that when you're afraid of being punished by God?"

"Sort of. And besides . . ."

Joséphine sighed, feeling discouraged.

"I'm afraid of being a big disappointment in bed."

"And that's why you won't spend a night making love with Philippe?"

"No, not at all!"

"Of course it is!"

"Well it's true that I sometimes I think he must've been with women a lot less inhibited than me."

"So that's where virtue springs from! I always suspected that people were virtuous out of laziness or fear. Thanks, Jo. You just proved me right."

Joséphine said she had to get off the phone because she was going to be late to the co-op owners meeting.

"Will your dishy neighbor with the hot eyes be there?" asked Shirley.

"Yeah, I expect so."

"And you'll go home together arm in arm, chatting."

"You really are obsessed!"

Shirley didn't deny it. "We're on Earth for such a short time, Jo. Let's enjoy it!"

"You planning to spend the night here?" asked Merson. "'Cause the rest of us are going home."

"I'm so sorry! I was daydreaming!"

"So I noticed. You didn't say a word!"

Merson's phone rang. While he answered it, Joséphine headed out the door.

Hervé Lefloc-Pignel caught up with her and suggested they go back to the building together.

"Would you mind if we walked? I love Paris at night. I often go out walking. It's my way to get exercise."

Joséphine thought of the man chinning himself from the tree branch on the night she was attacked. She shivered and moved away from him.

"Are you cold?" he asked solicitously.

Jo smiled, but didn't answer. Memories of the attack often came back to her, in painful little spasms. She thought about it, without really thinking about it. Until they arrested the man with the smooth soles, he would remain a danger crouching in her mind.

They took boulevard Émile-Augier, walked along the former rail line, and headed toward Parc de la Muette. The springtime weather was chilly, and Joséphine raised her raincoat collar.

"So what did you think of your first co-op meeting?" he asked.

"It was horrible! I had no idea it could get so nasty!"

"Mademoiselle de Bassonnière often goes too far," he said in a measured tone.

"You're being nice. She really attacks people!"

"I should learn to control myself. I always get sucked in. Even though I know her, she gets to me every time."

He seemed angry at himself, shaking his head like a horse choked by its halter.

It was getting late, and dark purple clouds began to streak the sky. Eager for the first warmth of spring, the chestnut trees put out their green branches as if appealing for sweetness. Joséphine imagined them as booted giants rousing themselves after a long winter. The sound of conversation came from apartment windows, and the animation coming from the open ones contrasted with the echo of their footsteps in the deserted streets.

A big dog crossed their path and stopped under a streetlight, looking at them for a moment, as if wondering whether to approach or avoid them. Joséphine put her hand on Lefloc-Pignel's arm.

"Can you see how he's looking at us?"

"He is so ugly!"

It was a big, black shorthaired mastiff with a slanted, amber eye. Its broken left ear was dangling, and the other one had been chewed down to a stump. A long scar could be seen along his right flank, flesh pink and swollen amid the hairs.

The dog gave a low growl, as if to warn them not to move.

"Do you think he's a stray?" asked Joséphine. "He doesn't have a collar."

She was looking at the dog tenderly, and he seemed to have eyes only for her. His gaze separated her from Lefloc-Pignel, as if he were sorry that she wasn't alone.

"The Black Dog of Brocéliande! That's what they called Bertrand du Guesclin. He was so ugly his father couldn't stand looking at him. He got back by becoming the greatest warrior of his generation. He was winning tournaments at fifteen, fighting in a mask to hide his looks."

Jo stretched a hand out to the dog, but it backed slowly away, then turned and trotted off toward Parc de la Muette, a tall black shape melting into the darkness.

"Maybe his owner is waiting for him under the trees," said Lefloc-Pignel. "A hobo. They often have big dogs as companions, have you noticed?"

"We should leave him on Mademoiselle de Bassonnière's doorstep," Jo suggested. "She'd be in a fix!"

"She would turn him over to the police."

"For sure! He's not chic enough for her."

Lefloc-Pignel smiled sadly, then continued as if he were still thinking about what Mademoiselle de Bassonnière had said.

"You don't mind being in the company of a peasant?"

Joséphine smiled.

"I don't come from very high-class people either, you know. We're both in the same boat."

"You're sweet . . ." He went on quietly, on a more confidential tone.

"But she's right, you know. I'm just a little guy from the sticks. Abandoned by his parents, taken in by a printer in a little village in Normandy. From her uncle, Mademoiselle de Bassonnière has gotten files on everybody. She'll soon know everything about you, unless she already does!"

"I couldn't care less. I don't have anything to hide."

"We all have our little secrets. Think about it."

"I already have. It's no go."

Then she thought about Philippe and blushed in the darkness. She said, "If your secret is to have grown up in a village in the countryside and been taken in by a generous man, there's no shame in that! It could even be the start of a Dickens novel. I like Dickens. People don't read him much anymore."

"I'm told you wrote a book that sold very well."

"It was my sister Iris's idea. She's the complete opposite of me: beautiful, lively, elegant, at ease wherever she goes. When we take the freeway out to her place in Deauville, I look at the little villages off in the distance. I can see little farms surrounded by groves of trees, thatched roofs, and barns, and I start thinking of stories by Flaubert and Maupassant."

"I come from one of those little villages. And my life would make a novel."

"Tell me about it."

"It's not very interesting, you know."

"Please! I love stories."

They were walking at the same pace, neither too slow nor too fast. Jo was tempted to take his arm, but resisted. Hervé Lefloc-Pignel wasn't a man to allow public displays of affection.

"In those days my village was lively and animated. Both sides of the main street were lined with shops. A general store, a grocery store, a barber, a post office, a bakery, two butchers, a florist, and a café. I've never gone back, but I doubt there's much left of the world I used to know. That was . . ."

He searched his memory.

". . . more than forty years ago. I was just a little boy. The man's name was Graphin, Benoît Graphin. His print shop was called Imprimerie Moderne. The words were painted green on a pine board. He worked all the time, day and night. He wasn't married and didn't have children. He taught me everything. I grew up surrounded by machines. In those days printing was a craft. He set all the type by hand, lining up the lead characters in galleys. I have wonderful memories of that. A peasant's memories."

Lefloc-Pignel looked bitter as he said it.

"Mademoiselle de Bassonnière is a wicked woman," said Joséphine. "Pay no attention to what she says."

"Yes, but it's my past, and nobody gets to touch it. Out of bounds. I loved that man. When I was ten, he sent me to boarding school in Rouen, so I could get a decent education, he said. I came to see him on weekends and during my vacations. But as I grew up I started to find the print shop boring. I was young. I wasn't interested in what he was teaching me anymore. I think I looked down on him because he worked with his hands. What a fool I was!"

"You should hear the way my daughters talk when they're trying to teach me how to use the Internet: like I'm mentally retarded."

"When children know more than their parents, that creates authority problems."

"Oh, I don't care! I don't mind if they think I'm a bit slow."

"You mustn't let them. You deserve to be respected as a mother and an educator. I think discipline issues are going to be critical in the future. Absent fathers are already a huge problem in children's educations in society today. Personally, I want to restore the image of the *pater familias*."

"One can also teach them that a father can be gentle and affectionate," said Joséphine, glancing heavenward.

Lefloc-Pignel shot her a hidden glance, quickly averted. He had a secretive and cautious air. She felt he wasn't quick to share personal information but when he did he was capable of great disclosure.

"When the work in the concierge apartment is done, Iphigénie wants to throw a little party and invite all the tenants."

They were entering the park, and Joséphine shivered again. She moved closer to Lefloc-Pignel, as if she thought the killer could be sneaking up behind her.

"That's not a great idea," he said. "Nobody talks to each other in the building."

"My sister will come."

Joséphine had said that to convince him to come. Iris was still her *Open Sesame!*, the magic key that opened all doors.

"Then I'll drop by, if you like" he said. She couldn't help thinking he would find Iris attractive. And Iris would be surprised to see her getting along with such a handsome man.

At the elevator, they parted with a little nod. Lefloc-Pignel had withdrawn again, and Jo found it hard to believe this was the same person who had just opened his heart to her.

Sibylle de Bassonnière raised the lid of her garbage can and grimaced at the fishy smell. She decided she would bring the can downstairs right away. She had eaten salmon that evening, and it smelled. *That's it, I'm not buying salmon anymore. It's expensive, it sticks to the pan, and it stinks.*

She put on her bathrobe and slippers, then a pair of rubber gloves, and picked up the can. She usually took it downstairs every evening at ten thirty—it was a ritual. Tonight, she'd briefly considered waiting until the next morning, but decided not to. *A ritual is a ritual, and you have to abide by it if you want to keep your self-respect.*

She pursed her lips in a greedy little pout. *All in all, I don't regret the salmon. It's my weekly treat, and I deserve it.* She thought back to the evening meeting. *I really got to them tonight, Lefloc-Pignel, Van den Brock, and Merson: a clean sweep! All three of those scoundrels are in my files. Lefloc-Pignel is a clodhopper in a good marriage, Van den Brock is a dangerous impostor, and Merson is a shameless sexual degenerate.*

Thanks to her uncle, her mother's brother, she was the only person in the complex to know some of these things. He'd been in the police at the Interior Ministry and kept files on everybody. When she was a little girl, she would climb into his lap with a newspaper, and say, "Tell me how they arrested this one." He would whisper in her ear: "You won't tell anybody will you? It's a secret." She would nod, and he'd describe the stakeouts with their betrayals, recklessness, rivalries, shootings. And always drama and bloodshed.

That was how she learned Lefloc-Pignel's background, his long odyssey as a child constantly taken in and tossed out, the foster homes each grimmer than the next, then his lucky marriage to the little Mangeain-Dupuy girl and his rise in society. She also knew why Van den Brock had left Antwerp to come practice medicine in France. "A medical error?" she would whisper to him as they left the annual meetings where she confronted her three victims. "More like the perfect crime." And what about the oversexed Merson, who regularly attended orgies, cheerfully joining rounds of revolting sexual couplings. It wouldn't look good if word got around.

Mademoiselle de Bassonnière had them in her sights and would fire her warning shots once a year. The co-op meeting was her big night, and she started preparing for weeks in advance. Van den Brock nearly gave up the ghost tonight! She had the complete file on his "medical error." She chuckled to herself, imagining the launching of a new trial. What with all his mistresses, past and present, there would be a lot of dirty laundry to air. She savored the heady feeling of power.

She stepped into the elevator, holding the garbage bin and its smelly salmon at arm's length, and pressed the button for the ground floor. The arrival of the new tenant, the one who looked like a deer caught in the headlights, had galvanized her. There was nothing in the Cortès woman's file. The novel supposedly written by her sister? That was yesterday's news. The husband, on the other hand . . . She recalled her uncle's motto: Everyone has a secret, some little bit of nastiness. By exploiting it, you can pressure them to serve or support you.

She crossed the courtyard and opened the door to the garbage room where the big gray cans were kept.

I'm glad I put on rubber gloves. She lifted the heavy lid of the nearest can, stepping back to avoid being assaulted by the stench. *This is disgusting!*

She didn't hear the door to the room as it creaked open behind her.

She was leaning over the big can when she was suddenly jerked backward and stabbed in the chest, first once, then again and again.

She had no time to scream or call for help. Falling forward onto the garbage can, her lank spinster's body collapsed across the lid, then bumped against another can before flopping to the floor. She turned, letting herself fall. *I haven't told everything yet. There are many more people whose shameful secrets I know, many people who might hate me. I love having people hating me, because you don't hate the weak, you only hate the strong.*

Sprawled on the ground, she could see the shoes of the man stabbing her. They were stylish, rich man's shoes, English shoes with rounded tips, brand-new shoes with smooth soles that flashed white in the darkness. He was bent over now, rhythmically stabbing her. She could count the blows, and it was like a dance, she counted them as they struck her. In her mind they got mixed up with the blood in her mouth, the blood on her fingers, the blood on her arms, the blood everywhere. *Is this revenge?* she wondered. *Did I guess right? They're all entangled in secrets that are too heavy for them to bear.*

She slowly bled onto the floor, her eyes closed, thinking, *Yes, yes, I knew it. They all have something to hide, even that gorgeous man posing in his underwear on those billboards. The handsome man with the romantic shock of brown hair was so attractive! My uncle had files on him, too: several arrests for drunkenness or drugs, resisting arrest, disorderly conduct. He has the looks of an angel, but he behaves like a lout.*

She'd learned his name, his address, everything about what he did. Above all, she learned his secret. The secret of his double life. Maybe she shouldn't have sent him that anonymous letter. She had been careless. She had gone outside her circle. Her uncle had always told her to pick her target carefully, to stay safely out of range.

Stay out of range. I forgot.

Mademoiselle de Bassonnière let herself slowly sink into the pain and a velvety unconsciousness, a pool of warm, sticky blood. With a finger of her left hand, she touched the blood. It felt viscous. *Could he have identified me after getting my letter? How did I slip up, for him to find me?*

She was startled to realize that she was still thinking, even so close to death. The brain goes on working as the body empties itself, the heart hesitates to beat, the breath slows in exhaustion.

She felt her attacker kicking her, shoving her inert body behind the big garbage bin, the one in the back that was taken out only once a week. He'd rolled her in a length of dirty carpet and shoved her into the corner so she wouldn't be found right away. *I wonder how long it will take them to find me. How do they determine the time of death, again?* Her uncle had explained that they studied the dark stain under the skin. She would have a black stain on her stomach. She felt a beer can roll against her arm, and she smelled an empty bag of peanuts. She was surprised to find that she remained conscious while the strength drained out of her. She didn't have the energy to go on fighting.

She was surprised, surprised and very weak.

She heard the garbage room door closing, a rusty creak in the silence of the night. She counted three more heartbeats, then gave a little sigh and died.

PART IV

♦ ♦ ♦

◆　◆　◆

$\mathcal{R}$eaching into her Birkin bag, Iris took out a Shiseido compact and checked her makeup. They would be at St. Pancras soon, and she wanted to look her best when she got off the train.

She had clipped in her hair extensions and applied purple-gray eye shadow and mascara. *Ah, those eyes of mine! I never tire of looking at them.* She pulled up the collar on her Jean-Paul Gaultier shirt, pleased that she had chosen the lilac jersey pant-suit that set off her figure so well. The purpose of her trip was simple: to seduce Philippe all over again and assume her rightful her place in the family.

Iris's seatmate on the train couldn't take his eyes off her. He looked to be about forty-five, with a strong features and broad shoulders. *Philippe will come back to me,* she thought. *And if not, I'll seduce someone else! I have to be realistic. I'm running out of options.*

Iris leaned back in her seat. It had been smart to tell Alexandre that she was coming before mentioning it to Philippe. That way, he couldn't tell her not to come. Everything hinged on this visit.

A shiver ran down her spine.

What if she failed?

Her gaze wandered out to the gray London suburbs, the little houses jammed together, the spindly gardens, the clotheslines, the broken lawn furniture, the graffiti-scrawled walls. They reminded her of the projects outside Paris.

What if she failed?

She played with her rings, stroked her Hermès handbag and her cashmere shawl.

What if she failed?

She didn't want to think about it.

She nodded when the man next to her offered to lift down her suitcase, and thanked him with a polite smile. The whiff of cheap cologne she caught when he raised his arms to grab the bag told her all she needed to know: He wasn't worth wasting time on.

Philippe and Alexandre were waiting for her on the platform. *How handsome they look!* She felt proud of them, and didn't turn back to the man who'd gotten off the train with her but now slowed his pace when he saw that she was being met.

They had dinner at a pub at the corner of Holland Park Avenue and Clarendon Road. Alexandre told them he'd gotten the best history grade in his class. Philippe congratulated him, and so did Iris. She wondered if they would share a bed or if he'd planned another sleeping arrangement.

Philippe's apartment looked just like the one in Paris, which was hardly surprising, since he had decorated both of them.

He set her suitcase down in the foyer. Alexandre went to bed after a polite good-night kiss, and the two of them found themselves alone in the big living room. Iris settled onto a long sofa and watched as Philippe turned on the stereo and chose a CD. He seemed so closed off that she wondered if she'd made a mistake in coming. She wasn't sure her eyes were still as blue as ever. She fiddled with her hair. She kicked off her shoes, and folded her long legs underneath her in a pose both defensive and expectant. She felt like a stranger in the apartment. She hadn't sensed Philippe responding to her, even for a second. He was affectionate and polite, but was keeping her at a distance. *How did we get to this point?* She decided to stop thinking. She couldn't imagine life without him. Remembering the man in the train's cologne, she curled her lip in disgust.

"Alexandre seems well," she said.

Philippe smiled and nodded.

"I'm happy living with him," he said, as if talking to himself. "I didn't know that he could make me so happy."

"He's changed a lot. I hardly recognize him anymore."

How could you? he thought. *You never knew him!* But he said nothing. He didn't want to open hostilities by talking about Alexandre, who wasn't the problem. The problem was this marriage that never seemed to quite end, just dragged on and on.

He looked at Iris, elegantly draped across the sofa, noting the slender arm, the long neck, the full mouth. He divided her into components and each took a blue ribbon as the most beautiful component. *Did she take any pleasure, being with me? I've held this woman in my arms, and I don't know a thing about her. But that's not my problem anymore. My problem tonight is to put an end to her illusions. I noticed her looking around to see where I put her suitcase, wondering where she's going to sleep. Well, we won't be sleeping together, Iris.*

"I brought you some presents," she finally said, to break the silence.

"That was nice of you."

"Where did you put my suitcase?" she asked playfully.

You know perfectly well, he almost said.

"In the foyer."

"In the foyer?" She sounded surprised.

"That's right."

"Ah."

She stood up and got a blue cashmere sweater and a box of calisson candies from her bag.

"Calissons?" exclaimed Philippe in surprise when she handed him the lozenge-shaped white tin.

"Do you remember our weekend in Aix? You bought ten boxes of them so you could have them everywhere: in the car, at the office, at home! I thought they were too sweet."

Her voice was bright and melodious, but Philippe could hear the underlying, unsung chorus: We were so happy then, you loved me so much!

"That was a long time ago," he said, trying to remember.

He put the box on the coffee table as if refusing to travel back in time to an invented happiness.

"Oh, Philippe! It wasn't that long!"

She was sitting at his feet now, her arms around his knees. She looked so beautiful, he pitied her. Left to her own devices, without the protection of a man to love her, Iris's weaknesses made her such easy prey! *Who will protect her when I'm not there?*

"It's like you forgot that we loved each other."

"I'm the one who loved you," he corrected her quietly.

"What do you mean?"

"It was a one-way street. And it's all over."

She had gotten up and was staring at him in disbelief.

"All over? That's impossible!"

"No it isn't. We're going to separate and get a divorce."

"Oh no, I love you, Philippe! I love you! All the time in the train I thought about you, about us. I told myself that we were going to start all over again, from scratch."

She had seized his hand, and was squeezing it. "Darling—"

"Please, Iris, don't make this harder than it is. You know perfectly well how things stand between us."

"I've made mistakes, I know. I behaved like a spoiled little girl. But now I know. I know—"

"You know what?" he asked, weary of her explanations even before hearing them.

"I know that I love you. I've changed, I'm not the same person."

He looked at her in disbelief.

"You think that just saying so makes it true, don't you? Life isn't that simple, darling."

The term of endearment revived Iris's hopes. She laid her head on his knees and stroked his leg.

"Please forgive me for everything!"

"Iris, please! You're embarrassing me!"

He shook his leg, as if to get rid of an annoying dog.

"But I can't live without you!"

"I won't cut you off."

"What about you? What are you going to do?"

"I don't know yet. I want to change my life. For a long time you were my reason for living, then it was my work, which I was passionate about, and now it's my son, whom I've only recently discovered. I got tired of my job, and you did everything to make me tired of you. What's left is Alexandre and a desire to live differently. I know how to be happy now, and this new happiness doesn't have anything to do with you. You're its opposite, in fact. So I see you, I recognize you, but I don't love you anymore. It's taken a long time. It's like our marriage was an eighteen-year hourglass, the time it took for those tiny grains of sand to fall from the top to the bottom."

Iris raised her face to him, a face lovely and tense, and marked with doubt.

"But that's impossible!" she cried again, seeing the determination in his eyes.

"It's become possible. You know we don't have feelings for each other anymore, Iris. So why pretend?"

"You're in love with someone else, aren't you? I felt it the moment I got here. So what about *my* love?"

"It isn't love, it's vanity. You'll heal quickly. I'm sure you'll find another man."

"You should've told me not to come, then."

"As if you ever asked me! You pushed your way in here. I didn't say anything, because of Alexandre, but I didn't ask you to come."

"All right, let's talk about Alexandre, then. I'm taking him back with me, if things are like that. I won't leave him here with your . . . your mistress!"

She'd spat the word as if it felt dirty in her mouth.

Philippe grabbed her by the hair and pulled it hard enough

THE SLOW WALTZ OF TURTLES

to hurt. He put his mouth close to her ear and quietly said, "Alexandre is staying with me, and that's that. It's not even open for discussion."

"Let me go!"

"Did you hear me? You and I can fight if we must, but you're not going touch him. You can tell me how much you want as a settlement, and I'll pay it. But you aren't getting custody of Alexandre."

"We'll see about that! He's my son!

"You've never paid him the slightest attention, you've never been concerned about him, and I won't let you use him to blackmail me. Got that?"

Iris bowed her head and said nothing.

"As for tonight, you're sleeping at a hotel. There is a very nice one right next door. You'll spend the night there, and tomorrow you'll leave without making a fuss. I'll tell Alexandre that you weren't feeling well, and went back to Paris. From now on, you'll visit him here. We can work out the dates together."

She freed herself and stood up, then declared, "If you want war, you'll have war!"

Philippe burst out laughing.

"How do you plan to fight, Iris?"

She looked pale and disheveled. The blue of her eyes had lost its sparkle. The corners of her mouth curved down, like that of an aging gambler who has lost it all. Her long black hair hung in lank strands. She was no longer the gorgeous Iris Dupin, but a defeated woman who could see her power, beauty, and wealth disappearing.

"Have I made myself clear?"

Iris didn't answer. She didn't want to cry. She was stunned, stumbling down a long tunnel into darkness. From now on she would suffer. She didn't know exactly when but soon the tunnel would collapse, turning her life into a pile of rubble. She wanted to delay it as long as possible. Philippe was slipping away from her and she hated him for it. *He is mine!* she kept telling herself. *No one can take him away from me. I own him.*

The day after the co-op meeting, Joséphine decided to go running. Zoé was still asleep—it was Saturday and she didn't have any classes—so Jo left her a note on the kitchen table.

In the elevator she ran into Merson, who was going for a bike ride. He was wearing tight cycling shorts and a fanny pack and carrying a helmet.

"A little jogging, Madame Cortès?"

"A little pedaling, Monsieur Merson?"

"I gather there was another shindig in the basement again last night."

"I don't know what they do down there, but they seem to be enjoying themselves."

"Youth must have its way. We've all spent time hanging out in basements, haven't we, Madame Cortès?"

"Speak for yourself, Monsieur Merson."

"Ah, you're doing your shy virgin number again."

"Are you coming to Iphigénie's party this evening?"

"Is it this evening? It'll be a bloodbath. I fear the worst."

"No, the people who come will behave themselves."

"If you say so, Madame Cortès. In that case I will come, but only because it's you."

"Bring your wife. I'd enjoy meeting her."

"Touché, Madame Cortès."

"Have a good day, Monsieur Merson. And remember, six o'clock in the concierge apartment—with your wife!"

They parted and Joséphine ran off, grinning.

Stopped at a light, Jo was jogging in place when she looked up and noticed a big billboard. The model in the ad was Vittorio Giambelli, Luca's twin brother. He was modeling underwear, his arms folded across his chest, looking sullen. Manly, but sullen. Above his head, a colorful banner displayed the slogan: BE A MAN, WEAR EXCELLENCE. No surprise that Vittorio is depressed. Seeing yourself in tight underpants plastered across the walls of Paris can't do much for your self-respect.

The light changed and Joséphine trotted across the street, thinking that she ought to return Luca's key. *I'll stop by his place while I'm out shopping with Iphigénie. If I run into him I'll say I can't stay because she's waiting in the car.*

She hopped over a low wall onto the wide promenade leading to the lake. She recognized the Saturday morning *boules* players. On Saturday they played in pairs. The women brought picnic lunches in coolers: rosé wine, hard-boiled eggs, and cold chicken in mayonnaise.

Joséphine started a first lap around the lake, running at her usual pace. She had her landmarks: the red and ocher boat-rental shed; the benches along the course; the clump of bamboo growing into the path that forced runners to the left; the dead, upright tree she had dubbed "the Indian," which marked the halfway point.

It was still a little too early to see the mysterious walker. On Saturday he showed up around noon. The weather was nice, and Joséphine wondered if he might take off his scarf or his watch cap.

She could see what he looked like, decide if he looked friendly or grumpy. *Maybe he's a celebrity who doesn't want to be bothered,* she thought. Some of the joggers smelled of soap, others of sweat. Some stared at the women, others ignored them. It was a ballet danced by a crowd of regulars, all circling, sweating, and suffering together, then circling some more. Jo enjoyed belonging to this world of whirling dervishes. Her mind gradually emptied, she could feel herself floating. Problems fell away like flakes of dead skin.

The ringing of her cell phone brought her down to earth. Iris's name appeared on the screen, and Joséphine stopped to answer the call.

"Jo?"

"Yes," said Joséphine, panting.

"Am my disturbing you?"

"I'm out running."

"Can I see you this evening?"

"We're already seeing each other, Iris. Or did you forget the party at my concierge's? And we agreed to have dinner together afterward. Don't tell me you forgot!"

"Oh, that's right."

"So you did forget!" Joséphine felt hurt.

"No, it's not that but . . . I absolutely have to talk to you! I'm in London and what's happened is terrible, Jo, terrible!"

Iris's voice was breaking.

"What's wrong?" Joséphine asked in alarm.

"Philippe wants a divorce! He says it's all over, that he doesn't love me anymore. I think I'm going to die, you hear, Jo?"

"Yes, yes," she murmured.

"There's another woman in his life."

"Are you sure?"

"Yes. I suspected it from the way he talked to me. He just looks right through me, Jo. It's like I'm invisible. It's awful!"

"You must be imagining things!"

"No I'm not, I swear. He told me that it's finished, that we're going to get a divorce. He sent me to stay at a hotel, can you imagine? And this morning when I went to see him, he'd already gone out. You know how he likes to go to a café alone and read the newspaper in the morning. So I talked to Alexandre, and he told me everything!"

"What did he tell you?" asked Joséphine, her heart in her mouth.

"He said his father is seeing a woman, that he takes her to the theater and the opera. That he often spends the night with her, but comes back at dawn hoping Alexandre won't notice. He knows everything, I tell you! He even knows her name, Dottie Doolittle. Oh, Jo, I think I'm going to die!"

I'm going to die too, thought Joséphine, leaning against a tree for support.

"I'm so unhappy, Jo! What's to become of me?"

"Maybe Alexandre made up the whole story," suggested Joséphine, clinging to that slim hope.

"He seemed very sure of himself. He told me all that, sounding like a little professor. You know, calm and detached. He even used a funny word. He said that the woman was probably 'transitory.' That was nice of him, wasn't it? He said it to make me feel better. Oh, Jo!"

"Where are you now?"

"At Saint Pancras station. I'll be in Paris in three hours. Can I come to your place?"

"I have to go run errands with Iphigénie."

"Who's that?"

"My building's concierge. I promised to take her shopping for her party things."

"I'm coming over anyway. I'll wait at your place."

Joséphine hung up, feeling devastated. "You can make the people who love you look away, but not the people who desire you. I love and desire you." She had believed him. She had taken those loving words, stitched them onto a banner, and draped it around herself. *I know nothing of love's intricacies. . . . I am such a fool!* Jo's legs began to fail her, and she plopped down on a bench. She closed her eyes and said the words, "Dottie Doolittle." *She's young and pretty, she wears little earrings, she has a charming gap in her teeth, she makes him laugh, she isn't anyone's sister, she dances rock 'n' roll and sings* La Traviata, *she knows Shakespeare's sonnets and the* Kama Sutra. *She's pushed me aside the way you sweep dead leaves away.*

Jo felt a breath on her arm and snapped her eyes open in alarm.

A huge black dog was looking at her, his head tilted to one side.

"Du Guesclin!" she cried, recognizing the black stray from the night before. "What are you doing here?"

A thread of saliva hung from his chops. He seemed upset to see her so sad.

"I'm unhappy, Du Guesclin. Really unhappy."

He tilted his head to the other side as if to show he was listening.

"You're funny dog! You still don't have an owner, do you?"

He nodded, as if to say, *That's right, I don't have an owner.* And he stayed like that with his head oddly cocked, the thread of sticky saliva on his lips.

"What do you expect from me, huh? I can't take you home."

She stroked the long, swollen scar on his right flank, the stiff hair crusted here and there.

"It's true, you really are ugly. Hervé Lefloc-Pignel was right. You've got eczema, someone chopped off your tail, one of your ears is hanging and the other one's just a stump. You're no prize beauty, that's for sure!"

He raised a vitreous gaze to her and she realized that his bulging right eye was milky.

"Oh, my God, someone put your eye out, too! You poor thing!"

Du Guesclin allowed her to pet him as she talked, neither growling nor pulling away. Bowing his head under her caress, he closed his eyes with pleasure.

"You enjoy being petted, don't you? You're probably more used to being kicked."

He moaned quietly as if in agreement, and Joséphine smiled.

She looked for a tattoo in his ear and on his inner thighs, but found nothing. He lay down at her feet, panting, and she understood that he was thirsty. She pointed at the dirty water of the lake but immediately felt ashamed. What Du Guesclin needed was a nice bowl of clean water.

Checking the time, Joséphine realized she was going to be late. When she stood up, he followed her, trotting by her side.

People gave them a wide berth when they approached.

"You see, Du Guesclin?" she said, chuckling. "You scare people."

She stopped and looked at him.

"What am I going to do with you?"

She groaned.

He rocked his hips from side to side, as if to say, *Come on, stop thinking. Just take me home with you.* His good eye, which was the color of old rum, pleaded with her, watching for her consent. Eye to eye, they took each other's measure: he, waiting confidently, she, hesitantly calculating.

"Who will look after you when I go to the library to work? What if you start barking or howling? What will Mademoiselle de Bassonnière say?"

Slyly, he slipped his muzzle into her hand.

"Du Guesclin!" she moaned. "That's not fair!"

She continued her walk and he followed, his nose at her heels. He stopped when she stopped, trotted along when she started up. He froze at the first red light, moved again when she did. He matched his pace to hers and didn't get tangled in her feet.

He followed her to her building, and slipped in behind her when she opened the door. He waited for the elevator to arrive and when it did, sneaked into it as skillfully as a smuggler dodging a customs patrol.

"You think I don't see what you're doing?" asked Joséphine, pressing the button for her floor.

Du Guesclin continued to give her a look that said his fate was in her hands.

"Listen, we'll make a deal. I'll keep you for a week, and if you behave yourself, it'll be another week, and so forth. Otherwise, I'm taking you to the SPCA."

He yawned widely, in apparent agreement. They walked into the kitchen, where Zoé was eating breakfast. When she looked up, she cried, "Wow, that's no lap dog, is it? I'm sure he's a stray. You see how he's looking at us? Can we keep him, Mommy? Please say yes! Please, please, pretty please?"

Now Zoé was talking to her again, and her sweet cheeks were flushed with excitement. Joséphine pretended to hesitate, and Zoé begged her.

"I've always dreamed of having a big dog, Mommy! You know that."

Du Guesclin looked at them from one to the other, from Zoé's anxious entreaty to Joséphine's apparent calm. In fact, Jo was thrilled to be reconnecting with her daughter and was relishing it in silence.

She spread her arms wide and Zoé rushed to her.

"Do you really want us to keep him?"

"Oh yes! If we don't, no one's gonna want him. He'll be all alone."

"Will you take care of him, and walk him?"

"I promise! Come on, say yes!"

As Zoé looked beseechingly at her, Jo had a question she was dying to ask, she but didn't. She would wait until Zoé chose to open up to her. She hugged her daughter and, sighing, nodded.

"Oh, Mommy, I'm so happy! What are we going to call him?"

"Du Guesclin. The Black Dog of Brocéliande."

"Du Guesclin," repeated Zoé, petting the dog. "I think he needs a good bath. And a good meal."

Du Guesclin wagged the stump of his tail and followed Zoé to the bathroom.

"Iris is coming over," Jo called from the hallway. "Let her in, please. I'm going to run some errands with Iphigénie."

She heard Zoé say, "Yes, Mommy," while talking to her new pet.

Feeling happy, Jo went downstairs looking for Iphigénie. She would have to buy some dog food for Du Guesclin.

"Hey, I just got a dog!" she announced.

"Now you're really stuck, Madame Cortès. You'll have to take him out at night and not be afraid of the dark!"

"He'll protect me. With him around, no one will dare attack me."

"Is that why you got him?"

"You know, that didn't even occur to me. I was just sitting on a bench and . . ."

"He showed up and glommed onto you, right? You're really something! You'd pick up just about anybody! Okay, I have my list, let's get going."

Joséphine checked to make sure she had Luca's key, while thinking that a few months ago she would've been thrilled to have it.

"I want to stop at a friend's for a minute to drop off a key."

"I'll wait in the car."

Stopping in front of Luca's building, she looked up at his windows. To her relief, the shutters were closed; he wasn't home. In her notebook, she quickly wrote, *Dear Luca: I'm giving your key back. It wasn't a good idea. Good luck, Joséphine.* As Iphigénie deliberately looked away, she reread the note, scratched out the words *It wasn't a good idea*, then copied it onto a fresh sheet of paper. She found an old envelope in the glove compartment and slipped the note inside. She would leave it with the building porter.

The concierge was vacuuming her apartment. She opened the door, the cleaner hose draped over her shoulder like a metal boa constrictor. Joséphine introduced herself and asked if she could leave an envelope for Monsieur Luca Giambelli.

"Don't you mean Vittorio Giambelli?"

"No. Luca, his brother."

That's all she needed, for Vittorio to run across a note from the "dimwit."

"There isn't any Luca Giambelli here!"

"Of course there is," said Joséphine with a smile. "A tall man with dark brown hair hanging in his eyes who always wears a duffel coat."

"Vittorio," the woman firmly repeated, leaning on the vacuum cleaner hose.

"No, Luca! His twin brother."

The concierge shook her head as she untwisted the boa.

"Never heard of him."

"He lives on the fifth floor."

"That's Vittorio Giambelli. There's no Luca."

"For heaven's sake, I've been here before! I can describe his apartment. I also know he has a twin brother named Vittorio who's a fashion model and lives somewhere else."

"Well, that's the person who actually lives here. I've never seen the other one! Didn't even know he had a twin. He never mentioned it. I'm not crazy, you know."

The woman was getting annoyed and looked about to close the door.

"Can I come in to talk for minute?" asked Joséphine.

"Okay, but it's not like I don't have other things to do."

She put the vacuum cleaner aside and reluctantly waved Jo in.

"The man I know is called Luca," explained Joséphine, clutching the envelope. "He's writing a book on the history of tears for an Italian publisher. He spends a lot of time in the library. Looks like a perennial student. He's dark, melancholy, rarely laughs."

"I'm telling you there isn't any Luca, just Vittorio! I ought to know. I bring up his mail, and on the envelopes it's written Vittorio, not Luca."

"But I've been here, and I know it's Luca Giambelli's place."

"And I'm telling you there's just one person and that's Vittorio Giambelli, who works as a model. Who loses his papers, loses his keys, loses his head and spends the night at the police station! So don't come telling me there are two of them when there's just one! That's just as well, because having two guys like him would drive me nuts!"

"It can't be," muttered Joséphine. "It's Luca."

"Vittorio. Vittorio Giambelli. I know his mother, I've talked with her. He's caused her a lot of misery. He's her only son, and she doesn't deserve this. I saw her like I'm seeing you. She was sitting on that chair right there."

The woman pointed to a chair whose current occupant was a big gray cat, asleep.

"She was crying, telling me all the awful things he did to her. She lives not far away, in Gennevilliers. I can give you her address, if you like. I'm sorry, ma'am, but I think he's been telling you stories. It's too bad he isn't here. He's gone to Italy, to Milan, for a runway job. He must've made up this Luca person to seem more interesting. He hates people knowing that he models for magazines, makes him crazy! But that's how he earns his living. Still, at his age! He really ought to settle down."

"This is unbelievable!"

"The man lies like a rug, he does. And this'll end badly, I'm telling you. Because as soon as you cross him, he goes berserk. Some of the tenants have asked to have him kicked out, so you can imagine. Once, he went after some poor lady who asked him to autograph one of his pictures. He yelled at her, you should've seen it. Threw a drawer right in her face! There are people running around loose who really ought to be locked up."

"I would never have thought . . ." stammered Joséphine.

"You're not the first woman this has happened to. Or the last, unfortunately."

"Please don't tell him I came by, all right? I don't want him to know that I know. Please, it's important."

"Hey, whatever you like. It's no skin off my nose, I don't look to hang out with him. So what about the key? You gonna keep it?"

Joséphine kept her envelope. She didn't trust the concierge not to talk to Luca. She would mail it to him.

She pretended to leave, waited until the woman closed the door, then returned and sat on the stairs. The vacuum cleaner could be heard humming in the apartment. She needed a moment to regain her composure before joining Iphigénie. So Luca was the half-naked man scowling down from the billboard. He despised himself as a model but had some self-respect as an intellectual and a researcher. This double life explains why he was always so distant, thought Joséphine. Being too involved would've forced him to reveal too much. He couldn't let his guard down.

Back in November, just before she was attacked, he had told her, "I have to talk to you, Joséphine, it's important." Maybe he wanted to confess, to free himself from the lie. And at the last minute he didn't have the courage, and didn't come.

Joséphine headed for the car, where Iphigénie was waiting. Jo sat down heavily and turned on the ignition, staring into space.

"Are you okay, Madame Cortès? You look all pale. Did something go wrong?"

"Yes, it did, actually," Joséphine said with a sigh as she drove toward the Intermarché store.

They filled two shopping carts with food and drink. Iphigénie was thinking big. Joséphine, unsure that many people would show up, tried to rein her in.

Iphigénie ticked off canapés and sandwiches, soft drinks and wine, paper napkins, plastic glasses, olives, peanuts, sliced roast beef, and cervelas sausages. Studying her list, she added bottles of Coca-Cola for the children and whiskey for the grown-ups. Joséphine bought a big bag of biscuits for older dogs, wondering how old Du Guesclin could be.

Iphigénie proudly took out her purse at the register, and this time Joséphine let her pay. The cashier asked if they had a loyalty card.

"This is where I get to add points to your card!" said Iphigénie, tickled at the idea of topping up Joséphine's account. Jo handed the card over.

"How many points are on it now?" asked Iphigénie eagerly.

The cashier raised an eyebrow, glanced at the register screen, and said, "Right now, none."

"What?" exclaimed Joséphine. "I've never used any of them."

"That may be, but the account's at zero."

"Well, that's strange, Madame Cortès!"

"I don't get it," muttered Joséphine, feeling embarrassed.

Bold in the face of adversity, Iphigénie wheeled on the cashier.

"You must be mistaken," she said. "Why don't you get your boss?"

The cashier, tired of being twenty years old and stuck behind a cash register, mustered the strength to press a button. This summoned a neatly dressed gray-haired lady, the bookkeeper and cash register supervisor. She listened to them with a wide, ingratiating smile, then asked for a moment while she checked. After a moment she came back, prancing along if she were crushing cigarette butts as she went.

"Everything's as it should be, Madame Cortès. A number of purchases were made on your card at various Intermarché stores over the last three months."

"That can't be!"

"Oh, yes, madame. I checked, and—"

"But I'm telling you that—"

"Are you sure you're the only person on the account?"

Antoine! Antoine had a card too!

"My husband . . ." Joséphine managed to say. "He—"

"He must've used it and forgot to tell you," said the woman. "Because I double-checked, and the purchases were certainly made. I can give you a detailed list with dates, if you like."

"No, don't bother," said Joséphine. "Thanks very much."

The bookkeeper flashed a last bright smile and walked away, pleased to have settled the problem.

"Your husband has some nerve, Madame Cortès! He's not living with you, but he's ripping off your points. Doesn't surprise me one bit! Men are all like that, taking advantage of us. I hope you give him a real talking to the next time you see him!"

Iphigénie continued to vent her spleen against the male gender. She was still fuming when she slammed the car door and muttering long after Joséphine drove away from the store.

"I don't know how you manage to stay so calm, Madame Cortès! Haven't you noticed? Bad things never come alone, but in bursts, like gunfire. For all we know, your troubles aren't over yet."

"Are you saying that to make me feel better?"

"You should check your horoscope for today."

"That's the last thing I feel like doing! Besides, I've already hit bottom. I can't imagine what else could happen to me!"

"The day's not over!" said Iphigénie with an ironic cackle, which she followed with a trumpeted raspberry.

The party in Iphigénie's apartment was in full swing. Up until the last minute, she and Jo were arranging chairs, spreading anchovy paste on sliced bread, and opening bottles of wine, Coca-Cola, and champagne. The champagne was a gift from the tenants in Building B.

Iphigénie had guessed right: Building B was out in force, while the only representatives of Building A so far were the Mersons and their son Paul, along with Joséphine, Iris, and Zoé.

"Mommy! He's eating all the canapés!" said little Clara, pointing at Paul Merson, who was shamelessly stuffing his face.

Iphigénie rapped Paul's fingers and turned to his mother.

"Don't you feed your son, madame?"

"Paul, please behave!" said Madame Merson limply.

"They give birth to children and don't even raise them right!" groused Iphigénie, glaring at Paul.

He made a face at her, wiped his hands on his jeans, and grabbed a chicken in aspic drumstick.

One couple—he had bad teeth and she wore a cheap suit—was telling an old lady plastered in white powder about the spike in the neighborhood's real estate prices. Another was congratulating Iphigénie on her lottery win, thanking heaven for rewarding her.

"Games of chance aren't moral, but you certainly deserve it, for all the hard work you do to keep up the building!"

"Try telling Mademoiselle de Bassonnière that!" Iphigénie replied. "She's always criticizing me and trying to get me fired. But I'm not leaving, now that my apartment's become a palace!"

"Oh, come on, Mademoiselle de Bassonnière isn't as bad as all that," said an old man sporting a Legion of Honor rosette and a beret. "She defends our interests as best she can."

"She's an old witch!" exclaimed Merson. "As a matter of fact, I noticed that you weren't at the tenants meeting the other evening."

Observing the scene from an IKEA chair in a corner, Iris was feeling that she had fallen pretty low. At this moment she should have been in Philippe's handsome apartment, arranging knick-knacks to put her stamp on the place or storing her cashmeres. Instead she was in a concierge apartment listening to meaningless gossip and turning down insipid canapés and cheap champagne. The men weren't interesting, except for Monsieur Merson, who was staring hungrily at her. It was so like Joséphine to hang around such ordinary people.

That was the moment that Hervé Lefloc-Pignel chose to walk in with Gaétan and Domitille, followed by the Van den Brocks and their two children. Lefloc-Pignel was tall and smiling, the Van den

Brocks as mismatched as ever. He, wanly waving his long beetle claws. She, smiling brightly, her eyes rolling around like marbles.

The atmosphere subtly changed. Suddenly everyone seemed to be standing at attention.

Joséphine caught Zoé anxiously looking at Gaétan. So he's the one! He walked over and whispered something in Zoé's ear that made her blush and look down.

The arrival of the Building A troops put a damper on the festivities. Iphigénie felt it, and hurried to offer them some champagne. She was all smiles, and Joséphine could tell she was feeling ill at ease.

Lefloc-Pignel, who had come without his wife, congratulated Iphigénie, and so did the Van den Brocks. To Joséphine's surprise, people were soon crowding around the new arrivals as if they were royalty. Despite the complaints, money, a nice apartment, and fancy clothes all command respect. People are critical from a distance but they kowtow up close.

Sitting in her corner, Iris waited for her sister to introduce her. When Joséphine made no move to do so, she stood up and walked over to Lefloc-Pignel.

"I'm Iris Dupin," she said, a picture of shy, elegant beauty. "Joséphine's sister."

As he gallantly bowed to kiss her hand, Iris noted the charcoal alpaca suit, the blue and white striped shirt, the necktie with its heavy, gleaming knot, the discreet pocket handkerchief, the athletic torso, the understated elegance and ease of a handsome man accustomed to elegant salons. She breathed in his Armani eau de toilette and caught a whiff of Aramis on his carefully combed black hair.

When Hervé Lefloc-Pignel raised his eyes to her, Iris felt buoyed by a wave of happiness. And when he smiled, the smile was like an invitation to the dance. Joséphine observed them in fascination. He leaned toward her the way you might bend to smell a rare flower, and she yielded to him with studied reserve. Neither said a word, but each seemed magnetized by the other. They were silent, surprised, smiling. Despite the conversations swirling around them, they didn't take their eyes off each other. They swayed this way toward some, that way toward others, but tremblingly, dizzyingly returned to each other.

When Joséphine came back from her shopping trip, Iris had asked who would be at the party, and if she really had to go.

"You can do whatever you like."

"No! Tell me about it."

"It's just a neighborhood get-together," she said to cut her sister's questions short. "Neither Putin nor Obama will be there!"

Iris looked hurt.

"You don't care that I'm suffering! You don't care that Philippe has thrown me away like an old sock. You pretend to be the soul of charity but you're really just selfish!"

Joséphine stared at her in astonishment.

"I'm selfish because I don't take an interest in you, is that it?"

"I'm unhappy. I'm about to die and you go off to run errands with some—"

"What about you, Iris? Did you ask me how I was doing? No, you didn't. How about Zoé? Or Hortense? No. Have you said a word about my new apartment or my new life? No. All you're concerned about is you, you, you! Your hair, your hands, your feet, your clothes, your wrinkles, your moods, your humors, your . . ."

Joséphine was choking now, unable to control what she was saying. She was spitting out words the way a sleeping volcano erupts, blasting the old lava plugging its crater.

"The last time we had lunch together, after you postponed it three times for reasons so trivial they made me want to cry, you did nothing but talk about yourself. You bring everything back to you, all the time!"

They went down to the concierge apartment in stony silence. Zoé chatted for three, describing Du Guesclin's astounding progress: he had submitted to his first bath without complaint and hadn't even whined when they went out. Two of them helped prepare for the party, with a silent Iris sulking in her corner. She helped as little as possible, and snubbed the first guests, then the ones who followed.

Until Hervé Lefloc-Pignel appeared.

Joséphine walked over to stand by Iphigénie and whispered, "Your little party's a big success! Are you happy?"

Iphigénie handed Jo a glass of champagne and raised her own.

"To my fairy godmother's good health!"

They drank in silence, observing the ballet of people around them.

"Just the same, all this stuff will have to be cleaned up and put in the garbage cans tomorrow!"

"I'll help, if you like."

"No way! Tomorrow's Sunday, you can sleep late."

"But we'll have to straighten everything so La Bassonnière doesn't complain!"

"Oh man, why doesn't she just mind her own business!" exclaimed Iphigénie. "She's so nasty! There's some people, you really wonder why God lets them live!"

"Iphigénie, don't say that! You'll bring her bad luck!"

Zoé didn't go down to the basement that night; she stayed with her mother and her aunt. But she felt like singing and shouting. During Iphigénie's party, Gaétan had whispered, "I'm in love with you, Zoé Cortès." She had turned into a pillar of fire. He continued quietly talking to her while pretending to drink from his glass. He said really crazy things like, "I love you so much, I'm jealous of your pillows!" Then they moved apart so as not to attract attention, and she noticed how tall he was. Could he have grown since the night before? Later he came back and said, "I won't be able to come to the basement tonight, so I'll leave my sweater on your doorstep. That way, you can go to sleep thinking about me." At that, the cork in her throat popped, and she said, "I love you too," and he looked at her so seriously she almost cried. She would get the sweater from the doormat before going to bed, and sleep with it.

"What are you thinking about, darling?" asked Joséphine.

"About Du Guesclin. Can he sleep in my room?"

Iris finished the bottle of Bordeaux and rolled her eyes.

"Having a dog is so lame. You have to take care of it! Who's gonna take him out tonight, for example?"

"I will!" cried Zoé.

"No," said Joséphine. "You're not going out this late. I'll do it."

"See? It's already starting," said Iris with a sigh.

Zoé yawned, kissed her mother and aunt good night, and went off to bed.

"That good-looking neighbor of yours, what's his name again?"

"Hervé Lefloc-Pignel."

"Han'some man!" she said, raising her glass. "Ver' handsome!"

"He's married, Iris."

"Still, he's attractive. You know his wife? What's she like?"

"A fragile blonde, a bit unstable."

"Oh? They must not be a very close couple. He came without her this evening."

Joséphine began to clear the table. Iris asked if there was any more wine left. Joséphine offered to open another bottle.

"I like to drink in the evening," said Iris. "It calms me."

"You shouldn't be drinking with all those pills you're still taking."

Iris heaved a long sigh.

"Say, Jo, can I stay here at your place? I don' feel like goin' home."

Joséphine was leaning over the trash, scraping the plates before putting them in the dishwasher. If Iris stays here, that'll be the end of my closeness with Zoé. Whom I only just now reconnected with.

"Don' look so pleased, little sister!" said Iris sarcastically.

"That's not it. It's just that . . ."

Joséphine caught herself; Iris had so often had them over to her place. She turned to her sister and lied: "Our life here is so quiet, I'm afraid you'll be bored."

"Don' worry 'bout me! I'll keep mysel' busy. 'Less you really don' wan' me here."

"You should stop drinking, Iris," said Joséphine, holding a

plate. "You're talking nonsense. Think of your son. Think of Philippe."

"What about Philippe?" Iris snapped. "Who's probably gettin' it on with Miss Doolittle at this very moment! And what a funny name, Dottie Doolittle! She probably has little ringlets and dresses all in pink!"

As she measured soap powder into the dishwasher, Jo wondered if Dottie was a blonde or a brunette. "Transitory," Alexandre had called her. That meant Philippe wasn't in love, he was just fooling around. He'd find another one and then another, and another. Joséphine was only one flower in a daisy chain.

"Wonder if he cheated on me when we were together," Iris continued, draining her wineglass. "I don' think so. He loved me too much. God, how he loved me! You remember?"

She smiled into emptiness.

"And then one day it stops and you don' know why. A great love should be eternal, don' you think?"

Joséphine abruptly bowed her head, and Iris burst out laughing.

"You take everythin' so tragically, Jo. This is just the way life is. But you can't know, you've never really lived."

Noticing that her glass was empty, Iris refilled it.

"I don' have anythin' left. I'm nothin'. My life is finished, Jo. Destroyed, washed up, on the junk heap."

Joséphine saw the fear in her sister's eyes, and her anger fell away. Iris was trembling, desperately hugging her chest.

"I'm afraid, Jo, you have no idea. He said he'd give me money, but money doesn' replace everythin'."

Iris's head was lolling. She played with her hair, pulled out a strand, rolled and unrolled it, hid behind it.

"In any case, it's too late. I'm screwed. I don' know how to do anything. And I'll wind up all alone."

Joséphine gave her a long look, trying to gauge how much sincerity there was in that fear. At her feet, Du Guesclin yawned widely. She thought of the real Du Guesclin's motto: "Let valor grant what appearance has denied." *She's dreaming of a ready-made solution, looking for ready-to-wear happiness. She's the princess waiting for the prince, who'll take care of everything, and she won't have to lift a finger. She's lazy and weak.*

"Come on, Iris, you need to get some sleep."

"You'll be there, won' you, Jo?" she said, slurring her words. "You won' leave me?"

Iris was slumped over the kitchen table, limply fumbling for her glass. Joséphine took her by the arm, stood her up, and gently led her to Hortense's room. She stretched her out on the bed, undressed her, took off her shoes, and got her under the covers.

"You'll leave the hallway light on, won' you?"

"I'll leave it on."

"You know what I'd like? I'd like somethin' really big. A big love, like in those Middle Ages of yours, a gallant knight to carry me off and protect me. Life's too hard. It scares me . . ."

Iris rambled for another few moments, then rolled on her side and fell deeply asleep. In moments, Joséphine heard her snoring.

She took refuge in the living room, stretching out on a sofa and wedging a cushion behind her back. *Events are all mixed up in my head. I have to take things one at a time. Philippe, Luca, Antoine,* she thought with a sad smile. *Three men, three lies. Three ghosts haunting my life.*

Closing her eyes, she saw the three phantoms dancing by

under her eyelids. Then the round stopped, and Philippe's figure emerged. In her dream his dark eyes shone, she saw the glowing tip of his cigar, smelled the smoke as he blew first one, then a second smoke ring, rounding his mouth. Then he was on Dottie Doolittle's arm, taking her by the coat collar, pressing her against an oven in his kitchen and kissing her, setting his warm, soft lips on hers. Joséphine felt a cold pain gnawing at the pit of her stomach that grew and grew. She put her hands on her body to keep the pain from spreading.

Feeling alone and very unhappy, she laid her head on the armrest and wept quietly into her sleeve. She was crying steady little sobs when she suddenly started hearing an echo of her sobs, and a moaning that matched her own.

Raising her head, she saw Du Guesclin. He was lying with his feet together and his head back, and he was howling at the ceiling. He played the howl like a musical saw, amplifying and softening it, repeating it, his eyes closed in a siren of despair. Joséphine jumped up and hugged him, kissing him all over, muttering "Du Guesclin! Du Guesclin!" Eventually, she calmed down and just stroked him, the two of them looking at each other, surprised by her flood of tears.

"What are you, really? You're not a dog, you're a person!"

He felt warm under her fingers, and harder than a concrete wall. His paws were muscular and strong. He got to his feet and looked up at her.

"That's right, you haven't been out yet! You're really a remarkable dog. Want to go?"

He wagged his hindquarters. She smiled, reflecting that Du Guesclin would never be able to wag his tail, that no one could tell if he was happy or not. *I should buy a leash,* she thought, then changed her mind. *I don't need a leash. He's never going to leave me. I can tell just by looking at him.*

He was hopping from foot to foot, waiting for her to get ready to go.

When she came back upstairs, she opened Zoé's bedroom door and Du Guesclin went to lie down at the foot of the bed. He circled his cushion a few times, sniffing it, then flopped down with a sigh.

Zoé had something woolen wrapped around her shoulders. Joséphine walked over, saw that it was a sweater, and touched it. Seeing her daughter's happy face and the smile on her lips, she understood that it was Gaétan's sweater.

"Don't be like me," she whispered. "Don't pass love by, thinking that you're so unused to it that you don't recognize it."

She blew on Zoé's warm forehead, on her cheeks, and on the damp strands of hair on her neck.

"Sleep, my beauty, my love. Mommy's here to love you and protect you."

"Mommy," mumbled Zoé in her sleep. "I'm so happy. . . . He said he loves me, Mommy . . . loves me . . ."

Joséphine leaned close to catch what her dreaming daughter was saying.

"He gave me his sweater. . . . I think I may have zsa zsa zsu after all."

Zoé shuddered a little and sank deeper into sleep. Joséphine pulled up the covers, straightened the sweater, and quietly left the room. Out in the hallway, she leaned against the wall. *This is what happiness is,* she told herself, *getting my little daughter's*

love back, touching her, blowing on her fingers, listening to her
breath, holding onto this moment, making it last, entering into it,
savoring it.

Junior was one, and decided it was time to strike out on his own.
He'd waited long enough.

He stood up, took a few hesitant steps, and fell back on his
diapered butt. He tried again, and kept trying until he was able
to walk across his room without difficulty. Putting one foot in
front of the other wasn't that hard, and it made his life a lot easier.
He was starting to wear out his elbows and knees with crawling.

He looked up at the bedroom door handle. Why in the world
had they locked him in? Everything in the household was going
to hell. His mother lay prostrate in bed. His father was in despair,
having scratched his skull raw. The apartment was so quiet, you
could hear a pin drop. No more visitors, no drunken lunches, no
cigar smells to tickle his nose, no friendly tussles of Dad grabbing
Mom and her yielding with that throaty laugh he liked so much.
Nothing. Deep silence, people stumbling about like corpses,
choked sobs in tight throats.

How happy Marcel and Josiane had been when he was born!
"It's a miracle!" they shouted. They lit candles, said prayers, were
beside themselves with happiness. Marcel especially. He couldn't
get over it. Held up the baby like a trophy, showed him off, sat him
on a corner of his desk and told him all about business. Junior found
it fascinating. *The Old Man was as clever as a fox, selling his junk all*
over the world. You should hear him, bullshitting his customers!

Junior was delighted when Marcel took him to the office. He
couldn't really participate, because he was still trapped in this

inarticulate, clumsy baby body, but he thrashed around in his chair, sending him signals. Sometimes Marcel understood. He would look at Junior as if he were seeing things, but he listened. He spoke to him in Chinese and English, read him profit and loss statements, financial analyses, and white papers. Junior had no complaints. The Old Man spoiled him. He at least understood that he was different, and far from being troubled, was thrilled.

Today was Sunday, May 24. Junior had been walking for two weeks and was itching to get out of his room. But though he listened for some sound from the apartment, he didn't hear anything. The silence made him uneasy. Where was his father? What was his mother up to? Why didn't anyone come for him? His stomach was rumbling, and he wouldn't mind a little lunch.

Junior decided to take action. He pushed a chair over so he could reach the door handle and get out. He opened the door, headed down the hallway, and glanced into the living room and the laundry. Seeing no one, he tottered to his mother's bedroom, and what he saw there made him scream. A long scream burst from his chest that shattered Josiane's ears, seemingly waking her from a dream.

She had set a chair out on their sixth-floor balcony and was standing on it. She was wearing an ankle-length white nightgown and stood swaying, irresistibly drawn to the void. Eyed closed and lips pale, she was clutching a photo of her man and her son to her heart.

As if suddenly roused from lethargy, Josiane opened her eyes to see her baby standing at her feet. He was watching her and screaming, and holding out his tiny hand.

"Arrgh!" he yelled, stepping between her and the emptiness.

"Junior?" she blurted, recognizing him. "You know how to walk? I never realized!"

"Grumphgrumph," he said, inwardly cursing the baby skin he was trapped in.

"What happened?" she asked, rubbing her brow. "What am I doing here?"

She looked down at the chair and the void beyond, and nearly fell. Straightening up, arms outstretched, she tumbled onto her son, who had put out his little arms to catch her.

The two of them crashed to the floor and rolled across the parquet. The thud of their falling bodies brought a cavalcade of footsteps, and shouts of, "Oh my God! I don't believe it!" Marcel arrived, red-faced and disheveled. There were Josiane and Junior, looking pale and bruised! He wrung his hands, dropping the bag of warm croissants he'd gotten them as a treat.

Junior snagged one of the croissants and stuffed it in his mouth. He was famished.

On that same Sunday, Hortense was having brunch at Fortnum & Mason with Nicholas Bergson, Liberty's artistic director. She liked Liberty, a big department store whose style was both old-fashioned and avant-garde. Its entrance on Regent Street looked like an old Alsatian house. Hortense often spent time there, and it was while wandering the aisles, taking notes and pictures of pertinent details, that she met Nicholas. He was very attractive, if you overlooked how short he was. He was funny, had a new idea every minute, and had that intriguing English way of always putting distance between himself and other people.

They were discussing Hortense's end-of-year project, the

portfolio she would present in order to get accepted into the next class. Of a thousand students, only seventy would go on. As her theme, she had chosen "Sex is about to be slow," an original and ambitious choice. She was sure nobody else would come up with the same idea, but wasn't sure she could illustrate it. In addition to presenting a sketchbook, she had to create a runway show with six outfits. She had six ensembles to draw and execute and then just a quarter of an hour on a catwalk to present them. She was focusing on details, the details that would infiltrate seduction into minutia, creating the setting for a slow blossoming of sexual desire: an all-black dress closed with an elaborate knot; a seemingly bare, trompe-l'oeil back; a shadow across a cheek; a veil hiding a smoldering eye; a shoe buckle on an arched heel. Nicholas would be able to help her. *He really isn't that short,* she decided. *He just has a long torso. A very long torso.*

He had invited Hortense to her favorite tea salon—the one on the fourth floor at Fortnum & Mason—but her mind was elsewhere. *This is the third time in a row Gary has turned me down for Sunday brunch.* The fact that he'd refused didn't bother her so much as the polite tone he had used. Lurking behind politeness is often reserve, embarrassment, a hidden secret. For Gary and Hortense these Sunday brunches were a ritual. *Something very important must be going on for him to ditch me. Something . . . or someone.* That second possibility was something Hortense didn't like at all.

She wrinkled her nose, and Nicholas thought she was disagreeing with him.

"No, I assure you," he said. "Black and desire go so well together that you must create an ensemble that's black from head to foot."

"You're probably right," said Hortense taking a bite of scone and a sip of Lapsang souchong tea, with that delicious hint of the cedar it had been dried on.

How long had it been since she'd seen Gary? It must have been the night she'd invited him to the restaurant and they'd walked around London by night. They hadn't seen each other since she moved in with Li May. She'd been very busy with the move, her classes, the year ending, and organizing her runway show. She had skipped three or four Sundays, and when she called, eager to make up for lost time, Gary was polite. How awful! When had they ever been polite with each other? One thing she liked about knowing him was being able to share her private thoughts without being embarrassed. And now he was becoming polite!

She bit the rim of her teacup. Nicholas hadn't noticed anything.

There must be a girl involved, she thought, setting down her cup. *Gary's independent, he marches to the beat of his own drum and I love that about him. But I don't like to feel that he's slipping away from me. I don't like it when men are too distant but I don't like it when they are too close. . . . Phew! It's all too complicated!*

"And don't worry about finding models," Nicholas was saying. "I'll get you six of the slowest and sexiest ones around. I can think of three right off the top of my head."

"But I can't afford to pay them," said Hortense, relieved to have her pointless daydreams interrupted by this generous offer.

"Who's talking about paying? They'll do it for free. Saint Martins is a prestigious school, and the show will attract everyone who is anybody in fashion and the media. The girls will come running."

It was bound to happen, she thought, her attention wandering. *He's as handsome as a prince from* The Arabian Nights, *smart, witty, rich, cultivated. He's the catch all the girls dream of—and*

I've missed my chance! I do not want Gary to fall in love with another girl! It must have taken him by surprise. That's why he was polite and distant, he didn't know how to tell me about it. Hortense felt like she had the weight of the world's sorrow—or what she imagined the world's sorrow to be—on her shoulders. *No!* she thought. *That's not like him. Either he was pursuing one of his many slutty conquests, and she was taking up all his time, or he had decided to lock himself in to read* War and Peace *from cover to cover, the way he did once a year.*

"Sex is about to be slow but nobody is slow today, because if you want to survive you have to be fast." That would be Hortense's parting shot. She could end her show with one of the models collapsing, apparently dead, while the others started walking very quickly, relegating slow desire to the subplot of a second-rate novel. Not a bad idea.

It was when she and Nicholas were waiting for the fourth-floor elevator that the real horror happened.

Hortense was standing off to one side, swinging her new purse. She figured it cost 600 or 700 pounds. Nicholas had given it to her so casually she wondered if he hadn't nicked it from a shipping container and slipped it under his arm when he left the store.

He was on the phone, saying, "No, no!" while she practiced shifting the purse from one hand to the other, putting it first under her right arm, then her left, admiring her reflection in the mirror as she twirled and spun, when the door suddenly opened and a gorgeous woman stepped out of the elevator.

She was one of those creatures so elegant that people stopped in the street to stare. She was wearing a tight black dress, ballet flats, long black gloves, and a huge pair of sunglasses that accented a charming upturned nose and a delicate red mouth. An enigmatic beauty, an intoxicating emanation of femininity. Hortense's jaw dropped. To steal her secrets, she was prepared to follow this ravishing creature to the ends of the earth.

She turned to gaze after the apparition, and when she turned back to the elevator, Nicholas was holding the door open, and a man inside was hastily picking up the contents of a bag that had spilled. She could hear him saying, "Sorry. . . . Thanks a lot."

I wonder what he looks like, to be with that beautiful woman?

He looked like Gary.

Seeing Hortense, he jerked back as if he'd been splattered with boiling pitch.

"Are you coming, Gary love?" the beautiful creature called.

Hortense closed her eyes so as not to hear.

"Coming!" he said, giving Hortense a peck on the cheek. "We'll talk, okay?"

She opened her eyes. This was a nightmare.

"Shall we go?" asked Nicholas, who had finished his phone call.

Hortense stepped into the elevator and slumped against the wall. She was sure the elevator would go straight down to Hell.

"Care to make a jaunt to Camden?" Nicholas was asking. "Last time, I found a pair of Dior cardigans for ten pounds. A real bargain!"

Hortense looked him over. *His torso really is too long,* she thought, drawing closer. *But he has beautiful eyes and an appealing mouth. Looks a little like a pirate. A pirate . . . That's seductive, intriguing, dangerous. Maybe if I focus on the pirate part . . .*

"I love you," she said.

"Do you really mean that?"

"No. I just wanted to see how it felt. I've never said it to anyone."

"Ah," he said, feeling disappointed. "I thought it was a little—"

"A little too soon. You're right."

She took his arm and they walked out to Regent Street.

Suddenly a thought hit her.

"She's old!"

"Who is?"

"That woman in the elevator, she's old!"

"Come now, don't exaggerate. She's Charlotte Bradsburry, Lord Bradsburry's daughter. Claims to be twenty-six, but she's actually twenty-nine."

"A hag!"

"An icon, my dear. An icon of the London scene! She has a degree from Cambridge, a scholarly interest in literature, follows everything that's happening in art and music. Occasional philanthropist, and generous, to boot. She has a reputation for spotting talent. She lends her time and her connections to young unknowns, and they quickly become famous."

"Twenty-nine! It's time she croaked."

"She's not only beautiful, she's the editor in chief of *The Nerve*. You know, the magazine that—"

"*The Nerve!*" moaned Hortense. "I am so screwed!"

"Why, darling?"

Nicholas had hailed a taxi, and it stood waiting for them.

"Because I intend to take her place!"

On that same Sunday, May 24, Joséphine decided to take a midafternoon break. She'd been working all day on the history of the Carmes monks' striped habits for her *habilitation* thesis and decided to take Du Guesclin for a walk.

For her part, Iris spent the afternoon lying on the living room sofa. She watched television and gossiped, the phone wedged between her chin and shoulder, while putting cream on her hands and feet. *She's going to get grease stains on my sofa,* Joséphine groused when she passed Iris the first time, on her way to the kitchen make a cup of tea. The second time she passed, Iris was still on the phone and still watching television—Michel Drucker was interviewing Céline Dion. This time she was rubbing her forearms. By Joséphine's third passage, Iris had changed position and was doing three things at once: watching TV, chatting on the phone, and doing a back bend to tighten her butt.

Zoé had asked her mother's permission to go to the movies. "I'll be back in time for dinner, I promise," she said. "I've already done all my homework for Monday, Tuesday, and Wednesday." Joséphine was wondering when she would take the time to explain why she had been so resentful and upset with her all this time. Zoé had changed her clothes six times in a row, bursting into her mother's bedroom asking, "What you think of this? Does it make my ass look big?" and "With these, you can't see my fat thighs," and "Mommy, does this look better with boots or flats?" and "Should I wear my hair up or down?"

Zoé kept coming in and out of Jo's room. She began her question in the hallway, ended it in front of her mother, then returned with a new outfit and a new question. Feeling torn between the thirteenth and the twenty-first centuries, Joséphine was having trouble focusing on her work. Discrimination because of the striped robes was a good story to illustrate her chapter on colors.

"Just wear a white T-shirt," she advised Zoé. "It flatters your complexion, and you can wear it with anything."

"Ah . . ." said Zoé, unconvinced.

She went off to try a new outfit.

Sprawled at Jo's feet, Du Guesclin dozed. She closed her books, pinched her nostrils—a sure sign of fatigue, with her—and decided that some fresh air would do her good.

She got up, put on a jacket, and walked through the living room with a gesture to Iris to say she was going out. Her sister shifted the telephone slightly in response, then resumed her conversation.

Joséphine slammed the door and stormed down the stairs with Du Guesclin.

She was enraged, fury was filling her black as coal smoke. She was so angry, she was practically choking. *Am I going to have to stay in my room to have some peace and quiet in my own apartment? Tiptoeing to the kitchen to get myself some tea so as not to disturb Iris's chats?* The anger grew; her brain was practically smoking. That morning, Iris hadn't lifted a finger to set or clear the breakfast table. Instead, she'd asked for toast—just lightly toasted, not burned to a crisp, please—and did they happen to have any of that good Hédiard honey?

Joséphine crossed the boulevard and entered the park. *Hm, I didn't see Luca's billboard. I must've passed it without noticing.* It felt strange to still be saying "Luca" instead of "Vittorio." Kicking an old tennis ball aside, she picked up her pace.

Nearby, Du Guesclin was coming and going. He trotted along, his muzzle at ground level, breathing in the smells, his nose checking on the other quadrupeds that had gone before him. He moved ahead, in large or small circles, but always came back to Joséphine, the center of his life.

Daylight revealed the scars on his flank, a sickly pink left by severe burns. Two black stripes on his muzzle gave him a Zorro mask. He wandered away, sniffed another dog, sprinkled a bush or a tree branch, went off, and then came back to throw himself at Joséphine's feet, joyously celebrating their reunion after such a long separation.

"Du Guesclin, stop it! You're going to trip me!"

He gazed up at her adoringly as Jo stroked his muzzle from his nose to his ears. He took three steps leaning on her, paws tangled in her feet, broad shoulders pressing against her thighs, then went exploring again, to catch a falling leaf. He would shoot off so fast it almost frightened her, then stop dead, suddenly aware of some prey to be sniffed out.

In the distance, Joséphine saw Lefloc-Pignel and Van den Brock walking around the lake. They looked like two friends out for a walk on a Sunday afternoon, away from their wives and children, discussing serious things. She would have liked to know what they talked about. They were both wearing red sweaters on their shoulders and looked like two brothers dressed by their mother. They looked preoccupied and were shaking their heads. They seemed to be disagreeing about something. Was it the stock market? Investments? Antoine never had any luck in the market. Every time he invested in a stock that promised quick and comfortable returns, the stock "took a tumble," as he put it. He once invested all his savings in the Eurotunnel, and that time he just said, "It took a real tumble." *And now he's stealing my Intermarché reward points. Is he a bum carrying plastic bags and living in the Metro?*

And what about Dottie Doolittle? Does she really exist or did Iris invent her to justify her separation from Philippe? She talks nonsense, sometimes. It's terrible to admit that your husband has left you because of who you are. It's easier to say that he's leaving you for someone else. I should go see him. I won't ask any questions, just sit down and look him in the eye.

She could go to London . . .

My English publisher wants to meet me. That's a thought; I could use that as an excuse. Going for a walk or a run always gave Jo ideas. Glancing at her watch, she decided it was time to go home.

Iphigénie was about to empty her wastebaskets, and Joséphine offered to help.

"We can just leave the stuff by the door to the garbage room."

"All right," said Jo. "Du Guesclin! Come back here right now!"

He had shot like an arrow into the courtyard and was furiously sniffing at the door to the garbage room.

"What in the world is he up to?" asked Joséphine in surprise.

Now he was scratching at the door, and trying to push it open with his muzzle.

Joséphine picked up a bag full of paper plates and plastic glasses, and headed for the garbage room. Behind her, Iphigénie was dragging two big trash bags.

The moment they opened the door to the garbage room, Du Guesclin bolted inside, his nose to the ground and claws skittering on the concrete. It was fetid and oppressively warm inside. A smell of rotting meat caught Joséphine by the throat.

"What can he be looking for?" she asked, holding her nose. "It really stinks in here. I'm going to wind up thinking La Bassonnière is right!"

She put her hand to her mouth, on the verge of throwing up.

"Du Guesclin?" she muttered, feeling queasy.

"He must've spotted an old sausage," said Iphigénie.

The smell was all-pervasive. Du Guesclin had seized a corner of an old, rolled-up carpet with his teeth, and was pulling it away from the wall. His back arched, he was straining to drag it toward the door.

"He wants to show us something," said Iphigénie.

"I think I'm gonna puke."

"Yes! Look there, behind the . . ."

They came closer, pushed a couple of big garbage cans out of the way, and stared at the ground. What they saw horrified them: a pale woman's arm protruding from the dirty carpet.

"Iphigéniiiiie!" screamed Joséphine.

"Don't move, Madame Cortès! Maybe it's a ghost!"

"No, Iphigénie, it's a body!"

The arm sticking out seemed to be waving for help.

"We should call the police! Stay here, I'll go make the call."

"No! I'm coming with you." said Joséphine her teeth chattering.

Du Guesclin kept tugging on the carpet. His face covered with foam and spittle, he now uncovered a pale, grayish face under a hank of sticky black hair.

"Mademoiselle de Bassonnière!" yelped Iphigénie. *"She's been—"*

Joséphine leaned against the wall so as not to collapse. The terrified women stared at each other, unable to move, as if the corpse was ordering them to stay near her.

"—killed," said Jo.

"It sure looks that way."

They stood stock-still, staring at the body's decomposing,

grimacing face. Iphigénie recovered first, blowing her signature raspberry.

"Well, she looks as mean as ever!"

The police, in the person of Capitaine Gallois and two uniformed officers, showed up quickly. They set up a security perimeter and surrounded the garbage room with yellow crime tape. Gallois walked over to the body, knelt down, and studied it. Then she started speaking aloud, enunciating clearly, like a student reciting a lesson. "One can observe that the process of putrefaction has already begun, so death must have occurred some forty-eight hours ago." She lifted de Bassonnière's nightgown and ran her fingers over a black mark on the stomach. "Abdominal stain, caused by gas forming under the skin. The skin turns black but remains supple and slightly swollen. The body turns yellowish." Lowering the nightgown, she said, "She probably died Friday evening or Friday night."

Gallois noticed flies above the body and gently waved them away. Then she called the prosecutor and the medical examiner.

Lips pursed, the imperturbable captain studied the body lying at her feet. Nothing in her face betrayed the least sign of horror, disgust, or surprise. In answer to her questions, Joséphine and Iphigénie told her how they had found the body, described the party in the concierge apartment, Mademoiselle de Bassonnière's missing it—"No surprise, everybody in the building hated her!" Iphigénie couldn't help saying—the garbage cans, the role played by Du Guesclin.

"How long have you had the dog?" asked Gallois.

"I found him in the street yesterday morning."

Jo was immediately sorry she'd said "found," tried to take

the word back, stammered guiltily. She didn't like the way Gallois talked to her. She projected a dull animosity that Jo didn't understand. She noticed a brooch hidden under the collar of the woman's blouse, a heart with an arrow through it.

"Do you have something to say to me?" asked the captain abruptly.

"No, I was just looking at your brooch, and—"

"No personal comments, please."

The medical examiner arrived, followed by a forensic photographer. The examiner took the temperature of the body—88 degrees Fahrenheit—noted the external injuries, measured the stab wounds, and called for an autopsy. Then he went to speak with the captain. Joséphine caught snatches of their conversation: ". . . wear on the shoes?" ". . . resistance?" ". . . surprised by the attacker?" ". . . think the body was dragged in, or was she killed here?" Meanwhile the forensic photographer, crouched at the victim's feet, took pictures from every possible angle.

"We'll need to question the neighbors," said Gallois.

"It's probably an assault, and the crime must have been committed in the middle of the night, late Friday or early Saturday, when honest folks are asleep."

"The building has a keypad," she remarked. "People can't just come and go as they please."

"Oh, you know, those codes . . ." The medical examiner gestured dismissively. "They only reassure the naive. If somebody wants to get in, they'll manage, unfortunately."

Then the prosecutor arrived, a thin blond man with a crew cut. He introduced himself, shook hands with his colleagues, then listened to their respective conclusions. He bent to look the body over, talked with the medical examiner, and seconded the call for an autopsy.

"Size of the blade, strength of the blows, depth of the wounds, signs of bruising, strangulation . . ."

A man accustomed to such scenes, he ticked off the various points to be covered with neither passion nor haste.

"Did you notice if the rubber carpet pad was soft or hard?" he asked. "Did it leave any marks on the body?"

The doctor answered that the pad was soft and flexible.

"Any fingerprints?"

"Not on the pad. Still too soon for the body."

"How about footprints in the garbage room?"

"No sign of any. The killer must've been wearing smooth soles, or wrapped his feet in plastic bags."

"And you're sure there are no fingerprints?"

"None. Used rubber gloves, probably."

"Send me the photos as soon as they're ready," said the prosecutor. "We'll start by questioning the neighbors, and draw up a profile of the victim. See if she had enemies or romantic problems, whether she'd ever been attacked or had a record. You know, the usual routine."

He gave a sign to the captain, and they went off together to a corner of the courtyard. The prosecutor's eyes lit on Joséphine. Gallois was probably telling him that she had been attacked six months earlier and had waited nearly a week before coming to the station to report the incident.

Why are they looking me like that? They can't think I'm involved, can they? Jo once again had a terrible feeling of guilt.

Under the prosecutor's steely gaze, she wanted to shout, "But I didn't do anything!"

Then she thought of Zoé and asked if she could go upstairs to her.

"Not before you've been questioned," said Gallois.

They started with Iphigénie, and then it was Jo's turn. As the captain took notes, she described the Friday co-op meeting and the confrontations with Merson, Lefloc-Pignel, and Van den Brock. She added what Merson had told her about the two times de Bassonnière had been assaulted, but made it clear that she hadn't witnessed the events herself. She saw Gallois write *Ask M. Merson* in her notebook.

"Can I go upstairs now? My daughter's waiting for me at home."

Gallois let her go, but only after asking on what floor and in what part of the building she lived, and telling her to stop by the station to sign her deposition.

"Oh, I nearly forgot," said the captain, raising her voice. "Where were you Friday night?

"At home, why?"

"I'm asking the questions here."

"I came back from the co-op meeting with Monsieur Lefloc-Pignel around nine o'clock, and I stayed home."

"Was your daughter with you?"

"No, she was down in the basement with other children from the building. In the Mersons' storage area. She must've come upstairs around midnight."

"Around midnight, you say. You're not sure?"

"I didn't check the time."

"You don't happen to remember something you might have watched on television or listened to on the radio?"

"No, I don't. Will that be all?"

"For the time being."

There's something about me she just doesn't like, thought Joséphine, as she waited for the elevator.

Zoé wasn't home yet, and Iris was still lying on the sofa in front of the TV, the phone wedged between her ear and her shoulder.

On that Sunday May 24, Gaétan and Zoé parted at the entrance to the square in front of the building. "My father would kill me if he saw us!" he said. "You go in by the front, I'll go in by the back." They kissed one last time, tore themselves from each other's arms, and then walked away backward so as to keep looking at each other for as long as possible.

I'm so happy! Zoé said to herself as she crossed the square's lawn, breathing in the ground's damp, earthy smell. *Everything is beautiful, everything smells good. There's nothing better than love.*

Love makes you want to bounce around and kiss everybody. Beautiful things become very beautiful, and shitty things become who cares? I really don't care that Mom kissed Philippe. After all, maybe she's in love too. Maybe she's got a balloon in her heart, like I do.

I'm not mad anymore because I'm in love! I have the feeling that life is going to be a long road full of laughs and kisses, sniffing his sweaters and making plans. We'll have lots of children, and we'll let them do whatever they like. Not like Gaétan's father. He seems really weird. The kids aren't allowed to have friends over. They aren't allowed to talk at the table. They have to raise their hand and wait for permission to speak. Watching television and listening to the

radio are forbidden. Sometimes in the evening, he'll want every-
thing to be white: clothes, food, tablecloth, napkins, the kids' paja-
mas. Other days it'll be green and they'll eat spinach and broccoli,
green lasagna and kiwi. Gaétan's mother is so unhappy, she's con-
stantly scratching her arms. They're all afraid she's gonna do some-
thing stupid like cut her wrists or jump out the window. And
Gaétan hasn't told me everything. He'll start to say something, and
then he'll shut up. A very odd family! 'Course, all families are odd,
even mine. I have a mom who kisses her brother-in-law in the kitchen
on Christmas Eve!

When Zoé saw the three police cars pulled up outside their
building, she thought she was going to die. *Something's happened*
to Mommy!

She raced to the door and then into the building. Seeing the
crowd gathered in the courtyard, she stopped dead. *Oh, my God,*
Mommy jumped out the window! She was sad because I didn't tell
her everything that was happening, in detail. She's always hungry
for details. Use the wrong word, and tears come to her eyes. I'll never
hide anything from her again, I'll never make her unhappy, I prom-
ise I'll tell her everything if she'll just stand up and not die!

From the back, Zoé saw Monsieur Lefloc-Pignel talking with
a blond man with a crew cut. Monsieur Van den Brock was with
a stern-looking policewoman with dark hair. Monsieur Merson
was chatting with Iphigénie.

"When did they find her?" asked Merson.

"I already told you twice! You aren't listening! Madame Cortès and I found her rolled up in the carpet. Actually, the dog did;
he smelled her."

"Do they have an idea who might've done it?"

"Hey, I don't work for the police! Just ask them!"

Zoé heaved a huge sigh of relief. *Mommy isn't dead!* She looked around for Gaétan, but didn't see him. He must've slipped in and gone upstairs already.

She raced up the stairs and through the front door, passed the living room where Iris lay talking on the phone, and burst into her mother's bedroom.

"Mommy! You're alive!"

Zoé ran to hug her mother, burying her nose in her chest, seeking her smell.

"I was so afraid! I thought the cops were here for you!"

"For me, why?" Jo whispered, rocking her.

"I thought that you . . ."

"That I was dead?"

"Yes . . . Oh, Mommy!"

The two of them burst into tears, hugging the breath out of each other.

"Life is so complicated sometimes," Zoé finally said. "And sometimes so simple. It's hard to figure out." She sniffled, and wiped her nose on her mother's shoulder. "I was really angry when I saw you kissing Philippe."

"That's why we have to talk, lovey. Always. Otherwise the misunderstandings pile up, and we stop understanding each other. We stop listening. Do you want me to tell you about Philippe?"

"I think I know."

"Because of Gaétan?"

Zoé turned beet red.

"We don't always choose things," Joséphine continued. "Sometimes love comes crashing down and knocks you out. I did everything I could to avoid Philippe."

Zoé took a strand of her mother's hair and wrapped it around her finger as Jo continued. "In the kitchen that evening, I didn't expect . . . It was the first time, Zoé, I promise. And the last, for that matter."

"Are you afraid to hurt Iris?"

Joséphine nodded.

"And you haven't seen him since?"

"No."

"And does that hurt?"

"Yes," said Jo, sighing. "It hurts."

"And Iris, does she know?"

"I think she suspects, but she doesn't really know. She thinks that I'm secretly in love with him, but he's ignoring me. She can't imagine that he might fall for me."

"Anyway, with Iris it's always all about her."

"Don't say that, darling. She's your aunt and she's going through a hard time."

"Stop always forgiving her, Mommy! You're too nice!" Zoé paused. Then as if coming back to reality, she asked, "What were all those people doing in the courtyard?

"It's Mademoiselle de Bassonnière. They found her body in the garbage room."

"Oh, did she have a heart attack?"

"No, they think she was killed."

"Wow! A crime in our building! It's gonna be in the newspapers!"

"Is that all you have to say?"

"I didn't like her, and I'm not gonna pretend. She always looked at me as like I had parsley growing out of my nose!"

The next day, Joséphine had to go to the station to sign her deposition. The building's tenants had all been called in, one after another, to say exactly what they were doing the night of the crime. Capitaine Gallois handed Joséphine her statement from the day before to sign. As she was reading it, the captain got a phone call. The man on the line, who must have been a superior, had a loud voice, and Jo couldn't help overhearing.

"I'm in the back of beyond in the seventy-seventh"—meaning Seine et Marne—"but I'll send a team to take over the case. Have you finished interviewing the witnesses?"

Gallois said that she had.

"There's been a new development," he said. "The victim was the niece of a former Paris police commissioner. So this is a big deal. We can't afford any screw-ups. Follow procedure to the letter, and I'll relieve you as soon as I can."

Gallois hung up, looking preoccupied. After a long silence, which she filled by bending and straightening some paper clips, she asked, "Did you walk your dog on Friday night?"

I must have, thought Jo, and the idea rattled her. It meant that when she took Du Guesclin out she would have walked past the garbage room, maybe even passed the killer. She sat there for a few seconds under Gallois's stern gaze, trying to remember. She hesitated, her mouth open and her fingers knitting an invisible strand of wool. As she concentrated, she put her hands on her knees to keep their fidgeting from making her look so guilty.

"Try to remember, Madame Cortès, it's important. The

murder was committed Friday evening and the body was found Sunday evening. You must have gone out with your dog on the evening of the crime. Didn't you hear or notice anything?"

Jo's hands had resumed their nervous knitting, and she forced them to lie still while she focused on what happened had Friday evening. She had left the co-op meeting and walked home with Lefloc-Pignel. They had talked along the way. . . . He had told her about his childhood, being abandoned on that Normandy road, the print shop and. . . . Suddenly Joséphine relaxed and smiled.

"I only got Du Guesclin on Saturday morning!" she cried, relieved at dodging the long shadow of prison bars. "How stupid of me!"

The captain looked disappointed. She read Joséphine's signed statement one last time and said that she could go. She would be called back if she was needed.

Monsieur and Madame Van den Brock were waiting out in the hallway.

"Good luck!" Joséphine whispered. "She's tough!"

"I know," said Monsieur Van den Brock with a sigh. "They already questioned us this morning, and they've asked to see us again."

"I really wonder why they're having us come back," said Madame Van den Brock. "It's that policewoman, especially. She has something against us."

Joséphine stepped out into the street, feeling shaken. She walked across to a café and took a seat on the terrace. Lefloc-Pignel was sitting three tables farther on, writing in a notebook, and he waved her over.

He was wearing a handsome bottle-green linen jacket with a perfectly knotted green-and-black striped tie.

"So how was the interrogation?" he asked with a look of amusement.

"Painful," breathed Joséphine. "I'm going to wind up thinking that I killed her!"

"Ah, you too!"

"That woman has a way of asking questions that chills my blood."

"She's not very friendly, that's for sure," said Lefloc-Pignel. "She spoke to me in a way that was . . . abrupt, let's say. It's unacceptable."

"She must suspect all of us," said Joséphine with a sigh, relieved to find that she wasn't the only one to have been mistreated.

"Just because she was killed in the building doesn't necessarily mean the killer is one of us! Monsieur and Madame Merson, who went in before I did, came out furious. I'm anxious to hear the reactions of the Van den Brocks. They're being grilled right now, and I promised I would wait for them. We have to stick together and refuse to be treated this way. It's a scandal!"

Lefloc-Pignel's jaws were clenched in an angry snarl.

Just then, the waiter came over to take their orders.

"A mint cooler," said Lefloc-Pignel.

"The same for me," said Jo.

"Do you have an alibi?" she asked. "Because I don't. I was home alone, which doesn't help me much."

"When we parted Friday evening I stopped by to see the Van den Brocks. I was still furious at Mademoiselle de Bassonnière's behavior. We were up until midnight, talking about that . . .

shrew. About the outrageous way she attacks us at every meeting. It's getting worse and worse. Or rather it was, because it's over now, thank God. But that night, I remember that Hervé was even considering filing a complaint."

"So Monsieur Van den Brock's first name is Hervé, like yours?"

He flushed, as if he'd been caught at an intimate moment.

"Yes, it is."

That's odd, thought Joséphine. *It's not a common first name. Before this I didn't know any Hervés, and now I know two of them!*

When the waiter brought the drinks, Lefloc-Pignel paid, and Joséphine thanked him. She was feeling better, having talked to him. He was taking matters in hand. He would protect her. She was part of a new family, and for the first time she found herself liking her neighborhood, her building, and her fellow tenants.

"Thank you," she murmured. "I feel better, talking with you." In the same confidential mode, she added, "It's hard to be a woman alone. You have to be strong, energetic, and decisive, and that's not really me. I'm rather slow. Very slow, actually."

"Like a little turtle?" he suggested, looking at her kindly. "I love turtles," he continued in a low voice. "They're very affectionate animals, you know, very faithful. They're really worth your while."

"Thank you," she said, smiling. "I'll take it as a compliment."

"I was given a turtle one day when I was little boy. She was my best friend, my confidante. I took her everywhere with me. Turtles live a long time, unless they have an accident . . ."

He stumbled on the word *accident.*

Lefloc-Pignel watched as Joséphine gracefully raised her glass and sipped her mint drink.

"You're very touching," he said quietly. "It makes one want to protect you."

He spoke without boasting, in a gentle, affectionate tone in which she detected no hint of seduction. She raised her head, smiled at him, and confidently suggested, "So, can we call each other by our first names now?"

Lefloc-Pignel jerked back slightly and turned pale, stammering, "No, I don't think so." He turned away, as if to talk to someone who wasn't there, put his hands on the table, then pulled them back and set them on his knees.

Startled, Joséphine straightened in her chair and apologized profusely. She didn't understand why his attitude had changed so suddenly. "I didn't mean to . . . I didn't mean to force you. . . . It was just so that we would become friends. I'm so clumsy, sometimes. But I really didn't mean to upset you."

Twisting on her chair, she tried to find words to repair what he had clearly taken as an unbearable intrusion. Lacking anything more to say, she stood up, thanked him, and left.

At the corner, she turned around and saw the Van den Brocks joining him on the café terrace. Van den Brock had his hand on Lefloc-Pignel's shoulder, as if to reassure him. Maybe they've known each other for a long time. It must take quite a while to become friends with that man.

The door to the concierge apartment was ajar, so Joséphine knocked and entered. Iphigénie was having coffee with a woman holding a poodle, an old white-haired gentleman, and a girl in a muslin dress who lived with her grandmother on the third floor of

Building B. They were describing their interrogations with supporting details and exclamations, while Iphigénie served cookies.

"So that makes two dead women in the neighborhood," said the woman with the poodle. "In six months!"

"That's what they call a serial killer," said Iphigénie knowledgeably.

"And both of them, the same way. Stabbed from behind, with a thin blade, so thin you apparently don't even feel it go in. Zip! Just like butter. Surgical precision. Zip! Zip!"

"How would you know that, Monsieur Édouard?" asked the lady with the poodle. "You're making things up!"

"I am not! I am re-creating the crime," he said, setting her straight with some irritation. "The chief told me about it. He took the time to talk to me, you see!"

He smoothed his shirt front, as if to underscore his importance.

"Well, you had reasons for resenting her too," said the lady. "She didn't like you very much, and that's why we stopped seeing you at the co-op meetings."

"I wasn't the only one," he protested. "She frightened everybody."

"It did take courage to go," she agreed. "That woman knew everything. Everything about everybody! She sometimes told me things . . ."

She took on a mysterious look.

"Things about people in the building," she whispered, obviously waiting to be begged for further details.

"Because you were her friend?" asked the girl eagerly.

"Let's just say she liked me. You can't live alone all the time, you know. You have to let down your guard sometimes, even if you're Mademoiselle de Bassonnière. So once in a while I'd have a shot of Noilly Prat at her place in the evening. She'd drink two little glasses and get tipsy, and then she'd tell me unbelievable things. One night she showed me a picture of a very handsome man in the newspaper and said she'd written him a letter!"

"A man, imagine!" giggled Iphigénie. "La Bassonnière!"

"I'm telling you, I think she was smitten!"

"Unbelievable!" exclaimed the old gentleman. "You're going to make me start liking her."

"What do you think of all this, Madame Cortès?" asked Iphigénie, getting up to make more coffee.

"I'm wondering who could have hated her so much to want to kill her."

"That depends how thick a file she had on her killer," said the old gentleman. "People will do anything to save their necks or their careers."

"She sure was living dangerously!" said Iphigénie. "It's actually surprising she lived as long as she did. Not that it makes us feel any safer."

Everybody in this complex is bizarre, thought Joséphine, *even the lady with the poodle! And what about me? I'm bizarre, too. If these people sitting here having coffee knew that I was almost stabbed to death six months ago, that my husband, who supposedly died in a crocodile's jaws, is living in the Metro, that my former lover is a schizophrenic, and that my sister is about to throw herself at Hervé Lefloc-Pignel, they would choke on their cookies.*

"I just don't understand women," muttered Gary, his knife in the air. The master of tomatoes Provencal was chopping parsley, garlic, basil, sage, and ham, which he intended to spread on sliced tomatoes before baking them.

He had invited his mother to dinner and parked her in the big arm chair he used as an observation post when he watched the squirrels in the park. They were celebrating Shirley's birthday: the big four-oh, a round, solemn number. "I'll do the cooking, you can blow out the candles," he'd told her on the phone.

"The deeper I go, the less I understand them," he said now.

"Are you talking to me as a woman or as a mother?"

"Both."

"What is it that you don't understand?"

"You women are so . . . pragmatic! You think about details, you forge ahead, following some implacable logic, you or-ga-nize your life! Why is it that the women I meet all know exactly where they're going, what they want to do, and how they're going to do it. Do-do-do! That's all they talk about!"

"Maybe because we deal with physical stuff so much of the time," said Shirley. "We knead, we wash, we iron, we sew, we cook, we scrub, and we slap away men's wandering hands. We spend our time doing, not dreaming!"

"Well, I'd like to meet a woman who doesn't know how to *do* anything, who doesn't have a career plan, doesn't know how to count, or drive, or even take the Tube. Someone who lives surrounded by books and drinks gallons of tea while stroking her old cat in her lap!"

Shirley was aware of her son's liaison with Charlotte Bradsburry. Gary hadn't told her anything, but the London rumor mill kept grinding out details. They had met at a party at Malvina Edwards's, the high priestess of fashion. Charlotte was coming out of a two-year relationship with a married man who had broken up with her on the phone, with his wife whispering the fateful words into his ear. All of London was talking about that one. "Honor and reparations!" cried Charlotte, who smilingly downplayed the story while looking for a new partner, eager to still the sharp tongues all too happy to bloody the editor of *The Nerve*, a magazine known for skewering its targets with refined cruelty.

And then she had met Gary.

He was younger than she was, but he was attractive, mysterious, and best of all, not known within Charlotte's little circle. With Gary, she created mystery, questions, suppositions. She remade herself. Gary was handsome, but didn't know it. He seemed to have money, but didn't know that either. He didn't work, played the piano, walked in the park, read endlessly. He was either nineteen or twenty-eight, depending on the topic being discussed. If you asked him about daily life, the hassle of riding the Tube, or the price of apartments, he looked like a startled teenager. But mention Goethe, Tennessee Williams, Nietzsche, Bach, Cole Porter, or Erik Satie, and he suddenly aged into an expert.

He looks like an angel. A sexy angel, she thought. *If I'm not quick enough, someone will steal him away.* So she seduced him, and they'd been inseparable since. She slept at his place, he slept at hers, she threw herself into educating him as a man of the world, and would soon turn the unformed boy into an exquisite being.

"What about Hortense? What does she say?" asked Shirley.

"About what?"

"You know very well what I mean. Or rather who."

Gary was carefully mincing the parsley and the ham, and

adding pepper and sea salt. He tasted the mix, added a clove of garlic and some bread crumbs.

"She's sulking. She's waiting for me to call her, and I don't. Besides, what can I tell her?"

He spread the stuffing on the tomatoes, opened the pre-heated oven, and set the timer, frowning.

"That I'm dazzled by this woman, who treats me like a man and not a pal? That would hurt her feelings."

"But it's the truth."

"It's a truth I don't feel like telling. I'd tell it badly, and besides—"

"Ah, man flees instead of talking! That great classic!"

"It's just that if I talk to Hortense, I'm going to feel guilty. Worse, I'll feel I'd have to run down Charlotte or downplay our relationship."

"Guilty, why?"

"Hortense and I made a silent vow never to fall in love with anybody else until we were both old enough to love each other. I mean really love."

"Wasn't that a little rash?"

"I didn't know Charlotte then. It was before."

Actually, it felt like the last century. Gary's life had turned into a whirlwind. The hunt for sluts was over, making way for the enchantress with the long neck; the lean, muscular shoulders; the arms more nacreous than a string of white pearls.

"And now I'm in a fix. Hortense doesn't call me. I don't call her. We don't call each other."

Gary had opened a bottle of Bordeaux and was sniffing the cork.

Shirley no longer felt comfortable discussing her son's romantic life with him. When he was a boy, they had talked about everything. They had grown up together hand in hand, sharing a deep secret, always united in the face of threats and dangers. But Gary was a grown man now with hair everywhere and big arms, big feet, and a big voice. Shirley felt almost intimidated. She'd rather let him do the talking.

"Do you care for Charlotte?" she eventually asked, clearing her throat to cover her embarrassment.

"She's beautiful, intelligent, curious, cultivated, and funny. I like sleeping with her, I like the way she slips into my arms, lets herself go, and makes me feel like a wonderful lover. She's a woman, an apparition! And she's not a slut."

"What about this vintage Bordeaux. Is that Charlotte, too?"

"No, I found it earlier when I was looking for the meat grinder. Before Hortense left, she hid all sorts of gifts around the flat so I wouldn't forget her. I open my closet, and a sweater falls out. I move a pile of plates, and a package of my favorite cookies appears. I reach for my vitamins in the medicine cabinet, and I find a note: 'I bet you miss me already.' She's funny, isn't she?"

Hortense woke up drenched with sweat. She'd had the same terrible nightmare again. She was in a damp, tiled room full of white steam. A man built like a beer keg with a dark, hairy chest crisscrossed with scars stood over her, swinging a long, studded whip. He grimaced, revealing black teeth he used to bite her all over. Huddled in a corner, she screamed and struggled as the man whipped her. She got to her feet and ran to a door that she somehow got through, and found herself running down a dirty, narrow street, bruising her feet on the cobblestones. She was cold and sobbing, with no one to give her shelter or protect her. She could hear the curses of the men chasing her. She tumbled to the ground, a big hand grabbed her by the scruff of the neck, and . . .

That's when she woke up, covered with sweat.

Three o'clock in the morning! She would never be able to get back to sleep! And she couldn't ever go knocking on Gary's door again, either. Or phone him in the middle of the night to say, "I'm frightened." Gary was sleeping with Charlotte Bradsbury.

Hortense grabbed a pillow and clutched it, stifling her sobs. She missed Gary's long arms. Only Gary's long arms could banish her terrors.

And they weren't available, because of another woman.

Hortense went to Google, typed "Charlotte Bradsbury," and blanched at the results: 132,457 hits! The damn woman showed up under every possible heading: the Bradsbury family, the Bradsbury estate, the Bradsburrys in the House of Lords, the Bradsburrys and the royal family, Charlotte Bradsbury's magazine, her parties, her pronouncements on fashions, her wit. She was quoted even when she didn't say anything!

People seemed to be fascinated by the smallest detail of her life: how she dresses, how she lives. Charlotte Bradsbury apparently gets up at six every morning, goes running in the park, takes a cold shower, has three walnuts and a banana with a cup of tea, then walks to her office. She reads all the world's press, meets with designers, writers, and creatives, digests all this and writes her editorial. At noon she eats an apple and a cashew. When she goes out in the evening she doesn't stay at any gathering more than half an hour, and she goes to bed at ten. That's because it's in bed that Charlotte Bradsburry likes to read, listen to music, and dream. "It's very important to dream in bed," says Charlotte Bradsburry. "That's where I get my ideas."

Bullshit! fumed Hortense, gnawing on the crust of a sandwich. *You don't have any ideas, you feed off other people's!*

America lay adoringly at Charlotte Bradsburry's feet. *Vanity Fair, The New Yorker,* and *Harper's Bazaar* were all begging her to come, but Charlotte Bradsburry remained wonderfully English. "Why live anywhere else? Other countries are pygmies!" A short video showed her head on, in profile, from the side, in a long dress, a cocktail dress, jeans, and running shorts.

When Hortense came across a column titled "Charlotte Bradsburry's latest conquest," she gasped. It was illustrated with a slideshow of Charlotte and Gary at an opening of Francis Bacon drawings: he, smiling and elegant in a green and blue striped jacket, and she, slender, hanging on his arm, smiling widely behind her sunglasses. The caption: "Charlotte Bradsburry smiles." *I killed myself trying to get into that show!* Hortense raged. *Nearly got trampled at the entrance. And no way to get an invitation! Yet those two spend ten minutes there and promise to return for a private visit!*

She typed "Hortense Cortès." Zero hits.

Life is too hard for people just starting out, she moaned. Gary had set the bar too high. Charlotte Bradsburry was turning out to be a tough cookie.

Hortense picked up the last piece of cheese from her plate and thoughtfully chewed it. Then she caught herself. *What the hell am I doing, eating a sandwich in the middle of the night? Hundreds of calories will turn into layers of fat on my butt and hips while I'm asleep! Charlotte Bradsburry is turning me into the Michelin Man!*

She ran to the bathroom, stuck her fingers down her throat, and vomited up the sandwich. She hated doing this, she never did it, but this was an emergency. If she were ever to confront her omni-Googled rival, she would have to banish every last speck of fat from her life.

Hortense went back to bed feeling angry and sad. *Have I ever been sad?* She thought hard about it and couldn't recall feeling this specific lukewarm mix of emotions. It was somewhat nauseating, bordering on helplessness and melancholy.

She switched off her night table light—the one with the cheap pink shade she'd draped with a tulip-red scarf to warm up the room—and forced herself to think about her upcoming fashion show. She absolutely had to succeed. The school took just seventy students out of a thousand, and she had to be one of them. She couldn't lose sight of her goal.

In two weeks it'll be me, Hortense Cortès, standing on the runway with my creations, she told herself. *That Charlotte Bradsburry woman doesn't create anything, she just feeds on the zeitgeist.* She opened her eyes, delighted. *It's true! Someday they'll be talking about me instead of her, and I'll be the one with one hundred thirty-two thousand four hundred fifty-seven Google hits, if not more!*

"I'm the best, a fashion queen!" she sang.

Shivering with pleasure, she pulled the sheet up to her chin and savored her revenge. Then she uttered a little shriek. *Oh my God! Charlotte Bradsburry will be at the show! She'll be in the front row, with her perfect outfit, her perfect legs, her perfect look, her disdainful little pout, and her big sunglasses. The Saint Martins show was the fashion event of the year. Plus Gary was sure to accompany her. He would be sitting in the front row, right next to her.*

Hortense's nightmare was starting again.

A different nightmare.

In the Eurostar taking her to London, Joséphine was ruminating. She had escaped from Paris, leaving her sister and daughter behind. Zoé had gone off to her friend Emma's to prepare for her *Brevet* exam. "I want to pass with honors," she'd said, "and when I'm with Emma, I study." The idea of being stuck alone with Iris in the big apartment had sent Joséphine running to buy a ticket for London. She entrusted Du Guesclin to Iphigénie and packed her suitcase, claiming she had to attend a conference in Lyon on lordly mansions in the medieval countryside.

Four days all to myself, and incognito! In three hours she would step onto the platform at St. Pancras. She hadn't alerted anybody of her arrival, neither Hortense, Shirley, nor Philippe. On the advice of her English publisher, she'd reserved a room in a boutique hotel near Holland Park, in Kensington. She was having an adventure.

Alone, alone, alone, jolted the train. *In peace, in peace, in peace,* she echoed. *English, English, English,* chorused the wheels. *French, French, French,* intoned Joséphine as she watched the passing fields and forests that English armies had so often crossed during the Hundred Years' War.

The English were at home in France, and regularly went back and forth between the two countries. Edward III spoke only French. Royal patent letters, letters between queens, religious institutions, and the aristocracy were all written in French or Latin, as were statutes and wills. Henry of Grosmont, Duke of Lancaster and Du Guesclin's opposite number, even wrote a book of devotions in French! When Du Guesclin dealt with him, he didn't need an interpreter. The concept of nation didn't exist. You belonged to a lord and a domain, and you fought to uphold your lord's rights. It didn't matter whether you went into battle under the colors of the king of France or of the king of England, and some soldiers switched sides for better pay. Du Guesclin himself remained faithful to the kingdom of France his entire life, and a chest full of gold *écus* wouldn't have changed his mind.

Joséphine heard the announcement that the train was about to enter the tunnel under the Channel, a twenty-five minute crossing. Twenty-five minutes in darkness. Some passengers chatted nervously. Jo merely smiled. She felt she was emerging *from* a tunnel.

Located at 135 Portland Road, the hotel was called Julie's. "It's nice and cozy," said Edward Thundleford, her publisher. "I hope it's not too expensive," said Joséphine, embarrassed at even mentioning this. "Please, Madame Cortès, you're my guest! I'm looking forward to meeting you. I loved your novel and am very proud to be publishing it."

He was right: Julie's looked like a box of English bonbons. The decor of the ground-floor restaurant was strikingly original, and the dozen tan and pink rooms upstairs featured deep, flower-pattern carpets and curtains soft as clouds. The guestbook recorded visits by Gwyneth Paltrow, Robbie Williams, Naomi Campbell, U2, Colin Firth, Kate Moss, Val Kilmer, Sheryl Crow, Kylie Minogue, and other names Joséphine didn't recognize.

She stretched out on the red counterpane and reflected that life was good. She would stay in this luxurious room and never go out. She would order tea and toast with marmalade, she would slip into the old-fashioned bathtub with dolphin-back feet, and relax. She would savor it all. She would count her toes, pull the bedspread over her head, and make up stories based on the sounds from the other rooms, spinning tales about couples, quarrels, and lovemaking. *Does Philippe live close by?* she wondered. *It's funny, I wrote down his phone number but not his address in Notting Hill.* She always felt lost in London, a city that seemed so big she'd never taken the time to study its layout. I could ask Shirley where he lives and stalk him, she thought, stifling a laugh. How would that make me look? First, she would go see Hortense.

Mr. Thundleford said the 94 bus would take her straight to Piccadilly.

"That's where my daughter's school is!"

"Then you won't be far away, and the trip is very pleasant. You go along the park for a while."

That first evening, Joséphine stayed in her room, eating dinner facing a luxuriant rose garden whose heavy blossoms bumped against the window panes. Then she walked barefoot on the bathroom's dark floor and jumped into a scented bath. She tried all the soaps, shampoos, conditioners, creams, body washes, and exfoliants. Her skin now soft and glowing, she turned down the big bed, slipped under the covers, and lay a long time studying the ceiling scrollwork. *It was a good idea to come. I feel new, as if I left the old Jo behind in Paris.* Aloud, she said, "Tomorrow I'll surprise Hortense when she comes out of class."

The reunion didn't happen quite that way. Joséphine was punctual, of course: At three minutes past noon she was in the main hallway at Saint Martins. Groups of students with thick folders straggled out of the classrooms, chatting and nudging each other good-bye with their shoulders. No sign of Hortense. By one o'clock, Jo still hadn't seen her daughter, so she went to the office and asked the big woman there if she happened to know Hortense Cortès, and when her classes would be over.

"You a member of the family?" asked the woman, looking at her suspiciously.

"I'm her mother," answered Joséphine proudly.

"Oh!" She sounded surprised.

In her eyes, Joséphine read the same surprise she used to see in the other mothers' eyes when she walked Hortense in the Courbevoie park. They all assumed she was a nanny, as if she and Hortense couldn't possibly be related.

Jo took a step back, embarrassed.

"I'm her mother," she repeated. "I've come from Paris, and I wanted to surprise her."

The woman checked a register and said, "She should be out any moment now. Her class is over at one fifteen."

"Then I'll wait . . ."

Joséphine went to sit on a beige plastic chair, feeling pretty beige herself. She was nervous. The woman's look had stirred up old memories, of Hortense's disapproving looks at her clothes when she picked her up at school, the slight distance she maintained between them when they walked in the street, her exasperation when Joséphine lingered to chat with a shopkeeper. "When are you going to quit being friendly to everyone? It's annoying. It's not like we know those people!"

She was on the verge of leaving when Hortense appeared in the hallway, alone. She looked pale and preoccupied, as if she were trying to solve some problem. She was alone, and ignoring the boy running after her with a piece of paper she had dropped.

"Hello, darling," said Joséphine, stepping into her path.

"Mom! I'm so happy to see you!"

She did look happy, too, and Joséphine felt a rush of joy. She offered to carry her armload of books, but Hortense refused.

"No, leave them alone. I'm not a baby anymore!"

"You dropped this," yelped the boy, holding out a photocopy.

"Thanks, Geoffrey," she said, turning her back to him and leading her mother away.

"He looks very nice," said Joséphine turning around to say good-bye to the boy.

"He sticks to me like glue! And he has no creativity! I put up with him because he has a big flat and I'd like him to rent me a room for cheap next year. But I have to straighten him out first, make sure he doesn't get the wrong idea."

They went to a coffee shop near the school. Sitting at a table, Joséphine studied her daughter's face. Hortense had bags under her eyes and looked a bit frazzled. But her hair, pulled back in a black headband, looked lustrous enough to grace a shampoo ad.

"Is everything all right, darling?"

"If it were any better, I couldn't stand it. What about you? What are you doing in London?"

"I came to see my English publisher, and to surprise you. You seem a little tired."

"I've been running around like mad. The show's at the end of this week and I'm far from ready. I'm working night and day."

"Would you like me to stay and see the show?"

"I'd prefer if you didn't. It would make be too nervous."

Joséphine felt a twinge of hurt feelings, and then had a nasty thought. *I'm her mother and I'm paying for her studies, but I don't have the right to be there? That's too much!* Frightened by the strength of her reaction, she asked a question to cover her upset.

"What's the reason for having the fashion show?"

"It's the final stage of your admission to this prestigious school. Remember, the first year is probationary. They don't accept many students, and I want to be among the happy few."

Hortense's gaze had hardened and seemed to be slicing the air as if to dissolve it. Her fists were clenched, thumbs in. Joséphine gaped at so much determination and energy. *And she's just eighteen!* she thought. Her love and deep attachment to Hortense swept any resentment away.

"You're going to make it," she whispered, giving her daughter an admiring look that she immediately quashed for fear of annoying her.

"Well, if not, I'm going to die trying!"

"Do you see Shirley and Gary from time to time?"

"I don't see anybody, Mom. I work day and night, I don't have a minute for myself."

"But we can have dinner together some evening, can't we?"

"Sure, but it mustn't be too late. I have to sleep. I'm worn out. You didn't pick a good time to come."

She seemed distracted. Joséphine tried to interest her with the news about Zoé, Mademoiselle de Bassonnière's death, and Du Guesclin's joining the household. Hortense listened, but with a polite absence that made it clear that her mind was elsewhere.

"I'm happy to see you," Joséphine finally said, putting her hands on Hortense's.

"Me, too. Really, I am. It's just that I'm exhausted and obsessed by this show. It's terrifying to have your whole life turn on just a couple of minutes! Everybody in London who matters will be there, and I don't want to look like a dork."

They separated, promising to have lunch together—the next day, if Hortense's schedule allowed.

Joséphine ate dinner alone, with a book: a Penguin edition of Saki's *Collected Short Stories*. She loved his dryly sarcastic writing. "Reginald closed his eyes with the elaborate weariness of one who has rather nice eyelashes and thinks it's useless to conceal the fact." Saki nailed the character in just a few words; no need for psychological details or long descriptions. "'One of these days,' he said, 'I shall write a really great drama. No one will understand the drift of it, but everyone will go back to their homes with a vague feeling of dissatisfaction with their lives and surroundings. Then they will put up new wallpaper and forget.'"

Jo closed her eyes, savoring the lines along with her club sandwich. Today was Friday, and she was letting herself live alone and free until Tuesday. *What is Philippe doing right now? Is he having dinner with Dottie Doolittle? Is he taking her home, going upstairs with her? Tomorrow or the day after, I'll go sit down with him, look deep into his eyes, and I'll know if this Dottie Doolittle business is true or not. Tomorrow I'll brush my hair until it crackles, slather mascara on my lashes. I won't even have to talk to him. I'll know just by looking.* She had time only to repeat, *Just by looking* . . . before falling peacefully asleep.

Joséphine had now been walking the circuit, around and around, since eight o'clock. She was playing the part of a casual tourist out to explore the city, but in fact, she was relentlessly circling the same cluster of streets: Holland Park Avenue, Portland Road, Ladbroke Road, Clarendon Road, then back to Holland Park.

It had rained during the night, and the steam rising from the sidewalks glowed dawn-pink before turning gold as it caught the morning sunshine. The target of Joséphine's surveillance was the Ladbroke Arms, the pub where Shirley claimed Philippe ate breakfast outdoors every morning.

The night before, Jo had eaten dinner with Edward Thundleford. They discussed the translation of Jo's book and the cover art, press releases, print runs, and English title. He escorted her back to her hotel and invited her to his office on Peter Street for the day after tomorrow. Jo accepted, though she would have preferred to spend the time wandering around town.

"I didn't dare turn down his invitation!" she later told Shirley, sitting on the carpet across from the big fireplace in her friend's living room.

"You can waste your whole life being polite, you know."

"But he's charming, and he's doing a lot for me."

"He's going to earn a ton of dosh thanks to you. Ditch him and come clubbing with me. I'll show you dirty underground London."

"I can't. I promised."

"Oh, Joséphine, try to be a bad girl!"

"I'm actually starting to, believe it or not."

In the living room, the two of them worked out a strategy for running into Philippe "by accident." Everything was planned, timed, and prepared.

"He lives right here," said Shirley, pointing on a map to a street near Notting Hill.

"That's where my hotel is!"

"And he eats breakfast here . . ." She pointed out the pub that Joséphine was now circling. "So you get up early, make yourself beautiful, and start patrolling at eight o'clock. Sometimes he gets there earlier, sometimes later, but you start your stroll at eight."

"What should I do when I see him?"

"You say, 'Philippe, what a surprise!' You come over, give him a peck on the cheek. Make sure he doesn't think that you're available and ready to be carried off. Then you casually sit down—"

"How does a person sit down casually?"

"You don't fall flat on your face, the way you usually do. You look like a woman who just happened by, you're busy, you check your watch and your phone and—"

"I'm never going to manage this!"

"Sure you will. We'll rehearse it."

So they rehearsed. Shirley played Philippe, sitting at a table with his nose in a newspaper. But Joséphine kept muffing her lines, and the more they rehearsed, the worse she got.

"I'm not going!" she cried. "I'll look stupid!"

"You're going and you'll look intelligent. Just walk around and around him until he grabs you and hauls you off to bed."

So she was now walking. And walking. It was already eight

thirty, with no man in sight. *This is crazy! He'll never believe it. I'll turn red, I'll knock my chair over, I'll be sweating bullets, and my hair will be all greasy.*

She continued her appointed rounds. *Why am I pushing fate? I should leave it to luck.*

She stopped in front of a perfume shop. *Should I buy some perfume? Maybe some of that intoxicating Eau des Merveilles, from Hermès.* She would spray some on her neck and wrists before going to sleep, even some on the light bulbs. Then she checked the store's business hours. It didn't open until ten.

Jo resumed her forced march, stopping at a newsstand near the Tube station to buy a paper. *Stand up straight! You're slouching.* She straightened and slipped the newspaper under her arm. *Slow down and take it easy. Maybe he's there now. I'm so nervous! Relax, it'll be fine.*

She was walking the fourth side of her quadrangle, just a few yards from the pub, when she saw him. From the back, sitting at a table. He put down his cell phone, opened the paper, called the waiter over and gave his order. Then he crossed his legs and began to read.

It was magical to observe Philippe without his knowing. Just by looking at his back, she could see the end of his night and the start of the day, his taking a shower, kissing his son off to school, his hungry anticipation of bacon and eggs with a cup of espresso, the hope of a new day. He was yielding himself to her, unguarded. She was deciphering his back. She lent him dreams and warmed him with her kisses, and he surrendered. She reached out her hand and drew a caress in the air.

He didn't belong to anyone else, Joséphine now knew. She

could tell by the way he turned the page of his newspaper, the way he raised the cup to his lips, the relaxed ease of his every movement.

They weren't the gestures of a man in love with another woman. Nor those of her sister's husband. They were the gestures of a free man.

Who was waiting for her.

Tonight is my last night. Jo will be here tomorrow. Tomorrow will be too late.

Iris went to the closet containing the fuse box and flipped the circuit breaker. The lights went out, the refrigerator hiccoughed and died, the stereo in the living room fell silent. Quiet. Shadows. Time to take action.

She went downstairs and knocked on the Lefloc-Pignels' door. It was nine fifteen. The children would have eaten dinner, and madame would be cleaning up in the kitchen. Monsieur would be free.

Lefloc-Pignel opened the door, his bulk filling the doorway, a severe expression on his face. Iris lowered her eyes, looking repentant.

"I'm terribly sorry to bother you, but my electricity went off all of a sudden, and I don't know what to do."

He hesitated, then said he would come up as soon as he finished something.

"I'll be there in ten minutes."

He closed the door before Iris had time to peek into the apartment, but it seemed strangely quiet for a place housing a family with three kids.

When he joined her later, she asked, "Are your children already in bed?"

"Every night at nine o'clock. That's the rule."

"And they obey?"

"Of course. That's the way they were raised. There's never any argument."

He opened the closet with the fuse box and smiled, indulgently amused.

"It's nothing. The circuit breaker just tripped."

He flipped it back up and the lights came on, the refrigerator hummed to life, and music started playing out in the living room.

"You're wonderful," said Iris, clapping her hands.

"It wasn't hard."

"I'd be lost without you. Can I give you something to drink? A glass of whiskey or some herb tea? I bought fresh mint at the market this morning."

She took out a bouquet of mint wrapped in tinfoil and gave it to him to smell. *Tea would be perfect,* she thought. *We can talk while I'm fixing it. He'll relax, and I'll find some way to get to him, leave my mark.*

"I'd enjoy some mint tea," he said.

She put the water on to boil, feeling his eyes on her, following her every move. She was wondering how to lighten the mood when he took the initiative.

"Do you have children?" he asked.

"One boy, but he doesn't live with me. He lives with his father in London. I'm in the process of getting a divorce, which is why I'm staying with Joséphine."

She readied a tray with a teapot and two cups. Took out

two small white napkins and carefully folded them, as if she'd taken lessons on being the perfect housewife. That's the kind of detail he would notice. She could feel him watching her. She shivered.

"His father is demanding custody and—"

"You aren't going to give him up, are you?" Lefloc-Pignel asked abruptly.

"Oh, no! I'm going to fight to get him back."

"I'll help you, if you like. I can find you a good lawyer."

"That's nice of you."

"It's normal. You mustn't separate a boy from his mother—ever!"

She poured the water over the mint, and carried the tray into the living room. She made the tea, handed him a cup. He looked up at her and said, "Your eyes are very blue. Very big and set wide apart."

"When I was little, I hated having such widely spaced eyes."

"I imagine you were a pretty little girl."

"And very insecure!"

"You must have gained self-confidence fast."

"A woman is only self-confident when she's loved. I'm not one of those liberated women who can live without a man's attention."

Iris had neither self-esteem, pride, nor fear of seeming ridiculous. She was all strategy: Hervé Lefloc-Pignel had to fall into her trap. He was handsome, rich, and brilliant—the perfect prey. *I* have *to seduce him! So what if he has a wife and three children? Who cares? Everybody gets divorced these days, and he would be the last man to want to stay with a wife who mopes around all day in a bathrobe. It's not as if I would be breaking up a tight-knit couple.* She was prepared to take his children in as well. She was the wife he needed. By giving herself to him, Iris reasoned, she would practically be doing him a favor.

She turned up the radio a little and offered him some more tea. He held out his cup, and she poured, allowing her hand to touch his. She rested her hand close, hoping he would take it. Then she brushed the sleeve of his jacket, almost caressingly, but he didn't make a move.

There was something imperious in Lefloc-Pignel's attitude, the habit of a man accustomed to being obeyed, and Iris found herself drawn to it.

They listened to the eleven o'clock news on the radio together, and exchanged a look of surprise that so much time had passed without their noticing. They didn't say anything, as if there was no need. They were already happy. They looked as if they knew something would happen, but didn't know what.

Philippe tried to shift his cramped arm, but Joséphine protested.

"Don't move. We're so comfortable."

Touched, he repressed a grimace. The tenderness radiating from their entwined bodies was certainly worth an attack of pins and needles. He hugged her, smelling a vaguely familiar perfume in her hair. Seeking to identify it, he moved down to explore her neck, her shoulder, the insides of her wrists. She shivered and pressed against him, reviving a desire that had briefly subsided.

"Again," she murmured.

And again they forgot everything.

There was an almost religious fervor in the way Joséphine sur-rendered in making love. As if she were struggling to ensure that, amid the ruins of the world, the light between two people making love, two souls who truly loved each other and were not just going through the motions, would endure. A spark that transformed a simple rubbing of bodies into a blazing fire. This thirst for the absolute might have frightened Philippe, except that he wanted nothing more than to drink at its source.

The future tastes like a woman's lips, he thought. *They're the conquerors, the ones who push back the frontiers. We men are ephemeral innocents who slip into their lives to play our parts, but they have the main roles. That suits me just fine,* he said to himself, smelling Joséphine's perfume. *I want to learn to love the way she does. To love the way you set off on an adventure. Any man who thinks he knows what's happening in a woman's mind is crazy or a fool. Or pretentious.*

He would never in the world have imagined Jo tracking him down at an English pub. Yet there she'd been, right in front of him, wanting to know. Women always want to know.

"Joséphine!" he exclaimed. "What you doing here?"

"I came to see my British publisher. They bought the English translation of *A Most Humble Queen,* and there were a lot of details to be taken care of."

She seemed to be reciting a lesson, and he interrupted her. "Sit down and tell me the real story, Jo!"

She pushed away the proffered chair. Crumpling the rolled-up newspaper she was holding, she lowered her eyes and blurted, "I really wanted to see you. I wanted to know if . . ."

"If I was still thinking of you, or had completely forgotten?"

"That's right!" she said, relieved, looking him in the eye, looking for the truth.

He listened to her, touched. Joséphine didn't know how to

lie. All she could do was blush and get right to the point, without detours.

"You wouldn't have made a very good diplomat, Joséphine."

"I wanted to see you. I wanted to know if you'd forgotten the kiss in the kitchen, if you had forgiven me for, well, pushing you away the way I did our last evening, and I wanted to tell you that I've often thought about you even if it's always complicated, there's Iris, and I'm still her sister, but I can't help it, I think about you and I think about you and I needed to know if you thought about me or if you'd completely forgotten me, because in that case you have to tell me so I can do everything I can to forget you, even if it makes me very unhappy, and I know that this is all my fault and . . ."

She looked at him, out of breath.

"Do you plan to stand there in front of me all day?" he asked. "You look as if you were on stage reciting lines! It's making me uncomfortable. I have to look up to talk to you."

She collapsed into a chair, muttering, "This isn't the way it was supposed to go!" In dismay, she noticed that her paper's newsprint had blackened her fingers. Philippe took his napkin, dipped it in hot water, and gave it to her. He watched in silence as she cleaned up. When she was done, she let her arms hang on either side of her body, thinking that she had completely failed in executing the plan she'd worked out with Shirley. He took her hand and held it.

"So you'd really be unhappy if—" he began.

"Oh, yes, I would!" she cried. "But I would understand, you know. I've been . . . I don't know . . . Something I didn't like happened that night and everything got mixed up in my head. I felt very frightened and I thought it was because of you."

"And you're not sure anymore?"

"That is . . . I think about you a lot."

He brought Joséphine's hand to his lips, and whispered, "And I think about you too, a lot."

"Oh, Philippe! Do you mean that?"

He nodded, suddenly looking serious.

"Why is it so complicated?"

"Because we complicate everything."

"And we shouldn't?" she asked.

"Don't talk, or it'll all up start again, and make us even more confused."

That's when she made her crazy move. She leaned over and kissed him, kissed him as if her life depended on it. He had just enough time to throw some money on the table before she grabbed his hand and dragged him off. The door to her hotel room was barely closed when he felt her nails on the back of his neck and she was kissing him again. He had to pull her head back so he could talk.

"We have all the time in the world, Joséphine. We aren't thieves."

"Yes, we are."

"You're not a thief, and neither am I. And anyway, there's nothing wrong with what's going to happen."

"Kiss me! Kiss me!"

As they walked across the room, they traveled back in time. They breathed in the scent of stuffing and turkey, felt the hot oven on their backs, felt the palms of their hands, heard the children in the living room. They tore off each item of clothing as if they were shedding stones from their memory, undressing without taking their eyes off each other so as not to lose precious seconds because they knew their minutes were counted, plunging into a space-time and a space-innocence that they wouldn't soon find again and which they couldn't afford to waste. They stumbled to the bed and it was only then, when they'd finally reached the shore they sought, that they looked at each other with the triumphant if shaky smiles of startled voyagers.

"I've missed you so much, Joséphine."

"Me too! If you only knew!"

Those were the only words they could say, the only words aloud. And then night fell in the middle of the day on the big bed and they stopped speaking.

The next day, Philippe took Joséphine to the train station. They had spent the night together, had written on each other's skin the words of love they didn't dare yet say. He'd gone home at dawn to be there when Alexandre woke up. Joséphine felt a strange twinge, hearing the door close. *Did he do that when he slept at Dottie's place?* Then she realized she didn't give a good goddamn about Dottie Doolittle.

She was leaving for Paris, and he was flying to Kassel, Germany, for dOCUMENTA, one of the biggest contemporary art exhibitions in the world.

He held her hand and carried her suitcase. He was wearing a yellow tie with little Mickey Mouses in red pants and big black shoes. Jo pointed to it, smiling.

"It's from Alexandre," he explained. "He bought it for me for Father's Day. He makes me wear it when I fly. Says it's a good luck charm."

They separated at the customs counter, kissing amid harried passengers brandishing passports and tickets and bumping them with their rolling suitcases. They didn't make each other any promises, but could see the same silent commitment, the same gravity, in each other's eyes.

Sitting in car eighteen, seat thirty-five, window, Joséphine stroked the lips he had just kissed. A refrain echoed in her mind: *Philippe, Philippe.* She hummed, "in love forever," from "Strangers in the Night," and wrote *forever* with her finger on the window.

Joséphine listened to the train noises, the passengers' comings and goings, the ringing cell phones, the laptops booting up. She wasn't afraid anymore. She felt chagrined at not being able to see Hortense's show, but caught herself. That's just Hortense, that's the way she is. *I'll never change her, and it doesn't mean she doesn't love me.*

At the Gare du Nord, Joséphine bought a copy of *Le Parisien* and went to stand in the line for a taxi. A headline jumped out at her: "Policewoman Killed in Parking Lot." Jo had a terrible premonition and read the article, standing stock-still, holding up people trying to get her to move, to gain a few extra steps. Capitaine Gallois, the police officer with the stern, pursed lips, had been stabbed to death near her white Clio in the police station parking lot.

The young woman's body was found lying on the ground yesterday at 7 A.M. She had gotten off duty late the previous night. Surveillance cameras showed a hooded man in a white raincoat approaching her, then stabbing her. This is the third attack of this sort within the last few months. "We are pursuing all possible leads," said sources close to the investigation, which has been assigned to the judiciary police departmental service. Police are considering the possibility that the killing is linked to other recent attacks. Investigators are troubled by the fact that Capt. Gallois was killed while she was investigating one of those crimes.

PART V

♦ ♦ ♦

♦ ♦ ♦

*W*hen Hortense opened her eyes, she realized she was in her room in Paris—and on vacation! Lying under the sheets, she sighed and stretched. The school year was over, and it had ended gloriously: She was now one of the seventy students enrolled at the prestigious Saint Martins school. She, Hortense Cortès, raised in Courbevoie by a mother who bought her clothes at Monoprix and thought Repetto was a brand of pasta. *I am the best, I am exceptional, I am the very essence of French style!*

Hortense's part of the fashion show had been the most refined, the most inventive, and the most perfectly executed. Nothing flashy, no plastic constructions, cardboard petticoats, or tarpaper masks. Just line and style. Closing her eyes, Hortense could see her "Sex Is about to Be Slow" presentation unfold: the models swiveling along, the swirl and fall of the fabrics, Nicholas's soundtrack, the photographers clustered at the foot of the runway, and the slow parade of the six models drawing sighs of ecstasy from a blasé audience weary of looking at beauty. *I'm now part of the school that produced John Galliano, Alexander McQueen,*

Stella McCartney, and Luella Bartley, the current toast of New York. Me, Hortense Cortès! Where do I get so much genius? she wondered, stroking the sheet.

She had triumphed. The sleepless nights and gray days, the frantic errands to find exactly the right embroidery, braid, and pleats she wanted, and no others. She assembled her creations, tore them apart, spread out the pieces, started over. Then suddenly everything began coming together, turning into a dream. Nicholas managed to get Kate Moss herself to model the final creation in a cloud of glittering black and white, a towering wig, and a black satin mask that she ripped off at the end of the runway, arching her back and murmuring, "Sexxx isss about to be slooow." The place went wild. "Sex Is about to Be Slow" became a catch phrase. A T-shirt manufacturer offered to immediately print a thousand shirts with the phrase, and people fought over them at the school's after-party.

It's you and me, Gucci, Yves Saint Laurent, Chanel, Dior, Ungaro!

Naturally there was one wrong note, but only one. That tramp Charlotte Bradsburry was at the end of the runway, taking notes for her rag and frowning while everyone else clapped, annoyed to see Gary leap to his feet and applaud, caught up in the enthusiasm.

To Hortense, the sight of Gary in the front row next to Charlotte felt like a punch in the stomach. He'd left messages for her, but she hadn't answered. She was ignoring him. She flashed a polite smile when she stepped on the runway and took a bow, but she didn't wink at him. Quite the contrary! She had Nicholas join her and put his arms around her.

"Kiss me," she whispered.

"Right here, in front of everybody?"

"Right here, right now. A lover's kiss."

"What will you give me an exchange?"

"Whatever you like."

Which is how Hortense wound up agreeing to join him on a cruise to Croatia, after a possible internship at Gaultier.

They kissed, and Gary looked away. "Touché!" Hortense murmured, her lips stretched in a fake smile. She let herself relax in Nicholas's embrace, radiant as a happy bride.

She rolled onto her stomach and hugged her pillow. *My next show will be "Glory Is Grief Bursting with Happiness." An homage to Madame de Staël. I'll design dresses for haughty queens with bloody hearts. I'll play with red, black, and purple. Long folds will fall like dry tears. It'll be violent, majestic, wounded.*

Joséphine was straightening the living room, with Du Guesclin dogging her every step. *God, that mutt sticks to her like glue,* thought Hortense. *I couldn't stand it for a second. Plus, he's ugly!* She always felt like kicking him.

"Girls, could you please not leave your things all over the place? This isn't a living room anymore, it's a dump! And do you realize what time you're getting up?"

"Oh, cool it, Mom!" said Hortense. "Drop the housekeeping for a moment and sit down and listen to me."

Joséphine sat, with her shoulders slumped and her eyes empty.

"What's the matter with you?" asked Zoé, struck by her mother's lack of energy. "You look completely out of it."

"It's nothing. I'm tired, that's all."

"That's not it," said Hortense. "I know you, Mom. There's something else going on."

Wringing her hands, Joséphine said, "I haven't told you everything. And now that the three of us are together, I have to tell you."

Sadly, she told them about the man with the red turtleneck in the Metro.

"It couldn't possibly be Daddy!" said Hortense angrily. "He hated red, said it was vulgar. He would've gone naked rather than put on a red sweater. And a turtleneck, to boot? You wouldn't think you spent nearly twenty years with him! He was punctilious about things that didn't matter, and overwhelmed by the rest. Wake up, Mom! Try to remember. Did you see the man again? Did he get in touch with you?"

Jo shook her head.

"In that case, you've imagined it."

"Well, there is one other weird thing," Joséphine said, and told them about the missing Intermarché points.

"What about that? Doesn't that prove he's alive? Just two of us had that card, him and me."

"Maybe somebody stole it."

"But didn't use it right away? Waited two years before using it? That doesn't make sense. He's come back, he's ashamed to show himself because he's fallen so low. In the meantime, he's surviving by using my Intermarché points."

Du Guesclin lay at Joséphine's feet and was looking from one of them to the other as if following the discussion.

At that point, Zoé spoke up in a small, shaky voice: "The

Intermarché points, that was me. I took the card from your wallet six months ago and I started using it."

"What for?" asked Joséphine.

"It was Paul Merson. When we had parties in the basement he said everybody had to chip in, and I didn't dare tell you because you would've asked me lots of questions and—"

"Who's this Paul Merson?" asked Hortense, intrigued.

"A boy who lives in the building," said Joséphine. "Zoé often goes downstairs to hang out with him and other kids. Go on."

Zoé took a deep breath and continued.

"Gaétan and Domitille don't have any money because their father is very strict. So I used the points on the card to shop for everyone."

"You lied to me!" said Joséphine. "You lied and you stole from me!"

"It was when we weren't talking to each other," she stammered, blushing. "I couldn't tell you that. You were doing dumb things and so was I."

Joséphine sighed, thinking, *What a waste!* Hortense tried to understand, but seeing how upset her mother and sister were, she gave up.

Marcel had asked Madame Suzanne into the living room. Junior was in his Baby Relax chair, showing his red gums while chewing on a piece of Cantal cheese. Josiane was slumped in an arm chair, wrapped in a mohair shawl, trembling. *Why are they all looking at me like this? And what am I doing in my bathrobe at seven in the evening?* She hadn't been taking very good care of herself for some time now.

Madame Suzanne was on her knees in front of Josiane, massaging her right ankle. Holding the foot in her soft hands, she was pressing a series of specific points. Her eyebrows had come together like basket handles and she was breathing heavily.

"I can feel that she isn't aligned properly," she said after a few minutes. "Someone has set her adrift." She paused. "Josiane, listen to me carefully. Do you have any enemies, that you know of?"

Josiane weakly shook her head.

"Have you deliberately or accidently hurt someone who might seek revenge to the point of wanting you dead?"

Josiane thought about this, but couldn't think of anyone she might have offended.

Madame Suzanne rubbed her foot, her leg, and closed and opened her eyes. Marcel was following her every move.

"I had the doctors run every test imaginable," he said. "There's nothing wrong with her."

They looked at each other, perplexed. Junior was writhing in his chair and crying loudly.

"Be quiet, Junior," said Marcel. "This is serious."

"No, leave him alone," said Madame Suzanne. "He's trying to say something. Go ahead, angel, tell us."

Junior started squirming in his Baby Relax and making funny gestures: He mimed a propeller turning over his head while making loud sounds with his mouth.

"That child wants to tell us something," said Madame Suzanne. "He's trying to communicate in his own way."

Junior gave her a wide smile and a thumbs-up, as if to say, *Good for you, lady. You're on the right track*. Then he went back to imitating a helicopter taking off.

"You'd think we were playing Pictionary," said Marcel in astonishment. "He really is trying to talk!"

"Have you had a relationship with an airline pilot?" Madame Suzanne asked Josiane, without taking her eyes off the child.

"No, never. Not a pilot, sailor, or soldier. I don't like uniforms."

"How about somebody who wears a halo or a big hat?" asked Madame Suzanne, closely following Junior's insistent gestures.

"A shepherd?" suggested Marcel.

Junior shook his head

"A cowboy?"

Junior looked exasperated.

"How about a mariachi?"

Junior glared at him. Then he started imitating an animal: He bleated, and pretended to have a pair of horns and a beard.

"I don't think it could be a goat," said Madame Suzanne dubiously. But Junior persisted, and pointed at her to show that she was on the right track.

"An old goat?"

He clapped for all he was worth, then encouraged her by doing his overhead propeller gesture.

"An old goat wearing a propeller or a big hat?"

Junior gave a cry of joy and relief, and fell back in his chair, exhausted.

"Henriette!" shouted Marcel, in a burst of inspiration. "It's Henriette!"

Clapping, Junior was so excited he nearly swallowed his cheese, but Marcel was watching and snatched it out of his mouth.

"So it's true! She's the one who put a spell on my honeybunch!"

Kneeling again, Madame Suzanne was at last able to enter

Josiane's soul and divine her fate. She called for silence, and a cathedral-like hush fell on the living room.

"Yes, it's someone by the name of Henriette," she murmured, still bent over Josiane's foot.

"How is this possible?" asked Marcel, as pale as someone who has seen a ghost.

"It stems from envy and a hunger for money," Madame Suzanne continued. "She's going to see a woman, a very fat woman with pink hearts all over her apartment, a woman who can channel evil, and who is working on Josiane. . . . I can see them together. The fat woman is sweating and praying to a plaster statue of the Virgin. The woman with the big hat gives her money, a lot of money. She gives a photo of Josiane to the fat woman, who casts spell after spell on it. . . . I'm seeing photographs with pins stuck in them!"

She paused.

"This is going to be painful and difficult, but I think I can do it."

Concentrating on Josiane's feet and calves, she took her hands in hers and started muttering strings of incomprehensible words and formulas that sounded like low Latin. Marcel listened, fascinated. Junior nodded. They made out a sentence demanding "that the evil come forth." Josiane gasped, and vomited a little bile.

"She'll pull through," said Madame Suzanne, "but she'll be exhausted."

Wrapped in her mohair shawl, Josiane began shaking all over, and then slid to the floor, motionless.

"That's it, she's liberated. A strange case, your Josiane. A mixture of postpartum depression and bad luck, as if her weakness had made her vulnerable. She was open to evil influence, and this Henriette person took advantage of it."

"So it really exists?" asked Marcel.

"Yes, unfortunately. This isn't the first case I've seen."

"What the heck is wrong with Mom?" asked Hortense, who was having breakfast in the kitchen with Zoé. "She's really not herself."

It was twelve thirty, and the girls had just gotten up. Joséphine had fixed them breakfast like an absent-minded ghost. She put coffee in the teapot and honey in the microwave, and she burned the toast.

"All these murders . . ." said Zoé thoughtfully. "That stuff can mess with your head. She was called back down to the station after that lady cop was killed. They called in everybody in the building."

"But when I saw her in London she was fine," said Hortense. "Seemed excited, even."

"When did you see her?" asked Zoé in surprise.

"Two weeks ago. She had a meeting with her English publisher."

"Mommy was in London? She told me and Iris she was going to Lyon for a conference."

"Nope. She was in London. I saw her with my own eyes."

"Why did she lie to us? That isn't like her."

Zoé and Hortense looked at each other, puzzled.

After a moment, Zoé spoke again.

"I think I know," she said mysteriously.

Then she fell silent, as if to gather her thoughts.

"C'mon, out with it!" ordered Hortense.

"I think she went to see Philippe and she didn't say so because of Iris."

"Philippe? Why would she tell us a lie just to see Philippe?"

"Because she's in love with him."

"With Philippe!" exclaimed Hortense.

"I caught them kissing in the kitchen on Christmas Eve."

"Mom and Philippe? You're out of your gourd!"

"No I'm not."

"Well, I'll be damned! Mom's love life is a never-ending source of fascination to me! I thought she was going out with Luca. You know, the cute guy from the library!"

"She dumped him. Out of the blue. In fact, I better tell her that I've seen him hanging around the neighborhood. I don't know if they're getting along."

"So she dumped Luca," said Hortense in awe. "Does Iris suspect anything?"

"No, 'cause Iris has been off on another planet for a while. She wants to get her hooks into Monsieur Lefloc-Pignel. She's having lunch with him today."

"Who is Lefloc-Pignel?"

"A guy in the building. I don't like him, but he's got a lot of class."

"The good-looking man I met at Christmas?"

"Yeah, that's the one. I really can't stand him. Gaétan's his son."

Zoé was dying to tell Hortense that she was in love with

Gaétan, but held her tongue. Hortense wasn't sentimental, and Zoé was afraid she would shoot her down with some wisecrack. *If I tell her about the big balloon in my heart, she'll die laughing.*

"Mom's really changing, isn't she? Swapping spit with Philippe! That's hot!"

"Yeah, but she's sad, too."

"You think it didn't work out with Philippe?"

"If it had worked out, she wouldn't be sad!"

Hortense frowned thoughtfully.

"Will you give me a hug?" whispered Zoé.

"Frankly, I'd rather not. That's not really my thing. But I can give you a friendly thump on the back."

Zoé burst out laughing. Not only was Hortense super classy, but she was funny, too.

"You have anything going on this afternoon?"

"No."

"We could watch *Thelma and Louise.*"

"Zoé, no! We've already seen it a hundred times!"

"Yeah, but I love it! When Brad Pitt gets undressed and then later when the truck blows up. And the end, when the two go flying!"

Hortense hesitated.

"C'mon, say yes! It's been too long since we watched it together."

"Okay, Zoé-cannoli. But just once!"

Zoé shouted in triumph and they tumbled onto the sofa together in front of the television.

They wound up watching the movie twice. As they played and replayed the scene where Brad Pitt takes off his T-shirt, Hortense thought of Gary and was angry at herself, and Zoé wanted to tell her about Gaétan, but didn't. They cheered when the truck exploded, and at the end, when the two women drove off the cliff, they held hands and screamed. *There are lots of ways of being happy*, thought Zoé. *Like being with Hortense and Gaétan. They aren't the same, but they both feel good.*

"I'm gonna tell you a secret," she whispered. "The most wonderful thing in the world happened—"

Zoé didn't have time to finish her sentence. Iris walked into the living room just then, dropped shopping bags crammed with clothes that spilled at her feet, and collapsed into an arm chair.

"Is your mother home?"

"She's in her room," the two girls answered together.

"She spends all her time in a room. That's lame."

"You spend all your time in stores," teased Hortense.

Iris ignored the jibe. Holding up the bags, she said, "I think Hervé Lefloc-Pignel is crazy about me!"

"He brought you all that stuff?" asked Hortense, almost choking.

"I told you: He's crazy about me."

"But he's married," protested Zoé. "And he has three children!"

"He took me to lunch at a heavenly restaurant in the Hotel Lancaster. After each bite, I thought I had died and gone to heaven. Then we went for a walk on the Champs-Élysées and avenue Montaigne, and he bought me presents at every store. A real Prince Charming!"

"What a great attitude," muttered Zoé.

"I'm going to put all these things away in my room."

———

Iris took her purchases from the bags one by one and laid them on the bed. With each item, she remembered the way Hervé had looked at her. She chuckled as she caressed a Bottega Veneta bag, a big padded tote of supple silvery leather. She'd been dreaming of having one. She had also chosen an ivory cotton dress with matching sandals that fit her perfectly. It could almost be a wedding dress.

They'd had lunch together, gazing into each other's eyes. He talked about his business affairs, explaining that the world's fifth largest plastics company was buying the fourth and might become the worldwide leader. Then he apologized. "I must be boring you. One shouldn't talk business with a pretty woman! Let's go shopping, to reward you for indulging me." Iris hadn't refused. For her, the height of masculinity was a man who was forever buying her presents. They parted at a taxi stand, where he kissed her hand and said, "I have to go back to work, unfortunately!" What a lovely man!

Hervé's first presents. He's getting bolder. Soon we'll have our first kiss, then our first night together, maybe even a weekend! And I'll wind up with the "Wedding March" playing and a ring on my finger! Tra-la-la! I can't get married in white, of course, but the ivory dress would do perfectly. If we got married in summer. . . . She lay back on the bed, holding the dress against her body.

She would just have to be patient. Hervé wasn't the kind of man to paw you or drag you off to a corner to jump you. He phoned in the morning to see if she was free for lunch, met her in a restaurant, and behaved with such gallantry that no one could believe that they were intimates. *But we aren't intimates yet! He still hasn't kissed me.*

Iris noticed that he always chose places where he wasn't known. She never saw him on weekends. On Monday morning, she set the phone on her pillow and waited for it to ring. She had a special ringtone for him. She let it ring three or four times before picking up. *Face it, I spend most of my time waiting. But I don't have much choice, do I? At least August will be here soon, and his wife and children will go on vacation to their big house on Belle-Île.*

Iris unwrapped a white blouse that had a high collar to hide the wrinkles on her neck. She pulled out the pins and the cardboard backing, and spread the shirt on the bed. As she did, she pricked her finger with a pin, and was dismayed to see a drop of blood fall on the beautiful Bottega Veneta dress.

Henriette came out of the Buzenval Metro station, turned right into rue des Vignoles, and stopped in front of Chérubine's rundown building to catch her breath. Her right toe was hurting and her sciatica sent pain shooting down her hip. *I'm too old to be taking the Metro.*

She began her slow ascent of the building's stairs, gagging at the reek of old boiled cabbage, resting at each landing until she finally reached the third floor. *Six hundred euros just to stick pins in a picture! That's no bargain! And I haven't seen any more results.* For all the time Henriette had spent lurking under Marcel's windows, she hadn't seen a single body crumpled on the sidewalk. She'd talked to the police, in vain. No accidents, no suicides. *At this rate my bank account is going to run as dry as an unplugged bathtub. This is my sixth payment. Six times six is thirty-six, so I've wasted three thousand six hundred euros. That's much too much! I must be crazy to put my faith in impossible nonsense.*

A sign above the doorbell read: RING THIS DOORBELL IF YOU ARE LOST. *Am I lost? Am I the kind of woman who loses her wits over a man? Absolutely not!* She looked at the doorbell for a long time and said aloud, "Well, I'm not ringing it!" She turned around and left.

I almost lost my way, Henriette thought, riding the number nine train back. *What do I care if Josiane and Marcel are making whoopee? I'm happier without him, aren't I? He did me a favor, by taking off. He gave meaning to my life, which to be honest didn't have very much. These days I'm high on life, as those young idiots like to say.*

Just yesterday, Henriette stole food at Hédiard. That's right, stole it! While the sales clerks were down in the basement gossiping or pretending to work, she had opened her big shopping bag and filled it up: red Sancerre, balsamic vinegar (81 euros for a small bottle), foie gras, fruit jellies, chocolates, cucumber soup, soupe au pistou, cashews, pistachios, calissons, spring rolls, sliced roast lamb, eggs in aspic, and every cheese within reach. She had grabbed everything she could. The shopping bag was so heavy it almost threw her shoulder out, and a trickle of warm sweat ran down her arms. But what a pleasure it was! *Besides, it's only fair,* she thought. *I used to steal from the poor, now I'm stealing from the rich! Life is exciting. I put my brain on pause when I let the fat lady take the reins.*

Henriette blessed this July day, when she'd finally gotten her common sense back.

Joséphine was feeling blue.

She was living cloistered in her bedroom. Stacks of files were piled around her bed, and she had to step over them to go to sleep. She no longer felt like going down to Iphigénie's brightly painted apartment. It had become gossip central, where people spent all their time discussing the recent killings. The craziest rumors were flying around.

Everybody had their favorite suspect, pointing out the telling details, the shifty eyes, the white raincoats.

Reduced to a pained silence, Monsieur Sandoz sat alone in a corner, gazing adoringly at Iphigénie. He was singing her a wordless love song, but Iphigénie had other fish to fry and lent him only half an ear.

"She's afraid to tell me I'm too old for her," Sandoz told Joséphine quietly, keeping his hands out of sight because he was afraid his nails were never clean enough. "But I'm doing everything I can to be nice."

"Maybe you're trying too hard," said Joséphine, whose own unhappiness was reflected in Sandoz's melancholy. "Eagerness and attraction don't always go together. Quite the contrary. That's what my elder daughter tells me, and she's an expert at seduction."

"I just can't pretend I don't care," he said. "People read me like an open book."

Joséphine sighed, lost in thought. *We have the same problem. I'm also transparent and predictable. One day was enough for Philippe to get bored.*

————————

It had been sixteen days since they parted on the St. Pancras train platform. Jo ticked off the days in little lines in the margin of a notebook. At first she started by counting the hours, but then gave up. The sight of too many lines depressed her. It had been sixteen days since she'd last heard from him. Each time the telephone rang, her heart started to race, sprinting up a mountain only to tumble back down, like Sisyphus. It was never him. *Why doesn't he call?*

He'd gone from bed to bored.

He didn't like the way I smelled, the little varicose vein on my left hip, the taste of my mouth, the little fold on my right knee, the curve of my upper lip, the feel of my gums. . . . I snored, I was too eager, I wasn't eager enough, I was stupid, I was clumsy, I don't know how to kiss, I make love like a garden gnome.

Desire . . . it's a perfume that can't be bottled. You can curse it, beg for it, wring your hands, offer to pay any price, but it remains flighty and fey.

Joséphine sank deeper into her favorite chair. The seat was cushioned, the armrests padded, and the firm back supported her nicely. *My love lies in pieces: a kiss against the oven, a Sacha Guitry quote, an escapade in London . . . and then a long wait that leaves me panting.*

She had spotted Luca from afar among the trees in the square, lurking around the building, his hands in his duffel coat pockets. She and Du Guesclin hid behind a tree and waited for him to leave. What did he want? Did his concierge tell him that she had stopped by and now knew his double identity. She was frightened, though she was afraid to admit it. What if he attacked her? When Du Guesclin saw Luca, he growled and his hair stood up.

The criminal division detectives seemed to think the killer was someone in the building. At one of their meetings, the new police officer on the case, an Inspector Garibaldi, told Joséphine that the investigation was focusing on the tenants.

"Why didn't you immediately file a complaint when you were attacked in November?" he asked. "Were you protecting the attacker? Do you know him? You just happened to go to London when Capitaine Gallois was killed. Were you creating an alibi?"

"I went to see my English publisher. I can prove it."

"I'm sure you're aware that she didn't like you."

"I noticed that."

"She had a rendezvous, a meeting, with you the day after the day when . . ."

"I didn't know that."

"She left a note, as it happens. Want to read it?"

Garibaldi handed her a sheet of paper on which Gallois had written *Dig RV, Dig RV, Dig RV* in felt-tip marker.

"She must've wanted to question you at that rendezvous. Did you two get into an argument about something?"

"No," said Joséphine. "I was surprised by her hostility. I figured there was just something about me she didn't like."

"Hah! So that's what you call being questioned? You better come up with something better than that. Or find a good lawyer, because you're in deep trouble."

Joséphine burst into tears.

"But I'm telling, I didn't do anything!"

"That's what they all say, madame! The worst criminals

always deny everything. They swear on their mother's grave that they're innocent."

Garibaldi drummed his fingers on his desktop, then said, "Okay, you can go now. But there's something fishy about your situation. I'd think it over, if I were you."

Joséphine ran into one of her neighbors every time she came out of the inspector's office. They were waiting on the pine benches in the shabby hallway. They were already feeling guilty and didn't dare talk to each other. Monsieur and Madame Merson complained; Pinarelli *fils* smiled mysteriously, as if he knew some exclusive secrets and was there only to round out the crowd; and Monsieur Lefloc-Pignel and the Van den Brocks were outraged.

Why would the killer be one of us? Mademoiselle de Bassonnière had files on everybody, not only the people in Building A! And just because I knew two of the three victims doesn't make me an accomplice. Dig RV. *You don't even say that. You* make *a rendezvous, you don't* dig *it.*

Jo wrote the two letters in her notebook:

RV, RV, RV.

Rendezvous, but also Reported Vaguely, Reasoning Vapid, Remain Vigilant, Regarding Victim . . .

Zoé appeared in the doorway and gave her a worried look.

"What are you doing, Mommy?"

"I'm working."

"Are you really working?"

"No, I'm just doodling."

Zoé came to sit on the chair arm. Joséphine handed her the sheet covered with *RV*s and tried to think of a way to head off her daughter's curiosity. She didn't feel like talking about the investigation.

"Ah," said a disappointed Zoé, putting the sheet down. "You're practicing writing text messages?"

"No," said Joséphine in surprise. "Just the opposite. When I send a text I'm careful to write out each word. I hope you do the same thing. Otherwise you'll forget how to spell."

"Oh, I do, but the other kids don't. You know what Emma sent me the other day?"

Zoé took a pencil and next to Joséphine's RVs wrote:

"It's a five-letter message: URAQT."

Jo tried to decipher it, in vain.

"It doesn't mean anything."

"Yes, it does. Think about it."

Joséphine read the letters backward, forward, and upside down but couldn't come up with anything. Zoé waited, proud at having figured it out on her own.

"Okay, I give up."

"Say the letters out loud," said Zoé. "To get it, you always have to read them aloud."

"U ar a cue tee. It still doesn't mean anything."

"Sure it does. It's 'You are a cutie.'"

"I would've never guessed!"

Zoé snuggled against her mother, wrapping her arms around her neck. She was at the age when you can move from being a woman to a child in a moment, from wanting a kiss from a boy to wanting a hug from your mom. Jo slipped her hands under Zoé's T-shirt and pulled her close. She had trouble imagining her in Gaétan's arms, even if their intimacy was probably still innocent.

"You're the prettiest mommy there is."

"And you'll always be my baby."

"I'm not a baby anymore! I'm big!"

"I know, but you'll always be my baby."

After a pause, Zoe said, "There's nothing to do today."

"Are you bored?"

"C'mon, Mommy, ditch your work and let's take Du Guesclin for a walk."

Joséphine so enjoyed having Zoé lying relaxed against her, she was prepared to do whatever she wanted.

"All right, my love." She pushed her papers aside and stood up.

"But just the two of us, okay? Let's not take Iris."

Joséphine grinned.

"You really think she'd want to walk around the lake with such a broken-down mutt?"

"Oh no! She'd much rather flounce around with handsome Hervé. . . . 'Do you think so, Hervé?' 'You know, Hervé.' 'Tell me, Hervé, since you're such a handsome Hervé. I can hardly wait for our next rendezvous, Hervé!'"

Joséphine fell back into her arm chair, stunned.

"What did you just say?"

"Er, nothing."

"Yes you did," said Joséphine in a shaky voice. "Repeat what you just told me."

"That she prefers parading around with handsome Hervé. Monsieur Lefloc-Pignel, if you like! She thinks he's gonna get a divorce and marry her. That's not right, you know. He's got a wife and three kids. I'm not crazy about him, but still, it's wrong."

Zoé continued, but Joséphine was no longer listening. Could *RV* be "Hervé"? What if Capitaine Gallois was referring to Hervé Lefloc-Pignel and Hervé Van den Brock? Dig into the matter of the two Hervés. She had learned something, or was about to, when she was stabbed.

Joséphine remembered how upset Lefloc-Pignel had been when she'd wanted to call him by his first name. They were at the café across from the police station, after she'd been questioned, and he'd suddenly turned hostile and cold.

"Oh, my God!" she murmured, sprawled in her chair.

"What's the matter, Mommy?"

She absolutely had to talk to Inspector Garibaldi.

The next day, Joséphine went to police headquarters, at 36 Quai des Orfèvres.

She waited for an hour in the long hallway, watching busy men hurrying by, calling to each other, talking loudly, and slamming doors. When the doors opened bursts of laughter and snatches of conversations came from the offices, then were cut off when the doors closed again.

Garibaldi eventually asked Jo into his office and had her sit down. The inspector was wearing a handsome red shirt, and his black hair was combed back tightly, as if held by rubber band. He gave her a penetrating look, and Joséphine felt her ears getting warm. She ran a hand through her hair and told him everything: the scene with Hervé Lefloc-Pignel at the café, how his manner changed when she wanted to use his first name, and how she'd learned that he and Van den Brock were both called Hervé.

"So there I was, thinking about what you said instead of working on my *habilitation* thesis, and I went back over that 'Dig RV' business. I wrote 'Dig RV' on a sheet of paper, and thought it looked wrong. I'm very aware of style and words, probably because of my literary training, and I was contemplating the words when my daughter came in."

Joséphine continued, making an effort to be clear and accurate. When she got to the matter of URAQT and RV meaning Hervé, Garibaldi slammed his hand on his desk and shouted, "Son of a bitch!" making both his files and Joséphine jump.

"Excuse my language," he said, calming down. "I think you've just given us a huge clue, Madame Cortès. Can I ask you not to tell a soul about our conversation? Nobody, you understand? Your safety could be involved."

"Is it that important?" she asked in a small, worried voice.

"I want you to step into the next office. They'll take your testimony in writing."

"You want me to make a deposition?"

"Yes, I do. You're mixed up in a strange business. We don't know all the ins and outs yet, but you've raised a detail that could be critical for the rest of the investigation."

Joséphine started feeling her courage returning.

"Can I ask why you suspected me?" she asked.

"It's our job to be suspicious of everyone around the victim. The killer is often someone they know. What struck us about you, was your keeping quiet after being attacked. In a situation like that, anyone else would've run to the nearest police station and told the whole story. Not only were you reluctant to tell anyone about the attack but you waited several days and then refused to file a complaint. As if you knew the guilty party and wanted to protect him."

"I can tell you why now," said Jo. "At first, I was thinking of Zoé. But later I thought it might have been my husband."

"Antoine Cortès, right?"

The inspector pulled a file from the stack on his desk and opened it. Turning the pages, he read aloud: "Died at age forty-three, killed by a crocodile in Kilifi, Kenya. . . . Worked for two years managing a crocodile farm for a Chinese businessman, Monsieur Wei. . . . Lived at . . ." The inspector laid out Antoine's entire life.

"He's dead, Madame Cortès. You know he is. The French embassy investigated, and that's what they concluded. What makes you think that he might have faked his death and still be alive?"

"I thought I saw him in the Metro one day."

"You wouldn't be the first person that's happened to."

"Just the same . . ."

"Madame, I'm telling you, he's dead. And this file absolutely proves it."

Raoul Frileux, known to a very few as "the Toad," was passing through London and having lunch with Philippe. He had chosen the restaurant at Claridge's and was scraping his short, square fingernails across the white tablecloth.

"You know what gets chicks today? Money, period. Hell, I'm no beauty, and I get them all. One of them turned me down at a cocktail party recently, and later, she called me. That's right! She must've found out what I was worth, and she came crawling. And the cunt paid for it, too. I don't need to tell you, but I treated her like shit."

"And you don't feel any shame?"

"Fuck no! I'm just paying them back. Where's that asshole waiter? Has he forgotten us?"

The Toad checked the time, flashing a big gold Rolex.

"Very chic!" said Philippe.

"Having money is so fucking nice! You don't have to lift a finger. They lie right down and spread 'em. What about you, Philippe? How's your sex life these days?"

"None of your business."

"You know, I never really understood you. You could've had any woman in town, and you never did. You're really nuts. You had a law firm that was a gold mine and you ditched it. You had the most beautiful woman in Paris, and you ditched her, too. By the way, I plan to put the moves on your wife."

"Iris?" Philippe was so surprised, he almost choked.

"You have any others?"

He shook his head.

"She's on the market, isn't she?"

"You could put it that way."

"She's on the market, and she won't be there for long, so I'm launching a hostile takeover. I thought it would be sporting to give you fair warning. Does that bother you?"

"Do whatever you like. We're getting a divorce."

Frileux looked disappointed, as if most of Iris's charm might lay in Philippe's still loving her.

"I called her the other evening," he went on. "Invited her to dinner, and she accepted. We're getting together next week. I have a reservation at the Ritz."

"She must have fallen pretty low," said Philippe.

"Or else she needs money. She's not as young as all that, you know. She's lowering her sights, so this is my chance. I need to get married again, anyway. It helps in business, and in that department, there's no one better than Iris."

"Because you plan to marry her?"

"Sure. Ring on the finger, prenup, the works. We won't have kids, of course, but I don't care. I've got two of them already, and what a pain in the ass they are!"

Frileux burst out laughing, showering his plate with spittle and a stray piece of unchewed food. He picked up a roll and buttered it. He already had three spare tires around his waist and was working on a fourth.

"Be careful with Iris!" said Philippe. "She doesn't have a heart. It's a sheet of ice."

"No sweat. I know how to skate!" said Frileux, lifting a pudgy foot in a gleaming Tod's loafer level with the tabletop. "So I have your blessing, right? It won't fuck up our business relationship?"

"It's a closed case. Over and done with."

And I'm not lying, thought Philippe, dismayed to find himself talking like the Toad.

Philippe walked home after the lunch. He'd been walking a lot since moving to London; it was the only way to learn his way around the city. "England built London for its own use, but France built Paris for the world," wrote Ralph Waldo Emerson. To get to know London, you have to use shoe leather.

He stopped at a newsstand and bought *Le Monde* and *The Independent.* Walked up Brook Street, past the handsome white buildings in Grosvenor Square, thought of the Forsythes and *Upstairs, Downstairs,* turned at Park Lane, and entered Hyde Park. Couples lay on the lawn, asleep in each other's arms. Children played cricket. Women on lawn chairs with rolled-up jeans worked on their tans. An old gentleman dressed all in white stood motionless on the grass, reading a newspaper. Kids crouching on skateboards zipped in and out among the joggers.

He would go as far as the Serpentine and come back on Bayswater.

Joséphine had left eighteen days before, and he'd been silent for eighteen days. After eighteen days, what can you say to a woman who comes, takes your hand, and gives herself to you without calculation? That he couldn't handle so much generosity? That he was petrified?

My arms would never be long enough to hold all the love Joséphine was offering. She shouldn't have left. I would have filled the room with her words, her gestures, her moans. I would've whispered, telling her not to go too fast, that I was a beginner. I was able to manage a kiss at a train station, and repeat it without thinking against an oven, but when suddenly everything became possible, then I was at a loss.

Philippe had let one day go by, then another, and a third, and eventually eighteen. And maybe nineteen, twenty, twenty-one.

A month . . . three months, six, a year.

It will be too late. We will have turned into statues, she and I. How can I explain to her that I'm not the person I was? I've changed address, country, wife, occupation. I may as well change my name. I don't know anything about myself any more.

On the other hand, I know what I don't *want to be anymore, and where I* don't *want to go.*

"Hey, Mommy, what are we doing this summer?"

Zoé threw a stick for Du Guesclin to fetch.

"What would you like to do?"

"I dunno. All my girlfriends are away."

"What about Gaétan?"

"He's leaving tomorrow. He and his family are going to Belle-Île."

"Didn't he invite you along?"

"Oh, no! His dad doesn't even know we're seeing each other. Gaétan has to do everything in secret."

"What about his mother? You never talk about her."

"She's neurotic. She scratches her arms and takes pills all the time. Gaétan says it's because of the baby they lost. You know, he was run over in a parking lot. He says it really screwed up their life as a family."

"How could he know? He wasn't born then!"

"His grandma told him. She said that before, they were completely happy. That his mom and dad used to laugh together, that they held hands and kissed. After the baby died his father changed overnight. He went crazy. But hey, what about summer vacation?"

Joséphine thought about it. Hortense was going to Croatia, so Zoé would be all alone.

"Would you like to go to Deauville, to Iris's place? We could ask her to lend us the house. She's staying in Paris."

Zoé made a face.

"I don't like Deauville. It's full of rich people flashing their wads of money."

"That's no way to talk!"

"But it's true! There's nothing there but parking lots, shops, and people with lots of money."

Du Guesclin trotted along beside them with a stick in his mouth, waiting for Zoé to play with him.

"Alexandre e-mailed me. He's going to a riding camp in Ireland, with ponies. He says there's still room. I'd like that."

"There's a good idea! E-mail him back and say that you'll go with him. Find out how much it costs. I don't want Philippe paying for you."

Zoé started playing with Du Guesclin again but was throwing the stick listlessly, almost mechanically. She scraped the tips of her shoes along the ground.

"What's the matter with you, Zoé? Did I say something you didn't like?"

"Why don't you call Philippe?" she mumbled, looking at her feet. "I know you went to London and you saw him."

Joséphine took her by the shoulders and said, "You think I've been lying to you, don't you?"

"Yes," said Zoé, her eyes still lowered.

"In that case, I'll tell you exactly what happened, all right?"

"I don't like it when you lie."

"Maybe, but you don't tell a daughter everything. I'm your mother, not your girlfriend."

Zoé shrugged.

"I mean it," said Jo. "That's important."

"Then let's have it," said Zoé, getting impatient.

"It's true that I saw Philippe in London. We had dinner together, and we talked a lot."

"And that's all?" asked Zoé with a sly smile.

"That's none of your business!" cried Joséphine.

"Because if you want to get married, I have no objections! I wanted to tell you that. I thought it over and I think I understand." Looking serious, Zoé continued, "Being with Gaétan, there are lots of things I understand now."

Joséphine smiled, and said, "Then you'll understand that the situation is complicated. Philippe is still married to Iris, and we can't forget about her just like that." Jo snapped her fingers.

"Yeah, except that Iris forgets."

"Yes, but that's her problem. So to get back to the matter of vacations, it's best if you work out the details with Alexandre, and I just handle the practical matters. I'll pay for your session at the camp and I'll put you on the train to London."

"But you won't talk to Philippe? Did you have a fight?"

"No, but I'd rather not talk to him right now. You say you're big, that you're not a baby anymore. Now's the time to prove it."

"All right," said Zoé.

Joséphine put out her hand to shake on their agreement.

Iris heard the phone ringing, but it wasn't Hervé's ringtone. She opened one eye and tried to read the time on her watch. Ten in the morning. She had taken two Stilnox pills to help her sleep, and her mouth felt pasty. She answered the phone to hear a loud, forceful man's voice.

"Iris? Iris Dupin?" he barked.

"Mmm, yes," she said, holding the phone away from her ear.

"It's me, Raoul!"

The Toad! At ten in the morning! She vaguely remembered that he had invited her to dinner the week before and that she had said . . . *What did I say?* It had been in the evening, she'd had a drink, and didn't quite remember.

"I'm calling to confirm our dinner at the Ritz. You haven't forgotten, have you?"

I must've said yes.

"Nnnnooo," she mumbled.

"Good. Till Friday then, at eight thirty. The reservation's in my name."

What is his last name again? Philippe always called him the Toad, but he must have a name.

"Is that all right or would you like someplace more . . . how should I put it? More intimate?"

"No, no, that suits me fine."

"For a first meeting, I thought it was perfect. The food's excellent, the service is impeccable, and the setting is very pleasant."

He sounds like the Michelin Guide! Iris slumped back on her pillow. *How did I get to this point? I have to stop taking sleeping pills. I have to stop drinking.*

Evenings were the worst, when sterile regrets and fears came crashing down on her. She didn't have an ounce of hope left. Having some wine was the only way to mask the fear, to still the little inner voice that shoved reality in her face, the voice that said, "You're old, you're alone, and time is racing by." A drink or two. Or three. She looked at the empty bottles lined up in mock regiments near the kitchen trash bin, counted them in dismay. *I'm stopping tomorrow. Tomorrow I'm drinking only water. Or maybe just one glass, to give me courage. But only one!*

Iris hung up feeling disgusted. The Toad was inviting her to dinner! *My God! Have I sunk so low that the Toad thinks he can hold me in his arms?* Tears came to her eyes and she began to sob. She would've liked never to stop, to drown in tears and sink into an ocean of salty water.

She sobbed harder. *What man will want me? Soon the Toad will be my only hope. Hervé absolutely has to make up his mind.* She would pressure him, make him speak from the heart. They had been seeing each other almost every day for several weeks, and he still hadn't kissed her.

She was meeting him at six that evening in a bar on place de la Madeleine. He would be driving his family to Belle-Île the next day. *When he comes back, I'll have him all to myself. No more wife, no more children, no more family weekends.*

Iris showed up exactly on time, because Hervé couldn't stand her being even a minute late. In the beginning she would flirtatiously make him wait ten or fifteen minutes, but it put him in such a foul mood she had a hard time cheering him up.

"What's ten little minutes compared to eternity, Hervé?" she had teased him, leaning close so her long hair brushed his cheek. But he drew back, offended.

"I'm not neurotic," he said. "I'm precise and ordered. The world is in such bad shape today because there is no order left. I want to restore order to the world."

The first time he delivered this tirade, Iris looked at him with amusement, but she quickly realized that he wasn't joking.

This evening he was sitting in a big red leather arm chair in the back of the bar, his arms crossed on his chest. She sat down next to him with a tender smile.

"Are the suitcases all packed?" she asked playfully.

"Yes, they are. Mine's the only one left, but I'll pack when I go home this evening."

She absent-mindedly ordered a glass of champagne when he asked her what she wanted to drink.

"But you don't need a suitcase, since you're not staying there." She said this with a somewhat tense smile.

"Of course I am. I'm spending two weeks with my family."

"Two weeks!" she exclaimed. "But you told me—"

"I didn't tell you anything, dear. You came to that conclusion on your own."

"That's not true! You're lying! You told me that—"

"I'm not lying. I told you I was coming back before them, but not that I was just dropping them off."

She tried to hide her dismay and control the shaking of her voice, but the shock of disappointment was too much. She gulped her champagne and ordered another one.

"You drink too much, Iris."

"I do whatever I like," she grumbled. "You lied to me!"

"I didn't lie to you. You've been imagining things!"

He glared at her now, a hint of fury in his eyes. She felt like a little girl who had done something stupid and was being punished. Something in her snapped.

"You are too a liar!" she yelled. "A liar!" Her voice shattered the quiet mood in the bar, and the waiter serving the next table glanced over in surprise.

"You promised me—"

"I didn't promise you anything," he said. "You're free to think so if you like, but I'm not going to continue this stupid argument." His voice was harsh. He sounded distant, already on his island. Iris buried her nose in her champagne glass.

"But what am I going to do then?"

Iris put the question to him, but she was really talking to herself. *I've waited for this month of August with so much impatience, imagining nights of love, kisses, dinners out on restaurant terraces. An early honeymoon before the real, official one.* A honeymoon that now seemed unlikely to happen. She fell silent, waiting for him to speak. He looked at her with a slightly contemptuous expression on his face.

"You're a child, Iris. A spoiled little girl."

She nearly answered that she was forty-seven and a half and had wrinkles in her bosom, but caught herself in time.

"You'll wait for me, won't you?" His question was actually an order.

Iris sighed and said "Yes," draining her glass. *Do I really have any choice?*

August began. It was hot, and the stores were closed. You had to walk a quarter of an hour to buy bread, twenty minutes to find an open butcher shop, half an hour to reach the produce aisle at Monoprix. Then you staggered home carrying your purchases, stumbling toward the shadows cast by trees standing motionless in the city's damp heat.

Joséphine stayed locked in her room, working. Hortense had gone to Croatia, Zoé to Ireland. Lying on the sofa by a fan, Iris alternated between the TV remote and her cell phone, dialing numbers that didn't answer. Paris was deserted. All the city held was the Toad, who was as faithful and frisky as ever. He called every evening to invite Iris to dinner under the stars. She claimed to have a headache, but turned him down in a provocative way.

"Maybe tomorrow," she said. "If I'm feeling better."

When he protested, she repeated "I'm tired," but then added "Raoul" in a softer tone that always won the Toad over.

"We'll talk again tomorrow, beautiful!" he croaked. Raoul hung up, pleased to hear Iris Dupin using his first name. *I'm getting there!* he said to himself, pinching the seat of his pants to loosen them. *I'll get her into bed sooner or later, then I'll hustle her butt down to City Hall.*

Iris was in no hurry to repeat their evening at the Ritz. Watching Raoul, she had tried to ignore the sound of his chewing, his wiping his fingers on the tablecloth, and his habit of reaching down to adjust the seat of his trousers. He talked with his mouth full, sprayed her with saliva, and puckered greasy lips in a kiss that made her cower in her chair. He winked at her as if to say, "It's a done deal." He didn't actually say those words, but she could read them in his bright, determined eyes.

Still, she hesitated to send him packing. She didn't have any news of Hervé. She could imagine him walking over grassy dunes with a sweater knotted over his shoulders enjoying a cool evening breeze, sailing with his sons, playing badminton with his daughter, strolling with his wife. He would be slim and elegant, his hair a bit sticky from the sea air, his lips curled in an enigmatic smile. *He looks very serious, but he knows how to be seductive. He's so unreachable, he's become irresistible. The Toad isn't in the same league, but he's hanging in there, with his pockets full of money and his finger itching for a ring. He doesn't just want to show me off, he wants to marry me.*

Iris was weighing this, but didn't feel anything had to be decided just yet.

She'd reached that point in her contemplation when the doorbell rang. It was Iphigénie, looking for Joséphine.

"Madame Cortès, would you mind coming downstairs with me? There's a leak in the Lefloc-Pignel apartment, and I have to check it out. But I don't want to go in there alone. They might claim I swiped something!"

"Can I come too?" asked Iris, who was eating dinner.

"Sorry, but no, Madame Dupin. They wouldn't want people in their apartment."

"He'll never know! I'd so love to see where he lives."

"Well, you aren't going to! I don't want to get into trouble."

Iris sat back down and pushed her plate away.

"To hell with you, all of you! Get out of here!"

Iphigénie turned on her heel and blew a raspberry. Joséphine followed her out.

"She's really something, that one! I can't believe you two are sisters."

"I can't stand her anymore, Iphigénie. It's awful. She's turning into a caricature of herself. How can a person change so fast? She was the most elegant, sophisticated, distinguished woman in the world, and she's become—"

"A bitter old crow. That's what she is!"

The Lefloc-Pignel apartment lay in semidarkness; the two women entered on tiptoe.

"I feel like a burglar," whispered Joséphine.

"And me, a plumber," said Iphigénie, who headed for the kitchen to turn off the water.

Joséphine wandered around. In the living room, all the furniture was covered with white sheets. It looked like a convention of ghosts. She could make out two side chairs, a wing chair, a sofa, and a piano. The center of the room was dominated by a large rectangular box like a coffin on a catafalque. She lifted a corner of the sheet to find a huge, dry aquarium filled with stones, flat rocks, tree branches, pieces of bark, roots, potsherds, water dishes, and reeds. What do they keep in here? Ferrets? Tarantulas? Boa constrictors? And what do they do with them when they go on vacation?

Jo stepped into what must be the master bedroom. The double curtains were drawn and the shutters closed. She flipped a switch and a large milk-glass chandelier lit up the room. A crucifix with a piece of boxwood and a picture of Saint Thérèse of Lisieux hung above the bed. Joséphine walked over to look at the framed family photos on the wall. There were monsieur and madame, smiling on their wedding day: long white dress for the bride, morning suit and top hat for the groom. Isabelle Lefloc-Pignel looked as if she were taking her first communion. Other frames held pictures of the three children's baptisms, the various stages of their religious education, family Christmases, horseback rides, tennis games, and birthday parties. Next to the photos Joséphine noticed a document in a golden frame, its headings in bold, uppercase letters. She stepped closer and read:

Extract from a Catholic
Home Economics Manual for Women
(Published in 1960)

You have been married before God and man.

You must rise to meet the challenge of your mission.

When He Comes Home in the Evening

Have a delicious meal waiting for him. This is a way of letting him know that you've been thinking of him and that you care about his needs.

Be Ready

Take a fifteen-minute rest before his return, so as to be relaxed. Touch up your makeup, put a ribbon in your hair, and look fresh and attractive. He has spent the day with people weighted down with work and worries. His hard day needs to be lightened, and making that happen is one of your duties. Your husband will feel he has reached a haven of rest and order, and that will also make you happy.

Seeing to his comfort will bring you enormous personal satisfaction.

Reduce All Noise As Much As Possible

The moment he arrives, turn off the dishwasher, dryer, and vacuum cleaner. Encourage the children to be quiet. Greet him with a warm smile and show sincerity in your desire to please him.

Listen to Him

It is possible that you will have a dozen important things to tell him, but the moment he comes home is not the right time. Let him speak first, and remember that his topics of conversation are more important than yours.

Never Complain If He Comes Home Late

Or leaves to have dinner or seek entertainment elsewhere without you.

Don't Greet Him with Your Complaints and Problems

Help him get comfortably settled. Suggest that he relax in a comfortable chair or lie down in the bedroom. Speak softly and soothingly. Don't ask him questions, and never challenge his judgment or his integrity. Remember, he is the master of the house and as such will always exercise his will with justice and honesty.

When He Has Finished Eating, Clear the Table and Do the Dishes Quickly

If your husband offers to help, decline the offer, because he may feel obligated to repeat it later, and after a long day of work he doesn't need any extra chores. Encourage him to indulge his favorite pastimes and show an interest in them, but without making him feel you are intruding on his domain. Try not to bore him when you talk, because the things that are of interest to women are often fairly insignificant compared to those of men.

Once you have both retired to the bedroom, prepare to get into bed quickly.

Make Sure You Look Your Best When You Go to Bed

Try to look attractive without being provocative. If you must apply cream or put your hair in curlers, wait until he is asleep, as it might shock him to go to sleep seeing such a spectacle.

Concerning Intimate Relations with Your Husband

It is important to remind yourself of your marriage vows, and in particular your obligation to obey. If he feels he needs to go to sleep immediately, so be it. In all things, be guided by his desires, and never pressure him in order to provoke or stimulate an intimate relation.

If Your Husband Suggests Coupling

Accept it with humility, while remembering that a man's pleasure is more important than a woman's. When he reaches orgasm, a small moan on your part will encourage him and will largely suffice to indicate any pleasure you may have experienced.

If Your Husband Suggests One of the Less Common Practices

Be obedient and resigned, but show a possible lack of enthusiasm by keeping silent. It is likely that your husband will then fall asleep quickly. Adjust your clothing, freshen yourself up, and apply your cream and hair products.

You Can Then Set the Alarm

So as to be awake shortly before him in the morning. This will allow you to hand him his cup of tea when he wakes up.

Reading this, Joséphine shuddered.

"Iphigénie!" she called.

"What is it, Madame Cortès?"

"Come here, quick."

Iphigénie came running, wiping her arms with a rag. She had found the leak and turned off the water. She ran a hand through her lemon-yellow hair.

"Did you see a mouse?" she asked, amused.

Joséphine pointed at the framed text. As Iphigénie read it, her mouth rounded in astonishment.

"The poor woman! No surprise that she's exhausted and never goes out. But maybe it's a joke, just for laughs."

"I don't think so, Iphigénie."

"Too bad your sister can't see this! She doesn't do a damn thing from morning till night, and this might give her some ideas."

"Not a word of this to Iris!" hissed Jo, a finger to her lips. "She would mention it to him, and that would cause all sorts of trouble. That man scares me."

"And this apartment creeps me out. There's not a shred of life in it. She must spend all her time cleaning. I bet the kids don't have much fun, either. He must be a real tyrant."

They locked the front door and went home, Iphigénie to her colorful apartment and Joséphine to her book-lined bedroom.

The heat of August filtered through the kitchen's closed shutters. A heavy, motionless heat that lifted only for a few hours at night, to return crushingly at first light. It was only ten in the morning, but the sun was already firing its burning rays at the white metal shutters like a flamethrower.

"I don't understand the weather anymore," said Iris, sighing, sprawled in her chair. "Two days ago, there was talk of turning on the heat, and this morning we're dreaming of glaciers."

"There aren't any seasons anymore," muttered Joséphine, aware that it was becoming a cliché but too lazy to come up with a different reply.

"By the way, Luca called twice!" said Iris, moving her head to follow the oscillating fan. "He absolutely wants to talk to you. I said you would call him back."

"Oh, my gosh! I forgot to send him his key. I'll do it right now."

She slowly got up, found an envelope, wrote Luca's address, and slipped the little keys inside.

"Aren't you going to write him a note? As good-byes go, that's pretty curt."

"What was I thinking?" said Joséphine, sighing. "I'll have to get up again."

"Be strong!"

Jo came back with a sheet of paper and tried to think of what to say.

"Tell him you're going on vacation with me to Deauville. That way, he'll leave you alone."

Jo wrote: *Luca, here is your key. I'm going to my sister's in Deauville. Enjoy the rest of the summer, Joséphine.*

"There!" she said, sealing the envelope. "And good riddance!"

"I wouldn't complain! He's very handsome."

"Maybe, but I don't want to see him anymore."

"Want me to read your horoscope?"

"Mmmm . . . okay."

"All right. 'General: Things will be stormy from August 15 . . .'"

"That's today," remarked Joséphine, tipping her neck to expose some hot, damp skin to the fan's cool breeze.

"'. . . through the end of the month. Hang on, it could get violent and you won't come through unscathed. Heart: An old flame will come to life, and you will be transported. Health: Expect cardiac palpitations.'"

"Sounds like it's going be pretty lively," muttered Joséphine, exhausted at the idea of being caught in a storm. "What about yours?"

Iris took an ice cube from the pitcher of iced tea Joséphine had made, ran it over her blazing temples and cheeks, and read:

"Let's see now . . . 'General: You will face a sizable obstacle. Use charm and diplomacy. If you choose to respond with violence, you will lose. Heart: A confrontation will occur. It will be up to you to win or lose. It could go either way.' Wow! That's not very encouraging!"

"What about health?"

"I never read health," said Iris. She closed the newspaper, folded it, and fanned herself. "I'd like to be a penguin sliding on an icy toboggan."

"We'd be more comfortable splashing around in Deauville."

"Don't mention that place! A while ago the radio said a terrible storm hit there last night."

Iris reached languidly for the radio to listen for other weather reports and turned up the volume, but an ad was playing. She turned the sound down again.

"At least it would be a little cooler," said Joséphine. "I can't stand this anymore."

"You can go, if you like, I'll give you the keys. But I'm not budging."

He'll be here tomorrow, Iris thought. *If he keeps his promise. He still hasn't given me any news. I can't believe I called him a liar! I have to learn to . . .* Iris glanced down at her horoscope. . . . *"use charm and diplomacy." I'll crawl as low as a pregnant snake, be as shy as a harem novice. Why not?*

To her astonishment, Iris found herself wanting to obey him, to submit.

No man has ever made me feel this way before. Could this be the sign of true love? Not to have to play a role anymore, to give yourself body and soul to a man, saying, "I love you. Do whatever you want with me." Strange, how absence can amplify feelings. Or is it Hervé and his attitude that causes this surrender? He left behind an angry woman; he will return to find a submissive lover. I want to slip into his arms, put my life in his hands. I won't protest. I will quietly murmur, "You are my master." That's what he wanted to hear the night before he left, but I wasn't able to say it. Two weeks of painful absence have made the words blossom on my lips. He's coming back tomorrow, tomorrow. He said two weeks.

Iris had finally ended the Toad's hopes by admitting that she was in love with another man. He'd merely snapped his platinum card down on the check and said, "It doesn't matter. My time will come."

"You really are confident, Raoul!"

He had straightened, as proud and resplendent as a Roman

emperor in his toga returning from a victorious campaign. She liked his martial tone. She loved men who were strong, determined, brutal. *They make me tremble, my body bends toward them. I feel dominated, possessed, taken, filled. I like raw strength in a man. It's a quality that a woman rarely admits to liking, frightened by the crudeness of the confession.* Smiling vaguely, Iris started seeing Raoul in a new light. He's really not that ugly, all things considered. And that gleam in his eye, like a challenge . . .

But there was Hervé. Uncompromising Hervé. Not a word, not a message in two weeks. She trembled, sitting on her chair, and ran her hands through her long hair to hide her turmoil.

"Go to Deauville. The house is empty! The reporter on the radio talked about downed trees and roofs torn off. You can check to see if the storm did any damage. You'd be doing me a favor."

And I won't have Jo underfoot when Hervé gets here. She could spoil everything.

She turned up the volume on the radio.

"It would do me good," said Joséphine. "But do you really think . . . ?"

Along with love, Joséphine was learning deceit. She looked at her sister, all innocence, waiting for her to repeat her invitation.

"It's a fine idea, believe me," said Iris, waving the newspaper like a limp palm frond.

"Would you mind if I left right away?"

"Right now?" asked Iris, taken aback.

She looked at Joséphine and saw her clutching the iced tea pitcher, looking determined and impatient.

She pretended to hesitate, then agreed.

"Sure, if you like. But drive carefully."

Joséphine arrived early in the afternoon, to hear the shriek of seagulls circling low over the house and to breathe the damp, salty air. From the top of the driveway leading to the front door she saw the closed shutters, and sighed. During the drive, she'd imagined that Philippe would be there, waiting for her.

He wasn't.

Suddenly a gust plucked a tile from the roof and sent it crashing at her feet. Joséphine raised a hand to protect herself and looked up. Half the roof had blown off. In places, all that remained were bare rafters and thick batts of fiberglass insulation flapping in the wind like the layers of a mille-feuille pastry. It was as if a huge rake had passed over the house, stripping off some rows of tiles while leaving others. She looked at the trees in the yard. Some were still upright, shaking slightly; others were split open like chopped leeks.

She decided to wait until she spoke with Monsieur Fauvet, the local roofer, before telling Iris about the extent of the catastrophe. For now, she just texted her to say that she'd arrived safely.

Iris woke up, gripped by an anxiety that prickled in her whole body. She lay in bed, feeling oppressed. Today was August 16. He had said two weeks. She put her phone on the pillow and waited.

He wouldn't call right away. Those days were over. She realized she had crossed an unforgivable line when she called him a liar. And in public, too! She remembered the stunned look on the waiter's face when she'd yelled, "You are too a liar!" Hervé wouldn't easily forgive her for that. He'd already sentenced her to two weeks of silence. There would be other punishments.

Iris stared at the phone, begging it to ring. *I'll say . . . I have to choose my words carefully, so as not to offend him. I'll tell him I surrender. I'll say, "Hervé, I have waited for you and I understand. Do with me whatever you like. I'm not asking for anything, just the weight of your hands on my body, shaping me like a lump of clay. And if that's still too much, order me to wait, and I'll wait. I'll remain cloistered, and lower my eyes when you appear. I will drink when you so order it, eat if you command me to, purify myself of my pointless angers and girlish impulses."*

She sighed with a joy so intense she thought she would faint.

He has taught me love. I was seeking this ineffable happiness by accumulating things, and I realize I'm attaining it by abandoning them. By yielding, by letting everything go . . . he has placed me in my life. I'm going to get up, put on the ivory dress he bought me, put a ribbon in my hair, and sit waiting by the door. He won't phone, he'll ring the bell. I'll open the door, eyes lowered, my face free of any expectation, and I will say . . .

The hour of truth was approaching.

Iris spent all day listening for his footsteps, checking and rechecking her phone to make sure it was working.

He didn't come that evening.

The next morning, Iphigénie rang the doorbell.

"Isn't Madame Cortès home?"

"She left town for a while."

"Ah," said Iphigénie, disappointed.

"The building must be empty," said Iris, to keep the conversation going.

KATHERINE PANCOL

"There's just you and Monsieur Lefloc-Pignel, who came in yesterday evening."

Iris's heart leaped. He was back! He would call her. She closed the door and leaned against the jamb, limp with joy. She had to get ready and make sure no one would come between them.

She went to the stairwell and called down to Iphigénie that she was leaving for a few days to visit a girlfriend, and to please hold the mail. Iphigénie shrugged, and said, "Have a nice vacation. It'll do you good."

The refrigerator is full, she thought. *I won't have to go out.*

Iris took a shower, put on the ivory dress, fixed her hair, and removed her red nail polish. Then she waited. She spent the day waiting. She didn't dare turn the volume up on the television for fear of not hearing the phone ring, or missing a furtive knock on the door. *He knows I'm here; he is making me wait.*

In the evening she opened a can of ravioli. She wasn't hungry. To bolster her courage, she drank a glass of wine, then another. She thought she heard music in the courtyard. When she opened the window she heard opera, then the sound of his voice. He was on the telephone, talking business: "I'm reading the file on the merger . . ."

She shivered, closed her eyes. He will come, she kept repeating to herself.

She waited all evening, sitting by the window. The opera ended, the light went out.

He didn't come.

She wept, sitting on her chair in her ivory dress. I mustn't get it dirty. My beautiful wedding dress.

♦ 354 ♦

She finished the bottle of wine, took two Stilnoxes, and went to bed.

He had let her know that he was back by turning the music up loud.

She had let him know that she submitted by not coming down and ringing his doorbell.

That first night, Joséphine slept on a sofa in the living room. The house was a wreck, and the roof over the bedrooms was gone. When looking up, one saw nothing but the heavy black sky, bolts of lightning, and slanting sheets of rain.

A thunderclap woke her during the night, and Du Guesclin started howling. She started counting, "One . . . two . . ." to calculate how far away the storm was. She hadn't reached three before a flash of lightning lit up the yard, followed by the deafening sound of a tree falling. She rushed to the window in time to see the big beech tree in front of the house crash down onto her car, which collapsed in a terrible screech of crushed steel. *My car!*

She ran to the light switch, but the electricity was off. Another flash of lightning confirmed that her car had been flattened.

The next day she phoned Monsieur Fauvet. The roofer's wife told her he was overwhelmed with calls.

"All the houses around here are damaged," she said. "You're not the only one! He'll come by sometime this morning."

Jo would wait. She put buckets under the various leaks.

Hortense called, saying, "I'm going to Saint-Tropez. Some friends invited me."

Zoe called, too, but the connection was so bad that Jo only caught one word out of two. She heard, "Everything's fine . . .

batteries running down . . . I love you . . . staying an extra week, Philippe agrees . . ."

"All right," Jo said into the lengthening silence.

She went into the kitchen, opened the cabinets, took out a package of cookies and some jam. All the stuff in the freezer is going to spoil. I should call Iris and ask her what to do.

When she phoned, she described the situation in the least alarming way possible. She did say that the electricity was out, and about the freezer.

"Do whatever you like, Jo. I really don't care."

"But it'll all go bad!"

"It's not a big deal," said Iris wearily.

"You're right. Don't worry, I'll take care of it. Are you doing okay?"

"Yes. Hervé is back. I'm so happy, Jo. So happy. I think I'm finally discovering what love is. I've been hopin' for this moment all my life and now it's here. Thanks to him. I love you, Jo. I love you."

"I love you too, Iris."

"I haven't always very been nice to you."

"Oh, Iris! That doesn't really matter."

"I haven't been nice to anybody, but I think I was waitin' for something big, something very big, and I've finally found it. I'm learnin'. I'm sheddin' parts of myself little by little. I don't use makeup anymore, can you imagine? One day Hervé said he didn't like artifice, and rubbed off my blush with his finger. I'm preparing myself for him."

"I'm happy that you're happy."

"Oh, Jo. So happy. . . ."

Iris's voice was slurred, dragging some syllables out and skipping others. *She must've gotten drunk last night,* thought Joséphine sadly. Aloud she said, "I'll phone you tomorrow to let you know what's happening."

"Don't bother, Jo. Just take care of everythin', I trust you. Let me live my love. I feel like I'm sheddin' an old skin. I wan' to be alone, you understand? We don't have much time to be together, I want to use it to the fullest." She giggled like a schoolgirl. "I may even move into his apartment."

Joséphine remembered the austere bedroom with the crucifix, the picture of Saint Thérèse of Lisieux, and the commandments for the perfect wife. Lefloc-Pignel wouldn't be moving Iris into his apartment any time soon.

The next evening Iris heard first opera, then his voice on the telephone. She recognized *Il Trovatore*, hummed a tune, sat on her chair in her beautiful ivory dress. Ivory. Ivory tower. We're each in our ivory tower. Then she leaped to her feet, thinking, *Maybe he thinks I've gone! Or that I'm still sulking. Yes, of course. Besides, it's not up to him to come to me, but to me to go to him. As a penitent. He doesn't know that I've changed. He can't imagine it.*

Iris went downstairs and shyly knocked on his door. He opened it, looking cold and imperious.

"Yes?" he asked, as if not seeing her.

"It's me."

"It's me, who?"

"Iris."

"That isn't enough."

"I've come to apologize."

"That's better."

She stepped through the doorway, but he stopped her with a rigid finger.

"I've been frivolous, selfish, and ill-tempered," she said. "But during these last two weeks all alone I've understood many things. If you only knew."

She reached out her arms, offering herself. He stepped back.

"Will you now obey me in all ways from now on?"

"Yes."

He waved her in, but stopped her immediately when she went to go to the living room. He closed the door behind her, and said, "I spent a very bad vacation because of you—"

"I'm sorry."

"Don't interrupt when I'm speaking!"

She slumped to a chair, stung by his authoritarian tone.

"On your feet! I didn't tell you to sit down!"

She stood up.

"You're going to have to obey, if you want to go on seeing me."

"I do, I do! I want you so badly!"

He jumped backward in alarm.

"Don't touch me! I'm the one to decide, I give permission. Do you want to belong to me?"

"With all my heart! It's the only thing I hope for. I've learned so many—"

"Be quiet!"

She felt a little stirring of pleasure between her legs. She lowered her eyes, ashamed.

"That's better. Are you ready to accept my rule?"

"I am ready to accept your rule."

"You're going to go through a period of purification to rid you of your demons. You will stay at home, strictly obeying my instructions. Are you ready to hear them? Nod if you are, and from now on keep your eyes down when you are in my presence. You will raise them only when I tell you to."

"You are my master."

He slapped her hard, slamming Iris's head against her shoulder. She touched her cheek. He grabbed her arm and twisted it.

"I didn't tell you to speak! Be quiet! I give the orders here!"

She nodded yes. She could feel her cheek swelling and burning. She wanted to touch the burn. Again she felt the stirring between her legs, and almost fainted with pleasure. She bowed her head and whispered, "Yes, Master."

He remained silent for a moment as if testing her. She didn't move, her eyes downcast.

"You're going to go upstairs and live cloistered for as long as I decide, and follow a schedule that I will give you. Do you accept my rule?"

"I accept it."

"You will get up every morning at eight o'clock. You will carefully wash yourself all over. The smallest part of you must be clean. I will check. You will then kneel and review your sins. You will write them down on a sheet of paper that I will collect. Then you will say your prayers."

"I don't have a prayer book," she said, eyes lowered.

"I will lend you one. Then you will do the housework. You will clean everything perfectly, working on your knees, with bleach. Bleach smells good and it kills germs. You will scrub the floor while offering your work to God's mercy, and you will beg his forgiveness for your former dissolute life. You will do the housework until noon. If I come by, I don't want to see a speck of dirt or dust, or you will be punished. At noon you will be allowed to eat a slice of white ham and some rice. And you will drink water. I want no colored food, is that clear? Say yes if you have understood."

"Yes."

"I want you to be dressed as simply as possible. In white. Do you have a white dress?"

"Yes."

"Good. You will wear it all the time."

"Yes, Master."

"Hair pulled back, no jewelry, no makeup. In the evening you will eat the same meal. No alcohol allowed. You will drink only water. Tap water. I will come up and throw away all the wine bottles. You drink. You're an alcoholic. Are you aware of that? Answer me!"

"Yes, Master."

"In the evening you will sit on a chair waiting, in case I decide to pay a surprise visit. In complete darkness. I want no artificial light. You will live by daylight. You will make no noise. No music, no TV, no humming. You will recite your prayers in a whisper. If I don't come, you will not complain. You will remain on your chair in silence, meditating. The least infraction will be punished. I will have to hit and punish you, and I will reflect on the just punishment that will hurt you physically, which is necessary, as well as spiritually. You have been strutting around like a prideful little girl and must be brought down."

She crossed her hands behind her back, keeping her head down.

"Be ready for my unexpected visits. I forgot to tell you that I will lock you in, to make sure you don't escape. You will give me your key ring and swear that no other keys are available. You still have time to withdraw from this purification program. I'm not forcing you to do anything. This is your free choice. Think it over, and say yes or no."

"Yes, Master. I'm surrendering to you."

He gave her a sweeping backhand slap.

"You didn't think about it, you just rushed to answer! Speed is the demon's modern shape. I said to think it over."

Iris looked down and remained silent. Then she murmured, "I'm prepared to obey you in all things, Master."

"Good. You are amendable. You are on the path to rehabilitation. We are now going up to your place. You will slowly climb each step with your head bowed and your hands behind your back, as if climbing the mountain of repentance."

Hervé had Iris walk in front of him. In the foyer, he took down a riding crop and whipped her legs to keep her moving. She jerked upright, and he whipped her again, warning her to never show discomfort or pain when he struck her.

In Joséphine's apartment, he emptied all the wine bottles into the sink, chuckling nastily. He talked to himself in a nasal voice about vice, repeating the word, muttering that vice was everywhere in the modern world, that there was no end of it, that the world needed to be cleansed of all its filth, that this impure woman was going to cleanse herself.

"Remember, I can show up at any time, and if the work isn't done—"

"I will be punished."

He slapped her again with all his might, and she moaned. He had hit her so hard her ear was ringing.

"You don't have the right to speak without my permission!"

She started crying. He hit her again.

"Those are false tears. Soon you'll be shedding real tears, tears of joy. Kiss the hand that punishes you."

She leaned down and delicately kissed his hand, barely daring to brush it with her lips.

He seized her hair and pulled her head back.

"Lower your eyes so I can inspect you."

He ran a finger over her face, and was pleased to see she was wearing no makeup.

"You've begun to understand, apparently!"

He chuckled.

"You like rough treatment, don't you?"

He leaned close, drew her lips back to make sure her teeth were clean, plucked out a scrap of food with his fingernail. She could smell him, the smell of a strong, powerful man. *This is the way it should be*, she thought. *To belong to him. Belonging to him.*

"If you are obedient in everything, if you become as pure as a woman should be, we will be joined together."

Iris stifled a little moan of pleasure.

"We will walk together toward love, the only love, the one that must be sanctioned by marriage. On the day of my choosing, you will be mine. Say, 'I want and desire this,' and kiss my hand."

"I want and desire this."

She kissed his hand. He sent her off to sleep.

She got into bed. He came close and stroked her head.

"Go to sleep now."

Iris closed her eyes. She heard the door close behind him and the key turn in the lock.

She was a prisoner. A prisoner of love.

Twice a day, Joséphine called Monsieur Fauvet, and twice a day she spoke to his wife. Every gust of wind was tearing off more tiles, she said. It was dangerous, the house was leaking, her cell phone would soon be dead and she wouldn't be able to call.

Madame Fauvet said, "Yes, yes, my husband will come over as soon as he can," and hung up.

It rained on and on. Even Du Guesclin didn't want to go outside. He slouched out onto the ruined high terrace, sniffed the wind, and raised a leg against the broken ceramic pots. Then he came back inside, sighing.

Joséphine slept in the living room, took cold showers, and raided the freezer, eating ice cream: Ben & Jerry's, Häagen-Dazs chocolate chocolate chip and pralines & cream. Du Guesclin licked the lids. He gazed up at her adoringly and waggled his hips, waiting for her to give him another lid.

Jo's cell phone rang, with a text message. It was from Luca!

You know, Joséphine. You know, don't you?

She didn't answer, thinking, I know, but I don't give a damn. I'm with Du Guesclin nice and safe under a shattered roof and a pink mohair blanket that tickles my nose.

The cell rang again. Another text from Luca.

Aren't you going to answer?

She didn't answer. Her phone would die soon and she didn't want to waste her last resources on Luca Giambelli—or rather Vittorio.

On a shelf she found an old edition of *Cousin Bette* by Balzac. She opened it and sniffed the binding. The book smelled of the sacristy, of priestly garb, of mildew. She would read it by candlelight once it got dark.

Maybe I should have told Inspector Garibaldi about Luca, so he could add him to his list of suspects. She pulled the blanket close, smoothed the long mohair threads, and picked up the book. She was interrupted by a third call, a third text message.

I know where you are, Joséphine. Answer me.

Her heart started to pound. Could he be telling the truth?

She tried to reach Iris, in vain. She was probably out having dinner with handsome Hervé. Jo checked to make sure all the doors were locked. The big picture windows had certified shatterproof glass, but what if he came in through the roof? There were openings everywhere. He could just climb up onto a balcony . . .

I'll blow out the candle. He won't know I'm here. Oh, but he'll see the flattened car under the tree.

A volley of text messages followed:

I'm on the highway, I'll be there soon.

Answer me, you're driving me crazy!

You won't get away with this!

I'm getting closer, and you won't be so proud.

Bitch! You bitch!

I'm at Touques.

At Touques! Jo looked at Du Guesclin in alarm, but he didn't stir. His head resting on his paws, he was waiting for her to resume reading or to open another container of ice cream.

She wanted to call Garibaldi, but only had his work number. She tried Iris again, got her voicemail again.

Jo's cell phone rang, with another text message.

The yard's beautiful, so close to the sea. Go to the window and you'll see me. Get ready.

Jo went to the window. Trembling, she held onto the frame and peered out. The night was so dark that she could only see giant shadows moving in the wind. Trees bending, branches cracking, leaves torn off in a gust and swirling to the ground . . . *It's as if they're being stabbed. Right in the heart. A hand goes around your neck and squeezes and squeezes, you're being held in a vise while the other hand sinks the knife in. The night I was attacked, Luca wanted to talk to me. "I want to talk to you, Joséphine, it's important." He wanted to confess, he got scared, he decided to kill me instead. He left me for dead.*

Joséphine was shaking so hard, she couldn't bring herself to step away from the window. *He's going to come in, he's going to kill me, Iris isn't answering, Garibaldi doesn't know what's going on, Philippe is in a pub, laughing with Dottie Doolittle, I'm going to die all alone. My girls, my little girls . . .*

Big tears were running down her cheeks. She wiped them off with the back of her hand. Du Guesclin's ears went up and he started barking.

"Be quiet! You're going to get us spotted!"

He barked louder, paced around the living room, stood at the window and put his paws on the glass.

"Stop it! He's going to see us!"

She sneaked a peek outside and saw a car coming down the driveway, headlights on. They threw a blaze of light across the room, and Jo dove to the floor.

Now Du Guesclin was barking furiously, panting, bumping into furniture in the dark. Gathering her courage, Joséphine stood up and looked around for a place to hide. Maybe the laundry room. It has a heavy door, with locks. *I hope I have some battery left. I'll call Hortense, she'll know what to do. She never panics.*

Down on all fours, Joséphine scuttled toward the laundry room. Du Guesclin was standing at the front door, head down and shoulders hunched, as if about to charge the enemy. She whispered, "Come on, we're retreating," but he stood guard, menacing and frothing at the mouth, his fur standing on end.

Joséphine heard steps on the gravel. Heavy steps. The man was coming closer. He was confident, he knew he would find her there. He came closer still. She heard a key turn in the door, unlocking first one lock, then a second and a third.

"Is there anyone here?" A man's voice.

It was Philippe.

———

One morning Iris was startled to wake up to find Hervé standing at the foot of her bed. She hadn't heard the alarm clock! She didn't raise her hand to protect herself from the riding crop that would punish her sin. Instead, she lowered her eyes and waited.

He didn't beat her. Didn't note the slightest infraction of the rules. Instead, he walked around the bed, slashed the air with the crop, and said, "You won't eat today. I put slices of ham and some rice on the table, but you aren't allowed to touch it. You will spend the day on your chair reading your prayer book, and I will come in the evening to see that the slices of ham are intact. You're filthy! This job is harder than I thought. You must be cleansed from head to foot to become a beautiful bride. You may drink two glasses of water. I put them on the table. You will drink them while thinking of the spring that flows and purifies you. Is that clear?"

She murmured, "Yes, Master." The hunger that had gnawed at her the night before now awoke in her stomach like an animal.

"To be sure that you have been obedient in studying your prayer book, I'm going to give you a passage you must memorize and recite to me without making a single mistake. The slightest stumble will be punished in a way that will make you remember the lesson. Do you understand?"

She lowered her eyes, and whispered, "Yes, Master."

He hit her with the crop.

"I didn't hear you!"

"Yes, Master," she cried, tears falling onto her chest.

He picked up her prayer book, leafed through it, and found something that seemed satisfactory.

"This is an excerpt from *The Imitation of Christ*. It's called 'Resisting Temptation.' You've never been able to resist temptation. This text will teach you how.

He cleared his throat and began reading aloud: "No one is so perfect or so holy but he is sometimes tempted; man cannot be altogether free from temptation. Yet temptations, though troublesome and severe, are often useful to a man, for in them he is humbled, purified, and instructed. The saints all passed through many temptations and trials to profit by them . . ."

He continued reading for a long time, in a monotonous voice. Then he put the book on the bedspread and said, "When I visit you tonight, I want you to recite this by heart, with all of the humility and care I demand."

"Yes, Master."

"Kiss the master's hand!"

She kissed his hand.

He turned on his heel, leaving her helpless with hunger and pain, motionless under the white sheets. She cried for a long time, her eyes wide open, without moving, without protesting, her arms along her body, her hands open on the bedspread. She had no strength left.

"Jo! The door's jammed shut! I can't get it open!"

"Philippe . . . Is that you?"

He had left his headlights on, but she wasn't sure she recognized him against the pitch-black darkness.

"Did you lock yourself in?"

"Oh, Philippe! I was so scared! I thought that . . ."

"Try to open the door!"

"Just tell me that it's really you!"

"Why? Were you expecting someone else? Am I interrupting something?"

She laughed with relief. It really was him. She ran to the door and tried to open it, but it was stuck.

"Philippe, it rained so much, the frame's swollen! When I got here it was so cold I turned the heat all the way up. It must've warped the wood."

"It's because I replaced all the doors and windows. There used to be drafts everywhere and I got tired of heating the garden, so I replaced them. They're new and a bit stiff. You just have to push."

"But I was able to get in!"

"They must've seized up after you turned on the heat. Try again!"

After making sure the bolts were pulled back, Joséphine did so. "No luck!" she said.

"It's always hard at first. Let me see . . ."

He must've moved away, because his voice was coming from some distance away.

"Philippe, I'm frightened! I've been getting text messages from Luca. He's on his way here! He's going to kill me!"

"No he won't. I'm here. Nothing can happen to you."

Jo could hear his footsteps on the gravel. He was walking along the house, looking for a way in.

"I installed security doors and windows everywhere. There's not a single opening. The house is like a safe."

"Philippe, he's coming," said Joséphine, now panicky. "He's the one who's been stabbing those women. I now know it's him!"

"Your old boyfriend?" he asked, sounding amused.

"Yes. I'll explain, it's complicated. It's like those Russian dolls, there are lots of stories one inside the other. But I'm sure it's him."

"It can't be! You're panicking for no reason. Why would he come here? Step back from the door. I'll try to break it down."

Joséphine took two steps back and heard the sound of his body slam against the door. It shook, but didn't yield.

"Shit!" cried Philippe. "I'll never manage. I'll go take a look in back."

"Philippe, be careful!" shouted Joséphine. "He's coming, I tell you."

"Jo, stop panicking! You're imagining things!"

She heard his steps on the gravel, moving away. She waited, gnawing on her finger. Luca was going to come, the two men would fight, and there wouldn't be anything she could do. She pulled out her cell phone to call the police, but was so rattled she couldn't remember the number. Then the phone died. The battery was dead.

The crunch of footsteps returned. She went to the window and saw Philippe in the glare of the headlights. She waved to him, and he came closer.

"Nothing doing! Everything's stuck! Calm down, Jo."

He put his hand on the window, and she pressed hers against it, through the glass.

"Luca terrifies me! I didn't have the time to tell you everything when we were in London. He's crazy! Violent!"

She had to shout to make herself heard.

"He's not going to do anything to us! Stop panicking!"

She could hear him slump down against the door.

"I'm going to have to spend the night outside."

"Oh, no," she moaned. There was the terrace where Du Guesclin relieved himself, but it was too high to be reached from the garden.

She sat down as well, leaning against the door. With a finger, she started scratching at one of the panels, as if to drill through it.

"Philippe, are you there?"

"If I spend the night out of doors, I'm going to rust."

"The bedrooms are soaked and there's almost no roof left. I've been sleeping in the living room on the big sofa with Du Guesclin."

"Is that a suit of armor?"

"My protector."

"Hello, Du Guesclin."

"He's a dog."

"Ah."

Philippe must've changed position, because through the door she could hear him moving. In her mind's eye she saw him sitting with his knees bent, arms hugging his legs, collar turned up. The rain had stopped. The only sound now was a sharp, imperious two-note song that the wind played as it whistled through the tree branches.

"See what I told you? He isn't coming," Philippe said after a while. "You were frightened for nothing. And even if he comes, he'll find me and that should calm him down. But I'm sure he won't come."

Joséphine felt at peace, listening to him. She leaned her head against the door panel and breathed quietly. Philippe was there, right on the other side. She wasn't afraid of anything anymore. He had come, alone. Without Dottie Doolittle.

"Jo?"

He paused, then said, "Are you angry with me?"

Suddenly she was close to tears.

"Why didn't you call?" she asked.

"Because I'm a jerk."

"There's nothing worse than silence," she moaned. "You start imagining the most horrible things. There's nothing to hang onto, not even a scrap of reality to get angry about. I hate silence!"

"But it's so handy, sometimes."

Joséphine sighed.

"You've just been talking. See, it's not so complicated."

"That's because you're on the other side of the door."

She burst out laughing, a laughter that drove her fear away. Philippe was there, Luca wouldn't come. He would see another car next to hers under the tree. He would realize she wasn't alone.

"Philippe, I feel like kissing you!"

"We're going to have to wait. This door seems to have other ideas. Anyway, I'm not easy. I like to be desired."

"I know."

"Have you been here long?"

"It's been three days. At least I think so . . ."

"And it's been raining like this for three days?"

"Yes, nonstop. I've tried to get Fauvet, but—"

"He called me. He's coming with his workmen tomorrow."

"He called you in Ireland?"

"I was back by then. When I got to the camp to pick up Zoé

and Alexandre, they said they wanted to stay on, so I went back to London."

"Alone?" asked Joséphine, scratching harder at the door.

"All alone. You won't lose me again, Jo."

"I even thought you'd fallen back in love with Iris."

"No, it's really all over with Iris," he said sadly. "I had lunch with her new love. He asked me for her hand."

"Hervé Lefloc-Pignel? He was in London?"

"No, Raoul Frileux, my partner at the firm. Why Lefloc-Pignel?"

"I probably shouldn't tell you this, but she's apparently in love with him. They're having a grand love affair in Paris right now."

"Iris with Hervé Lefloc-Pignel? But he's married!"

Jo was tempted to ask if it hurt his feelings, but kept quiet. She didn't want to talk about her sister, didn't want Iris to come between them. She waited until he resumed the conversation.

"Joséphine, I wanted to tell you. . . . Someday I might not be able to keep up with you. And if that day comes, I want you to wait for me. Wait until I finish growing up. I'm way behind in that department!"

They spent the night talking, on opposite sides of the door.

Fauvet showed up in the morning and freed Joséphine, who had to resist jumping into Philippe's arms. She settled for leaning against him and rubbing her cheek on his jacket sleeve.

She telephoned Inspector Garibaldi and told him about the harassment she'd suffered at Luca's hands and what he'd said in his text messages. She described his indifference, his split personality, his violent outbursts.

"We know all about that," said the inspector.

"So you've already been investigating him?"

"This conversation is over, Madame Cortès."

"You mean you know who the killer is?"

But Garibaldi had already hung up. Joséphine was thoughtful as she turned her attention back to Philippe and Fauvet, who were inspecting the roof and making a list of repairs to be made.

When Philippe came over to her, she quietly said, "I think they've arrested the killer."

"Is that why he didn't come here? Because they caught him in time?"

He put his arms around her shoulders and said she should forget about it.

They took off for Étretat and checked into a hotel, leaving their room only for tea and cake. From their bed, they watched the rain sluice down across the window. Sprawled on the carpet, Du Guesclin sighed, shifted position, and went back to sleep.

They decided to take their time returning to Paris.

"Do you want to try just traveling back roads?" asked Philippe.

"Yes."

"Get lost on back roads?"

"Sure, why not? That way, we'll have the most time together."

"Jo, now we can have all the time together we like."

It was raining so hard, they actually did get lost. Joséphine turned the road map every which way, and Philippe joked that he would never choose her as a co-pilot.

"But you can't see a thing! Let's get back on a highway. Too bad."

Taking route D313, they drove through little villages. They could barely see through the rapid sweep of the windshield wipers. Eventually they came to a town called Le Floc-Pignel.

Philippe whistled.

"Hey, Hervé's important. He even has a town named after him!"

As they very slowly drove through the village, Joséphine spotted an old shop with peeling paint. A sign in faded green letters on white read IMPRIMERIE MODERNE.

"Philippe! Stop the car!"

He pulled over, and she got out to look at the building. Seeing a light inside, she gestured to Philippe to join her.

"What was the man's name again?" she muttered to herself, trying to remember what Lefloc-Pignel had told her.

"Who's that?"

"The man who took Lefloc-Pignel in. It's on the tip of my tongue!"

His name turned out to be Benoît Graphin. An old man, frosty white with age. He looked surprised when he opened the door, but invited them into a big room full of machinery, books, pots of glue, and printing plates.

"Sorry about the mess," he said. "I don't have the energy to straighten up."

Joséphine introduced herself, and the moment she said the name Hervé Lefloc-Pignel, the old man's eyes lit up.

"Tom," he murmured. "Little Tom!"

"You mean Hervé."

"I called him Tom. Because of Tom Thumb, you know."

"So what he told me is true, that you took him in and raised him."

"Took him in, yes; raised him, no. She didn't give me the time."

He went to fetch a coffeepot from an old wood stove, offered them some, and opened a tin of cookies. He walked bent over, dragging his feet. He wore an old woolen sweater, threadbare corduroys, and slippers.

He dipped cookies in his cup, and refilled it when they soaked up the coffee. He moved mechanically, his eyes vacant, as if Joséphine and Philippe weren't there.

"You have to excuse me," he muttered. "I don't talk much anymore. Before, there were people in the village, stuff going on, neighbors. Now they've nearly all gone."

"I know," said Joséphine softly. "He told me about the main street, the stores, and about working with you."

"So he remembers?" Graphin asked, moved. "He hasn't forgotten?"

"He remembers everything. Especially you."

The old man took out a handkerchief and dabbed at his eyes. His hand shook as he put it back in his pants pocket.

"When I found him, he was no bigger than this. . . . Heaven sent him to me, little Tom."

"You mean he just showed up and knocked on your door?" asked Joséphine, smiling.

"Oh no! I was busy working and the machines were running." He gestured at the dust-covered printing machines behind him. "Made a hell of a racket. But I heard a sudden squeal of brakes, so I went to the window and looked out. And you wouldn't believe what I saw!"

He clapped his hands together as if he still couldn't believe it.

"A big car stopped right in front of my place, and a woman tossed him out. Like somebody getting rid of a dog. The kid just stood there by the side of the road. He was holding a turtle. He must've been three or four, I never knew. I had him come inside. He wasn't crying, just held his turtle. I figured the people would turn around and come back for him. He was as cute as anything. Nice, sweet, shy. He didn't know his name. In the beginning he didn't talk, actually. That's why I called him Tom. He only knew his turtle's name, Sophie. That was a good forty years ago, you know. I told the cops, and they said to keep him for the time being."

A piece of cookie fell into Graphin's coffee cup, and he got up to get a spoon. He sat back down heavily and continued, while fishing out the cookie.

"He never said Mommy or Daddy. Hardly talked at all. And then one day he just said, 'Keep me with you.' It really moved me, I'm telling you. I didn't have any kids. So the three of us just lived here: him, me, and his turtle. He loved that animal, and it was strange, but she was attached to him. I got used to having the kid and the turtle around. He went everywhere with me. I didn't take a step without him. I enrolled him in the village school. I knew the teacher, and he didn't make any fuss. The cops would drop by from time to time, have a cup of coffee. They said I really ought to register him, that maybe his parents were looking for him. I didn't say anything, just listened. I figured that if his parents wanted him . . . it wouldn't have been hard to come back and ask around, would it?"

"Of course not!" Jo and Philippe answered together, They were rapt, hanging on the old man's words, his milky eyes with their painful tears, the aged fingers dipping the cookies.

"So one day this woman shows up. A social worker, says her name's Évelyne Lamarche. A dry stick, bossy and impatient. She'd written 'RV Le Floc Pignel' in her notebook that day, and decided he was going with her. Just like that! Without asking us, me or him! When I protested, she said it was the law. She needed a name for him, and said he'd be called Hervé Lefloc-Pignel. She was going to put him in a foster home. I protested again, saying this already was his foster home. But she told me you had to be signed up on a list. Said there was lots of people waiting for children, and I had never signed up. Why would I? I never expected a kid, for God's sake!"

Graphin wiped his eyes again, folded his handkerchief and put it back in his pocket. He brushed cookie crumbs off the table with the sleeve of his sweater.

"He'd spent six years with me, and in three minutes, he was gone, just like that. He screamed when she carried him off. Scratched and bit her, kicked like mad. She threw him into her car and locked it. He was screaming, 'Papie! Papie!' That's what he used to call me. I thought I was going to die. I wasn't old then. My hair turned white overnight."

Graphin ran his hands through that white hair, smoothed his eyebrows.

"I don't know what they did with him, but wherever they placed him, he ran away. Always came back to me. People didn't listen to children in those days, so you can imagine, nobody cared what an abandoned child said. But I did tell him one thing. I said he should study hard in school, that's how he would get by. And he listened. He was always first in his class.

"One day, when he'd run away yet again, he showed up without Sophie. In the family where he was placed, the father was a real nut job. Used to be a paratrooper and scared everybody around him half to death. And he laid down the law: You had to fold hospital corners on the beds, clean the toilet with a toothbrush. If Tom did the slightest thing wrong, he was beaten. He had burn scars all over his body. The wife, she didn't say anything. She had a very strong, sick connection with her man. She had to get herself fixed up before he came home from work. She put on garter belts and stockings and sexy underwear. She'd parade around in front of the children in a bra and panties. The guy would come home and feel her up, and make the kids watch, to teach them about life.

"The man told Tom that if he wasn't always first in class he'd be punished. One day he got a bad grade, and this crazy guy grabbed Sophie, put her on the kitchen table, and killed her. Beat her to death with a hammer. And then he did a really horrible thing. He told Tom to throw Sophie's body in the garbage can. Tom attacked him. He must've been just thirteen, and the man beat the crap out of him. When he got here, he was all bloody. And you know what happened?

Graphin turned red and slammed his fist on the table.

"The social services lady came to get him! With her little brief-case and her tight little skirt and her little bun. And she took him away again. Tom hated that woman. Every time he ran away and came here, she'd find him and stick him with some other crazy family. They'd make him cut wood, work in the fields, clean the house, mow the lawn, paint, polish, pump out the septic tank. Barely gave him enough to eat, and they beat him. But this woman said he had to be broken. A real sadist, I'm telling you. It just made me sick. I stopped enjoying life, I let the shop run down.

"The last time I saw Tom, he showed up in the middle of the

night with a pal. They were both pretty drunk. They showed that bitch something, they said. Tom even said, 'I got my revenge. I reset the counters to zero.' I said, 'Tom, you don't get revenge by putting the counters to zero.'

"His pal laughed, and said, 'That's not Tom, that's Hervé. Why you callin' him Tom? You got something against Hervé?' I said, 'No, I don't have anything against Hervé, it's just that I call him Tom.' And he said, 'Well that's good, because my name's Hervé too. I was a welfare kid too, and that bitch Lamarche was on my case, too. She really fucked up my life!"

"What was the second Hervé's last name?" asked Joséphine.

"I don't remember. A weird name, Belgian. Van something. I've got it written down. Because after they left I wrote everything in a notebook."

"It's very important, Monsieur Graphin."

"You think so?" he asked, his white eyebrows shooting up. "Well, I'll find it for you. It's in a box. My box of memories."

He shuffled to a shelf with a dusty box, and asked Philippe to get it down for him. Graphin took out a notebook, carefully opened it, and leafed through it until he found a date he read aloud: "August second, 1983."

"Van den Brock! That's it, his name was Van den Brock. He'd taken the name of his adoptive family. But he spent two years in foster care before being adopted. That's how the two boys got to know each other. And they stayed close ever since. When they showed up that night, they were celebrating their graduation. They must've been twenty-three or twenty-four. The tall, rude one studied medicine. Tom graduated from Polytechnique and lots of other schools I can't remember anymore. They left at dawn, headed back to Paris.

"I never heard from Tom again. But one day I read in the local paper that he was marrying the daughter of a banker named Mangeain-Dupuy. The family owns a castle not far from here. I don't know if they really accepted him. After all, he was named for a little nothing village and didn't come from their world. Not long afterward, someone who worked at the castle told me how their first child died. It was horrible! Run over in a parking lot. Sort of like Sophie the turtle. Life plays us some pretty dirty tricks, I told myself. To put Tom through that—him, of all people! After that, I only heard about him from time to time.

"I don't know how you survive a childhood like that. Little Tom! He was so cute when he waltzed around the shop with Sophie. He danced very slow so she wouldn't get dizzy. He would slip her into his jacket and she stuck out her little head, and he talked to her. You see me, I never got married, I never had children, but at least I never made anyone unhappy."

"So they've known each other since they were kids," murmured Joséphine.

"I've heard people talk about Lefloc-Pignel, but I could never imagine he'd had a childhood like that," said Philippe. "Never."

Graphin looked him in the eye. His voice trembled as he said, "Because it wasn't a childhood, that's why!"

In the car, Joséphine was thoughtful. *So the two men knew each other. That must've been the trail Capitaine Gallois was following when she was killed.*

"Do you think we should warn Iris?" she asked. "It's a pretty violent story."

"She won't listen to you," said Philippe. "She never listens. She lives in a dreamworld."

Iris had been purifying herself for the last eight days.

For eight days she lived as a recluse in the apartment, eight days of getting up at seven thirty every morning so as to be clean when Hervé came to bring her food.

She knew it had been eight days because he reminded her. On the tenth day, they would be married. He had promised. It was an engagement, a solemn engagement.

"Will I have a witness?" she asked, her eyes lowered and her hands tied behind her back to a chair, as usual.

"There will be a witness for the two of us," he said. "Who will record our engagement before it becomes official in the eyes of others."

That suited her fine. She would wait for as long as it took for him to deal with the divorce papers. He never spoke of divorce, always of marriage. She didn't ask any questions.

They now had a routine. She was no longer disobeying, and he seemed satisfied with her. At times, he would untie her and brush her long hair while speaking lovingly. "My beauty, my lovely one, you belong to me alone. Promise you'll never let another man near you."

He woke her up in the morning. He set the ham and rice on the kitchen table. She had to be clean in her white dress. He ran his finger over her eyelids, along her neck, between her legs. He wanted no smell between her legs, so she scrubbed herself with

Marseille soap. His touching her there was the most terrible ordeal. She couldn't let herself go, and gritted her teeth to keep from giving a long moan of pleasure. He ran a finger over the TV screen to be sure there wasn't any static dust on it, another finger over the tiles, the floor, the chimney.

Then he would come back and stroke her cheek, a very gentle caress that made her cry. "You see, this is love," he said. "When you give up everything, when you surrender completely, blindly. You didn't know this before. You were living in such a false world, you couldn't. When everyone comes back to town, I'll rent an apartment for you. You'll be purified, and if your behavior is exemplary, maybe we'll relax the rules a little."

She savored the anxiety before the blows, the torment of expectation. *Have I done everything well? Will I be punished or rewarded?* Expectation and anxiety expanded her life. Every minute was important. Every second spent waiting filled her with an incredible happiness she'd never known before. She waited for the moment when she knew he was happy and satisfied or knew he was furious and violent. Her heart pounded and pounded. Her head spun. She let him strike her, then fell to his feet and promised never to do it again. Then he would tie her to the chair. For the whole day. At noon, he came back to feed her. She opened her mouth when he told her to, chewed when he told her to, swallowed when he told her to. At times, he seemed so pleased that they waltzed around the apartment. In silence. Without making a sound, which was even more beautiful. She leaned her head against him and he caressed her. He even lightly kissed her hair, which made her nearly faint.

One day when she had disobeyed and he tied her up, the

telephone rang. It couldn't be Hervé; he knew she was tied up. To her astonishment, she realized she didn't care who was calling. She didn't belong to that world anymore. She didn't feel like talking to other people. They would never understand how happy she was.

She did disobey in one way, however. She described her happiness in writing, on sheets of paper that she hid behind the stove. She told it all, in detail, and it was like reliving all the pleasure and all the fear. *I want to record this love that is so beautiful and so pure. I want to be able to read and reread it, and shed tears of joy.*

I have grown more in eight days than in forty-seven years of life.

She had become exactly the woman Hervé had wanted her to be.

"I'm happy at last," she murmured before falling asleep. "Happy at last."

And then the evening arrived when he came to get her, to marry her.

She was waiting, barefoot in her ivory dress, her hair undone. He had asked her to wait for him standing in the doorway like a beautiful bride ready to walk down the church nave. She was ready.

Roland Beaufrettot was in a rage that night. "Fucking society can't even get its shit together!" he muttered to himself, chewing on his pipestem. "Just lets people sink or swim, and fuck 'em."

He spat a stream of tobacco juice into the bushes.

Beaufrettot had been warned that a gang of ravers were out looking for a field to throw the "party of the century." *I'll show you a fucking party! Those drugged-out little shits aren't gonna fuck up my field.*

They say those degenerates go out at night, looking for places to party. Well, they won't be disappointed. They're gonna wind up at the end of my rifle, and no one will be the wiser. I'm not about to let a bunch of loud druggies tear up my fields.

Beaufrettot was hidden in the bushes, waiting for the ravers, when he heard the noise of a first car, and then a second, some distance in front of him. *Hm, I'll finally have a chance to see what a raver looks like up close. Just enough to get a quick look before I shoot their balls off, assuming they have any.*

The first car stopped and parked in the forest clearing so close to Beaufrettot that he stepped back so as not to be seen. It was late August, and a full moon hung in the sky, a lovely round moon as bright as a city streetlight illuminating the field he loved so much. The second car parked facing the first one, their hoods a dozen yards apart.

A tall man wearing a white raincoat stepped out of the first car. From the other, a very skinny, almost skeletal man emerged. The two of them talked for a moment and then the skinny man went back to his car, switched on his high beams, and started playing music. Beaufrettot thought it was gorgeous. Not the kind of music you might hear in a TV story about raves, but music that spins and soars, and a woman's voice, as beautiful as the moon on his field, echoing through the forest and touching the trees, the century-old oaks, the aspens, and the white and gray poplars that Beaufrettot's father had planted, and which he guarded jealously.

The man in the white raincoat switched on his high beams as well, creating a lattice of light crisscrossing the clearing. He helped a woman in a white dress out of the car. She had long black hair and was very beautiful. She was barefoot, but walked so lightly it was as if she weren't touching the ground, as if the thistles didn't scratch her feet.

That's a hell of a good-looking couple, for sure. Don't look like ravers, either. Hard to tell how old they are, in their forties, maybe. Elegant, and just a little show-offy, like people who've got money and are used to having people make way for them when they appear. And that music . . . the music! Beaufrettot had never heard such beautiful music.

These people aren't ravers, so they must be the organizers, scouting party locations. Beaufrettot lowered his rifle and took out a notepad and pencil. While he still had enough light, he wrote down the makes of the cars and their license plates. Then he put away his notebook and looked at the woman through his binoculars. *She's so beautiful! They can't be ravers. But if they're not, what the hell are they doing here?*

White Raincoat introduced Skinny to the beautiful, elegant woman. She bowed her head very slowly, with a lot of restraint, as if she were in her living room and receiving an honored guest. Then Skinny went to turn down the music a little. The handsome couple stood in the middle of the clearing, upright, handsome, romantic. White Raincoat had his arms around the woman and was holding her, but very chastely. Skinny came and stood before them, put his palms together like a priest, and began a ceremony. He said something to the woman, who answered with a few words that Beaufrettot couldn't hear. Skinny turned to White Raincoat and asked him a question. He answered loudly, "Yes, that is what I want." Then Skinny took their hands, pressed them together, and very loudly said, "I hereby declare you joined by the bonds of marriage."

So that's what it is! A wedding at nightfall in my field!

The woman leaned against White Raincoat, her long hair floating on her shoulders just as she floated in the man's arms, and they spun round and round in the clearing.

The couple was waltzing very, very slowly. Beaufrettot thought he'd never seen anything more beautiful. The woman was smiling, her eyes lowered, her feet naked on the grass. The man held her with a kind of quiet authority and grace that seemed to come from another age.

Then Skinny threw his arms in the air like a human semaphore, clapped his hands, and yelled "Now! Now!" From his pocket, White Raincoat took something that gleamed in the glare of the headlights and quickly plunged it into the woman's chest. He did this powerfully and methodically, holding her in his arms and counting, "One-two-three, one-two-three," as they waltzed.

I must be dreaming! thought Beaufrettot. *This can't be happening!* Under his very eyes, a man was stabbing a woman to death as they danced. The woman fell to the ground, a long white blot on the dark grass. Without looking at her, the man raised the thing to the sky, like a Druid offering, then handed it ceremoniously to Skinny. Beaufrettot thought it looked like the short knife you use to dispatch a stag when hunting to hounds. Then Skinny went to his car and came back with a kind of big garbage bag. The two men slowly bent the woman in half, slid her into the bag, and closed it. With one man at each end, they then carried it and threw it in the lake next to the field.

Beaufrettot was rubbing his eyes, stunned. He had dropped

his rifle and binoculars and was crouched in the bushes, staying well out of sight. He had just witnessed a murder as it was happening.

The two men returned to the clearing. From White Raincoat's car they took out a crate, opened it, and spread what looked like stones on the field, arranging them in a circle. They're covering up the evidence, thought Beaufrettot. Hiding the bloodstains. Then the men shook hands and separated. The cars' headlights disappeared in the dark and the noise of their engines gradually faded away.

"I'll be a son of a bitch!" Beaufrettot muttered to himself. "I can't fucking believe this!"

After waiting to be sure the cars weren't coming back, he emerged from the bushes. He wanted to see what the men had left on the ground to hide the evidence of their crime.

By the light of his flashlight he saw a dozen big brown and yellow stones arranged in a perfect circle. It was as if they were trailing each other, walking in a circle. He nudged one with the toe of his boot, and the stone moved. It stuck out a little leg, then a second, and a third. Beaufrettot shouted, "Goddamn fucking son of a bitch!" and took to his heels.

The next day he went to tell the cops the whole story.

They were back in Paris. Philippe had gotten them a room in a hotel. They wanted to spend some more time together without anyone knowing. Zoé and Alexandre would be arriving in two days. They had two days all to themselves, alone in an empty Paris. Joséphine dialed Iris's cell number again, but she didn't answer.

"It's strange, she's always glued to her cell. I'm worried."

"She probably turned it off," he said. "She doesn't want to be disturbed. Let her live her big love affair. They must've gone away for a couple of days."

"Doesn't it bother you at all, knowing she's with another man?"

"Jo, the only thing I want is for her to be happy, and I'll do whatever it takes for that to happen. With Lefloc-Pignel or someone else. But I'm afraid she's going to run into a brick wall with him."

He took Joséphine in his arms and she leaned against him, her mouth against his, motionless, savoring a kiss that went on and on. He kissed her, stroked her neck, his hand moved down to seize a breast and squeeze it. She pressed against him, pushed her tongue into his mouth, moaning. He led her to the bed, turned her over, and held her tightly in his arms. She sighed and said, "Yes, yes."

But then she noticed the time on the mahogany clock on the mantelpiece, and freed herself from his embrace.

"It's ten o'clock! I have to go see Garibaldi. I have a million questions I have to ask him."

Philippe grumbled, put an arm out to catch her.

"I'll be right back," she promised.

At 36 quai des Orfèvres, Joséphine was telling the cop at the front desk that she absolutely had to see Inspector Garibaldi when the man himself came hurrying down the stairs.

"Inspector! I have to talk to you! I have news."

But Garibaldi gestured to two police officers to follow him, and didn't stop. To an anxious-looking Joséphine he said, "I have news too, Madame Cortès, but I don't have the time now."

She ran alongside him.

"It's about the RVs!"

"I don't have the time, I tell you! Come to my office this afternoon."

Jo returned to the hotel and Philippe.

"He was in a hurry and going somewhere, but I'm seeing him this afternoon."

"Didn't he say anything?"

"No. He looked . . . how can I put it? I didn't like the look on his face."

Jo's cell phone rang with an incoming text.

"Who is it?" grumbled Philippe.

Joe got up to go to see.

"It's Luca."

"What does he say?"

"'So you were able to get rid of me!'"

"You're right, the man's crazy. Does this mean they haven't arrested him yet?"

"Apparently not."

"What are they waiting for?"

"I've got it!" exclaimed Joséphine. "That's where Garibaldi was rushing off to. He was going to arrest Luca!"

When Joséphine showed up for their meeting, Garibaldi was wearing a handsome black shirt. He gave instructions that they not be disturbed and offered her a chair. For some reason, he was nervously fiddling with his fingernails, and his nose and mouth were twitching. He cleared his throat several times before speaking.

"Madame Cortès, do you know if there's a way to contact Monsieur Dupin?"

Joséphine blushed.

"He's here in Paris."

"So he can be reached?"

She nodded.

"Could you ask him to come join us?"

"Has something bad happened?"

"I'd rather wait until he's here before I—"

"It's about one of my girls, isn't it?" Joséphine cried, jumping up. "I have to know!"

"No. This doesn't involve your daughters or his son."

Reassured, Joséphine sat back down.

"Are you sure?"

"Yes, madame. Can you phone him?"

Jo called Philippe's cell and asked him to come to the inspector's office. He arrived almost immediately.

"That was fast!" said Garibaldi sarcastically.

"I was waiting at a café across the street. I wanted to come with Joséphine, but she preferred to see you by herself."

"What I have to tell you is very unpleasant. You're going to have to be strong and stay calm."

"It doesn't involve the girls or Alexandre," said Joséphine reassuringly.

"Monsieur Dupin, your wife's body has been found in a lake in the Compiègne Forest."

Philippe paled, and Joséphine cried, "What?" She thought she hadn't heard right. *It wasn't possible. What in the world would Iris be doing in the Compiègne Forest?*

"That can't be true!" she blurted.

"But it is, unfortunately. It's definitely her body." Garibaldi sighed. "I'd like to know, which of you spoke to her last?"

"I did," said Jo. "On the phone, about eight or ten days ago."

"What did she tell you?"

"That she was having a grand love affair with Hervé Lefloc-Pignel and that she'd never been so happy. Also for me not to call her because she wanted to experience it in peace, and that they were going to get married."

"Then that's it. Lefloc-Pignel lured her to the forest by promising to marry her, there was a phony ceremony, and he stabbed her to death. A farmer saw the whole thing. He had the remarkable presence of mind to write down the two cars' license plates. That's how we were able to identify them."

"Who do you mean when you say 'them'?" asked Philippe.

"Lefloc-Pignel and Van den Brock are accomplices. They've known each other forever, and they acted together."

"That's exactly what I was coming to tell you this morning!" cried Joséphine.

"I've sent officers to Lefloc-Pignel's apartment and to Van den Brock's vacation place in Sarthe."

"All this could have been prevented if you'd only listened to me!" said Jo.

"No, madame. When I saw you this morning, your sister was already dead. I was on my way to take the testimony of the man who saw it."

He coughed, his fist in front of his mouth.

Holding Joséphine's hand, Philippe described their drive from Deauville, the stop at Le Floc-Pignel, and the printer's tale. Joséphine interjected that she'd heard about the village and the printer from Lefloc-Pignel himself.

"So he confided in you!" said Garibaldi. "That's surprising."

"He said I was like a little turtle."

"A little turtle who gave us some real help with that 'Dig RV' business."

Then the inspector revealed what he had discovered.

Going through de Bassonnière's papers, he'd learned Lefloc-Pignel's story, his having been abandoned as a child, where he got his name, his string of foster homes.

"We didn't make much of it right away," he said. "There's no shame in being a foster child and rising in society by marrying well. And you can't help but feel sorry for him after his baby was run over in a parking lot. Capitaine Gallois was the first to make the connection between the two Hervés."

"How did she come to that conclusion?" asked Philippe, holding Joséphine's hand. "It's not obvious."

"Her mother was a social worker with health and human services in Normandy. She too was involved in placing abandoned children. She had an older colleague named Évelyne Lamarche, a hard woman who seemed convinced those children were worthless. So worthless that she never bothered giving them a name that suited them or that they liked. She called all the boys Hervé. When Mademoiselle de Bassonnière was killed, Capitaine Gallois noticed the identical first names on the two men's statements and remembered the social worker. When she was growing up, her mother often mentioned Lamarche critically, saying, 'She's going to turn those children into wild animals.'

"Gallois checked the men's ages and had a hunch they might both have passed through Lamarche's hands. She figured the two might have had the same experience and known each other for a long time. So she followed the trail. She called her mother

to find out what had become of Lamarche. And she learned that
Évelyne Lamarche had been found hanged in her home near
Arras, the night of August second, 1983."

"That's the date the printer gave us!" Jo exclaimed. "It was
the last time he saw Lefloc-Pignel, and he was with Van den
Brock."

"So it all fits!" said Garibaldi. "Let me explain. There was an
investigation after Lamarche's death, because she wasn't known
to be depressed. She'd come back to her native village, near Arras.
She lived alone, without any friends or children. She became
known in town and was planning to run in the municipal elec-
tions. She'd died by hanging, but nobody thought it was suicide.

"This confirmed Capitaine Gallois's suspicion that she'd been
murdered. Had Lamarche paid with her life for humiliating those
children in the old days? The two Hervés were obvious suspects.
Gallois probably called them in, questioned them again, and may
have let something slip. She knew too much, and they decided to
get rid of her."

"Did you figure this out after Capitaine Gallois was killed?"
asked Joséphine.

"We were on their trail, but we were still feeling our way. Why
did Gallois ask her mother about Lamarche's death? Why hadn't
she told us anything about her investigation? And why leave that
note, 'Dig RV'? And then you had your brainstorm, Madame
Cortès, that 'RV' meant 'Hervé.' We knew then that we were getting close.

"Shortly after that, Capitaine Gallois's mother related the
conversation she'd had with her daughter and told us what she'd
found out. We followed a number of leads before concentrating

on that one. We also looked into the case of Vittorio Giambelli, a very disturbed man. He's a schizophrenic, but he's not a criminal. He even asked to have himself committed. He realized he was losing his grip after sending you a series of text messages and turned himself in. He seemed relieved to be apprehended. He should be hospitalized very shortly."

"So it wasn't him," murmured Joséphine.

"That's when we turned our full attention to the two Hervés. After Gallois's death and the RV business we knew we were on the right track, but we had to keep questioning everyone, so as not to tip the two main suspects off. Gallois's mother was a great help. She sent us photocopies of the local newspapers, and one of them carried a small item about an incident that happened the very evening of Évelyne Lamarche's death.

"The front desk clerk at a hotel near Arras had been assaulted by a pair of students. They claimed she had 'spoken rudely' to them, she objected, and one of them punched her. She filed a complaint the next morning, giving their names from the hotel guest register: Hervé Lefloc-Pignel and Hervé Van den Brock. The names weren't published in the newspaper; we got them from the police. There was no reason for the two to be in the area. They both came from Paris, and they spent only one night there."

"So you think they killed the social worker together," said Philippe.

"Lamarche had humiliated them when they were children. They wanted justice. They got away with it, and I think that first murder gave them the idea of doing it again.

"We tracked down the hotel clerk, and she remembered the incident very well. When we showed her a lineup of photos, she immediately recognized the two Hervés. The trail was getting warmer, but we still didn't have any solid proof. And without proof, there wasn't much we could do."

"And, of course, there's the problem of connecting the crimes," said Philippe, thinking aloud. "What do the victims all have in common?"

"As the inspector said, they humiliated them," said Joséphine. "I saw Madame Berthier and Lefloc-Pignel argue about his son's studies. Mademoiselle de Bassonnière attacked both men at the tenants' co-op meeting. I was there too. It was when I walked home with Lefloc-Pignel that he told me about his childhood. But what about Iris? What did she do to them?"

Said Philippe: "Knowing her, she must have expected so much from Lefloc-Pignel, fantasized so wildly about him, that she was crushed when he left on vacation. She probably got angry and called him every name in the book. She was feeling fragile and desperate, and he was her last hope."

"From then on we kept a close eye on the two men," said Garibaldi. "We knew Lefloc-Pignel was seeing your sister, so we stationed officers to watch the building around the clock. All we had to do was wait for him to commit another crime, and catch him red-handed. I mean before he committed it, of course. We never imagined he would attack your wife."

"But you used her as bait!"

"We saw Madame Cortès leave Paris, but we never saw your wife after that. We thought she had left town as well. We questioned the concierge, and she said Madame Dupin told her to hold the mail because she was going on vacation. So the officer watching the building focused only on Lefloc-Pignel."

"But she was in the damned place!" snapped Philippe. "You must've seen lights on, or heard something."

"No, nothing. There were no lights or noises on her floor, and the shutters were closed. She must have been living like a recluse. Didn't even go shopping. And Lefloc-Pignel stayed in his apartment at night. All the surveillance reports confirm this. He would come in, have a quick dinner, then go into his home office and stay there. He would listen to opera, talk on the phone, dictate correspondence. The office windows give onto the courtyard and were wide open. It's like an echo chamber, you can hear everything. Lefloc-Pignel never phoned Van den Brock. We figured he was lying low.

"The night of the murder, he fooled us into thinking he was at home. The routine was the same as the other evenings: opera, phone conversations, more opera. In fact, he must've recorded a tape of all that and played it while he left, got your wife, and drove her to the forest. When our officer was relieved at midnight, he had no idea that Lefloc-Pignel had flown the coop."

"But how could he kill Iris so coldly?" exclaimed Joséphine.

"In the eyes of a serial killer, the victim is nothing. Or at most a way of realizing his fantasies. These people are very often very intelligent and very unhappy, you know. People who suffer enormously and express that pain by inflicting terrible suffering on their victims."

"Inspector, forgive me if I don't sympathize with Lefloc-Pignel's unhappiness," said Philippe angrily.

"I'm just trying to explain how it could have happened," said Garibaldi. "We would like to search your apartment, Madame Cortés, to see if Madame Dupin left any evidence of what her life was like those last eight days. Could you give us the keys?"

He extended his hand. After a nod from Philippe, Jo handed them over. Then she said, "I can't believe all this. It's a nightmare, and I keep expecting to wake up. But why was I attacked? I didn't do anything to him. When it happened, I barely knew the man."

Said the inspector: "One detail caught our eye, which Capitaine Gallois had already picked up on. When we took over the investigation, she told us you wore the same hat as Madame Berthier. A funny green hat with three layers. The night Lefloc-Pignel attacked you, I'm sure he mistook you for Madame Berthier in the darkness. He'd already had that argument with her. He saw the hat, you were both about the same size . . ."

"But wasn't he afraid of getting caught?"

"He had a ready-made alibi: Van den Brock said he was with him. The crimes connected the two men. One's rage fed the other's. And each time, they renewed the alliance they'd formed in their first killing."

"And I escaped that mayhem . . ." murmured Joséphine.

"In a way, he protected you," said the inspector. "He called you a 'little turtle.' You never provoked him, either physically or psychologically. You didn't try to seduce him, and you didn't question his authority."

The inspector paused, then added, "If I were you, I'd try to shield the children from all this. Keep them away from the papers for a while. Summer is a slow time for news, and this is the kind of story reporters love."

Hortense was the first to learn what happened. She was at Saint-Tropez having breakfast on the Sénéquier terrace with Nicholas. It was eight in the morning. Hortense liked to get up early.

She gave a shout, elbowed Nicholas, who nearly choked on his croissant, and immediately phoned her mother.

"Wow, Mom! Have you seen the paper?"

"I know, darling."

"Is what they say true?"

"Yes."

"It's horrible! What about Alexandre?"

"He's coming tomorrow, with Zoé."

"How did they take the news?"

"Alexandre was very quiet. He said, 'So she was dancing when she died,' and that's all. Zoé cried and cried. Alexandre got back on the phone and said, 'I'll take care of her.' That boy's amazing!"

"You want me to come look after the kids? I can handle it, and you're probably bawling your eyes out."

"I'm not able to cry," said Joséphine. "My tears are like dry stones in my throat. I can hardly breathe."

"Don't worry about it. It'll hit you all at once, and then you won't be able to stop!"

Hortense thought for a moment, then added, "I'll take them out to Deauville. I can turn off the TV and the radio. And no newspapers!"

"The house is being worked on. The storm took the roof off."
"Shit!"

"Besides, Alexandre will certainly want to come to the funeral. Zoé too."

"Okay, then I'll come up to Paris and take care of them there."

"The apartment is sealed. The police are looking for evidence of Iris's last days."

"All right then, we'll go to Philippe's. The whole gang."

"With all of Iris's things around? I'm not sure that's a good idea."

"We can't go to a hotel, for chrissakes!"

"Why not? That's where Philippe and I are."

"Well, that's a bit of good news, at last!"

"You think so?" asked Joséphine shyly.

"I sure do." Hortense paused. "You know, Iris's dying like that was perfect for her, waltzing in her Prince Charming's arms. She died in a dream. Iris always lived in a dream, never in reality. As deaths go, it suits her fine. Besides, I don't think she could've handled getting old. It would've been terrible for her!"

A pretty harsh eulogy, Jo thought.

"What about Lefloc-Pignel?" asked Hortense. "Is he in jail?"

"The police went to arrest him when I was with the inspector yesterday, but I haven't had any news since. There's been so much going on! Philippe went to identify the body. I couldn't bring myself to do it."

"The newspapers mentioned a second man. Who's that?"

"Hervé Van den Brock. He lived on the second floor."

"Is he pals with Lefloc-Pignel?"

"In a way."

"Okay, Mom. Tell Philippe to reserve a big room for Zoé, Alexandre, and me. And don't worry. I know it's hard, but you'll come through. You always come through. You're tough, Mom. You don't know it, but you are!"

"That's sweet of you to say. You're really sweet. If you knew how much I—"

At that, Joséphine started sobbing. Big, wracking sobs, and tears that erupted as if fired from a slingshot.

"You see," said Hortense with a sigh. "I told you it would come. And now you won't be able to stop."

Joséphine got off the phone, saying she had to call her mother.

"Hello!" Henriette barked.

"Mom, it's me, Joséphine."

"Well, well, Joséphine. A ghost from the past!"

"Have you read the papers, Mom?"

"I read the papers every morning, I'll have you know."

"And you didn't seen anything—"

"I read all the business news, and then I work on my portfolio. Some of my stocks are doing very well, others worry me, but that's the stock market and I'm learning."

"Iris is dead," said Joséphine.

"Iris, dead? What are you talking about?"

"She was killed, Mom. In a forest."

"You poor girl, you're talking complete nonsense."

"No, she really was killed."

"My daughter, killed? That can't be. How did it happen?"

"Mom, I don't have the strength to tell you right now. Call Philippe. He can tell you better than I can."

"You said it was in the papers. That's shameful! They shouldn't be allowed to—"

Joséphine hung up, unable to stop crying.

Philippe came out of the bathroom just then, wearing a white terrycloth robe. She ran to him, wiped her nose on the robe. He sat down and took her on his knees.

"It'll be all right," he murmured, kissing her hair.

"I can't help myself."

"That's normal. But think about it, and you'll understand. I lived with Iris for a very long time. I gave her everything, but she was like a bottomless well. She never had enough. She thought she'd finally found paradise with him."

It was six in the morning when the three detectives rang Lefloc-Pignel's doorbell.

When he opened the door, he was freshly shaved and was wearing a bottle-green smoking jacket and a dark-green ascot. He coldly asked them their business. The officers said they had a warrant for his arrest and ordered him to follow them. He raised a scornful eyebrow and asked them not to stand so close when speaking to him. He noticed that one of them smelled of stale tobacco.

"And what exactly are you bothering me about so early in the day?"

"A little dance in the woods," said one. "If you know what I mean."

"A farmer saw you and your pal stabbing the pretty lady," said another. "They're dragging the lake right now. Things aren't looking too good for you, blue blood. So comb your hair and come with us."

Lefloc-Pignel started, took a few steps backward, then asked if he could change his clothes first. The three detectives looked at each other and agreed. He led them inside and went into his bedroom with one of the men.

As the other two paced the living room, one noticed the turtles lying amid lettuce leaves and apple slices in a big glass enclosure.

"Nice aquarium!" he said, giving a thumbs-up.

"It's not an aquarium, it's a terrarium. In an aquarium you put water and fish. In a terrarium, turtles or iguanas."

"How do you know about this stuff?"

"I have a brother-in-law who's crazy about turtles. He pets them and cuddles them. Calls the vet the moment they catch cold. We can't dance or play music too loud in the living room, because the vibrations bother them. We practically have to keep our voices down. And when we walk, we have to do it very quietly."

"He sounds as wacko as the guy in the bedroom!"

"I don't make a big deal of it 'cause of my sister, but I think his elevator doesn't quite go to the top floor."

"This guy must be raising them. Look at all of them, sleeping."

"It's breeding season. They must be in getting ready to lay their eggs."

"Maybe that's why he came back early from vacation."

"With nut jobs, you're never disappointed."

The two detectives peered at the turtles, scratching at the terrarium glass, but the turtles didn't move.

The men straightened up.

"He's taking his sweet time getting dressed, isn't he?" said one with some irritation.

"Guys like that don't run around in sweat pants."

"Want to go see what he's up to?"

Just then, the third detective burst into the living room.

"I wasn't able to stop him!" he shouted. "He asked me to turn around while he changed his underpants, and he jumped. There wasn't anything I could do!"

They ran into the bedroom to find the floor dotted with little turtles. Scattered around them were yellow and green lettuce leaves, quartered apples, peas, cucumbers, and figs. The window was wide open. Leaning out, they saw the inert body of

Hervé Lefloc-Pignel sprawled in the courtyard. He was clutching a turtle, its shell shattered in the fall.

Hervé Van den Brock watched as a Citroën C5 pulled into the white gravel driveway leading to the house his wife inherited from her parents. He looked up from the book he was reading, dog-eared the page, and set the book on the garden table next to his chaise longue. He pushed away the packet of pistachios he'd been nibbling on. He didn't like the sound the car's tires made as they scattered gravel onto the short green grass, which a gardener tended with great care. He also didn't like the tone the two policemen used when they told him to follow them.

"What does this concern?" he asked, reproachfully.

"You'll find out soon enough," said one of the two, stubbing his cigarette out on the grass and flashing a police ID card.

"I would appreciate your picking up that cigarette butt. Otherwise I'll call my friend the prefect. He'll be disappointed to hear of your bad manners."

"He'll be even more disappointed to find out what you were doing in the Compiègne Forest the other evening," said the second, smaller man, casually dangling a pair of handcuffs.

Van den Brock paled.

"There must be some mistake," he said more quietly.

"You can explain it to us," said the smaller man, opening the cuffs.

"Those won't be necessary. I'm going with you."

He waved at his wife, who was repotting bamboo shoots in a garden shed.

"There's a little something I have to take care of, dear. I'll be back soon."

"Or never," cackled the man who'd stubbed his cigarette out on the lawn.

Joséphine's voice rose, pure and melodious, in the dark Père Lachaise crematorium crypt.

"Leave me, oh you wandering stars and inconstant thoughts, I beg you, and let me speak to the Beloved, let me savor the Beloved's presence. You are my joy, my happiness, my cheer, my joyous day. You belong to me, and I to you, and will forever. Tell me, oh my Beloved, why did you let my soul seek you so long and so ardently without finding you? I sought you through this world's voluptuous night. I crossed mountains and fields, as wild as an unbridled horse, but I have found you at last, and am resting happily, peacefully, and lightly on your bosom."

Jo's voice broke on the last words. She was barely able to say, "Henry Suso, 1295 to 1366," the poet who had written the lines she was offering as an homage to her sister. "Good-bye my love, my life's companion, my lovely beauty." She folded the sheet of paper she was holding and went to sit between her two daughters in the crypt.

There were few people at the crematorium: Henriette, Joséphine, Hortense, Zoé, Philippe, Alexandre, Shirley—and Gary.

He had arrived from London that morning with his mother. Hortense was surprised to see him in their Hotel Raphael suite. She had paused a moment, then came over, kissed him on the cheek, and said, "It was nice of you to come."

The coffin was covered with white roses and sprays of irises, their deep purple lit by dashes of bright yellow. A big photograph of Iris stood on a tripod. A string quartet played Mozart.

Joséphine had chosen texts for each of them to read in turn.

Henriette had refused to participate, claiming that she didn't need such playacting to express her pain. She was quite disappointed by the simplicity of the ceremony and the small turnout. She sat very erect under her big hat, without anything to dampen the pretty cambric handkerchief she dabbed at her eyes, hoping to produce a tear that would show the vastness of her sorrow. She had proffered a reluctant cheek for Joséphine to kiss. Henriette was one of those women who never forgive, and her entire attitude showed that in her opinion Death had chosen the wrong passenger.

Chin down, arms crossed on his navy blue blazer, Alexandre gazed solemnly at his mother's picture. He was trying to gather his memories of her, and his knitted brow showed that this was no easy task. All he caught of his mother were furtive moments: quick kisses, a hint of perfume, the quiet thud of shopping bags dropped in the foyer, her voice on the telephone, exclamations of surprise or delight, slim feet and painted toenails. When his father set a big white candle at the foot of the picture, Alexandre asked to light it, as a final homage. He said, "Good-bye, Mom" as he did, and even those words seemed too solemn for the lovely woman smiling at him. He tried to blow her a kiss, but stopped himself. *She died happy. She was dancing when she died. Dancing. . . .* And if he needed it, that thought reinforced his feeling that he hadn't had a mother in his life, but a lovely stranger.

Zoé and Hortense were sitting on either side of their mother. Zoé had slipped her hand onto Jo's and was squeezing it hard, imploring her not to cry. This was the first time Zoé had seen a coffin up close, and she was imagining her aunt's body under the carpet of white roses and irises. *She isn't moving, she can't hear us, her eyes are closed, she's cold. Does she want to get out, I wonder? She's sorry she's dead, but it's too late. She's never coming back.* And then Zoé immediately thought, *Papa didn't die in a nice box like that. He died naked and unprotected, fighting rows of sharp teeth tearing him to pieces.* The thought was too much for her and she slumped against her mother, sobbing. Joséphine hugged her, guessing at the terrible pain that Zoé was finally able to express.

Hortense looked at the paper on which her mother had printed the text she was to read, and sighed. Another of Mom's ideas! As if we're in the mood to read poetry. Oh well. She waited until the Mozart piece ended, and began to read the Clément Marot poem. She was annoyed to find her voice shaking. "I am not what I used to be . . ." Hortense coughed, composed herself, and bravely started again: "I am not what I used to be / and never will be again / my springtime and my summer too / have out the window flown."

Then she burst into tears at the thought that it would be just like Iris to lift the coffin lid, come sit down among them, ask for a glass of champagne, and put on a pair of fireman's boots and a little fuchsia Christian Lacroix top. Hortense stood there angrily weeping, her arms stretched out as if trying to push back the wave of tears breaking over her. *And that big dummy Gary looking at me with his sad, sympathetic eyes. He can't possibly make this any worse, he couldn't! He isn't going to come over and . . .*

She threw herself into Gary's arms, and he embraced her as if she were a bouquet of flowers. He rested his head on the top of hers and hugged her tight, saying, "Don't cry, Hortense." And the tighter he hugged her, the more she wanted to cry, but these were strange tears, tears for something she didn't really know, something softer, gayer, tears like a kind of happiness, of relief, of great joy that wrenched her heart. Gary was both there and not there, she held him and didn't hold him, a kind of reconciliation before another separation, perhaps—she didn't know.

She shook herself angrily, realizing that she'd never cried in her life, that this was the first time, and that it had to be in the arms of a traitor in the pay of Charlotte Bradsburry! She freed herself and went to sit next to her mother. She took her firmly by the arm to let Gary know that the moment of tenderness was over.

The cremation was announced, and they were told that they could wait outside. They left in orderly rows, with Joséphine holding her daughters' hands, Philippe holding Alexandre's, and Henriette, Shirley, and Gary bringing up the rear.

Philippe had decided to scatter Iris's ashes in the sea at their house in Deauville, and both Alexandre and Joséphine agreed. But when he told Henriette, she said, "My daughter's soul doesn't live in an urn. You can do whatever you like with her ashes. As for me, I'm going home. I have nothing more to do here." She waved and left.

Shirley went to visit the Père Lachaise tombstones with Gary, who especially wanted to see those of Oscar Wilde and Chopin. They took Hortense, Zoé, and Alexandre with them, leaving Philippe and Joséphine alone.

They sat down on a bench in the sunshine. Philippe had taken Joséphine's hand and was quietly stroking it.

An older blonde woman came walking toward them. She was wearing a hat, gloves, and a very well cut suit.

"Do you know her?" Philippe asked in a whisper.

"No. Why?"

They looked up to find the woman standing right in front of them, looking very dignified. Her drawn face spoke of sleepless nights, and the corners of her mouth fell in sad little commas.

"Madame Cortès and Monsieur Dupin? I am Madame Mangeain-Dupuy, Isabelle's mother."

Philippe and Joséphine stood up, but she signaled that it wasn't necessary.

"I read the obituary in *Le Monde*, and I wanted to tell you . . . That is, I don't know quite . . . This is a little delicate. I want to say that the death of your sister and your wife was not useless. It liberated a family."

She paused.

"Do you mind if I sit down? I'm not as young as I was, and these events have tired me."

Philippe and Joséphine made room on the bench, and Madame Mangeain-Dupuy sat down stiffly between them. She laid her gloved hands on her purse, and raised her chin. With her eyes on the patch of lawn in front of her, she began what felt like a long confession. Joséphine and Philippe listened without interrupting, deeply moved by the effort the woman was making to speak.

"My coming to see you may seem peculiar," she said. "My husband didn't want me to come. He thought my presence would be inappropriate. But as a mother and a grandmother I felt I had to."

From her purse she took a photograph, the very one that Joséphine had seen in the Lefloc-Pignels' bedroom: the wedding photograph of Hervé Lefloc-Pignel and Isabelle Mangeain-Dupuy. The older woman stroked it with the back of her gloved hands, then began to speak.

"My daughter Isabelle met Hervé Lefloc-Pignel at the Bal de l'X, at the Opéra. She was eighteen, he was twenty-four. She was attractive and innocent, she had just passed her *baccalauréat*, and thought herself neither beautiful nor intelligent. She very quickly fell in love and just as quickly wanted to marry him. When she told us about Hervé, we warned her that he might not be a suitable match. But she never did listen to us, and we eventually had to give our consent to their union. We learned to hide our feelings, and welcomed him as our son-in-law. He was certainly brilliant. Difficult but brilliant. He once managed to rescue the family bank from a terrible fix and from that day on we treated him as an equal. It was a blessed time. And then . . ."

She stopped, overcome with emotion, and her voice quavered.

"And then little Romain was born. He was a beautiful baby. He looked just like his father, who was crazy about him. And then the accident . . . The accident you know about happened. It was horrible. Hervé was the person who picked the baby up. He changed overnight. He became withdrawn, had terrible mood swings, practically stopped coming to see us. My daughter has never forgiven herself for Romain's death, and the birth of her other children didn't change anything.

"One day she asked to talk to her father. She told him that she wanted to leave Hervé, that her life had become a living hell. And my husband said something to her he has regretted ever since. He said: 'You wanted him, you got him, we warned you.'"

She paused, tucked a strand of hair back in her chignon, and smoothed it with her fingers.

"When we learned what happened to Madame Dupin, I thought of you, of course, but I also felt a great weight lifted from me. And from Isabelle! She came into my bedroom, just had time to say, "I'm free, Mom! I'm finally free!" and collapsed from exhaustion. She is now being treated by a psychiatrist. That's what I wanted to tell you, what I wanted you to know. Your wife, monsieur, and your sister, madame, did not die in vain. She saved a family."

Madame Mangeain-Dupuy stood up as stiffly as she had sat down. She took a letter from her purse and handed it to Joséphine.

"This is from Gaétan. He asked me to give it to you for your daughter Zoé."

"What is going to become of him?" murmured Joséphine, shaken by the long confession.

"We have enrolled all three children in an excellent private school in Rouen under their mother's maiden name. That way, they'll be able to have a normal schooling without being the target of every bit of gossip. I want to thank you for listening to me, and I apologize again for the strangeness of my approaching you."

She gave them a little nod and walked away as she had come, a pale silhouette from another era, a woman both strong and submissive.

The next day, they all found themselves in the Raphael suite. Philippe had ordered club sandwiches, Cokes, and a bottle of red wine.

Hortense and Gary were doing a kind of do-si-do of avoidance, attraction, and repulsion. She watched his cell phone like a hawk. When he suggested they go to the movies, she said, "Sure, why not?" But then his phone rang, it was Charlotte Bradsburry, and his voice changed. Hortense stopped on the threshold, glared at him, and canceled the movie date.

"Oh, come on, don't be silly!" he said, after hanging up. "Let's go!"

"I don't feel like it anymore," she said sourly.

"I know why," he said, smiling. "You're jealous!"

"Of that old hag? Not on your life!"

"Okay, since you're not jealous, let's go to the movies."

"I'm expecting a call from Nicholas. After that, I'll see."

"That little peacock?"

"You jealous?"

Joséphine and Shirley hid their laughter.

Philippe asked Alexandre and Zoé if they wanted to visit the Grand Palais and its glass-roofed nave.

"I'm coming with you!" cried Hortense. She was ignoring Gary, but he invited himself along and followed her.

"Alone at last!" cried Shirley when they'd gone. "Why don't we order another bottle of this excellent wine?"

"We're going to get drunk!"

Shirley phoned room service for the wine.

"It's the only way to make you talk."

"Talk about what?" Jo asked, kicking off her shoes. "I'm not saying anything, even if you torture me with good wine."

"You're looking very beautiful these days. Is it because of Philippe?"

Joséphine put two fingers to her lips, meaning she wasn't telling.

"Are you going to live together next year?"

Joséphine merely smiled.

"So you are going to live together!"

"It's too soon yet. We have to take it slow, for Alexandre's sake."

"And Zoé's."

"Yeah, Zoé too. It would be best if I spend some more time just with her. We'll go to London on weekends, or they'll come to Paris. We'll see."

The doorbell rang and a waiter delivered the wine. Shirley poured Joséphine a glass, and they toasted.

"To our friendship," said Shirley. "May it always be beautiful, and tender, and gentle, and strong."

Jo was about to answer when the phone rang. It was Inspector Garibaldi, saying she was free to return to her apartment.

"Did you find anything?"

"Yes, a diary your sister kept. It belongs to you, so I had it delivered to your hotel this morning. She had moved into another world. When you read it, you'll understand."

Jo rang the front desk, and they sent the package up.

"Do you mind if I read it right away?" Jo asked. "I can't stand waiting. I so much want to figure out what happened."

Joséphine opened the envelope to find some thirty sheets of paper inside. She dove in, and the more she read, the paler she got.

She silently held the pages out to Shirley, who asked, "May I?"

Jo nodded and ran to the bathroom.

When she came back, Shirley had finished reading and was staring into space. Joséphine sat down next to her and rested her head on her shoulder.

"It's horrible! How could she have ever . . ."

Shirley nodded. They passed the pages back and forth in silence, watching as Iris's elegant writing deteriorated into a tangled scrawl.

"That's what happened," said Shirley. "He ground her down

and infantilized her. You have to be incredibly strong to resist madness like that."

"Tell me I'm not surrounded by crazy people!" Joséphine cried. "Tell me I'm normal!"

Shirley gave Joséphine's panicky face an odd look, and murmured, "What's 'normal,' Jo? What isn't? Who knows? And who gets to decide?"

Joséphine put on her running shoes and called to Du Guesclin, who was lying in front of the radio listening to TSF Jazz and keeping time with his hindquarters. It was his favorite station, and he spent hours listening to it. When the ads came on, he wandered off to sniff his dish or roll at Joséphine's feet, baring his belly for a rub. Then he went back to listening. When a trumpet blew very high notes, he put his paws on his ears and shook his head, in pain.

"Come on, Du Guesclin, let's go!"

She had to get moving, go running again. She had to use her body to push away the wave of pain overwhelming her. She couldn't risk drowning in sadness a second time. *How can this be? How can it hurt just as much, each time? I'm never going to heal, never.*

Not long after Iris's death, she had phoned Henriette to ask for some photographs of Iris and herself when they were children. She wanted to frame them. Henriette said the pictures were down in the basement, and she didn't have time to go down and sort through them.

"Besides, Joséphine, I think it would be better if you stopped calling me. I don't have a daughter anymore. I had one and I lost her."

The same old waves had crashed down on Joséphine, sweeping

her away to sea, this time, she thought, to be drowned for sure. Since then, everything felt fuzzy. She was losing her grip. Nothing and no one could save her. She could count only on herself and her own strength to pull herself through.

That woman has the power to kill me every time. You never recover from having a mother who doesn't love you. It leaves a big hole in your heart, and it takes an awful lot of love to fill it up! You never have enough, you always doubt yourself, you feel you're not lovable, you're not worth a damn.

Maybe Iris suffered from that, too. Maybe that's why she ran toward that insane love, why she accepted and endured everything, thinking, "He loves me, he loves me!" Iris thought she had found a love that would fill the bottomless well.

And what about me, Du Guesclin, what do I want? I don't know anymore. I know my daughters love me. The day of the cremation, we came together, my hands in theirs, and it was the first time I felt that the three of us were one. I liked that arithmetic. Now I have to learn about love with a man.

Philippe had gone back to London, and it was Joséphine's turn to be silent. When he left he said, "I'll be waiting for you, Jo. I have all the time in the world." He kissed her gently, parting her hair as if he were parting the hair of a drowned woman.

"I'll be waiting for you."

She didn't know if she still knew how to swim.

When Du Guesclin saw her jogging shoes, he barked. She smiled. He lurched to his feet with the grace of a seal waddling across an ice flow.

"You really are fat, you know? You've got to move your butt a little."

He stretched, seeming to say, *It's been two months since we last went running. It's no surprise I've put on weight.*

At the Van den Brocks' floor, they ran into a real estate agent who was showing the apartment.

"I wouldn't want to move into a killer's apartment," she told Du Guesclin. "But maybe she won't bother mentioning it."

When they dragged the Compiègne Forest lake, divers found the bodies of three women in weighted garbage bags. Van den Brock was in jail, awaiting trial. The investigation was still going on. The farmer and the hotel desk clerk had been brought in, and they both recognized him. He denied everything, claiming he'd only been a witness, and powerless to stop his friend's murderous madness.

It was fall, and the leaves were turning. *It's been a year already! A year that I've been running around this lake. A year ago I was visiting Iris in her clinic and she was delirious.* Jo shook her head, to clear it of that thought. *It was a year ago that I thought I saw Antoine in the Metro, too. And it was a year ago that I walked around the lake trembling beside Luca the indifferent.*

Raindrops began to fall, and Joséphine picked up the pace.

"Come on, Du Guesclin! Let's play at running between the drops!"

She started running with her shoulders hunched and her head down, keeping her eyes on the trail to make sure she didn't slip on a branch or something. She didn't notice that Du Guesclin wasn't with her anymore. She kept running, elbows close, forcing her body, arms, and legs to fight against the waves, forcing her heart to work to become stronger.

Marcel was sending her flowers every week with a little note: *Hang in there, Jo. We're here and we love you. Marcel, Josiane, and Junior.* Could they be her new family? One that wouldn't stab her in the heart over and over again?

When she stopped and looked around for Du Guesclin, she found him far behind her. He was sitting down and looking off in the distance.

"Du Guesclin, come on! What are you doing?"

She clapped her hands and stamped her foot, yelling "Du Guesclin!" each time, but he didn't move. She walked back and kneeled down by him.

"Are you sick? Are you in a bad mood?"

He kept looking off into the distance with his nostrils quivering slightly, as if to say, *I don't like what I'm seeing. I don't like what's coming this way.* Jo was used to his moods. She first reasoned with him, then tried pulling and pushing him, but he stubbornly refused to budge.

She stood up and looked in the same direction, studying the lakeshore as far as she could. Suddenly she spotted the man in the scarf, marching along. How long had it been since she'd last seen him?

Du Guesclin growled, his eyes narrowed to sharp slits.

"You don't like him, do you?"

He growled again.

Before Jo had the time to interpret his answer, the man was standing in front of them. The scarves he used to wear tied around his neck were gone, revealing a youthful, attractive face.

"Is that your dog?" he asked, pointing at Du Guesclin.

"He's my dog and he's very handsome."

The man smirked, and said, "That's not the word I would use to describe Tarzan."

"His name isn't Tarzan, it's Du Guesclin."

"No, I know him and his name is Tarzan."

"Come on, Du Guesclin, let's get out of here."

Du Guesclin didn't move.

"That's my dog, madame."

"He certainly is not! He's mine!"

"He ran away from me, about six months ago."

That was troubling, because that was when Jo had found him. At a loss as to what else to say, she said, "You shouldn't have abandoned him!"

"I didn't abandon him. I brought him in from the countryside where he'd been living, and he ran away."

"There's no proof that he belongs to you. He doesn't have a tattoo, and he doesn't have any tags."

"I can produce witnesses who will all say that Tarzan belongs to me. He lived with me for two years in Montchauvet, at 38 rue du Petit-Moulin. He was a very good guard dog. Some thieves roughed him up a little, but he fought like a lion, and the house wasn't robbed. After that, even hardened crooks ran away when he appeared."

Joséphine could feel tears coming to her eyes.

"Didn't you care that he was practically cut to ribbons?"

"That's his job as a guard dog. That's why I picked him."

"So what are you doing walking around here, if you live out in the country?"

"I think you're being very pushy, madame."

Joséphine backed down a little. She was so afraid the man

would take Du Guesclin away that she was ready to bite. In a more conciliatory tone she said, "You don't know this, but I love him very much and we get along so well!"

Du Guesclin moaned, stressing the truthfulness and sincerity of what she'd said, and the man relaxed a little.

"To answer your unspoken question, madame, I'm a lyricist. I write song lyrics and modern opera librettos. I work with a musician whose studio is at La Muette. Whenever I'm due to I meet with him, I first take a walk around the lake, to concentrate. I lost Tarzan the day I came to Paris to board him with a friend. I was leaving for New York to record a Broadway musical comedy. He ran away, and I didn't have time to go looking for him. You can imagine how surprised I was when I saw him this morning."

"If you travel all the time, he's better off with me."

Du Guesclin gave a brief yelp in agreement.

The man looked at him for a moment, then said, "Here's what we're going to do. I'll talk to him, then you talk to him, and then we'll walk away in opposite directions and see who he follows."

Joséphine said she agreed.

The man crouched down near Du Guesclin and started whispering to him.

Joséphine moved away, turning her back on them.

When she turned around she saw the man take a package of little orange cookies from his pocket and give it to Du Guesclin to sniff. Smelling the cookies, he started to drool, producing two long threads of clear saliva. Then the man gestured to Joséphine that it was her turn to talk to Du Guesclin.

Joséphine took him in her arms and quietly said, "I love you, you big tub of lard. I'm crazy about you. And I'm worth a lot more than an orange cookie. He needs you to guard his nice house, but I need you to guard *me*. Think about that!"

Still drooling, Du Guesclin kept his eyes on the man, who was now waving the bag to remind him of the cookies.

"You aren't playing fair!" said Joséphine.

"We each choose our weapons!"

"Well, I don't like yours!"

"If you keep insulting me, I'll leave with my dog!"

Like two duelists, they turned their backs on each other and walked in opposite directions. Du Guesclin sat there for a long time, smelling the orange cookies gradually moving away. Joséphine didn't turn around.

Clenching her fists, she prayed to all the stars in the sky, to all her guardian angels on the Big Dipper handle, prayed for them to push Du Guesclin toward her, to make him forget the delicate scent of orange cookies. *I'll buy you much nicer ones. I'll buy you round cookies, flat cookies, cookies that are waffled, crunchy, velvety. Cookies with icing and dipped in chocolate. I'll invent cookies especially for you.* She kept on walking, her heart torn. *Don't turn around, or I'll see him running away, chasing after an orange cookie, and I'll be even sadder, even more desperate.*

She turned around, and there was Du Guesclin trotting along beside the Broadway lyricist, looking happy. He had forgotten her. She saw him nip a cookie, swallow it, and scratch at the package for another.

I'll never be a nice woman. Even an orange cookie can defeat me. I'm a loser, I'm ugly, I'm stupid, I'm not enough. . . . Not enough of anything.

Her head sunken in her shoulders, she plodded along, unable to bear watching Tarzan's little party. She didn't feel like running anymore, bounding along the dark water past the clumps of bamboo. *I absolutely have to come up with a good reason for his leaving me. Otherwise I'm going to be too sad. The wave will swallow me forever. . . . Mom will have won.*

First of all, he didn't belong to me. He and his owner had other routines, and life is often more about routine than free choice. Second, I'm sure he wanted to stay with me, but his sense of duty prevailed. I didn't call him Du Guesclin for nothing. He was born to defend a territory, he was faithful to his king, he never betrayed. He never changed sides, going over to the king of England. He embodies the tradition of his noble ancestor. I didn't put my trust in a traitor. And last of all, I didn't respect his warrior nature. I thought he was friendly and gentle because he had a pink nose, but he wanted me to treat him like a hardened soldier. I was going to turn him into a sissy; he got away just in time.

Joséphine struggled to hold back her tears.

No crying, no crying. That's just more saltwater, more drowning. Enough of that! Think about Philippe, he's waiting, he told you so. The man doesn't say things just to hear himself talk. But is it my fault that I'm in such a fog that everything falls apart before it reaches me, that I'm anesthetized? Is it my fault that I don't heal all at once, that I have to keep bandaging the wounds of my childhood? Du Guesclin would've helped me, for sure, but I have to learn to heal by myself. That's the price you pay to become really strong.

She had reached the little boat rental shed when she heard the sound of a thundering gallop behind her. She stepped aside so the demented runner wouldn't knock her over, looked up to catch a glimpse of him, and gave a shout.

It was Du Guesclin. He was running toward her, nearly tangled in his own feet, as if afraid that he'd never catch her again.

He was carrying the bag of orange cookies in his mouth.

The Yellow Eyes of Crocodiles

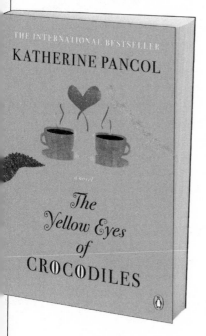

When her chronically unemployed husband runs off with his mistress, Joséphine Cortès, mother of two, is forced to maintain a stable family life while making ends meet on her meager salary as a medieval history scholar. When Joséphine's charismatic sister Iris charms a famous publisher into offering her a lucrative book deal, she makes a deal of her own: Joséphine will write the novel and pocket all the proceeds, but the book will be published under Iris's name. All is well—that is, until the book becomes the literary sensation of the season.